D0050526

## Books by Phillip Margolin

LOST LAKE
SLEEPING BEAUTY
TIES THAT BIND
THE ASSOCIATE
WILD JUSTICE
THE UNDERTAKER'S WIDOW
THE BURNING MAN
AFTER DARK
GONE, BUT NOT FORGOTTEN
THE LAST INNOCENT MAN
HEARTSTONE

## Coming Soon in Hardcover

PROOF POSITIVE

# PHILLIP MARGOLIN

## L O S T
# LAKE

HarperTorch
*An Imprint of HarperCollinsPublishers*

HARPERTORCH
*An Imprint of* HarperCollins*Publishers*
10 East 53rd Street
New York, New York 10022-5299

Copyright © 2005 by Phillip Margolin
Excerpt from *Proof Positive* copyright © 2006 by Phillip Margolin
ISBN-13: 978-0-06-073504-3
ISBN:10: 0-06-073504-X

First HarperTorch paperback printing: June 2006
First HarperCollins hardcover printing: March 2005

HarperCollins®, HarperTorch™, and ♥ ™ are trademarks of HarperCollins Publishers Inc.

Printed in the United States of America

Visit HarperTorch on the World Wide Web at www.harpercollins.com

10 9 8 7 6 5 4 3 2 1

FOR MY BROTHER,
JERRY MARGOLIN, SHERLOCKIAN EXTRAORDINAIRE,
AND HIS WIFE, JUDY, MASTER TEACHER,
THANKS FOR YOUR FRIENDSHIP AND SUPPORT.

# PROLOGUE

LOST LAKE, CALIFORNIA—1985

Deputy Sheriff Aaron Harney pulled his cruiser onto a grassy strip at the side of the road and rolled down his window. The clean mountain air felt good after the day's oppressive heat. He lit up and watched the smoke from his cigarette drift toward the diamond-bright stars that glittered above Lost Lake. Life didn't get much better than this.

Harney was a local boy who'd seen a little of the world during a hitch in the army and had decided that Lost Lake was the only place on earth that he wanted to live. There was fishing, there was hunting, and there was Sally Ann Ryder, his high school sweetheart. What more could you want out of life than a day outdoors and an evening with a cold beer and the woman of your dreams?

Harney's choice of career had been a no-brainer. He had been an MP in the military. The sheriff had been glad to sign him up. Harney had no political ambitions, and he did what he was told without complaint. Take tonight, for instance. There had been some vandalism in the expensive summer homes that were scattered along the shoreline of the lake, and Sheriff Basehart had assigned Harney to patrol them. Everyone was pretty certain that the vandalism was the work of townies, resentful of the fat cats who summered at the lake and then deserted to San Francisco at the first sign of bad weather. Harney even thought he knew which kids had broken the picture windows in the Fremont and McHenry homes. He doubted that the little bastards would be back at it tonight, but the sheriff wasn't taking chances with his biggest contributors, and Harney was perfectly content to cruise the lake on this beautiful summer evening.

From where he was sitting, the deputy could see the flat black outline of Congressman Eric Glass's modern log cabin on the far shore. Last year, Harney had been part of the security detail for the congressman's fund-raiser cookout. That was some house. In the back the lawn sloped down to the dock where the congressman moored his speedboat. You couldn't see the boat or the dock in the dark, but Harney remembered them and the narrow path that led through the woods to a tennis court. Imagine having your own tennis court. Harney wondered what the house had cost. A hell of a lot more than he could afford on a policeman's salary, that was for sure.

A scream shattered the stillness. Harney bolted upright and crushed out his cigarette. The mountain air played funny tricks with sound, but Harney thought that the scream came from Glass's place. He made a U-turn and gunned the engine.

It took five minutes to circle the lake, and Harney's imagination worked overtime as he drove. Police work in Lost Lake was calming down drunks at the Timber Topper, handling an occasional domestic disturbance, and handing out traffic tickets to teenage speeders. Harney had never had to deal with a bloodcurdling scream in the dead of night.

A long dirt driveway led from the road to the house. Harney killed his headlights and turned onto it. He wasn't in any hurry to find the source of that scream. When he couldn't put it off any longer, the deputy unholstered his gun, got out of his car, and stood in the dark, listening carefully. An owl hooted and a sudden gust of wind off the lake rustled branches in the forest. Somewhere in the distance he heard the sound of an outboard engine.

Harney walked slowly through the trees that bordered the drive until he reached the front lawn. He glanced around nervously, half expecting someone to leap out of the dark woods. Harney had radioed for backup, but the Lost Lake force was small and he would be on his own for a while. The deputy took a deep breath, crouched low, and raced across the lawn. He pressed against the side of the house, then edged forward until he could see through a window. There was light deep inside the house, but he couldn't hear any sound.

Harney sprinted past the window and tried the front door. It was locked. He remembered a door off the back terrace. The deputy spun around the corner. Nothing. He fanned his gun back and forth across the side lawn as he crept toward the back of the house. His chest felt tight. The brick patio was as he remembered it. A barbecue grill stood at one end. He could make out the silhouette of a speedboat bobbing next to the dock.

A noise drew his eye toward the footpath that led to the tennis court. A ghost staggered out of the woods. Harney stretched the muzzle of his gun toward the apparition.

"Hold it there," he commanded, trying to keep the fear from his voice. A woman froze, her eyes wide with fright. She was wearing a long white T-shirt, and she swayed back and forth on unsteady legs.

"He's dead," she said. She sounded dazed.

"Who's dead?" Harney asked as he searched the woods and the lawn for any sign of movement.

"Carl killed him."

The back door was open. Harney hadn't noticed at first, but his eyes were getting used to the dark.

"Is there anyone inside?" he asked.

"He's dead," the woman repeated as she stared into the darkness with eyes that did not focus. Harney wondered if she'd understood the question or even knew that he was there.

"Let's go inside," Harney said gently as he backed toward the house, scanning the yard while watching the woman out of the corner of his eye. He reached out slowly and touched her shoulder. The contact shook her and she stepped back, but her eyes focused on Harney for the first time.

"It's okay. I'm a sheriff's deputy. More police are coming."

Harney found a wall switch. They were in the kitchen. With the lights on he could see that the woman was beautiful. He put her in her mid-twenties. Her hair was blond and cut short, and her eyes were pale blue.

"You said someone was dead. Are they inside?"

She nodded.

"Can you show me where?"

The woman pointed down a hall that led to the kitchen. Harney remembered a home office mid-way down and a huge living room at the end of it. The light he'd seen from the front window was coming from the office. Harney closed the back door and locked it. Then he sat the woman at a small table in a nook that looked out at the lake.

"You said that someone named Carl killed someone. Is Carl still here?"

She shook her head.

"He's gone?" Harney asked to make sure.

She nodded.

"Okay, stay here. I'll be right back. Is that okay?"

She nodded again, but her body tightened and he could see that being left by herself terrified her.

"It'll be okay. My friends will be here soon."

Harney waited a moment for her response. When she made none, he edged down the hall with his gun leading the way. After a few steps, Harney got a whiff of an odor that brought to mind the day, last year, when he had answered a complaint about a domestic dispute and walked into a blood-bathed bedroom where a murder-suicide had just played out. The deputy swallowed hard and forced himself down the hall. When he reached the office he spun into the doorway. His stomach rolled and he fought the urge to throw up. In the background he heard the sound of sirens. In the foreground was Eric Glass.

The congressman was seated in a ladder-back chair. His arms and ankles were stretched tight and secured to the back of the chair with tape, making him vulnerable to any assault. Glass was wearing only cotton pajama bottoms. They were soaked with blood from the jagged wounds criss-crossing his torso. His head was tipped forward, and his chin rested on his chest. Harney crouched down and got a good view of Glass's bruised and bloodied face.

Bubble lights illuminated the living room and car doors slammed. Harney spoke into his radio, telling the officers to go around the back before he reentered the kitchen. The woman was sitting where he had left her. She was leaning forward, cradling her head in her arms. Harney unlocked the back door, then sat beside her.

"Who did this?" he asked quietly.

The woman looked up. She was exhausted. Her

eyes were red-rimmed and tears coursed down her cheeks.

"Carl killed him," she answered. "Carl Rice."

Aaron Harney heard the helicopter before he saw it. He shielded his eyes from the sun and scanned the sky until he found the source of the "whup-whup" sound dropping through the clouds toward the helipad on the hospital roof. Sheriff Basehart stood beside his deputy. He was a big man who had returned to Lost Lake after a brief career as a cop in San Francisco and had served as a deputy for a few years before running unopposed for sheriff when his predecessor retired. He'd held the post for eleven years.

The helicopter settled on the roof. A miniature tornado stirred up by the rotor blades threatened to rip the Stetson off Basehart's head, and he grabbed the brim that shaded his ruddy face. As soon as the helicopter's hatch opened, a stocky, muscular white man dressed in jeans and a light tan jacket jumped to the ground. He was followed immediately by a tall, wiry black man with a shaved head dressed in khakis and a denim jacket. They surveyed the rooftop before the stocky man nodded toward the interior of the copter. Seconds later, a tall, square-shouldered man wearing the uniform of a general stepped out of the plane, followed by a man with a styled salt-and-pepper mane dressed in a charcoal-gray business suit.

General Morris Wingate spotted the sheriff and strode across the roof. Something about him made Harney stiffen his spine and stand tall. If the General had given him an order, Harney knew he would have obeyed instantly, but General Wingate ignored Harney and focused on the sheriff. The General's aides stood a few steps behind the General and the other man, their eyes moving back and forth across the roof as if they were in a combat zone. Harney saw the butt end of a weapon under the black man's jacket.

"General Wingate?" Basehart asked.

The General nodded. "And this is Dr. Ernest Post. He's a psychiatrist. I want him to take a look at my daughter."

"I'm Earl Basehart, sir, the sheriff of Lost Lake. I'll do anything I can to help you."

"Thank you, Sheriff. What is my daughter's condition?"

"You'll need to speak to Dr. Stewart to get precise information, but he told me that she's in shock. Quite frankly I'm not surprised." He shook his head. "Seeing something like that." He shook his head a second time. "We had seasoned officers who were upset."

"Has she told you what happened?"

Basehart nodded toward Harney. "My deputy is the one who found her. Like I told you on the phone, she told him that a man named Carl Rice murdered the congressman. We haven't been able to get much more out of her. She was hysterical. We had her transported to the hospital, immediately. She's under sedation now."

"Have you found Rice?"

"Not yet. We have an APB out and we've

alerted the police in the surrounding areas. Unfortunately, he got a big jump on us."

"Do you have any information that would lead you to believe that Rice may still be in the vicinity? I'm concerned for my daughter's safety."

"We don't know where he is, but I have a deputy on duty outside your daughter's room. We're not taking any chances."

"Thank you, Sheriff," Wingate said. "My daughter means everything to me. I appreciate the thoroughness with which you've conducted this investigation and the way you've treated her."

"Sir, do you know anything about this fellow Rice that can help us catch him?"

"He went to high school with my daughter. He's been to my home."

The General paused. He looked upset. "Carl is a seriously disturbed young man who was recently discharged from the service because of mental problems. He can be violent. He learned that my daughter had moved to Washington and reestablished contact with her. Given his mental condition, I have no idea what he thought about the state of their relationship. He may have imagined that my daughter and the congressman were lovers and become insanely jealous. From what you told me about the state of the body, this sounds like a crime of passion."

"I'm trying to be delicate here, sir, but this is a murder investigation . . . "

"You do not have to walk on eggs with me, Sheriff. Please be blunt."

"Thank you. What was your daughter's relationship with the congressman?"

"She worked for Eric. That's all I know."

"Thank you, sir," Basehart said.

"I'd like to see Vanessa, if I could."

"Right away," Basehart said, reacting instantly. He led the way to the steel door that opened into the hospital from the roof. Harney rushed ahead to open it and followed Wingate, the doctor, Wingate's aides, and the sheriff inside.

The Lost Lake hospital had three stories and the General's daughter was in a private room on the second floor. The sheriff led the way. A deputy was on guard outside the door. He stood up when he saw the men approaching.

"Any problems, Dave?" Basehart asked.

"Everything's quiet."

"Okay. We're going in for a visit. You and Aaron stay out here."

The General, his aides, Dr. Post, and the sheriff entered the room. Harney was about to say something to the other deputy when he heard a scream exactly like the one that had shattered the peace of his cigarette break on the shore of Lost Lake. He drew his gun as he wrenched open the door. When he stepped into the room, the General's daughter was staring wide-eyed at her father as if she'd seen Satan.

# CHAPTER **ONE**

The organizers of the Portland Spring Art Fair had lucked out. It had been a very wet March in Oregon and the weather seers were predicting rain through most of April. But Mother Nature had redecorated in the nick of time, storing away the endless precipitation and gloomy black clouds for another day and setting out sunshine and clear blue skies for the weekend of the fair.

Ami Vergano had dressed in a multicolored peasant skirt and a white blouse with short puffed sleeves to celebrate the pleasant weather. Ami was just over five-four and still had the solid build of the gymnast she'd been until she grew in high school. She kept her brown hair short because it was easy to care for. Her big brown eyes dominated her face. Circumstances had turned Ami serious, but her wide, bright smile could light up a room.

Ami was delighted at the large crowds that were taking advantage of the first sunny days of spring to roam the Park Blocks in search of art. Her booth had attracted people since the fair opened, and three of her oils had sold already. She was putting the money from her most recent sale into her purse when someone spoke.

"I like that. Is it imaginary or did you paint a real scene?"

Ami turned and found a broad-shouldered man admiring one of her landscapes. His face had the tanned, leathery look of someone who spends a lot of time outdoors. Ami figured him for five-ten and in his mid- to late forties. He was dressed in jeans, moccasins, and a plaid long-sleeved shirt. His long hair was gathered in a ponytail, and he had a scraggly mustache and goatee. He brought to mind the hippies of the peace and love generation in the 1960s.

"That's a forest glade not far from my house," Ami said.

"I love the way you've captured the light."

Ami smiled. "Thanks. You have no idea how long I worked to get it just right."

"Dan Morelli," the man said, offering his hand. "I have the booth next door. I saw how many people have been going in and out of yours and decided to see what the fuss was all about."

"Ami Vergano," she said as she took Morelli's hand. It was large and comforting, like his smile. "What are you showing? I've been so busy that I haven't had a chance to look around yet."

"I build custom-made furniture. Take a peek if you get a chance."

"I will. Are you from around here? I haven't seen you at our shows before."

"First time in Oregon," Morelli said.

"Where's home?"

"No place, really. I was an army brat. We moved from town to town. I've been living in Arizona, but it's too dry. I like the woods, the ocean."

"There's not much of that in Arizona."

"No, there's not. Anyway, I heard about the fair and thought I'd see if I could get a few orders."

"How's it going?"

"Good. One fellow who stopped by just opened an accounting office and he wants a desk, bookshelves, and some other stuff. That should keep me busy for a while. Now I just have to find somewhere to stay and a place to work."

Ami hesitated. She didn't know a thing about Morelli, but he seemed nice. She made a snap decision.

"You might be in luck. I have an apartment over my garage that I rent out, and my studio is in a barn behind the house. It has plenty of room for carpentry. There's even a workshop and power tools. A student was renting but he had to leave school early because of an illness in the family, so the apartment is empty."

"I have my own tools, but that does sound just right. Can I drive out after the fair shuts down and have a look?"

"Sure."

"What's the rent?"

She told him and Morelli smiled shyly. "I can make that." He stepped out of Ami's booth and looked over at his own. "Got to go. Looks like I have customers. I'd better sell something now that I have to pay rent."

Ami laughed and waved. "See you around five."

Morelli ducked out, and Ami wrapped her arms around herself. Finances had been tight since her tenant left. She could use the extra money. And it would be fun to have another artist around the place. Morelli seemed nice. She hoped it would work out.

Ami Vergano closed the screen door as quietly as she could and stood on the front porch watching Daniel Morelli teach her ten-year-old son how to throw a curveball. They were in the front yard under the aged oak tree that Ami called Methuselah. Morelli was squatting beside Ryan and gently adjusting his fingers on the seams of a badly scuffed hardball that, along with his mitt, was her son's prize possession. Ryan's brow wrinkled as he concentrated on getting the grip right, oblivious of the darkness that was descending at the end of a perfect spring day.

Morelli was wearing jeans and a black T-shirt advertising a local microbrew. When he stretched out his arm, his biceps, triceps, and forearm looked like coiled rope. For someone approaching fifty, Morelli was in good shape. Ami knew that he ran for miles in the morning because she'd seen him returning to his apartment lathered in sweat when she was leaving for work. Once she'd seen him with his shirt off and had been impressed by the etched perfection of his physique. She had also been surprised to see more than one long scar cutting across his back and stomach.

"That's right," Morelli said, and Ryan grinned with pride. Her son was an energetic, gawky towhead who played Little League with a passion and loved anything to do with baseball. Since moving into the apartment over her garage three weeks ago, Morelli had kept pretty much to himself, but he and Ryan had struck up a friendship when her son learned that her lodger had played shortstop in middle school. There was no man in Ami's life, and Ryan gravitated toward any adult male who showed an interest in him. Ryan followed her tenant around like a puppy. Morelli didn't seem to mind. He appeared to enjoy explaining woodcraft to Ryan as well as the proper way to turn a double play.

Ryan looked so serious that Ami couldn't help smiling. She wished that she could freeze this tableau, but her duties as a mother forced her into the role of the Grinch.

"Time for bed," Ami said as the sun edged below the horizon.

"Can't I stay up a little longer?" Ryan begged.

Morelli stood up and tousled Ryan's hair. "We'll work on the curve tomorrow, little buddy. I promise."

"But I've almost got it."

"You do, but it's too dark now and this old man is getting tired. So listen to your mother."

"Okay," Ryan said reluctantly as he trudged up the porch steps and into the house.

"Thanks for playing with Ryan," Ami said. "If he gets to be too much for you, let me know."

"He's no trouble. He listens and tries real hard."

"But he can be exhausting. I'm serious. I appreciate the time you spend with him but don't feel bad about turning him down once in a while."

"Don't worry. He's a good kid. I enjoy working with him."

"Do you want a cup of coffee?" Ami asked. "I'm going to fix one as soon as I get Ryan tucked away."

"That sounds good."

"I've got some cake if you're interested."

"Coffee will be fine."

"Take a seat, then, and I'll be out as soon as I get Ryan settled."

There were several wicker chairs on the porch. Morelli plopped into one and stretched his legs. The spring evening was balmy, and he closed his eyes. He was just shy of falling asleep when the screen door snapped open and Ami handed him a mug.

"Did I wake you?" she joked.

"I did almost nod off. It's so nice tonight."

"How's the work coming?"

"I brought over the desk two days ago and Mr. DeWitt was real happy."

"Good. Maybe he'll get you some more orders."

"He already has. The real estate agent in the office next door to his wants me to build a desk for his home office."

"That's great."

They sat in silence for a while and sipped their coffee.

"This weather is perfect," Ami said after a while.

"You can't beat spring and summer in Oregon," Morelli answered.

"It's the winters that get me down, but once you get through December, January, and February the weather is fine."

Ami had turned toward Morelli when she spoke and she saw his eyes start to close again. She laughed.

"Looks like Ryan did you in."

Morelli grinned. "I am wiped. I put in a real full day."

"Don't stand on ceremony if you want to get to sleep."

"No, I think I'll sit a while more. I'm usually on my own and I'm enjoying the company."

"Have you ever thought of staying in one place and opening a store? Your stuff is good. I bet you could build up a clientele pretty fast."

"I'm a drifter, Ami. I get too restless."

Ami thought Morelli sounded a little sad when he confessed his wanderlust. She imagined that it must be lonely always moving from place to place. Then she remembered that solitary men who liked its vast and empty expanses had built the west. Morelli was just a modern-day version of mountain men like Jim Bridger and Joe Meek. He even looked as she imagined they would have looked with his long hair and hard, lined face.

They talked for a while more before Ami told Morelli that she had to finish up some chores. Morelli thanked her for the coffee and walked across the lawn to his apartment. As Ami watched him she remembered something he'd said earlier when they were discussing the weather. He'd just told her that you couldn't beat spring and summer in Oregon, but she was almost certain that the day they'd met, at the art fair, Morelli had told her that he'd never been in the state before.

# CHAPTER **TWO**

Vanessa Kohler hadn't chosen to conduct the interview with Terri Warmouth at the Cruise On Inn because the thirty-six-year-old shipping clerk had claimed she'd been abducted from its parking lot. Vanessa had chosen the tavern because it had cheap scotch and she could smoke there without getting dirty looks from her politically correct colleagues.

Vanessa was a hard-drinking, rail-thin chain-smoker with snarled blond hair and pale blue eyes. The forty-nine-year-old reporter paid no attention to her looks and favored baggy jeans and bulky sweaters, unless she was on assignment. Tonight, she'd cleaned up a little and was wearing a black leather jacket over a T-shirt and tight jeans.

Vanessa looked at her watch. It was almost nine, and Warmouth had said she'd be at the tavern at eight-thirty. Vanessa decided to give her another scotch's worth of time before heading home. Sam Cutler, her boyfriend, was out on an assignment at some rock concert anyway, and there was nothing on the tube. She could think of worse ways to spend her time than drinking in the ambience created by smoke, loud country music, and raucous pool players.

A sudden draft told Vanessa that someone had opened the door. She shifted her gaze from the scarred tabletop to the front of the tavern. A heavyset, big-haired woman wearing too much makeup was bathed in the red-green light of the jukebox. She cast anxious glances around the bar until Vanessa raised her hand. The woman hurried over.

"Vanessa Kohler from *Exposed*," she said as she handed Warmouth her card. The woman's hand shook when she took it.

"Sorry I'm late," Warmouth apologized. She sat down and laid Vanessa's card on the table next to a puddle of beer. "This is Larry's bowling night and his ride was late."

"Perfectly understandable," Vanessa said.

"I couldn't let him know I was going out. He'd want to know where I was going and who I was meeting. I just hope he doesn't call from the alley. I'll be up all night getting grilled."

She flashed a weak smile, looking for sympathy. It took Vanessa a moment to catch on. She flashed back a smile that she hoped conveyed female solidarity.

"Can I buy you a beer?" the reporter asked.

"That sounds good."

Vanessa signaled for the waitress and ordered a pitcher.

"So, Terri, you ready to tell your story?" Vanessa asked when the waitress left.

"Yeah, sure," she said, though she didn't sound so sure.

Vanessa placed a tape recorder on the table between them. "Do you mind if I record this so I can report what you tell me accurately?" she asked, omitting the part about the recording being primo evidence whenever a fruitcake decided to sue.

Warmouth hesitated but then said, "Sure, okay."

Vanessa pressed "record."

"This is going to be in the paper, right, with my real name and everything?" Warmouth asked.

"You bet."

"Because it's the only way Larry will believe it, if it's in *Exposed*. He reads it like the Bible, every week. He says it's the only paper he can trust."

"It's good to know we have such loyal readers."

"That's why I called you, on account of Larry being such a loyal reader."

"Right. So, as I understand it, you're pregnant?"

Warmouth looked down at the table and nodded.

"You've got to speak up for the recorder, Terri," Vanessa reminded her.

"Oh, right. Yeah, I'm . . . I got . . . "

"Pregnant."

"Right."

"And this was a surprise?"

Warmouth reddened. "Yeah, I'll say." She looked

up, her eyes begging for understanding. "Larry's going to know it's not his. We tried like crazy after we was married." Warmouth hesitated. "You ain't going to put this part in the paper, are you?"

"Not if you don't want me to."

"Well, don't. It would embarrass him something awful."

"What would?"

"The doctor told us I'm okay, but Larry's sperm don't swim so fast. I don't understand all of it, but it made him feel terrible, unmanly, you know. So, he'll know it weren't his kid."

"And whose kid will it be?" Vanessa prodded.

"The alien's."

"The ones who abducted you from the parking lot of the Cruise On Inn?"

"Yes," Warmouth answered in a little voice that Vanessa could barely hear over the noise in the bar.

"Tell me how it happened."

"I was here . . . "

"What night was this?"

"Same as tonight. Larry's bowling night."

"So, Larry didn't know you were out on the town?"

"Uh, no."

"Were you alone?" Vanessa asked, watching Warmouth carefully when she answered. Her interviewee ducked her head and turned deep red.

"Yeah, just me," she said.

"How come you came here? The Cruise On is pretty far from your house."

"It ain't so far from work."

"Been here with some of your pals from work, have you?"

"Some of my girlfriends," she answered too quickly.

"But that night you were on your own?"

"Yes. And it got late, so I knew I'd have to go so I'd be home when Larry got home. He doesn't like me going off on my own."

"Larry's the jealous type?"

"I'll say. He's always going on about how guys stare at me and accusing me of staring back, when I'm not. It's sort of flattering, but it can get on your nerves, if you know what I mean."

"You bet," Vanessa answered with a nod. "So, tell me about the aliens."

"Yeah, okay. So I went out to my car, which was over at the end of the lot, and I was just about to open the door when I heard this like humming sound, and I looked up and there it was."

"There what was?"

"The ship. It was big and spinning and it looked like a saucer, but with lights."

"Any special color lights?"

"Uh, green, I think. I don't remember real well. I was pretty shook. But it did look like a lot of those alien ships you write about in your paper. So it was probably from the same planet."

"Which planet is that?"

"They never said, but some of the other ones who got abducted knew the name of the planet and I bet it was one of those, since the ship was so similar."

"What happened after you saw the ship?"

"Well, that's where it gets hazy. I do recall a beam of light coming down. But after that it's like you get when you have an operation and they give you drugs."

"Some of our abductees have said it's like a good high."

"Yeah, sort of like that. You know how you sort of float. Well that's what I was doing. But I do remember I was strapped down on this table and I didn't have any clothes on. And this tall one was on top of me."

"Having sex?"

"I don't know what they do. I didn't really feel anything. And then I was back in the parking lot."

"Naked?"

"Uh, no, the aliens must have put my clothes on."

"And the ship was nowhere to be seen?"

"No, they must have left after they beamed me back down."

"Made their getaway before anyone could see them?"

"Yeah, made their getaway," Terri echoed softly.

Terri was crying. Vanessa switched off the tape recorder. She reached across the table and took Warmouth's hand.

"Larry's not going to buy this, Terri. I know you're hoping he will because he likes my paper, but he's going to know."

Terri's shoulders were shaking, and the tears were pouring down.

"Who is it? Someone from work?"

Warmouth's head bobbed up and down for a second. When she lifted her tear-streaked face Vanessa tried to remember if she'd ever seen anyone who looked so miserable.

"But he says it isn't his," Warmouth said between gulps for air. "He . . . he says I must have been sleeping around or it's Larry's."

"Sounds like a real nice guy," Vanessa observed.

Warmouth wiped her eyes. "I sure thought he was."

"So you can't count on this guy and you can't tell your husband."

Warmouth's head bobbed yes.

"What about an abortion?"

"How would I pay for it? Larry has all the money. If I asked him for some, I'd have to explain why I wanted it. He'd ask for receipts if I said I was buying something. He watches money like a hawk."

Vanessa made a decision. She reached across the table and picked up the business card she'd handed Terri Warmouth. Then she wrote a name and phone number on the back of it.

"You call this doctor, Terri. You tell her I told you to call. I'll clear it with her first thing in the morning, so call from work around ten. She'll take care of you."

"But the money . . . ?"

Vanessa squeezed Terri's hand. "Don't worry about the money. Just get this taken care of."

"I really want a baby," Warmouth sobbed. "I don't know if I can do it."

"That's up to you. You don't have to. Think about it. I know it's a hard choice." Vanessa paused. "You could leave Larry, you know. Leave him and have the baby."

Warmouth looked stricken. "I couldn't leave Larry. I love him."

"Would he accept a child that wasn't his?"

"No, never! He'd kill me. Being a man, it's real important to him. If he knew I cheated . . . and I love him. I don't want to leave him." She seemed to be in agony.

Vanessa stood up. "I'm going to call my friend in the morning. Then it's up to you." She dropped some money on the table and slipped the tape recorder back into her purse. "Come on. Let's get out of here." Vanessa smiled. "I'll walk you to your car. Make sure the aliens don't get you."

Terri Warmouth didn't smile back. "I wish they would," she said.

Vanessa drove from the tavern to the offices of *Exposed* to finish a story about a giant rat that was stealing slum babies. The rat was supposed to be as big as a German shepherd. Patrick Gorman, Vanessa's boss, had made up the story at the weekly staff meeting and assigned Vanessa to write it. Vanessa had thought it was disgusting and had protested, finally getting Gorman to agree that she could substitute Terri Warmouth's alien abduction tale if it panned out. But it hadn't.

The paper took up two floors of a remodeled warehouse within sight of the Capitol dome in a section of Washington, D.C., that teetered between gentrification and decay. Abandoned buildings and vacant lots—the habitat of junkies and the homeless—could be found within blocks of multicolored, rehabilitated row houses owned by young professionals. Vanessa unlocked the front door, relocked it, and walked past the Personals office. When she had started with the paper, the personals amused her. In recent years they had become bizarre enough to freak her out. She hoped that they were genuinely weirder, because the alternative was that she was getting old.

Vanessa walked up the stairs to the second floor and checked in with the security guard. He told her that no one else was around. That was fine with Vanessa. After her meeting with Terri Warmouth she craved solitude. Warmouth had exhausted her. Needy people always made Vanessa uncomfortable, which was odd considering her line of work. Supermarket tabloids lived off the exotic and psychotic tales told by people who had a tough time fitting into the real world. The people she interviewed talked themselves into believing in another Earth where the strange and wonderful occurred with enough frequency to let them escape from the demands of their drab existence.

Vanessa punched in her security code and used her key to get into the second floor, where the work of creating each edition was carried on. The office seemed bigger than it was because of the vaulted ceiling, which was painted gray like the thick cross beams. Vanessa fixed herself a cup of instant coffee in the staff kitchen before turning on the fluorescent lights that illuminated the cubicles where the reporters worked. Her cubicle was across the floor from a floor-to-ceiling bookshelf that held back issues of *Exposed* and other tabloids. It was filled with two black metal filing cabinets and a desk on which perched her file holder and computer monitor.

Vanessa was one of the lucky few with a window, but it was too dark to see anything outside. She sipped her coffee and toiled on her story to the accompaniment of the night noises that haunted the floor where the minions of *Exposed* worked for low wages and no prestige. Vanessa's salary at *Exposed* was ridiculous, but she didn't need the money. What she did need was access to press credentials and databases so that she could proceed with her research.

Vanessa lived in a redbrick row house in the Adams Morgan section of Washington. The area off Eighteenth Northwest was funky and crowded with Ethiopian restaurants, jazz nightclubs, bars, and pizza parlors. Most nights, a rowdy college crowd packed the streets. Vanessa enjoyed the chaotic scene, and her apartment was far enough from Eighteenth to muffle the noise. It was well after one when she opened the door to her fourth-floor apartment. She could afford something better, but she had lived in Adams Morgan for years. Her neighbors kept to themselves, and there was plenty of room for her research materials, which were mostly in the spare bedroom but had started to spill out into the living room. They consisted of the Warren Commission Report and books critical of it, tomes on the Roswell cover-up, and magazines with stories about the CIA's covert operations and the like. If a book or article alleged a government conspiracy, Vanessa had it or had read it.

Vanessa flipped on the lights. The sight of a parcel with a return address from New York made her heart sink. The package was sitting on a small table in the foyer where Sam had stacked the mail. Vanessa carried it into the living room. She switched on the lamp beside the sofa and sat down to the groan of aged springs, placing the package on top of the magazines and days-old newspapers that littered her coffee table. She stared at the package for a minute before ripping off the brown paper wrapper. A letter lay on top of her manuscript, covering the title and her assertion of authorship. Vanessa hesitated before picking up the letter. It was signed by an editor at Parthenon Press who was supposed to be open to new ideas and was not afraid to challenge the establishment. He had published a number of controversial exposés of government cover-ups. A book of his about a Marine who'd blown the whistle on a training maneuver that had left two recruits dead had just fallen off the best-seller list.

Dear Ms. Kohler: I read *Phantoms* with great interest. Unfortunately, I have decided that your book is not right for Parthenon Press. I wish you the best of luck placing your manuscript. Yours truly, Walter Randolph

Vanessa squeezed her eyes shut. She wanted to fling the manuscript across the room and break things. She fought to keep her rage in check and tried to dissipate her hostile energy by pacing the worn carpet that covered her hardwood floor. Something was going on here. It could be as simple as the fact that her press credentials were from *Exposed* instead of *The New York Times*. Of course, that level of credibility was closed to her. No reputable paper was going to hire someone with her history. But Vanessa was certain that something darker was at work.

Vanessa was a superb researcher and had ferreted out Walter Randolph's unlisted home phone number as part of her background check on the editor when she was deciding to whom she would send her book. Vanessa dialed a number in Connecticut and waited while the phone rang several times.

"Hello," answered a voice groggy with sleep.

"Walter Randolph?"

"Who is this?"

"Vanessa Kohler."

"Who?"

"*Phantoms*. You just rejected it."

"It's one-thirty in the morning, Ms. Kohler," Randolph answered, fighting to sound civil. "Would you please call me at work?"

"Who got to you?"

"I will not continue this discussion at this time."

"Was it my father? Did someone from the government visit you? Did someone threaten you or buy you off?"

"I rejected your book because of insufficient documentation, Ms. Kohler. There was nothing sinister about the decision."

"You don't expect me to believe that?"

Vanessa heard a sigh on the other end of the line. "I don't know how you got this number, but a call at this hour is a violation of my privacy. I am going to end it in a moment, but, since you insist on knowing, not only have you failed to verify your rather dramatic claims, but your past makes it highly unlikely that any publishing house would give them any credence."

"My past?"

"Your mental history, Ms. Kohler. And now I must hang up. I have a hard day tomorrow and I need my sleep."

"Who told you I was hospitalized, who told you that?"

But Vanessa found herself talking to a dead line. She slammed down the phone, redialed, and got a busy signal for her efforts. She was about to throw the phone at the wall when the front door opened and Sam Cutler walked in carrying his camera equipment. He was dressed in jeans and wore a tight black T-shirt under a windbreaker.

Vanessa was five-ten. Sam was a little taller—and solid, while Vanessa verged on anorexic. He was a few years older than Vanessa, and his gray-streaked brown hair was receding up front.

Sam stopped in his tracks and Vanessa froze, arm cocked, the phone a moment away from destruction. Sam saw the manuscript on the coffee table.

"A rejection, huh? I was going to hide it until I came home. Then I got a call and forgot."

The arm holding the phone dropped to Vanessa's side. "Someone got to the editor. I'm sure of it."

"How do you know that?" Sam asked, keeping his voice neutral because he knew that the slightest sign of doubt where this subject was concerned could push Vanessa into an uncontrollable rage.

"He knew I was hospitalized. How did he find out about the sanatorium if someone didn't tell him?"

Sam crossed the room. He knew better than to try for physical contact now. He hoped that standing close would calm her.

"Maybe there was something in the papers," he suggested. "Your father is big news right now. There might have been a sidebar about the family."

Vanessa shook her head vehemently. "They want to discredit me. There's no way they're going to let this get out."

"Who is 'they'?" Sam asked, knowing that he was treading on thin ice.

"My father, the military, the CIA. You don't think they were all involved? Once the truth gets out, Watergate will look like a tea party. They can't afford to let the public get even a hint of what I know."

Sam had been down this road before. "If that's true, why hasn't anyone tried to kill you?" he asked calmly. "Why hasn't anyone stolen your manuscript? You haven't made a secret of what you're doing. Everyone knows about your book. You even tried to interview that guy at the CIA, and nothing happened."

Vanessa glared at Sam. "You don't understand how they work. They could steal my manuscript, but they know I'd just write the book again. Besides, my attorney has a copy. And killing me would let everyone know that I was telling the truth."

"Everyone who? Come on, Vanessa. I respect what you're trying to do. I know you think you're right, but most people who know about this . . . Well, they don't believe it. And the CIA could make your death look like an accident, if they wanted to. You know that. No one would think you were killed to suppress your book. People would think you were the victim of a hit and run or had a heart attack or something like that."

Vanessa slumped down on the couch. "You're right," she said. She sounded very tired. "Randolph is right." She closed her eyes and laid her head back. "I'm an ex-mental patient and I don't have a shred of evidence that proves that the Unit ever existed. There never was much evidence, anyway—just a few sheets of paper, and they're gone."

"You look all in, babe. Let's get to bed. You'll think better in the morning. You'll figure out what to do when your mind is clear."

"He's going to win, Sam. He always wins and he's going to win again. I can't stop him, I never could. No one can."

Vanessa's hands curled into fists and her eyes snapped open. A vivid anger was sizzling in them.

"Do you know how my father made his bones in the intelligence community?"

"No, I don't."

"Think about this. Daddy was promoted very rapidly starting in early 1964, right after the Kennedy assassination."

Sam's mouth gaped open. "You don't think . . . ?"

"I think my mother knew. I think that's why he killed her, to keep her from telling the truth about who was really on the grassy knoll."

"Did your mother tell you she thought that . . . ?" Sam couldn't even finish the sentence.

"She was always upset on the date of Kennedy's death. When I asked her why, she would never tell me. And she looked scared to death if I asked while my father was in the room."

"Ah, Van," Sam said, dropping onto the couch beside her and wrapping an arm around her shoulder. "You've got yourself in a knot. You're not thinking straight."

Vanessa's rage disappeared as quickly as it had appeared. She laid her head on Sam's shoulder and started to cry.

"I hate him, Sam. I hate him. I wish he were dead."

# CHAPTER **THREE**

Ami Vergano grabbed her purse and locked the front door. Ryan stuffed his baseball in his mitt and charged toward the station wagon. Ami froze with her hand on the doorknob, wondering if she'd turned off the living room lights. Electricity cost money she couldn't afford to waste. Then she remembered the bag with Ryan's snacks. She reopened the door and dashed into the kitchen.

"We'll be late, Mom," Ryan yelled anxiously, reminding Ami of something she knew already. She was still wearing the navy blue pantsuit and powder-blue shirt she'd worn at work because she had not had time to change. A client had kept her on the phone forever and she'd had to drive home like a lunatic in order to get Ryan to his Little League game on time. Being a professional woman and a single mother sucked, but she wasn't a trust fund baby, she had to pay the bills. And Ryan made all the running around and stress worthwhile. Every time she started to feel sorry for herself, Ami looked at her son and real-

ized just how lucky she was, despite everything
that had happened.

When she graduated from law school, Ami had
never imagined herself living a frantic existence on
the edge of financial ruin. She was married to Chad
Vergano, the love of her life, and had just been
hired by a small Portland firm. When Ryan was
born, her future looked rosy. But life has a way of
playing tricks on us. When Ryan was five, Chad
died in a freak bicycling accident. They had only a
small life insurance policy, and neither of their parents was well off, so Ami had to depend on her
salary at the firm. Then the firm disintegrated.
Unable to find work with another firm because of a
horrid economic climate, Ami had been forced to
hang out a shingle. She had friends who fed her
work, and she was starting to build a clientele, but
the demands of parenting made it tough to take on
any case or client that would require too much of
her time. This meant living on a shoestring budget
and praying that she would never get sick.

Ami shut the front door and got into the car.
"Let's go," Ryan shouted impatiently as she fas-
tened his seat belt. Daniel Morelli hopped into
the back. As the adult, he should have been sitting beside her, but Daniel had turned out to be a
gentle, considerate soul who knew that Ryan
liked to sit in front and pretend to be the man of
the house.

Ryan's game was being played at a field behind
the local middle school, and Ami pulled into the
parking lot with three minutes to spare. Ryan
tore out of the car and raced toward his team-

mates, who were grouped around Ben Branton. Ben's son played third base and Branton Cleaners, the family business, sponsored the team.

Morelli watched Ami watching Ryan and smiled. "He's a handful."

Ami smiled back. "He's not so bad. He just gets so excited."

Ben Branton spotted Morelli and waved him over. The two men had met at Ryan's last game.

"Dan, I need a favor. Rick Stein usually helps me out, but Andy is sick so he's not here. Can you be my assistant coach today?"

"No problem. What do I do?"

Branton handed Morelli a roster attached to a wooden clipboard, and a mechanical pencil. He was explaining Morelli's duties when the umpire called the coaches onto the field. Ami settled in the stand between two other Little League moms.

Ryan's team scored a run in the second inning. Two innings later, the other team tied the score. Ami cheered good-naturedly like most of the other parents when Ryan got a hit. Barney Lutz was the exception. Lutz was a huge man with a beer gut and thick shoulders he'd developed doing construction work. His heavy black beard and perpetual scowl frightened Ryan. Barney's kid, Tony, was also a load and no one liked him or his father. They were bullies and sore losers. Ben Branton constantly had to deflect Tony's attacks on his teammates and opposing players. At games, Barney stood behind the backstop, jeering the opposing squad or ordering Tony and his teammates around. Ben

Branton's attempts to get Barney to tone it down were ignored.

The trouble started in the fifth inning when Tony hit a single and tried to stretch it to a double. Ben told Tony to stay on first, but his father bellowed at him to run. Tony was fat and slow. The right fielder pegged the ball to the second baseman with plenty of time to make the tag. Tony saw that he would be out at second and would never get back to first. Out of frustration, he stopped short of second base. When the second baseman tried to tag him, Tony threw out both hands. The kid was half Tony's size, and the blows sent him sprawling. The umpire and both coaches ran onto the field to see if the second baseman was okay. The kid was crying but was more shocked than hurt. As his coach attended to him, Ben pulled Tony Lutz aside and began bawling him out.

Two policemen had been watching the game. Ami had seen one of them urging on the pitcher for the opposing team and guessed that he was a parent. The officers moved to the edge of the infield when Barney Lutz headed for Ben. Morelli stood to one side, watching quietly.

"That was a terrible thing to do," Ben Branton was telling Tony when Barney Lutz reached him. Ben looked over at Tony's father.

"I can't let Tony play anymore today, and I'm not letting him play next week."

"Bullshit. My boy just plays aggressive baseball. The second baseman was blocking the bag."

Ben Branton was slender, bookish, and five inches shorter than Barney Lutz, but he held his ground.

"I'm suspending Tony."

"No, you're not."

"I have to, Barney. He fights all the time. That sets a very bad example for the other kids."

"Listen, you candy ass, my boy's got fire. If these spoiled brats played as hard as Tony we'd win some games."

"Hey," Morelli said, "could you tone it down? There are kids here."

Barney glared at Morelli. "I'm not talking to you, so fuck off."

"Barney," Branton said, "I'll have to suspend Tony for the rest of the year if you don't stop this scene."

"You're not suspending anyone, you faggot. I'm coaching from now on. So get the fuck off the field."

Barney turned toward Morelli. "Give me that," he said, making a grab for the clipboard. Ben grabbed Lutz by the forearm. Lutz wrenched his arm loose and pulled his hand back to punch the coach. Branton staggered away from the threatened punch and tripped over his feet. As the coach fell to the ground, Morelli chopped down with the side of the clipboard and shattered Lutz's wrist. Lutz went white from pain and swung his head toward Morelli, exposing his neck. Morelli drove the mechanical pencil into the bully's throat. The huge man's eyes went wide, his hands flew to his neck, and he crashed to the ground. Ben Branton stared in horror as Lutz gurgled and writhed in front of him.

The policemen had rushed forward as soon as

they saw Lutz start to swing. The big man was tumbling to the ground when the first officer grabbed Morelli from behind. Ami saw the policeman fly through the air. Dust rose where his shoulder hit the ground. Morelli transformed his hand into a spear and aimed his fingertips at the helpless policeman's throat. The other officer pulled his gun and fired. Morelli half-stood and turned. The officer fired again and Morelli collapsed in the dirt. All around Ami, people were gasping and screaming, but the only sounds that reached her clearly were Ryan's cries of "Dan, Dan," as he rushed toward his fallen hero.

Ben Branton had not moved from the time Morelli stabbed Barney Lutz until Morelli was shot by the police officer. Ryan's screams snapped him out of his trance. The policeman heard Ryan's footsteps and whirled around. "No!" Ben yelled when he saw the gun pointing at Ami's son. Ryan and the policeman froze. Ben ran to Ryan and scooped him up.

The policeman with the gun looked as startled as everyone else. In the stands, terrified parents were calling 911 on their cell phones. A mother from one team and a father from the other rushed up and told the officer they were doctors. The policeman who had tried to subdue Morelli was grimacing in pain from a shattered collarbone, but he told the doctors to tend to Lutz and Morelli.

Ami took her son from Ben. Ryan was staring at Morelli. Blood had pooled around his wounds, turning the brown dust rusty-red. Ami turned

Ryan so he would not see his wounded friend and started to walk off the field.

"Ma'am," the officer with the gun said. Ami stopped. He pointed at Morelli. "Do you know this man?"

"Yes. He's my tenant. He was helping the coach."

"I know you want to take your son away from here, but I need you to stick around. The detectives will want to ask you some questions."

Ami nodded and led Ryan from the field in a daze. Daniel Morelli had been living in her home for two months. She thought that he was a quiet, kind, and gentle man. She could not believe how wrong she had been.

# CHAPTER **FOUR**

"Best giant rat story I've read since the *Enquirer* piece about the prehistoric rodent that was terrorizing that island near Borneo."

It was almost five, and Patrick Gorman was standing over Vanessa's desk with a grin plastered on his face. Gorman was a fat man with heavy jowls and an alcoholic complexion. He was usually fun to work for because he didn't take himself or the paper seriously, but he could be demanding. For Gorman, UFOs and the Loch Ness monster were commodities, like sneakers for Nike. Produce, and Gorman loved you. Adversely affect his bottom line, and there was hell to pay.

"Stuff it, Pat," Vanessa said. She glared at her boss. "You owe me."

Gorman laughed. "You could have gone with the alien abduction."

Vanessa averted her eyes. "That didn't work out."

Gorman noted her rapid change of mood but didn't say anything. He respected his reporter and he wasn't going to ask her what had happened if she didn't want to tell him. Gorman knew that he was lucky to have someone as talented as Vanessa on board. Most reporters with her brains and ability fled to legitimate newspapers as soon as the chance presented itself. He knew why she couldn't move on, but he never held that up to her. Vanessa appreciated his tact.

"I've got something I want you to look at," Gorman said. "It's all over the news. There was a brawl at a Little League game in Oregon. A coach decked a cop and another cop shot him."

"You're kidding."

"That ain't the good part. The coach who got shot, he almost killed the parent of one of the kids by ramming a pencil into his throat."

Vanessa's mouth dropped. "You sure this is Little League? It sounds more like pro wrestling."

"I just caught a little of it on talk radio when I was driving in. Check it out and get back to me if you think there's something we can run with. Everyone's got an opinion. It's the Little League parent thing, too much pressure on the tots to excel, parents living vicariously through their kids."

Gorman walked away, but the phrase lingered in Vanessa's head. Parents living vicariously through their kids. No chance of that problem with her parents, she thought angrily. Charlotte Kohler had never had a chance to see her daughter grow up. She was dead, murdered, when Vanessa was thirteen years old—although Vanessa was the only one who had dared to accuse her father of murder publicly, and much good that did her.

And her father didn't need to live through her. He had his own plans. Her father had never shown much interest in her except when he destroyed her life. Then he had been very focused.

Vanessa shook off these bitter thoughts, knowing full well what would happen to her if she dwelled on them. She swung back to her computer and punched up the Little League story on the Internet. After reading a few accounts, she concluded that Gorman hadn't been kidding. An overbearing parent had been stabbed in the throat with a mechanical pencil, but quick work by an EMT had saved him. One of the cops had a broken collarbone and the assistant coach was in the hospital with two gunshot wounds. Vanessa decided that if she ever had a kid who wanted to play Little League she'd talk him into joining the Marines. It sounded safer.

Vanessa logged off her computer at eight and dialed Sam's extension.

"The Smiling Buddha?" Vanessa asked, naming a Chinese restaurant two blocks from the paper.

"You're on. Meet you in the lobby in ten."

Vanessa walked to the ground floor. As a practicing paranoid, she scanned the street outside while she waited near the front door. Two men were talking in a doorway across the way. They did not look threatening, but Vanessa didn't trust anyone. Inside her oversize purse with her cosmetics, address book, and tissues was an unregistered .357 Magnum loaded with hollow-point rounds. One advantage of being an army brat was her ability to shoot anything, anywhere. Her father had taught her about guns from an early age. She'd hunted deer and even bagged big game in Africa on a safari as a teenager. The togetherness had stopped when her mother died, but the skill remained.

"What did Gorman think of the rat tale?" Sam asked as they walked toward the restaurant.

"Loved it. He's such a prick. But he did put me onto something interesting. Real news, for once," Vanessa said, filling him in on the Little League massacre as they walked.

"Oregon is nice this time of year," Sam said. "See if you can wheedle a trip out there. Maybe ask him to send a photographer along."

"Sounds good," Vanessa said as they passed a clothing store. She stopped for a moment, apparently to look at the dresses in the window, but really to check the reflection from the other side of the street. The men from the doorway were a half-block back. One was tall, the other short and stocky. Both wore windbreakers and jeans. Vanessa's heart started to pound, but she didn't say anything to Sam, who tolerated her paranoid fantasies but never encouraged them.

An hour later, Vanessa and Sam were reading their fortunes. Sam was coming into big money, but Vanessa was supposed to be wary of strangers. It was after nine and there was a hint of rain in the air when they left the restaurant. They had taken separate cars to work, and they reached Sam's car first. He gave Vanessa a peck on the cheek and said he'd see her at home.

Vanessa looked for the two men who had been waiting outside the office, but the streets around the *Exposed* building were empty. A page from a newspaper flew down the street until the wind plastered it against a chain-link fence. Over the fence were the remnants of an abandoned warehouse that was destined to become some upwardly mobile couple's dream condo. Vanessa thought she saw someone moving through the rubble and hurried to her car.

A man was standing in the shadows of a doorway across the street. He wore a hooded sweatshirt and looked homeless, but people engaged in surveillance often used disguises. Vanessa locked her doors as soon as she was in the driver's seat. A face pressed against the glass of the passenger's window. Vanessa reached into her purse without thinking. She saw messy red hair and cheeks covered with stubble. Bloodshot eyes stared in at her. The man knocked on the window. Vanessa extended the Magnum. The man jumped back, his eyes wide with fright. Vanessa gunned the engine. Her car fishtailed down the street. She cut the wheel and raced down a side street, putting a building between her and the derelict. Just before she turned, she looked in her mirror. The man was standing in the middle of the street watching her.

Vanessa zigzagged through town until she was certain she wasn't being followed. The adrenaline was starting to wear off when she pulled into the dark end of a parking lot. Her hands were shaking. Who had sent the man after her? Had he been after her? Panhandlers had accosted her many times. That was an occupational hazard of working in the *Exposed* building. Had she overreacted? And what about the two men who had followed her and Sam to the restaurant? Maybe that was innocent, too. But what if it wasn't? What if they were spotters who kept the man in the hooded sweatshirt aware of her movements? And if there were three men working together, there could be more.

Sam! She had to warn him before he arrived at the apartment. They might be waiting for her. She pulled out her cell phone. Not Sam. If anything happened to him . . . She dialed Sam's cell. It was turned off. He would be home in minutes. Vanessa dialed 911.

"There are men at my apartment," she screamed hysterically, hoping the urgency in her voice would spur the dispatcher to action. "They're killing my boyfriend."

The dispatcher tried to get her to calm down, but she gave her address and disconnected the phone. If the cops got there fast enough, Sam might be okay. She started to tear up and gulped down air. She couldn't afford to be hysterical. She had to think.

Vanessa couldn't go to the apartment, but she didn't dare use a credit card at a motel or hotel. The people who were after her would trace her if she charged her account. Vanessa had just been to the ATM and had two hundred dollars less the price of her dinner. She started the car and drove into Maryland to a large motel run by a chain. She paid cash and gave the desk clerk the phony ID she always carried with her. Vanessa also carried real and counterfeit passports. As soon as she was in her room she called Sam.

"Thank God," Vanessa said when she heard his voice. "Are you okay?"

"Why wouldn't I be? Has something happened?"

"I can't talk now. Has anyone searched the apartment?"

"Searched the . . . Vanessa, what's going on? There were cops here when I got home. They said a woman told 911 I was being attacked. Was that you? Did you make that call to the cops?"

Vanessa was about to answer when she heard a voice in the background.

"Who's that?" Vanessa asked.

"One of the policemen. He wants to talk to you."

"I can't."

What if her cell phone call had been intercepted and the men at the apartment weren't really cops? She wanted to tell Sam to run, to leave town, but another man took the phone and started asking her questions. Vanessa cut the connection.

It seemed as if hours had passed since her meal with Sam and her flight to the motel, but it was only a little before eleven. She slumped down on the edge of the bed, exhausted. She had gotten a kit with a toothbrush and toothpaste from the front desk when she checked in. She brushed her teeth, washed up, stripped off her jeans, and crawled under the covers. When she closed her eyes she thought of Sam.

Vanessa had taken few lovers since getting out of the institution. Most men ran after learning that she'd been in an asylum. Those that thought screwing an ex-lunatic was kinky ran when they learned the depth of her obsession. Until she met Sam Cutler at a bar near her apartment three months ago, Vanessa had not been with a man for a little over a year. Sam was a freelance photographer who had worked all over the world. She had been reluctant to let him get close to her at first, but he had persisted and she had dropped her guard.

Sam could tell great stories, in bed he was creative and had endurance; but the best thing about him was that he was not judgmental. It had not fazed him when he learned that Vanessa was an ex-mental patient. When Vanessa told him about the Unit, he had calmly accepted its existence as a possibility. Vanessa had talked Patrick Gorman into giving Sam a job, and she had started to believe that she might find happiness at last. What if something happened to him now? What if he died because of her?

Vanessa felt empty inside and tired of her life. The people who were after her had so many resources and she had so few. She couldn't run forever. If they were hunting her, they would catch her eventually. She started to cry in the dark. After a while she drifted off to sleep.

*   *   *

Vanessa opened her eyes and jerked up, startled by the strange surroundings. Then she remembered where she was and why she was hiding in a motel instead of waking up in her apartment and getting ready for work. She felt sick. Had she panicked for no reason? Had she made a fool of herself? She recalled the events of the previous evening. While waiting for Sam she had noticed two men talking in a doorway across from her office, but were they talking about her? Did they even know that she existed? The men had walked slightly behind her in the same direction as the restaurant, but were they following her? And what about the bum who had knocked on her car window? Did she have any evidence that he wasn't just a homeless man looking for a handout? In the light of day her actions seemed absurd.

Vanessa felt so stupid. What would she do now? She couldn't go to work. She would have to face Sam. Would this be the last straw? Would he leave her? He had always tried to understand, but how much could he take? And what about the police? Would they arrest her for making a false report? No, the police would have no further interest in her. Sam would have seen to that. She flushed with shame as she imagined him explaining that his girlfriend was a former mental patient who imagined that people were plotting against her. The cops would have been angry at first, but their anger would have turned to sympathy for the poor bastard who was living with this loony. They would have shaken their heads as they left. The incident probably provided a few good laughs back at the station house.

Vanessa couldn't go home and she couldn't go to work. She was ashamed to face Sam. Checkout time was noon. She decided to stay in the room until she was forced to leave. Maybe she would think of something by then.

Vanessa ordered room service. While she waited for her food, she turned on Fox cable news in the middle of a report on a retired general, Morris Wingate. The General had left the military in the late 1980s and stayed out of the public eye for many years. In the early 1990s, he had invested heavily in Computex, a fledgling software company headed by a genius named Simeon Brown. Wingate's contacts in the military helped the company obtain lucrative contracts. A few years ago, Brown had died when his private jet crashed during a vacation trip to Greece, and Wingate had taken over the company. Last year, he had become a national hero by rescuing six of his employees who had been kidnapped while working on a reconstruction project in Afghanistan. The General had brought his men out alive after leading a private army into the rugged mountains on the border between Pakistan and Afghanistan. Now he was running neck and neck with the incumbent president, Charles Jennings, for their party's nomination.

"Terrorists must learn to live in terror of the might of this great country," General Wingate was telling a large audience in the ballroom of a hotel in Los Angeles. The diners were elegantly dressed. The announcer said that each seat had cost a thousand dollars. "Terrorists must learn that their families, their friends, and any country that harbors them will pay dearly for their cowardly acts. We must use force against force, and we must be merciless."

The sight of Wingate smiling down like a tin god at his wildly applauding audience made Vanessa furious. She switched to CNN, where the "Little League parent syndrome" was the topic of discussion. A bright-eyed blond listened with rapt attention while an eminent psychologist expounded on the dangers of parents' becoming too emotionally involved in their children's activities.

"That was fascinating, Dr. Clarke," the blond said. "And I think our viewers will find this equally fascinating. CNN has just obtained exclusive footage of the frightening melee at the Oregon Little League game from Ralph and Ginnie Shertz, the parents of a child on one of the teams."

The home movie had been videotaped with an expensive camera, and the picture was very clear; but Ralph Shertz was no Spielberg—the pictures jerked from one spot to another. The action started with a large bearded man shouting at a slender man with glasses. A third man with a ponytail was standing with his back to the camera. The large man threw a punch. Moments later he was clutching his throat and writhing on the ground.

When the camera refocused on the man with

the ponytail, he was throwing a policeman over his shoulder. A second policeman shot him. The man with the ponytail turned toward the officer. Vanessa's heart stopped. She ran toward the set and squinted at the screen. The man with the ponytail fell, and the policeman's back blocked out his face. The camera moved closer to the action and tipped down. The man with the ponytail was unconscious. Ralph Shertz had gotten a close-up of his face before the policeman who'd fired the shots slapped a hand across his lens.

The tape ended and Dr. Clarke began expounding again, but Vanessa did not hear a word he said. What she'd just seen energized her. Finally, she had a chance to prove that she wasn't crazy. First, though, she had to make certain that Sam was safe.

Vanessa took her wallet out of her purse. In one of the compartments was a yellowed business card with a number for the FBI. Many years ago, the man who had given it to her was an agent. Now she asked to be connected to the office of Victor Hobson, the executive assistant director for law enforcement services.

"Who may I say is calling?" Hobson's secretary asked.

"Tell him it's Vanessa Kohler."

"Does Mr. Hobson know what this is about?"

"Just give him my name and tell him I know where to find Carl Rice. He'll take the call."

There was dead air for a moment. Then Hobson was on the line.

"Vanessa, it's been years."

"I don't have time for chitchat, Mr. Hobson. Carl Rice is alive and I know where to find him."

"Where is he?" Hobson asked. Vanessa could tell that he was trying to suppress his excitement.

"I'll tell you as soon as you do one thing for me."

"And that is?"

"There's a man, Sam Cutler. He works with me at *Exposed*. He's a photographer. I want him protected."

Vanessa told Hobson the address of her apartment. "He'll be there or at the paper."

"Why do you think Mr. Cutler is in danger?"

"Some men tried to kill me last night. My father sent them."

Hobson was quiet. Vanessa squeezed the phone in frustration. If he thought she was crazy he wouldn't help her.

"You have to protect Sam while I make certain that the man I saw is really Carl."

"Then you're not sure?"

"I'm ninety-eight percent certain, but I won't know until I see him in person. It's been twenty years. People look different after twenty years. Keep Sam safe. I'll call you as soon as I know it's Carl. Do we have a deal?"

"I'll bring him in and offer him protective custody. Where can I reach you to let you know we have him?"

Vanessa laughed. "Nice try."

"Wait. Take down my cell phone number. I'll keep it on. You can call me anytime."

Vanessa wrote down the number. As soon as

she hung up she started packing. She had to leave the motel immediately. Hobson might have been running a trace as they spoke. She wasn't taking any chances, and she had to be on the next flight to Portland anyway.

# CHAPTER **FIVE**

The line went dead. Victor Hobson hung up the phone and leaned back in his chair. When he was younger, his cold gray eyes and craggy features had made him seem dangerous. Now, in his early sixties, he was still a hard-looking man, but his gray hair was thinning, he had developed a paunch, and he took pills to control high blood pressure. With bank robberies, drugs, and all his other federal criminal concerns he really didn't need the additional stress of having Carl Rice reappear; but Lost Lake was one of the more curious occurrences in a very eventful life, and Vanessa was a seriously disturbed woman, who was either a murderer or the key to a mystery.

Hobson ordered an agent to pick up Sam Cutler and bring him downtown. He did not believe that Cutler was in any danger, but Vanessa's friend might know where she was going. As soon as the agent was on her way, Hobson swiveled his chair until his back was to his desk. It was a sunny morning in Washington. From his window in the FBI building he watched the hustle and bustle on the street as he thought back to the last time he had spoken to Vanessa. It had been in the late 1980s, more than a year after she had been discovered wandering in a daze outside the summer home of Eric Glass and three months after she had been released from Serenity Manor, the private sanatorium where she had been living since her father, General Morris Wingate, had spirited her away from the hospital at Lost Lake. Hobson had not known it at the time, but he now believed that his assignment to investigate the murder of Congressman Glass had been the turning point in his career.

*The Shenandoah apartments in Chevy Chase, Maryland, were expensive and secure. The three buildings were set back from the street. A buffer of manicured lawn separated them from the spear-tipped wrought-iron fence that surrounded the property. Entry was gained only by satisfying the guard at the sentry box that you had business with the United States senators, federal judges, movie stars, and other members of the elite who resided in the gated complex.*

*Serenity Manor had refused to give Victor Hobson Vanessa's address without a subpoena. General Morris Wingate had told Hobson that he did not want his daughter disturbed. He also said that Vanessa had serious mental problems and would not be a reliable witness. It had taken a favor from a friend at the telephone company to run down Vanessa's location and his FBI credentials, plus a not too subtle threat, to get by the doorman and the* security guard at the reception desk in the wood-paneled lobby. As he rode the elevator to the twentieth floor, Hobson wondered what the Wingates were hiding. Their actions had always been suspicious, if explainable. Vanessa's father had taken her out of the hospital in Lost Lake by the time Hobson had arrived in town, supposedly to give her the superior care that Serenity Manor provided. All requests for interviews at the psychiatric hospital had been denied, allegedly for the protection of the patient. It would be too traumatic for such a fragile individual to have to relive the horrors of Lost Lake, he had been told.

"Who is it?" Vanessa asked nervously moments after Hobson rang her doorbell. He had come up unannounced. The doorman and the security guard knew that there would be consequences if they called ahead.

"Federal Agent Victor Hobson," he answered, holding his identification up to the peephole. "May I come in, Miss Wingate?"

"What is this about?"

"I'd rather not say out here in the hall where the neighbors can hear us."

"I don't want to talk to you."

Hobson played his trump card. "Carl Rice has killed again, Miss Wingate. I don't want him to hurt anyone else, including you."

There was no sound on the other side of the door. Hobson wondered if Vanessa was still standing there. Then locks snapped, chains rattled, the door opened, and Vanessa Wingate eyed him warily as she stepped aside to let him in.

*Hobson thought General Wingate's daughter looked hyperalert and scared. She was pale and drawn. Her clothes hung from her. The dark circles under her eyes told him that she did not sleep easily.*

*"Thank you for letting me in, Miss Wingate."*

*"It's Kohler," she said. "I no longer use my father's name."*

*Hobson remembered that Charlotte Kohler was Vanessa's mother. She had died in a car accident when her daughter was in middle school.*

*Vanessa shut the door and turned her back to Hobson as she led him into a spacious living room. A cigarette was smoldering in an ashtray on a polished mahogany end table. Vanessa sat on the sofa and picked up the cigarette. She hunched her shoulders as if it was cold, but there was a fire blazing in a marble fireplace and the temperature in the apartment must have been in the seventies.*

*"I had a hard time finding you," Hobson said. "I thought you'd be staying at your home in California, but your father said you moved out."*

*"I want nothing to do with him," Vanessa answered, her anger boiling up. "I don't communicate with him. He had me locked up."*

*"I was told that you needed psychiatric care because you were traumatized by your experience at Lost Lake."*

*Vanessa smiled coldly. "That's the party line, and the quacks at Serenity Manor were paid a lot of money to spout it."*

*"I tried to talk to you while you were in the hospital. The doctors wouldn't let me see you."*

"I wouldn't have been much use to you," she answered quietly. "They kept me drugged most of the time. The whole year is a blur."

"Do you remember what happened at the lake?" Hobson asked softly. He could see how skittish she was, and he was afraid of spooking her. Vanessa did not answer right away. She took a drag on her cigarette and stared into the distance.

"Miss Kohler?" he said, remembering to use her new name.

"I heard you. I'm just not sure I want to talk about that."

"It's important. Especially now that someone else is dead."

That got her attention. "Who did Carl . . . ?"

"General Peter Rivera."

Vanessa's brow furrowed. "I've never heard of him."

"He's a short man, stocky, with a dark complexion and a scar on his forehead."

She shook her head. "No. What makes you think that Carl killed him?"

"He was tortured and murdered in much the same way as Congressman Glass." Vanessa blanched. "And there's other evidence connecting him to the scene."

Vanessa smoked quietly. Hobson let her think.

"I was asleep in the guest room," Vanessa said without preliminaries. She was staring at the fire, not looking at Hobson at all. "It was on the second floor. I woke up and heard voices. That surprised me. I thought that we were alone in the house."

"Just you and the congressman?" Hobson asked.

She turned toward him. "It's not what you think. He'd been to the mansion in California to meet with my father. Eric was on the intelligence committee and my father was the head of the Agency for Intelligence Data Coordination. I had lunch with them once and dinner another time. When I started graduate school I interviewed for a job."

"He was your employer?"

She nodded. "We were just friends."

"Then why were you there, alone, at his house?"

Vanessa looked down. "It's personal. I don't want to discuss it." She sounded frightened. Hobson decided not to push.

"So you heard voices and . . . "

"Eric said something. I couldn't hear what he said but it sounded odd."

"Odd?"

"Like a gasp. He sounded as if he was hurt. I went downstairs to investigate. There was a light on in his office. I looked in." She squeezed her eyes shut.

"Are you okay?"

Vanessa did not answer Hobson's question. She just continued talking as if he had never asked it.

"Carl was standing with his back to me. He was all in black. I had no idea who he was at first. Then he turned around and I gasped. My hand actually went to my mouth. I remember that. I said, 'Carl,' and then I saw the congressman and . . . and I saw the knife. Carl was holding it and it was covered with blood. I ran. I think I screamed."

"Did he try to catch you?"

"No. I've thought about that. Carl was very athletic. If he'd wanted to catch me he could have, easily."

"But he didn't go after you?"

"I didn't look back. I just ran. But I'm pretty sure he didn't come after me. I ran into the woods. Then I heard a boat going across the lake, fast. Then the deputy found me."

"You've known Rice for some time, I understand."

"We dated in high school. Then he was drafted and we lost touch. I met him again in D.C. a few months before . . . Lost Lake."

"Do you know why Carl killed the congressman?"

Vanessa looked away. "No," she said. Hobson was certain that she was lying.

"Your father thinks Rice was jealous of Congressman Glass."

"I told you, there was nothing between us. We were just friends. I worked for him."

"When you renewed your acquaintance here, did Rice ever say anything that made you think that he had a grudge against the military?"

"No," she said too quickly. Hobson debated confronting her but decided to leave on a friendly note. He would talk to her again when he had more to work with.

"What are your plans?"

"I don't know. I was in graduate school when all this happened. Maybe I'll finish my degree," Vanessa answered, but it didn't sound as if that would happen anytime soon.

*"And you're staying in D.C.?"*

*Vanessa flashed a sardonic smile. "Is that question a polite version of 'Don't try to leave town'?"*

*Hobson smiled back. "No. You're perfectly free to go wherever you want."*

*He stood up and held out his card. "Thank you for talking to me, Miss Kohler. If you think of anything more, give me a call."*

*Vanessa took the card and put it on the end table without looking at it. She followed him to the door. When he was in the hall Hobson heard the locks snap back into place.*

*On the way to his car, Hobson thought about their conversation. He was certain that Vanessa was concealing information. Did General Wingate know what it was? Had the General rushed his daughter to Serenity Manor so that she would be unavailable to the authorities for questioning? As he neared his car something else occurred to him.*

*"Agent Hobson?"*

*Hobson turned. A black chauffeured limousine was parked at the curb. An elegantly dressed man with crystal-blue eyes and hair so blond it was almost white was holding open the rear door.*

*"Would you mind getting in?" he asked.*

*"Yeah, I would. Who are you?"*

*The man held out a laminated card that identified him as Charles Jennings, an agent with the CIA.*

*"Ride with me a bit," Jennings said when Hobson was done examining his credentials. "I'll get you back to your car after we've talked."*

*"About what?"*

*"Please get in. This is too conspicuous."*

Hobson hesitated. Then curiosity got the best of him and he climbed into the back of the car. It was spacious, with a wet bar, television, and telephone.

*"Okay, what's this about?"* Hobson asked as the car pulled away from the curb.

*"Your investigation into the murders of Congressman Eric Glass and General Peter Rivera."*

*"Why is the CIA interested in those cases?"*

*"That's something I can't explain right now."*

*"Then I guess I won't be able to discuss the investigations."*

Jennings smiled. *"I thought you might say something like that."*

*"I'm a serious person, Jennings. Even as a kid, I never liked playing games."*

*"Oh, this is no game, Agent Hobson. This is a matter of national security."*

*"And I'm supposed to take your word for that?"*

Jennings's smile widened. *"Everyone says you're a tough guy."*

*"I'm not tough. I'm just going by the book. I don't discuss my cases with anyone who asks. Quite frankly, Mr. Jennings, credentials like the one you showed me can be forged by enterprising reporters hot after a story."*

*"You see the telephone? Call the director and ask him if it's okay to talk to me."*

*"The FBI director?"*

Jennings rattled off the number of the director's inside line, which Hobson knew to be correct. He dialed without taking his eyes off the CIA man.

*"I know why you're calling, Agent Hobson,"* the

director said as soon as Hobson identified himself. "You are to cooperate completely with Mr. Jennings in this matter."

"Does that mean . . . ?"

"It means what I said. Complete, one hundred percent cooperation."

The director broke the connection. Hobson held the receiver for a moment before hanging up. Jennings was leaning back in his seat, at ease, in command.

"What do you want to know?" Hobson asked.

"I want to know everything you've found out about Carl Rice."

Hobson told him what he knew.

"What have you concluded?" Jennings asked when Hobson was through.

"That Rice is a disgruntled ex-soldier with a crush on Vanessa Wingate. He's probably responsible for the murders of Congressman Glass and General Rivera."

"Probably?"

Hobson hesitated.

"The director instructed you to cooperate fully, did he not?"

"That's what he said."

"Then please answer my question. Do you have any reservations about your conclusion that Rice is responsible for these murders?"

Hobson felt uncomfortable. "There was no physical evidence connecting Carl Rice to the murder at Lost Lake. Everyone is looking for Rice because Vanessa Wingate said he killed the congressman."

"Go on."

"No one saw Rice at the lake, except Vanessa. There are no fingerprints or other physical evidence connecting him to the murder scene. If Vanessa Wingate hadn't given us his name he wouldn't be a suspect."

"I'm not following you," Jennings said, though it was obvious that he did and just wanted Hobson to commit himself.

"The Lost Lake police decided that Vanessa didn't murder the congressman because the murder weapon couldn't be found and Vanessa had no blood on her. But what if she got rid of the knife and whatever she was wearing? Maybe she was naked when she killed him. She could have dumped the knife in the lake and showered."

Hobson's theory clearly intrigued Jennings. "What's led you down this path?"

Hobson shook his head. He looked troubled. "Why did General Wingate rush his daughter into a private sanatorium before I could question her? Why wouldn't the doctors at Serenity Manor let me talk to her? Maybe they were just being protective; maybe reliving what happened at the lake would have damaged her psychologically. But I get the impression that the General and his daughter are hiding something. Only I have no proof that they are and no idea what it might be, unless she killed Glass."

"What about General Rivera?" Jennings asked.

"There's nothing connecting Vanessa to his murder."

"And Rice?"

"The MO is the same as the Lost Lake murder;

*there were cuts on his chest and damage to his face, throat slit. Rice's hair and blood was found at the scene . . . "*

*"Were there signs of a struggle?"*

*"No."*

*"Interesting. If there was no struggle, where did the blood come from?"*

*Hobson shrugged.*

*Jennings asked Hobson to send him copies of the files of both cases. Then he ordered the driver to return Hobson to his car. They rode in silence until the limousine stopped.*

*"You have my card. I want to know any new developments as soon as they happen," Jennings said. "Most important, I want to be notified the minute Carl Rice is located, captured, or killed, day or night. That's a major priority."*

*Just before Hobson got out, Jennings said, "You'll be doing your career a favor by giving me your complete cooperation. I'm not the only person interested in these cases. There are very important people who want to know the truth about Lost Lake."*

Hobson had sent a copy of the case files to CIA headquarters, but there had been no new developments. Carl Rice had disappeared as if he had never existed. As far as Hobson could tell, Vanessa and Rice never made contact after Lost Lake.

Hobson had kept tabs on Vanessa. He learned that she was living on a hefty trust fund that had been established by her mother and that she'd

broken off all contact with her father. During the
year and a half after her discharge from Serenity
Manor Vanessa lived like a hermit. A move to her
current, less expensive digs had followed her hiring by *Exposed* after attempts at employment at
more reputable newspapers and magazines had
all failed.

After their conversation in the black limousine,
Hobson had not talked with Charles Jennings
again, but that wasn't the last he heard of Jennings. A few years after their brief meeting, Jennings was appointed director of the CIA. When
the administration changed, Jennings returned
to Pennsylvania and served two terms as a United
States senator. Four years ago, Charles Jennings
had been elected to the presidency of the United
States.

Over the years, Hobson had risen steadily
through the ranks until his recent appointment
as executive assistant director for law enforcement services. There were others as deserving of
promotion, some more deserving. Hobson always
wondered how important to his career the short
car ride from Vanessa Wingate's apartment house
had been.

The intercom buzzed, and Hobson's secretary
informed him that Sam Cutler was in his reception area. After the agent brought the photographer into his office he dismissed her. Cutler
looked around warily. Hobson smiled to put him
at ease.

"Sit down, Mr. Cutler. You're not in any trouble, if that's what you're worried about."

"Then why am I here?" Cutler demanded.

"Vanessa Kohler thinks you're in danger."

Cutler's shoulders sagged. "You're kidding? This is because of Vanessa?"

"She asked me to have you picked up and offered protective custody."

Cutler looked furious. "I don't believe this. Don't you know Vanessa is nuts? I just went through this with the D.C. police. She called 911 last night and said I was being murdered." Cutler tapped his temple angrily with his index finger. "She's crazy."

"It's not that simple."

"I'll tell you what it is, it's embarrassing. First, there were the cops last night. I have no idea what our neighbors think. Then an FBI agent drags me out of my office."

"I apologize, but Vanessa has gone somewhere and I need to know where she went. I was hoping you could help me. Believe me, it is important."

"This doesn't have anything to do with her father, does it? She's not making threats against him, is she? She went ballistic when he announced that he was running for president. That's what set off this recent round of insanity. She was fine before that."

"She hasn't made any threats against General Wingate."

Cutler looked as if he was at his wit's end. "I like Vanessa. I do, and I've tried very hard to deal with her problems, but it's getting to be too much. She's a brilliant woman, a terrific reporter. If it weren't for her mental problems she'd be going for the Pulitzer. But she has trouble separating reality and fantasy, and it's getting worse instead of better. What I don't understand is why the FBI is talking to her, much less giving credence to anything she says."

"I can't explain, but it is in connection with a case."

"Is she in trouble?"

"Not from us. Tell me, Mr. Cutler, has she ever mentioned a man named Carl Rice to you?"

"That sounds familiar." Cutler snapped his fingers. "He's in the book. Aw, no. Don't tell me it's about her book. I mean that's a total fantasy. I've read it. She doesn't have a shred of evidence to back up anything she says."

"What book is that?" Hobson asked, although he had read a copy that had been made from a manuscript that had been surreptitiously copied by an employee at a publishing house who was paid under the table by the FBI.

"She's written this exposé of her father. She claims that he ran a secret army unit during Vietnam that committed all sorts of crimes. Only she doesn't have a shred of proof."

"What does she say about Rice?"

"He was supposed to be one of Wingate's assassins."

Cutler took a deep breath. "You can't put any stock in these wild accusations, Mr. Hobson. When Vanessa was in her twenties she saw a very gruesome torture murder. She was staying at a congressman's house in California. I think that's what started her problems, because she was hospitalized for a year after that at some private sanatorium for the shock of seeing this guy killed. She says this old boyfriend of hers, Carl Rice, killed the congressman to get evidence he had about this army thing her father was supposed to be running. But you can't believe anything she says about General Wingate. She hates him. I mean, really hates him. Vanessa blames him for everything that's gone wrong in her life: her mother's death; being in that psychiatric hospital. She even thinks that he was involved in the Kennedy assassination."

"What?"

"She claims her father was the second gunman on the grassy knoll. Then she claims that she was never crazy and that he put her in a sanatorium to keep her from telling what she knows." He shook his head.

"You don't believe what's in the book?" Hobson asked.

"Hell, no. And I know where she got that stuff, too. She has a huge collection of books and articles about real clandestine government operations, like Phoenix, and a ton more about Roswell, Kennedy assassination conspiracy theories, and that sort of crap. Her book is a mishmash of the real stuff and what the conspiracy nuts believe."

"Do you have any idea where she went?"

"No. I talked to her last night, right after she called the cops, but she didn't tell me where she was. And this is the first I've heard that she was going anywhere."

"If she calls you, will you let me know where she is?"

Sam looked uncomfortable. "You swear that you're not going to arrest her, that she's not a suspect in anything?"

"You have my word. I'm concerned that she might find Carl Rice and he might hurt her."

"Then this Rice is real?"

"Yes. She did go out with him in high school, and she met him again right around the time that Congressman Glass was murdered. She told the police that Rice killed the congressman."

"So, she'd be in danger if she ran into this guy?"

"She might be."

Sam took a deep breath. "If she calls, I'll try to find out where she is."

"For the record, I promised Vanessa that I'd offer you protective custody."

Sam shook his head. "Just have someone drive me back to the paper, and promise you'll vouch for me if my boss asks any questions."

# CHAPTER **SIX**

As soon as Ami Vergano, attorney and single mother, was identified as the parent of the little boy who had rushed to Daniel Morelli's side, helicopters from the TV stations buzzed her house, reporters started knocking on her door at all hours, and the phone began ringing incessantly. Ami tried to explain that she was only Morelli's landlord, but the reporters wanted to know if he was her lover or Ryan's father. By the time they grew bored and moved on, Ryan was a mess. Ami had tried to shield him, but he had seen his friend shot and bleeding, he had heard some of the cruel unending questions, and he had seen the distress they caused his mother.

Two days after the fight at the ball field, Ami walked an uncharacteristically subdued Ryan to his fourth-grade homeroom. She extracted a promise from the principal and Ryan's teacher that they would not allow reporters, Ryan's classmates, or anyone else to talk to him about the incident at the ball field. Ami hugged Ryan and reluctantly drove downtown. Her office was in an old brick building on Front Avenue, across the street from a waterfront park that ran along the Willamette River. Ami might have been depressed, but the weather was balmy and the sun promised a happy day. In a few hours, speedboats would be tearing past sleek watercraft with multicolored sails and the park would fill up with dog walkers, women pushing strollers, and kids playing hooky.

An Irish bar occupied the ground floor of Ami's building. The entrance to the upper floors was between the bar and a travel agency. On the third floor, the elevator doors opened across from a firm that built websites. Down the hall to the right was an architect's office. At the other end of the floor was the suite where Ami shared space with a three-person law firm and two other sole practitioners. A Hispanic woman with a baby; a neatly dressed black man; and a blond woman wearing aviator glasses, a tan blouse, and jeans were seated in the reception area. Ami had no scheduled appointments, so she assumed that none of the people in the reception area were waiting for her. As she stopped at the reception desk to get her messages, the receptionist leaned forward.

"The woman in the tan blouse is here for you," she whispered. "She doesn't have an appointment."

After checking her messages to make certain that there was nothing urgent, Ami walked over to the blond.

"I'm Ami Vergano. I understand you want to see me."

The woman stood up. She didn't smile or offer a hand. "I hope you have some time free. If you're busy, I can wait."

"Can you tell me what this is about?" Ami asked warily. If this was another reporter, Ami was going to commit mayhem.

The woman looked at the other clients. "I'd prefer to speak to you in private."

Ami led the way to her broom-closet-size office at the rear of the suite. The window looked down on the bar's parking lot. Diplomas covered one wall, and another displayed a seascape that she'd taken as a fee from another artist for whom she'd written a contract with a gallery. There were two client chairs, a credenza that ran beneath Ami's window, and her desk, which was covered by pleadings, memos, letters, and law books. A picture of Ami, Chad, and Ryan stood on the credenza, and a picture of Ryan sat next to her phone.

"How can I help you, Ms. . . . ?"

"Kohler. Vanessa Kohler. I live in Washington, D.C. I flew into Portland late last night."

Ami's brow furrowed. "You didn't fly all the way to Oregon to consult with me on a legal matter, did you?"

"Actually, I did. I heard your name on CNN. They said that you're a lawyer. They also said that Daniel Morelli was living with you."

Ami glared at her visitor. "Are you a reporter?"

"Mrs. Vergano, I do work for a newspaper, but I'm not here for a story."

"What paper?" Ami demanded angrily.

Vanessa sighed. "I'm employed by *Exposed*. It's a

supermarket tabloid, not a daily. I assure you that my trip to Portland and this meeting have nothing to do with my job. I'm here on my own, not for a story. I knew Dan in high school and in D.C. in the mid-eighties. We were very close at one time. I want to hire you to represent him."

"Ms. Kohler, the press has made my life and my son's life hell for the past few days. I'm not sure I trust any reporter. But even if I believed you, I couldn't help you. I don't practice criminal law and my only contact with it is a required course I took during my first year in law school. I am not competent to represent anyone facing any kind of criminal charges, let alone something this serious.

"But even if I were a great criminal lawyer, I couldn't represent Dan. You never represent someone you know. And there's a potential conflict of interest. I'm a witness. I saw what happened. The DA could call me and I'd have to testify that I saw Dan stab Barney Lutz in the throat and throw that policeman to the ground. So, you see, there's no way I can do what you want me to do."

Vanessa leaned forward. She looked intense. "I don't care about all that. What I need is someone who can get me in to see Dan. I called the hospital. They said he's being held in a secure ward. They won't let anyone but his attorney visit him. You can get a message to Dan. Maybe you can get me in as another attorney or an expert witness."

Ami's anger boiled up again. "This sounds like a ploy to get an interview."

Vanessa gripped her hands tightly in her lap to

control her mounting frustration. "I told you, I am not here as a reporter. I care for Dan and I want to help him. I'm probably the only person who can help him. There are things I know, things he knows. He could use his knowledge to cut a deal."

"What things?"

"I'm sorry. I can't tell you that."

Ami decided to put an end to the meeting.

"Look, Ms. Kohler, this isn't going to work. I'd get disbarred if I lied to the police so you could see Dan. I might even be arrested. You're going to have to find another attorney."

"When you talked about Dan on TV, it sounded as though you cared for him."

"I do like Dan, but I've only known him for a short time."

"He's a very good man, Mrs. Vergano, but he's been wounded emotionally. He needs our help. I know how to help him, but I have to see him first."

"I'm sorry. I can't help you, Ms. Kohler."

Vanessa took a check for $25,000 out of her pocket and laid it on the blotter. Ami stared at the check longingly. How she could use $25,000.

"I must see Dan before it's too late," Vanessa said. She sounded desperate. "You have no idea how important this is. If you care about him at all, you'll help me. His life is in danger."

"From who?"

Vanessa shook her head. "You have to trust me on this. They may know that Dan is here already. If they don't, they'll know soon. Then it will be too late."

Vanessa Kohler made Ami very uncomfortable, but the money . . . it could be the beginning of a college fund for Ryan. She could use it to pay down some of her debt. And what if Morelli really was in some danger more serious than his legal problems? That was hard to believe, but so was what had happened on the baseball diamond. For a moment, Ami thought about taking the $25,000, but her conscience would not let her.

"You're asking me to put my livelihood at risk for a man I don't really know. You're going to have to give me more if I'm going to take this type of risk."

"I don't know what I can say. I thought you'd help because you knew him."

"The man I thought I knew was a gentle person. I'm having trouble reconciling that with what I saw."

"From what I can tell, he was protecting your son's coach from a beating."

"Yes, but there are limits. He stabbed Barney Lutz in the throat. He almost killed him. And what about what he did to the policeman?"

"The policeman came at him from behind. Dan didn't know who he was."

"He's a violent, dangerous man, Ms. Kohler, and my son was around him a lot. God knows what he might have done to him."

Vanessa stared hard at Ami. "You know in your heart that he would never hurt your boy. You know he's not like that."

"You said yourself that you knew him last in

the mid-eighties. People change. The man I saw two days ago is a killer."

Vanessa was on the edge of her chair, leaning forward like a runner at the start of a race. She gripped Ami's desk so tightly that her knuckles turned white and her eyes bored into Ami's with such intensity that Ami wondered if her visitor was dangerous.

"If Dan is a killer, I know who made him like that. This man is ruthless. Once he learns that Dan is in Portland, he won't stop until Dan is dead. The only way to keep him alive is to make a deal with the authorities. I can convince Dan to do that, but I have to meet with him face to face."

Ami tried to sort out her feelings. What if Kohler was telling the truth? Morelli was an enigma. What Dan had done had shocked and upset her because the Daniel Morelli who had lived at her house and had been so kind to her son was nothing like the man who had acted with such brutal efficiency at Ryan's game. She liked and respected the artist who had stayed with her, but the violent man who had almost killed Barney Lutz terrified her. Which one was the real Morelli? She decided to take a chance and try to help the man she thought of as a friend.

"Look, Ms. Kohler, I'll try to visit Dan. I'll give him a message from you. I'm not going to charge you $25,000, though, because I can't take the case. Write a check for a $1,500 nonrefundable retainer and I'll charge you by the hour. If you want help finding a real criminal lawyer, I'll do that, too."

Vanessa's shoulders sagged with relief. She smiled for the first time.

"Thank you, and let's make the retainer $5,000. I can afford it. There is one thing, though. I don't want anyone except Dan to know that I've retained you. Is that understood? No one can know that I'm in Portland or that I hired you. Can you promise me confidentiality?"

"I'll keep you out of it," Ami said. But as Vanessa ripped up her first check and began to write another, Ami thought about what she had just agreed to do and wondered what she had gotten herself into.

# CHAPTER **SEVEN**

As soon as the door closed behind her new client, Ami regretted her decision to visit Morelli. Her fear and doubt increased as she drove to the county hospital and peaked when she opened the door to the office of Dr. Leroy Ganett, the physician in charge of Morelli's case.

Ganett was a tall, angular man with unruly brown hair who sat with his back to the room's only window. His office was furnished with a dull gray metal desk and an old wooden bookshelf. Ami introduced herself, and Ganett waved her into a seat in front of a wall covered by his degrees and a picture of him in shorts and a T-shirt standing on a dock beside a gigantic marlin.

"What can I do for you, Mrs. Vergano?"

"Daniel Morelli is my client. I want to meet with him."

"No one told me that the court appointed a lawyer."

"I'm not court-appointed. I've been hired to represent Mr. Morelli."

Ganett frowned. "I don't know if I can let you see Morelli without the DA's approval."

Ami was afraid that Dr. Ganett would say something like this. She honestly had no idea whether the district attorney could prevent her from seeing Dan. She wasn't kidding when she told Vanessa Kohler that she knew next to nothing about criminal law. She did remember something that she'd seen on a TV lawyer show, though.

"Dr. Ganett, everyone in America has a right to counsel. It's guaranteed by the Constitution. The district attorney has no power to keep Daniel Morelli from his attorney. Neither does this hospital."

Dr. Ganett looked unsure of himself. Ami smiled and addressed him in her most reasonable tone.

"Look, doctor, I don't have any desire to make a federal case out of this visit, and I'm sure you don't want to have the hospital dragged into court over an issue it can't win."

Ami half hoped that Ganett would refuse to let her see Dan. It was an easy way out. But Ganett shrugged.

"There's a policeman on duty. If he doesn't object, I won't."

"Thanks. How is Mr. Morelli doing?"

"He's depressed and withdrawn. He hasn't said a word to anyone since he got here. But I'd be surprised if he wasn't depressed. He's been shot; he's facing criminal charges. Depression would be normal under these circumstances."

"What's his physical condition?"

"He was a mess when we got him. One bullet penetrated the spleen and grazed the left kidney. We had to remove the spleen. Then there was blood loss. He's on antibiotics and analgesics for the pain, and we're running some tests because he's spiking a fever, but considering everything, he's doing fine."

Ganett handed Ami a medical report. "Here. You can keep that. It's a copy."

Ami scanned the report, and Dr. Ganett translated the medical terminology that Ami did not understand. Morelli's white count showed a mild leukocytosis with a shift to the left. There were some old scars and evidence of plastic surgery and a flat plate of the abdomen showed metal fragments posterior to the right iliac crest compatible with shrapnel. The hematocrit was stable at 31.

"You wrote that the incision is healing," Ami asked. "What does that mean in terms of how long Mr. Morelli will be in the hospital?"

"I'm not releasing him to the jail tomorrow, if that's what you want to know. He still needs to be hospitalized. But he's pulling through nicely, so he may not be here long."

"Thanks. Can I see Mr. Morelli now?"

"Sure thing."

The security ward was on the third floor at the other end of the hospital. A muscular orderly dressed in white pants and a short-sleeved white shirt was reading a paperback western at a wooden table to the right of a metal door. In the center of the door was a small, square window made of thick glass. A push-button bell was affixed to the wall beside the door. The orderly put down his book when he saw Dr. Ganett and Ami approaching.

"Mrs. Vergano is with me, Bill. We want to see Mr. Morelli."

Bill talked into his radio. A few seconds later, the door swung open. Another orderly was waiting inside. Ami followed Dr. Ganett down a wide hall that smelled of disinfectant. The coffee-colored walls looked as if they could use a coat of paint. A long hall led off to the right. Dr. Ganett turned down it, and Ami saw a policeman seated in front of a door similar to the one at the entrance to the ward. As they got closer to the officer, Ami started to perspire and her stomach turned. She wasn't doing anything illegal, but she felt as though she was. Ami was certain that the policeman would see through her the moment he looked at her.

"Officer, I'm Leroy Ganett, Mr. Morelli's doctor. This is Ami Vergano, an attorney who's been hired to represent Mr. Morelli. She'd like to talk to him."

The policeman asked Ami for her bar card and picture ID. Ami handed him the card and her driver's license. While she waited for him to ask the incisive questions that would expose her, the policeman checked her face against her photograph.

"You'll have to leave your purse out here," the policeman said as he handed back her ID. "Don't give the prisoner anything. Okay?"

Ami nodded, finding it hard to believe how easy it had been to get in to see Morelli.

"Do you want me to come in with you?" Dr. Ganett asked.

"I have to see him alone. Attorney-client confidentiality, you know," Ami answered, successfully hiding her nervousness.

"Then I'll get back to my work," Ganett said as the officer opened the door to Morelli's room.

"Thank you for the help."

The doctor smiled. "No problem."

"Knock when you're through," the policeman told Ami before closing the door after her.

The hospital room was spartan. Two plain metal chairs and a squat metal chest of drawers stood against the wall. There were bars on the windows. Morelli's bed had been cranked up so that he was partially sitting. He stared at Ami without expression. His complexion was pale and his cheeks were hollow, but his gaze was intense. A nasogastric tube, leading from his stomach to his nose, was taped to the side of his left nostril, and a bottle containing a clear solution was suspended over the bed. It dripped its contents into another tube that had been inserted into Morelli's left forearm. Ami walked over to the bed and looked down at the injured man.

"Hello, Dan. How are you feeling?"

"Not great, but better than I did a few days ago."

"Dr. Ganett says you're doing well."

"Did he say what's going to happen to me?"

"You'll stay in the security ward of the county

hospital until you're well enough to be transferred to the jail."

"That's not good," Morelli said, more to himself than to Ami.

"Have you been locked up before?"

"In 'Nam," he answered softly, his mind far away from the reality of the hospital.

"Were you a soldier? Is that where you learned how to fight like that?"

The question snapped Morelli back to reality. "How did you get in to see me?" he asked, suddenly suspicious.

"What do you mean?"

"You're the only visitor I've had except for a detective and some guy from the DA's office. Why would they let you in?"

Ami reddened. "I told them I was your lawyer."

Morelli's eyes widened and he became agitated. "That's no good. You shouldn't have done that. Go out and tell them you're not."

"Why?"

"Just take my word. You need to stay away from me. It won't be good for you or Ryan if our friendship becomes general knowledge."

"It's too late for that," Ami answered bitterly. "The fact that we know you has been splashed all over the papers and TV. The media can't get enough of the story of the Little League game that turned into a bloodbath. They've made my life and Ryan's miserable."

"I'm sorry. I didn't know. I haven't seen a television or read a paper since . . . "

Morelli's voice trailed off. He looked very worried.

"Ryan misses you," Ami said.

"Did he see what happened?"

"Of course. You were lying there in a pool of blood. He thought you were dead."

Morelli's features softened and he hung his head. "I never wanted those kids to see that."

"Then why did you do it?"

The prisoner shook his head slowly. "I don't know. It just happened so fast. If I could, I'd take it back."

Morelli looked at Ami. He was distraught. "You have to go. I appreciate that you came, but don't come back, please. And tell Ryan that I'm okay. I don't want him worrying about me."

"I'll tell him, but I do have something I need to talk over with you before I go."

"What's that?"

"I really am your lawyer in a way. A woman hired me to represent you, this morning. She says that she can help you. I told her I couldn't handle your case. I don't know anything about criminal law. But I did agree to give you a message."

"Who is she?"

"Her name is Vanessa Kohler." Morelli looked stricken. "She says she knew you in high school and that you met again in the mid-eighties. She's staying at the Hilton in room 709. I have her phone number."

"No! You tell Vanessa I'm not going to see her. Tell her to stay away from me. Tell her to go home."

"But she thinks she knows a way to help you."

Morelli's features tightened. "Do as I say, Ami. Tell her to go home. And I don't want you coming around either. It's not safe to be around me."

"But Dan . . . "

"Get out," he yelled. "Get out now. I don't want to talk to you anymore."

Ami was upset when she left the hospital. She'd never imagined that Morelli would reject her assistance so forcefully. During the ride back Ami tried looking at the situation from his point of view, and her anger cooled. Dan was seriously wounded and facing incarceration. He was a man who loved the outdoors and he would probably end up in prison. His future was very bleak. As Dr. Ganett had said, it would be normal to be depressed in Dan's situation, and it was selfish to expect Morelli to be pleasant and grateful for her visit.

Morelli's reaction to finding out that Vanessa Kohler was in town was also understandable. He hadn't seen the woman since the mid-1980s. Ami had no idea what their relationship had been like twenty years ago. Vanessa was definitely odd. Maybe Morelli had never liked her and did not want her sticking her nose into his business.

In any event, Ami thought as she opened the door to the reception area, her work on Morelli's case was over. He'd made that crystal-clear. She would call Vanessa Kohler and tell her that Morelli did not want her to represent him and did not want to talk to either of them.

"Mrs. Vergano," the receptionist said, the moment Ami stepped into the waiting room, "these gentlemen are here to see you."

Two men in business suits stood up and studied her in a way that made Ami very uncomfortable. They both looked like take-charge types. The taller of the two was handsome in a male model sort of way. His sharp features would photograph well from any angle, but they were so perfect that they looked a little off, like a really good attempt at computer animation. The other man was shorter and bulkier. His hair was not blow-dried like the model's and his clothes were less expensive. Ami thought his nose had probably been broken. He had the look of someone who did not believe anyone, ever.

"Ami Vergano?" the taller man asked unpleasantly.

"Yes."

"I'm Brendan Kirkpatrick of the Multnomah County District Attorney's office. This is Howard Walsh, a detective with the Portland Police. We'd like a word with you."

"Sure," Ami said, forcing a smile. She knew this had to be about Morelli's case, and she felt like a kid who'd been caught with her hand in the cookie jar. "Come on back to my office."

As soon as they were in the office, Kirkpatrick and Walsh took seats without being asked.

"What's this about?" Ami asked, hoping that she sounded pristinely innocent.

Kirkpatrick fixed Ami with a look that told her he wasn't buying anything she had to sell.

"I just received a very disturbing call. You know Dr. Leroy Ganett, don't you?"

Ami didn't answer. Kirkpatrick smiled coldly. "He knows you. He told me that you showed up at the county hospital and told him that you were Daniel Morelli's attorney. Dr. Ganett says that you threatened to sue the hospital if he didn't let you meet with my prisoner. So, Mrs. Vergano, are you Morelli's attorney?"

"Yes," Ami answered as her stomach lurched like a car on a roller coaster.

"Well, that's interesting. The court didn't appoint you and Morelli hasn't made any calls or had any visitors until you forced your way into his room."

"Morelli was staying with you, wasn't he, Mrs. Vergano?" Walsh asked in a manner that implied that Morelli was more than just a tenant. Ami decided not to bite.

"He was my lodger."

"Did you tell Dr. Ganett that you were Morelli's lawyer so you could pay him a social visit?" the detective asked.

"No, I did not."

"Then who hired you?" Kirkpatrick demanded.

Ami concluded that these two thought they could bully her because she was a woman who had no clout. Her fear gave way to anger, but she chose to answer with a smile.

"I'm afraid that's confidential."

Kirkpatrick reddened. "This isn't a game, Mrs. Vergano. Your boyfriend attacked a police officer and almost killed a man. He . . . "

"Just one minute," Ami interrupted. "Daniel Morelli has never been my boyfriend, and I resent your insinuation. Now come to the point. Why are you here?"

"There's no reason to get upset," Walsh said, trying to calm everyone. "We've run into a problem, and it's made us a little nervous."

"What problem?" Ami asked.

"Morelli's ID is phony. We ran his prints and they don't show. From what we can tell, Morelli appeared in Portland two months ago. Before that, he didn't exist."

Ami was unable to hide her surprise.

"I believe you told the officer who interviewed you at the ball field that you met him at an art fair," Walsh continued.

"That's right."

"Did you know him before that?"

"No."

"Well, neither does anyone else we've talked to, and what with the phony ID and the way he handled himself at the ball game, we're concerned that he might be a terrorist."

Ami paled. She'd never considered this possibility. Morelli was definitely a trained fighter. Had he learned how to kill people with a pencil at an al-Qaeda training camp?

"We were hoping you could tell us who he really is, Mrs. Vergano," the detective said.

Ami shook her head. "I really can't. I've only known him for two months and he's always told me he was Daniel Morelli."

"Maybe the person who hired you knows his real name," Kirkpatrick prodded.

"I'm sorry," Ami answered apologetically. "I can't give you that information. It's confidential."

Kirkpatrick turned to Walsh. "You know what I'm thinking, Howard. I'm thinking that no one hired Mrs. Vergano. I'm thinking she made up a story about being Morelli's attorney so she could get in to see him."

"That would be a serious crime, Brendan."

"Obstruction of justice, at a minimum, Howard." Kirkpatrick switched his focus to Ami. "But the charges could get a lot worse if Morelli does turn out to be a terrorist."

"You can threaten me all you want, Mr. Kirkpatrick, but you know I'm not allowed to reveal the name of the person who hired me."

"*If* someone did hire you." Kirkpatrick looked around Ami's office. "From the look of your digs, you're not doing too well. Morelli's case is getting a lot of publicity. His lawyer will get a lot of press; maybe even get his or *her* face on Court TV. Have you been doing a little ambulance chasing?"

Ami stood up. "That's it. I want you out of my office."

"I think you went up to the hospital and lied your way in to see Morelli so you could sign him up," Kirkpatrick continued, ignoring Ami's outburst. "You can get disbarred for that."

"If you stay one minute more you'll be trespassing. Before you start threatening me with disbarment, you might think about what the bar would do if I told them how you've acted in my office."

Kirkpatrick smiled brazenly, completely unfazed by Ami's threat. "We know you're not Morelli's lawyer, Mrs. Vergano. Dr. Ganett got suspicious but he wanted to make sure of his facts before he called me. So he asked Morelli if you were his attorney. Morelli says you don't represent him."

"We can settle this difference of opinion easily enough," Walsh said. "Why don't you accompany us to the hospital? If the prisoner says that you're representing him, we'll apologize."

Ami felt trapped. She had lied to Dr. Ganett. She had never really represented Morelli. She couldn't unless he agreed. If she went to the hospital Morelli would tell Kirkpatrick and Walsh that she wasn't his attorney. But if she refused to go, they might arrest her.

"That's an excellent suggestion," Ami bluffed, "and I will expect both of you to apologize when Morelli tells you that I'm representing him."

"You'll be hiring your own attorney if he doesn't," Kirkpatrick fired back.

Dr. Ganett looked nervous when he saw Ami, Kirkpatrick, and Walsh walk into the area in front of the security ward. He nodded uncomfortably at the DA and the detective but could not bring himself to look Ami in the eye.

"It's good to see you again, Dr. Ganett," Kirkpatrick said, "I believe you already know Mrs. Vergano."

Ganett flushed when Ami's name was mentioned. "I hope I didn't cause any trouble."

"Not a bit," Walsh assured him. "Why don't you escort us down to Morelli's room?"

They waited outside the security door without speaking while the orderly radioed inside. Kirkpatrick and Walsh looked relaxed and confident. Ganett shifted from one foot to the other. Ami's mind was racing.

The door opened with a metallic snap and Dr. Ganett led the way to Morelli's room. Ami could not believe her predicament. In moments, she might be under arrest with her career in jeopardy. How would she support herself and Ryan if she were disbarred? She imagined the effect on her son of seeing his mother branded a criminal.

Morelli was sitting up when they entered. His eyes moved from Kirkpatrick to Walsh to Ami. When they reached her, she tried to communicate her distress. Morelli's expression did not change.

"Remember me, Mr. Morelli?" the deputy DA asked.

"Don't answer that," Ami cried out.

Kirkpatrick seemed shocked that Ami had the temerity to interrupt him. Ami turned to Kirkpatrick.

"My client has a right to consult with counsel before he answers any questions from a prosecutor or the police."

"What are you trying to pull?" Kirkpatrick asked angrily.

"I'm not trying to pull anything, Mr. Kirkpatrick. I'm giving my client the advice any responsible lawyer would. I would be totally incompetent if I let a client talk to the authorities without first conferring with him. That's what lawyers do, Brendan. They advise their clients."

Kirkpatrick turned red. Morelli looked from Ami to the deputy DA.

"Is this woman your attorney?" Kirkpatrick demanded, his rage barely under control.

"Don't answer that," Ami instructed.

"I'd better follow my attorney's advice, Mr. Kirkpatrick," Morelli said.

Kirkpatrick turned on Ami. "You think you're smart, don't you?"

"I think I'm this gentleman's attorney, and I also think you owe me an apology."

Kirkpatrick glared at Ami for a moment, then turned on his heel and walked out of the room. Walsh took their defeat with grace. He shook his head and tossed Ami a respectful grin.

"I would like to consult with my client, Dr. Ganett," Ami said firmly.

"Of course. I'm sorry. I was concerned that . . ." he stammered.

"That's quite all right," Ami answered magnanimously. "I'm glad that you were concerned enough to check on me. Most people wouldn't have been that conscientious."

"What was that all about?" Morelli asked as soon as they were alone. Ami sank into a chair and started to shake.

"Are you all right?" Morelli asked.

"Barely. That jerk Kirkpatrick accused me

of . . ." She shook her head, "all sorts of things. He said I was an ambulance chaser." She looked at Morelli. "They would have arrested me if you didn't say I was your lawyer. Thank you, Dan."

"My pleasure. Kirkpatrick is an asshole." He smiled. "I liked the way you handled him." Morelli laughed. "I thought his head was going to explode when you told him you wanted an apology."

Ami tried to be dignified for another moment, but all of sudden the tension that had been crushing her evaporated and she began to giggle uncontrollably.

"He was pretty upset, wasn't he?" Ami said.

"I don't think he likes people who stand up to him."

Ami blushed. She felt proud of herself for not backing down. Then she sobered up.

"There are two things we have to discuss," Ami said.

"Go ahead."

"You need a lawyer."

Morelli started to say something but Ami cut him off.

"I'm only going to represent you until I can get a good criminal defense lawyer to step in. But you need help."

"I don't know if I want help." Morelli looked sad and defeated. The sudden transformation shocked Ami. "I almost killed Barney, and I would have killed that cop if his partner hadn't shot me."

"Why did you do it?"

"When Barney swung, my training took over. I wasn't thinking," Morelli answered so softly that Ami had trouble hearing him. "I swore I'd never hurt anyone again, Ami. I've tried so hard." He shook his head. "Maybe I should just take what's coming and get it over. I'm so tired of running."

"Who are you, Dan?" Ami asked.

Morelli blinked. "What?"

"Who are you really?"

"I don't understand the question," Morelli answered warily.

"They checked your ID. It's phony. They ran your prints and they came up blank. Who are you?"

Morelli turned his head away from Ami. "I'm not anyone you'd want to know," he answered sadly.

"Dan, I want to help."

"I appreciate that, but you'd better go."

# CHAPTER **EIGHT**

Vanessa Kohler paced her room, feeling more like a caged animal than a hotel guest. From her window she had a view of the majestic snow-covered slopes of Mount Hood and sailboats cruising the Willamette River. The streets below were full of people taking advantage of the sun. She would have given anything to get outside and away from the recirculated hotel air, but she was afraid that she would miss Ami Vergano's call.

For a while, Vanessa had tried to distract herself by watching television, but the shows were vapid and so boring that she could not stick with them. The news channels were worse. They were obsessed with the presidential campaign and Morris Wingate's surge in the polls. Every channel showed her father smiling with smug superiority. It made her furious.

The phone rang.

"Ms. Kohler?" Ami asked.

"Why did it take you so long to call? Is anything wrong?"

"There were problems, but I think I've handled them."

"What kind of problems?"

Ami told Vanessa about her adventures with Dr. Ganett, Deputy District Attorney Kirkpatrick, Detective Walsh, and Daniel Morelli.

"Dan doesn't want to see you," Ami concluded. "He got upset when I tried to get him to talk to you. He's also pretty adamant about me getting off the case as quickly as possible."

"Shit."

"I tried, really. I'll take another shot at him after he's had some time to think, but I don't know if it'll make any difference."

Vanessa had some ideas but they weren't the kind that she could confide to an officer of the court.

"Okay," she told Ami, "you did your best."

"Do you want me to find him a good criminal lawyer?"

"Yeah."

"It will be expensive."

"The money is the least of our problems," Vanessa said.

"What does that mean?"

"I'm sorry, I can't tell you."

"Vanessa, who is Dan? The DA said that his ID is phony and they can't match his fingerprints. When I asked Dan for his real name, he got very upset."

"Believe me, you don't want to be burdened with that information."

"No lawyer is going to be able to help Dan

without knowing who he is. No judge will grant bail to a man with a fake identity."

"You're right, but I won't answer you."

"Was Dan in Vietnam?"

Vanessa hesitated. "I don't know."

"I think he was a prisoner of war. Did you know that?"

"No."

"But you know that he was a soldier?"

"I want to end this conversation, Ami."

"Kirkpatrick and Walsh think he may be a terrorist."

"I know that you're just trying to help, but I'm going to hang up now. Thank you for everything you're doing."

Vanessa cut the connection and tapped a cigarette out of the pack that lay next to the phone. She paced the room as she smoked. What were her options? There was only a limited amount of time before her father figured out Daniel Morelli's real identity.

It occurred to Vanessa that she had not spoken to Sam since she'd arrived in Oregon. Had Victor Hobson honored his promise to protect her lover? Was he safe? Vanessa looked at the clock. It was three hours later on the east coast. She dialed her apartment and Sam picked up immediately.

"Thank God you're okay," she said as soon as she heard Sam's voice.

"I'm fine, but I'm really worried about you."

"Did the FBI . . . ?"

"Your friend Victor Hobson had me picked up at work, Vanessa. It was very embarrassing, especially after having the police barge in the night before."

"Why aren't you in a safe house?"

"Because this is nonsense. I'm not in any danger."

"Damn it, Sam, you are in danger. You have to believe me. My father will stop at nothing once he learns what I know."

"Is this about Carl Rice, the guy in your book?"

"How do you know about Carl?"

"Hobson asked me about him. What have you gotten yourself into?"

"It's better if you don't know."

"Where are you, Vanessa? I'll come there. We'll be together. I'll help you get through this."

"I don't want you to come here."

"Please. You need help."

"I want you to get out of the apartment, Sam. I want you to go into hiding."

"Vanessa . . ."

"No. I won't tell you where I am. It will be even more dangerous if you're here. You'll be a distraction."

"Vanessa," Sam repeated, but he was speaking to a dead line.

Ami was more puzzled than upset when Vanessa Kohler ended their conversation. She knew that Vanessa wanted to help Dan. What she didn't understand was why Vanessa and Dan wouldn't give her the information she needed to do her job. Ami noticed the clock. It was time to pick up Ryan at school.

Ryan was waiting when Ami pulled next to the curb. He looked exhausted, and he didn't say anything when he slid into the seat beside her.

"How was school, Tiger?" Ami asked as she pulled into traffic.

"Okay," Ryan mumbled.

"I saw Dan today. I visited him at the hospital."

Ryan looked at her expectantly.

"He says, 'Hi,' and he wanted you to know that he's a little banged up, but okay."

"Really?"

"Yeah, really. When I saw him he was sitting up and talking just fine."

"Will he be coming home?" Ryan asked, his eyes wide and full of hope.

"No, Ryan. He's okay physically, but he hurt Mr. Lutz and that policeman, so he'll have to stay in jail until that's cleared up."

"But after that? Can he come home then?"

"That's a way off, Tiger. Let's wait and see."

Ryan got very quiet. His shoulders slumped, and he cast his eyes down. Ami felt terrible. She wasn't sure what would happen to Dan. He had been trying to protect Ben Branton when he hurt Barney Lutz, and there was no way he could know that a policeman had grabbed him when he hurt the officer. Maybe a good defense attorney would get him probation or a light sentence. Even if he got probation, Ami was certain that Dan would move on. He had no roots in Portland. Come to think of it, he didn't seem to have roots anywhere. She had asked him where he was from when they first met, and he had told her that he'd moved around a lot as a kid and didn't think of any place as home. She'd accepted the answer then, but in light of what she was finding out the answer seemed evasive.

Then she realized that the answer to the mystery of Daniel Morelli was some unknown lawyer's problem, not hers. Tomorrow, she would start asking her attorney friends for recommendations. When she found a good criminal attorney, she would give the name to Vanessa.

This realization helped her forget about Morelli for all of three minutes. He might be out of her legal life, but she couldn't get him out of her thoughts. There was something tragic about her lodger, a sadness that had bubbled to the surface during their brief meetings at the hospital. Ami was certain that Morelli's wounds and legal problems were not solely to blame for his fear and depression. Vanessa Kohler had said that he was "emotionally wounded." Who had inflicted Dan's psychological wounds? Maybe it was something that had happened in Vietnam when he was a prisoner. She imagined that their Vietnamese captors did terrible things to American prisoners of war. Did Morelli have a mental defense to his charges?

Ami remembered a case she had worked on when she was with her firm. The client had been a seriously disturbed veteran, and they'd used a psychiatrist as an expert witness on posttraumatic stress disorder. Victims of PTSD often reexperienced a traumatic event, like a rape, an earthquake, or a car accident, that was outside the range of ordinary human experience. Other symptoms included guilt feelings and reduced involvement with the external world. Many Vietnam War veterans suffered from PTSD. Ami had conducted the initial interview of the expert to see if he would help their case. She remembered him as being very smart and personable. Ami was definitely not going to continue as Morelli's attorney, but she hadn't found a new attorney for him yet. It would certainly assist whoever ended up with Morelli's case if she laid the groundwork for a defense. Ami was excited. First thing tomorrow she would start her search for Morelli's lawyer. But she would also try to remember the name of the psychiatrist.

# CHAPTER NINE

Dr. George French was in his late fifties and slightly overweight, but his clothes were hand-tailored so that the weight didn't show. French's gray-green eyes twinkled behind custom-made steel-rimmed bifocals. His skin was pale and his mustache and beard were salt-and-pepper like the fringe of hair around his otherwise bald head. When French walked into his waiting room, Ami Vergano put down the magazine she was reading.

"You're looking well," the psychiatrist said, flashing Ami an engaging smile.

Ami smiled back. "Thanks for seeing me on such short notice."

"Let's talk in my office. Do you want any coffee?"

"Coffee sounds great. I need to get my brain moving."

There was a small kitchen halfway to Dr. French's office. The doctor stopped there and filled two cups before continuing down the hall.

"I'm sorry your firm broke up."

"Me too."

"It must have been quite a shock."

Ami shrugged. "The associates never know what's going on. One morning the partners called us into the conference room and that was that."

"And you're out on your own now?"

"Yeah," she answered, embarrassed by her fall from the higher echelons of the law to the lowly ranks of the solo shingle hangers. "I'm scraping by. Mostly divorces, wills, contracts. I've got a small business that sends me all its work. If Microsoft or Nike asks you for the name of a good attorney, I'd appreciate the referral."

Dr. French laughed as he stood aside to let Ami into his office. A couch upholstered in burgundy leather sat against a pastel-blue wall under a grouping of sunny prints. Across from it, on the other side of the room, was a wide window that brought light and a skyline view into the room. The psychiatrist shut his office door and motioned Ami toward one of the two chrome-and-leather chairs that flanked a low glass coffee table. He took the other chair.

"I have someone I want you to see," Ami told the doctor.

"A client in a divorce?"

"No. Actually, it's a case that's been getting a lot of notoriety. Have you heard about the fight at the Little League game?"

"Who hasn't?"

"My son is on one of the teams that were playing and the man who was arrested was renting from me. He had the apartment over my garage. He's the person I want to talk to you about."

"Why me?"

"You're an expert on posttraumatic stress disorder."

"Ah, Mazyck," French said, mentioning the case he had been hired to work on by Ami's old firm. Gregory Mazyck was a veteran who had holed up in his house with a hostage. Dr. French had testified that Mazyck was suffering from posttraumatic stress disorder and believed the police were Iraqis and the hostage was his best friend, who had died in his arms during the Gulf War.

"How much do you know about what happened at the Little League game?"

"Not much."

"Okay. Well, Dan—Daniel Morelli, my client— is a carpenter. I don't know his age, but I'm guessing he's in his late forties. He travels around the country in a pickup truck. He doesn't have roots. Sometimes he lives in the woods for weeks at a time. He supports himself by doing odd jobs and building very beautiful handmade furniture. That's how we met, at an art fair on the Park Blocks. He had a booth next to mine, and he was trying to get orders for his furniture. Anyway, he needed a place to stay. I liked him. He seemed very gentle. My son really took to him. I never saw any sign that he was violent."

Ami told the psychiatrist about the fight.

"I asked him about what he did to Barney and the policeman. He said that he wasn't thinking; that his training took over. He seemed very remorseful about what he did, very depressed. He also told me that he'd been locked up in Vietnam. I asked him if he'd been a soldier, but he wouldn't discuss it. He also said that he had sworn not to hurt anyone again. I'm wondering if the sudden violence was connected to his experiences in Vietnam."

"I guess that's possible."

"I remembered your testimony. You said that combat experience could produce symptoms of posttraumatic stress disorder years after the event that caused the problem. I'd like you to talk to Dan and tell me what you think."

"All right."

"There's another thing," Ami said, "something weird. Dan's ID is phony and they can't find a match for his fingerprints."

"Now that is interesting. His prints would have to be on file if he was in the military." Dr. French stood up. "Let me check my schedule."

He walked over to his desk and talked to his secretary over his intercom.

"I've got a cancellation this afternoon," he told Ami, a moment later. "Would three be okay?"

Morelli was sitting up in bed when the guard let Ami and Dr. French into his room. The nasogastric tube and IV were gone, and some color had returned to his face. His long hair was fanned out behind his head, almost covering his pillow.

"You're looking a lot better," Ami said.

Morelli focused on Ami's companion. "Who's your friend?"

"This is George French. He's a psychiatrist."

Morelli smiled wearily. "That's going to be my defense, insanity? I can save you a lot of trouble, Ami. It won't fly. I'm sane."

"You don't have to be nuts to have a mental defense, Dan. Dr. French just wants to ask you some questions."

"Is this confidential? It stays between us?"

"Yes," Ami assured him.

Morelli shrugged and gestured toward the chairs that sat against the wall.

"Be my guest. I don't have anything better to do."

Ami and the doctor pulled the chairs over to the bed. George placed a yellow lined pad on his lap and scribbled a heading.

"Do you mind if I call you Dan?" he asked.

"You can call me anything you want, except late for dinner," Morelli quipped to indicate that he wasn't taking Dr. French's inquisition seriously.

French laughed. "I'd like to get some background before we talk about what happened at the ball field. Is that okay?"

Morelli looked a little uncomfortable, but he nodded his assent.

"Good. Let's start with an easy one. Where did you grow up?"

"California."

"Where in California?"

"San Diego."

Morelli had told Ami that he was an army brat who moved around. Now he was telling Dr. French something else.

"Any brothers or sisters?"

"No."

"Is your mother still living?"

"No."

"Father?"

"I have no idea."

"You didn't get along?"

"He walked out on us when I was young."

"Did your mother remarry?"

"No."

Dr. French made some notes before resuming the interview.

"Getting any deep psychological insights, Doc?" Morelli asked.

"Thirteen so far," French answered with a smile.

"Touché," Morelli replied. He was trying to upset George, but he was smart enough to see that the doctor wasn't biting.

"Why don't you tell me where you went to high school?" French asked.

"St. Martin's Prep."

George looked surprised. "You must have been pretty well off."

"Scholarship boy."

"So your grades must have been good."

"A's mostly."

"Any sports?"

"I did a lot of stuff in junior high. No organized sports at St. Martin's. I concentrated on my grades pretty much and kept to myself."

"What subjects did you enjoy?"

"Science, math. I liked physics."

"Did you like St. Martin's?"

Morelli shrugged. "Some of the teachers were pretty sharp. The kids were from a different world. We didn't have much in common."

"Did you have any close friends?"

A cloud descended over Morelli's features. "I don't want to get into that."

"You knew Vanessa in high school," Ami said.

Morelli looked upset. "Yeah, Vanessa. I knew her. But I'm not going there, so you can move on."

"Okay," Dr. French said agreeably. "What about college?"

Morelli did not answer.

"Mr. Morelli?" George prodded.

"No college. It was during 'Nam. I was drafted."

"You didn't want to go in?"

"I don't know what I wanted. It was complicated."

Ami thought that Morelli sounded sad and bitter.

"Where did you go through basic training?" Dr. French asked.

"Fort Lewis."

"This was your usual basic training?"

"Yeah." Morelli paused, remembering something. "There were the tests. I don't think they were part of the normal training."

"What tests?"

"We all took tests during basic training; IQ, language proficiency. Like that. At first, we took the tests in a group, but I started getting singled out after a while. I'd be called in on a Saturday morning or midweek night, and I'd take these tests with two or three other guys. We were told not to talk about them. They were real strict about that. But I did talk to this one guy once. He was curious about it, too. It turns out his folks were Russian emigrants, so he was fluent. He knew that one of the other guys spoke an Asian language and another one had majored in Russian in college."

"And you?"

"That's what I couldn't figure. I had high school French and my grades were good, but this guy spoke Russian like a native."

"Did anything else unusual happen in basic?"

"Well, it wasn't unusual. It was just unexpected."

"And that was?"

"My posting. We were asked to indicate a preference for AIT," Morelli said. When Ami looked puzzled, he explained. "Advanced Individual Training. I indicated OCS—officer candidate school—first, then Special Forces. I got Fort Holabird. It's just outside Baltimore."

"What went on there?"

"Intelligence training."

"And you didn't indicate a preference for that?"

"Nope. But mine was not to reason why, right? So I went along with the program."

"What did you learn at Fort Holabird?"

"Intelligence stuff. How to tail someone, how to break and enter, electronic surveillance."

"Bugging?"

"And other nifty skills." Morelli smiled. "We got to go on these field trips."

"Give us an example."

"Oh, I'd pick a name out of the phone book and follow the mark all day. Another time I bugged a business. I broke in at night and put the bug in place. We listened to hours of the most boring shit. A few nights later I broke in again and took it out."

"What would have happened if you were caught?"

"One guy was. The army smoothed things over. If it was cops, it was okay because they knew we did this stuff from time to time. If it was a civilian, they'd send over a colonel with a chest full of medals. First, he'd appeal to the guy's patriotism, then his pocketbook. If that failed, he'd let the guy know how difficult life can be, in a very subtle way, of course."

"Did anything happen at Fort Holabird that was unusual?" Dr. French asked.

Morelli nodded. "Around the end of my fourth month I was called out of training and told to report to an office on the base. There were two Green Berets waiting for me, both in full dress. They told me that they wanted me to apply for Special Forces training. They said that they were very impressed by my records and felt that I'd fit the mold. It was all low-key and very flattering. I was led to believe that I'd been singled out from all the others, and they hinted at clandestine missions and high-risk assignments.

"You have to remember that I was just a kid and very impressionable. Both of the Green Berets were out of a John Wayne movie. Their chests were covered with decorations. And there was the mystique of the Special Forces."

George smiled. "I assume that you signed up."

"You bet. As soon as I finished up at Holabird I went to Airborne at Fort Benning, Georgia, for three weeks to learn how to jump out of planes. After that it was the Special Warfare Center at Fort Bragg, North Carolina."

"What did you do there?"

"Intense physical and survival training. There were five-mile obstacle courses; we learned how to repel off mountains and build rope bridges; that sort of thing. The survival training was a bitch. They'd drop us in salt water in a remote coastal area. We'd learn how to get to shore and survive off the land. You know, what type of plants were edible in the region, how to build a fire, real Boy Scout stuff.

"Then there was specialty training. Your basic unit in the Special Forces was the A team. That's two officers and ten enlisted men. Each A team member has a specialty. There are combat engineers who train with explosives, medics, radio operators, language experts, weapons experts, and an expert in psychological operations. That was me."

"What exactly did you do?"

"I learned how to use medical and agrarian assistance, assassination, and fear to bring people around and get noncombatants to work for us, and I learned how to interrogate prisoners."

Morelli paused for a moment, as if he had recalled something that he wished he had not remembered.

"Anything else?" Dr. French asked in an effort to get the conversation going again.

Morelli's eyes refocused on the psychiatrist. "Practical operations," he answered. "My team would go out as a unit. We trained in Alaska and Panama; cold weather, jungle climates. After I finished up at Fort Bragg, I went to Fort Perry in North Carolina for training in advanced interrogation techniques. Then back to Bragg."

"Did you ever get to put your training to use?"

Morelli looked wary, but he nodded.

"What were some of your assignments?"

"I'd rather not say."

"Is that because they were classified?"

"I'm not going to discuss my assignments."

"All right."

Dr. French made some more notes. Ami thought Morelli's energy was decreasing. He closed his eyes while French wrote on the pad, and his last few answers had been given quietly.

"Ami told me that you were in Vietnam."

Morelli looked at Ami when he nodded.

"And you were a prisoner of war?"

Morelli nodded again.

"How long were you a prisoner?"

"About two weeks."

George tried to hide his surprise. "Why so short a time?"

"I escaped."

"Where were you captured?"

"I'd rather not say."

"This was Vietcong?"

"I'd rather not say."

"How did you get away?"

Morelli got a faraway look in his eyes. "I made up my mind that I was going. I'd had enough of the situation."

"Were you in a prison camp or a . . . ?"

"I wasn't any place you've heard of."

"But it was in Vietnam?"

Morelli didn't answer.

"Where did you go after your escape?" French asked.

"Into the jungle. I have a fair ability to get by in the woods without a map or compass. It worked out okay." Morelli closed his eyes again. "I'm getting tired, and I'd like to stop," he said.

"Fine," French agreed. "Just one more question. What was your final rank?"

"Captain."

Dr. French stood and Ami followed. "Thanks for talking to me."

Morelli didn't respond.

"I called a top criminal attorney about taking over your case, but he's out of town," Ami said. "I'll get back to you when I know more."

Morelli nodded but seemed uninterested.

"Vanessa is still in town. She still wants to talk to you. What should I tell her?"

"She has to leave. Tell her to go while she still can."

"Is she in some danger, Dan?"

"I'm tired," Morelli answered.

Dr. French touched Ami on the arm. "Let's let Mr. Morelli rest," he said. Ami was worried about Morelli, but the doctor was right. Her client had shut down and she knew they wouldn't get anything more out of him today.

"What do you think?" George asked as they walked to their cars.

"Dan was obviously not your typical GI," Ami answered enthusiastically. "Can you imagine what it must have been like for him after his escape from the Vietnamese?"

"Then you buy his story?" George asked, without revealing his own opinion.

"It certainly sounded real. Why, do you have doubts?"

"Last year, I was involved with a fellow whose defense to an embezzlement charge was that he worked for the CIA and was using the funds for a covert operation. He was very convincing and could look you in the eye and say the most outrageous things, but they were all lies. He had read every book ever written on the CIA and spy novels and newsmagazines. He had an encyclopedic knowledge of the history of the CIA and its workings."

"You think that Morelli is making this up?"

"He has the army training routines down, but those details are easy to learn. He could have known someone in the army or read about them in a library or online. Think about his story, Ami. Morelli wouldn't discuss the smallest detail of any of his missions. I'll tell you something else. I was in army intelligence during Vietnam. I've never heard of an American making a successful escape from a Vietnamese prison camp."

Ami's unlawyerly enthusiasm for Morelli's exciting story made her feel foolish. It had been a welcome addition to the life of someone whose excitement usually came mainly at her son's Little League games.

"Don't look so glum," George said with a light laugh. "I haven't drawn any conclusions about Morelli yet. I'm just not going to accept a story like this without hard evidence. I have a friend who may be able to get us a copy of Morelli's military records. Let's see what they say."

"What are the implications if he's telling the truth, George?"

Dr. French thought for a moment. "The stress he would have been under if he was in a Vietnamese prison camp could cause PTSD. But I'd have to have a hell of a lot more proof that he was a prisoner and a lot more information about his conditions of captivity before I'd give that opinion in court."

"Let me ask you something else. What if he made it all up, but he believes he was some kind of commando? Would that make him legally insane?"

"Well," George said slowly, "that would be paranoid behavior, but he's far too integrated to be paranoid schizophrenic. I don't see that at all. He has good contact with reality. By that I mean that he speaks rationally, he's aware of his situation, and his responses to questions are appropriate."

Dr. French paused. "Paranoid personality disorder is another possibility. The onset usually occurs in early adulthood. There's a pervasive distrust of others. People's motives are interpreted as being malevolent. But I don't really see that here. Morelli was willing to talk to us. He confided sensitive information to us, which someone with this disorder would be reluctant to do."

They walked through the parking lot with Dr. French deep in thought. When they arrived at Ami's car, French ventured another opinion.

"There's a possibility that Morelli is in a paranoid state, but that form of paranoia is extremely rare."

"Explain that to me."

"A person is in a paranoid state when he has a very tight delusional system that develops in early adulthood. It starts with a belief that an outside force, like the CIA, is controlling him. Once the delusion is in place the individual constructs an extremely complex delusional system that is based on it. If you buy the original premise, everything else in the system works logically and it's almost impossible to crack it. This type of individual is always in the delusional system, but he keeps his mouth shut because he learns that talking about it gets him into trouble and he is healthy enough to control it."

"Would he open up to us because he's afraid of going to jail?"

"That's possible, and you told him that his conversation was confidential. Opening up under those circumstances would be consistent with that type of paranoia."

"You said that a paranoid state is extremely rare."

"Almost as rare as meeting someone who's done what Morelli claims to have done. Look, it's more fun believing an exciting story like Morelli's than subjecting it to scrutiny, but that's what we have to do."

"Okay, get the military records. Call me if they confirm or rebut his contentions. Meanwhile, I'll work on finding a lawyer with criminal experience who can take over Morelli's case."

# CHAPTER **TEN**

Ami was in a good mood when she entered the office reception area two days after her meeting with Morelli and Dr. French. Ray Armitage, one of the top criminal defense attorneys in the country, had returned her call. He was in Colorado conducting pretrial motions in a murder case involving a member of the Olympic ski team, but he would be back in Portland on Monday and was interested in taking over Morelli's case.

Ami had called Vanessa as soon as she'd finished talking to Armitage. Vanessa was prepared to pay his retainer and any additional fees and expenses, even though they were steep. Ami was surprised that Vanessa had not asked if Morelli had changed his mind about meeting with her.

"Good morning, Nancy," Ami sang out.

"Am I glad you're here," the receptionist answered. "The phone has been ringing off the hook."

Ami looked puzzled.

"Don't you read the morning paper or listen to the news? They indicted your friend for the Lit-

tle League assault. It's on the front page. Everyone knows you're his attorney."

Nancy handed Ami the newspaper. The story
was featured beneath the fold, but it took up the
bottom third of the front page.

"Oh, and there was a call from that man Kirkpatrick."

"What did he want?"

"Morelli is being arraigned at the hospital at
one o'clock."

"Today?"

"That's what the message said. He called last
night after we forwarded the phones. The answering service took the call."

"And Kirkpatrick didn't bother to tell them to
try and reach me at home," Ami thought to herself. "That bastard is trying to sandbag me. How
am I going to handle an arraignment today, or
anytime?"

Ami had only the vaguest idea of what an arraignment was and no idea what one did at this
type of court appearance. She grabbed her phone
messages and fled to her office. Most of the calls
were from the press. She put the message slips on
top of a stack of unanswered mail and dialed
Betty Sato, a classmate from law school who
worked at the Multnomah County district attorney's office.

"Oh, my God!" Betty said when they were connected. "Ami Vergano, the world-famous criminal lawyer, is calling *me*. What did I do to deserve
this honor?"

"Stuff it, Sato."

Betty laughed.

"You read the papers, huh?" Ami asked.

"That, too. But Brendan Kirkpatrick found out that we were classmates and he pumped me about you. I've got to tell you, he's not your biggest fan."

"That's the least of my problems."

"Since when do you take criminal cases?" Betty asked.

"It's a long story," Ami answered, a bit concerned that Kirkpatrick was checking up on her. "That's why I'm calling you. You're my only friend who knows anything about criminal law. I just found out that my client is going to be arraigned this afternoon, and I haven't the foggiest idea what to do at an arraignment."

There was silence on Sato's end of the line. When she spoke, she used the tone that a nurse in a psychiatric hospital uses with an irrational patient.

"Can I say something, Ami? I mean, we're friends, right?"

"I know I'm in over my head, Betty. I'm talking to a very good criminal lawyer about taking over, but he can't meet with me until next week. So I'm stuck doing the arraignment."

"I'm glad you're getting someone to take this case." Ami could hear the relief in her friend's voice. "Brendan has a real hard-on for you and I'd hate to see you get hurt."

"Believe me I want to get off this case as soon as possible. But I can't do it today. So tell me what to do?"

"Okay, but you've got to promise not to tell

anyone I helped you. Kirkpatrick would barbecue me if he found out."

"I promise."

"It's simple. A chimpanzee can handle an arraignment. Kirkpatrick will give your client a copy of the indictment. You waive the reading but reserve the right to move against it for legal defects. Then you tell the judge that your client pleads not guilty and wants a jury trial. Also, make sure that Brendan gives you discovery of all the police reports, because that's when he has to do it—after there's an indictment."

"What about bail?"

"There will be an amount set already, but it will be high. Brendan's charged attempted murder and assault. It doesn't matter now, though. Your guy is in the hospital, so he's not going anywhere for a while. Let the lawyer who takes over deal with getting him out. Bail hearings get complicated."

"Okay. The arraignment seems easy enough."

"It is, but it's the last easy thing you'll do in this case."

"I told you I'm getting out, okay. Cut me some slack. I'm stressed out as it is."

"Sorry. I'm just concerned that you'll get hurt."

"I know. Thanks." Ami paused. "What did you tell Kirkpatrick about me?"

"That you'll sleep with him if he throws the case."

"Think he'll fall for it?"

"You're not staying on the case long enough to find out, remember."

"Seriously, what did you say?"

"The truth. You're really smart and hardworking, but I didn't think you took criminal cases."

"What's he like?"

"Brendan is as smart as you and single-minded. His wife died in a car accident three years ago and he has no children. The word is that he loved his wife and can't stand going home to an empty house. That's probably true because he's always in the office working. Nothing gets by him because nothing matters except his cases. He's arrogant and ruthless, but he's also dedicated and scrupulously honest."

"I told you I was getting off the case, Betty. No need to scare me anymore."

"You wanted to know."

"Thanks. Look, let's get together for dinner and a movie."

"Soon. It's been too long since we've seen each other."

"The problems of being a single mom."

"Spring for a sitter and we'll party."

Ami hung up. She felt calmer knowing that the arraignment was something that she could handle. Kirkpatrick's message said that it would be held at the hospital. If they did it in the secure ward, she would not have to be in open court where her gaffs would be magnified by public scrutiny. Ami took a deep breath. She could do this. There was a small law library in the conference room. She would read the statutes on arraignments and learn as much about the law as she could. She checked her watch and decided that she might even have time to go to the law library at the courthouse and read some criminal law textbooks.

Ami was about to stand up when her intercom buzzed and Nancy told her that Dr. George French was on line two. She picked up the receiver.

"Hi, George. What's up?"

"My friend tried to get Morelli's army records. They don't exist. No one named Daniel Morelli served in the Special Forces, or any other branch of the military, during Vietnam."

Ami thought for a minute while Dr. French waited. "That fits in with his ID not checking out. If he served, it must have been under another name."

"Or," French added, "he never served and he's feeding us a line."

"I'll confront him after the arraignment and get back to you with what I find out. Thanks."

Television crews and shouting reporters took up most of the space in the lobby of the building that housed the hospital security ward. Ami mumbled "No comment" as she ran the gauntlet from the front door to the elevator. When the elevator doors closed, the reporters were still clamoring for something they could print. Ami leaned against the wall, closed her eyes, and vowed that she would never take on another high-profile case.

When she arrived at Dr. Ganett's office Ami found Brendan Kirkpatrick chatting with Ruben Velasco, the judge assigned to arraign Morelli.

Velasco was a middle-aged Cuban whose parents had escaped from Castro's clutches and migrated from Miami to Oregon to work in a cousin's restaurant when their son was a teenager. Ami knew very few judges, and it was obvious that Kirkpatrick was not laboring under this disadvantage.

When Ami entered, Velasco stood and bowed slightly. He had dark curly hair, clear brown eyes, and an easy smile. When he welcomed her, Ami could hear traces of his Hispanic heritage. She shook hands with the judge and managed to look Kirkpatrick in the eye when she took his hand. His handshake was crisp and courteous but devoid of warmth. The judge introduced Ami to his court reporter, an elderly African-American named Arthur Reid.

"Arraigning Mr. Morelli in the hospital is a little unusual," Judge Velasco explained, "but Brendan was afraid that there might be constitutional error if your client wasn't arraigned as soon as Dr. Ganett deemed him competent to understand the proceedings."

Ami had read enough law during lunch to realize that there could be constitutional consequences if an arraignment was delayed, but she couldn't remember what they were, so she settled for nodding knowingly.

"We have one other issue to discuss before Dr. Ganett takes us down to see the patient. The press wants to cover the arraignment. Now I'm not about to let all the reporters you saw in the lobby into the security ward of this hospital, but

Brendan suggested that we let the media desig-
nate one newspaper reporter and one television
crew to represent everyone and we'll require that
all the papers and stations have access to their
pictures and notes. Is that okay with you?"

Ami had no idea whether she should object, so
she said she'd go along with whatever the judge
thought was best. Judge Velasco's brow wrinkled
for a moment. He wasn't used to defense attorneys being so reasonable, but he adjusted his features quickly and thanked God for small favors.

"Okay," the judge said, "let's get Dr. Ganett's
opinion of Mr. Morelli's mental state on the
record and we'll do this."

Twenty minutes later, Ami, Kirkpatrick, Judge
Velasco, and his court reporter walked into the
lobby outside the security ward, where a reporter
from *The Oregonian* and a crew from Channel
Four news were waiting. After the reporters
agreed to the ground rules for covering the arraignment, Dr. Ganett led everyone inside the
ward. The lights on the television camera flooded
the corridor with a bright, artificial light as they
walked to Morelli's room. With the cameras
rolling, Kirkpatrick made it appear that he and
the judge were very chummy and ignored Ami.
When the lights switched off and the camera
stopped recording, the DA dropped back to walk
beside her. He flashed a smug smile.

"I see you've got George French working for
you."

"Did your little snitch, Dr. Ganett, tell you
that?" Ami asked.

"Now, now, don't be catty. The policeman outside Morelli's room is under orders to report the names of Morelli's visitors."

"I suppose he listens in on all the attorney-client conversations, too."

"I'm surprised at you, Mrs. Vergano. That would be against the law."

Ami scowled at Kirkpatrick. The DA grinned. He was enjoying himself.

"So, are you going with PTSD?" Kirkpatrick asked innocently.

"Wouldn't you like to know?"

"Actually, the law requires you to tell me. You've heard of reciprocal discovery?"

Ami had heard the term, but she had no idea what the statutes required her to do. Before she could think of a witty rejoinder to cover her ignorance, the television camera started filming again and Kirkpatrick moved to the judge's side. When he saw the group approaching, the officer guarding Morelli stood up and unlocked the door to the prisoner's hospital room. Judge Velasco stood aside to let Ami in first. She walked to Morelli's bed, and Kirkpatrick and the judge followed her. Morelli looked confused for a moment. Then the camera crew entered the room and started filming. Morelli froze like a deer caught in a car's headlights. Then he threw his arm across his face and turned his head away from the camera.

"Get them out of here," Morelli shouted.

Ami turned to the judge. "Please. He's really upset."

"The press has a constitutional right to be here, judge," Kirkpatrick insisted. "If we were in court the press would be covering this."

"Not with TV cameras," Ami said, hoping that she was right.

Judge Velasco turned to the reporter from Channel Four. "You can stay but I want your cameraman to leave."

"Our attorney told us . . . "

"I don't care. The camera is causing a problem, so it goes," Velasco said firmly. "You'll have plenty of chances to film Mr. Morelli when he's in a courtroom. He's a patient in a hospital now, and I'm going to honor his wishes."

The reporter saw that it would be useless to argue, and he told the cameraman to wait in the hall.

"Is that okay with you, Mr. Morelli?" Judge Velasco asked.

Morelli lowered his arm. "Thank you, judge."

Kirkpatrick had given Ami two copies of the indictment. While the court reporter set up his machine, Ami gave Morelli his copy and told him what was going to happen during the arraignment. When Arthur Reid was ready, Judge Velasco read the caption of the case.

"Your Honor," Kirkpatrick said. "There has been a problem verifying the defendant's identity. We can't match his prints, his identification is false, and he doesn't show up in any of our databases. I'd like the court to ask the defendant if the name in the indictment is his true name."

Ami fought down her panic. The arraignment

was supposed to be easy. She wasn't supposed to have to make any decisions that could affect Morelli.

"The Fifth Amendment, Your Honor," she blurted out.

"What, Mrs. Vergano?" the judge asked, puzzled by her outburst.

"I'm advising my client to exercise his Fifth Amendment right to remain silent."

Kirkpatrick was annoyed. "We need to know the defendant's real name, Your Honor."

"No you don't," Ami said. "What if he had amnesia? You'd prosecute him as John Doe. So you don't need his name to go forward."

The judge held up his hand before Kirkpatrick could reply. "Mrs. Vergano's point is well taken, Mr. Kirkpatrick."

The DA glared at Ami but held his tongue. The judge read the indictment, and the rest of the arraignment went along without any problems. When the brief appearance was concluded, everyone but Ami left.

"How is Ryan doing?" Morelli asked as soon as they were alone.

"He's back in school. Being with his friends helps. He always asks about you when I get home from work."

"He's a good kid. He's tough. He'll be okay."

"Yeah," Ami answered, but Morelli could see that she was worried. He smiled.

"You know, for someone who says that she doesn't know a thing about criminal law, you're doing okay."

Ami flashed an embarrassed grin. "I pulled that Fifth Amendment thing out of thin air. It's what they do on TV. The lawyer always tells his client to plead the Fifth. Unfortunately, I haven't been watching much TV lately, so I'd better get another lawyer in here pronto."

"I don't know if I want another lawyer. You've got Kirkpatrick so upset that he might dismiss my case just so he doesn't have to deal with you."

Ami laughed. "Whether you want it or not, I'm out of here as soon as Ray Armitage agrees to take over."

"Who's he?"

"Just one of the best criminal defense lawyers in the country. He's in Colorado on the case of the Olympic skier. We've talked on the phone and he's definitely interested in representing you. He'll probably be on board early next week. Meanwhile, you're stuck with me and we have to talk."

"About what?" Morelli asked defensively.

"Just before I came over, Dr. French called me. He has friends in the military. They tried to get your records, but there is no record of a Daniel Morelli serving in the Special Forces or any other branch of the military during Vietnam."

Morelli turned his head away from Ami.

"Look, Dan, your health is improving. They're going to send you to jail soon unless we can get you bail. Someone like Ray Armitage can persuade a judge to set a low bail. You were defending Ben Branton when you stabbed Barney. Ben would have been hurt if Barney had hit him. And the policeman grabbed you from behind, so we can argue that you didn't know that he was a cop. But the judge isn't going to listen to those arguments if you're using a fake name and fake ID. Kirkpatrick will argue that you're a flight risk. How can we make an argument to refute that?"

Morelli turned back to Ami. He looked defeated and exhausted.

"If you knew my real name it would make matters worse."

"Why?"

"I went AWOL from the Army in 1985. Everyone thinks I'm dead. You have no idea the shit storm you'd stir up if certain people discovered that I'm alive. That's why I didn't want my picture taken. That's why you've got to figure out a way to get me out of here before I have to go to court. Once my face is in the news or in the paper they'll know I'm alive. They'll come for me."

"Who will come for you?"

Morelli closed his eyes. Ami waited patiently. She couldn't help feeling sorry for him. She could see that he was suffering.

"While I was in the army," he said so quietly that Ami had to lean forward to hear him, "I was recruited by an intelligence agency."

"The CIA?"

"No. The Agency for Intelligence Data Coordination—the AIDC—but I doubt there's a record that I ever worked for them in any capacity. The agency's charter does not permit it to employ people who did my type of work, and there is nothing on paper about this unit. I received verbal orders. As far as the army is concerned, the unit never existed."

"Why the secrecy?"

"Murder," he answered calmly.

"You murdered people?" Ami asked, not certain she'd heard him correctly.

Morelli nodded.

"Where?"

"Southeast Asia."

"That was okay, wasn't it? There was a war in Southeast Asia."

Morelli looked Ami in the eye. "That wasn't the only place. I've killed people in Europe and I've murdered Americans in the United States."

"But if you were ordered to . . . to do that?"

Morelli smiled sadly. "I'm not going to justify my actions. It was murder. There's no other way to look at it. And I did other things that were just as bad."

"Like what?"

"How much do you know about the Vietnam War?"

"Just what I learned in school in history class."

"Do you know what the Shan Hills are?"

"I've heard of them. They're in Burma, right?"

"They're part of the Golden Triangle, roughly 150,000 square miles of rugged mountain terrain in Burma, Laos, and Thailand. During the sixties and seventies about seventy percent of the world's illicit opium supply came from there. When the Kuomintang-Nationalist Chinese government collapsed in 1949, groups of Kuomintang soldiers fled China and settled in the Shan

States. Starting in 1950, the CIA began regrouping them for an invasion of southern China. That project failed, but the soldiers succeeded in monopolizing the opium trade.

"One of my jobs was to ambush mule trains carrying morphine base down from the Shan Hills. We would kill the guards and steal the product."

Morelli laughed.

"What's so funny?"

"I was just remembering. We were such cowboys. The first time we ambushed a mule train we blasted everybody and everything. I mean we killed the guards and the mules." He shook his head. "It turned out we'd also blown the packages with the morphine base all to hell and didn't have a thing to show for the raid."

Ami didn't think that it was funny in the least to kill people and animals, but she held the thought.

"What did you do with the morphine base?" she asked instead.

Morelli sobered. "We brought it to Laos, where Meo tribesmen on the CIA payroll processed it into heroin. Some of the heroin was flown to Saigon on Air America, an airline financed by the CIA. In Saigon, the regime sold the heroin. Some of the people who bought it were American GIs."

"Why would we help create GI addicts?"

"The CIA couldn't ask Congress for money to pay off the Saigon regime, so they provided a commodity."

"Didn't that bother you?"

"Of course it did, once I found out what was going on. But I didn't learn the full story until much later. I wasn't in on the big policy decisions. I was a grunt, a foot soldier. They told me to ambush the train and bring the product to a certain person. That's what I did. Then I went home. I didn't question my orders."

"You said that some of the heroin was sent to Saigon. What happened to the rest?"

"Some of it was traded to organized crime in the United States for favors."

"You're serious?"

Morelli nodded. "The rest was used to create a secret fund that financed the Unit's operations. The money was kept in secret accounts in offshore banks. Only a few people knew the access numbers to the secret accounts." Morelli got a faraway look. "I suspect those accounts no longer exist."

Morelli's story was growing more implausible with each new revelation, and Ami remembered what George French had said about the ability of people in a paranoid state to create believable stories that weren't true. Ami was about to ask for some specifics that she could investigate when she remembered a piece of trivia she had read recently.

"Did you know General Morris Wingate?"

Morelli looked startled. "Why are you asking me about him?"

"He was the head of the AIDC during the Vietnam years. I saw that in a profile of Wingate in *Newsweek*. So, do you know him? Maybe he could help you."

Morelli laughed. "He'd help me all right. He'd help me out of this world. I am Morris Wingate's worst nightmare. He's the man I'm hiding from."

"I don't understand."

"General Wingate recruited me. He gave me some of my orders. Vanessa is his daughter. If what I did for Wingate became public knowledge, he would go to prison. Do you see why I can't let my picture be published? Once the general knows I'm alive he'll have me killed. He has no choice."

Ami was stunned. She couldn't believe that Vanessa was Wingate's daughter or that Morelli had the power to topple the General. Then again she wasn't sure that she should believe what Morelli was telling her. Everything he'd said sounded crazy. Still . . .

"I think you'd better tell me everything from the beginning," Ami said.

"What's the use?"

"I don't know. Maybe we won't be any better off after I know everything. But I might be able to figure out some way to help you if I do. This is all between us anyway. I'm not going to tell anyone about it without your permission."

"I don't know."

"Please, let me help you."

"All right. I'll tell you about Wingate and the Unit."

"Why don't you start by telling me your real name?"

# CHAPTER ELEVEN

CALIFORNIA—1969 AND 1970

## 1

"Carl, hold up." Carl Rice was packing up his books at the end of his calculus class, and Vanessa Wingate's voice froze him like a direct hit from Captain Kirk's phaser. "You're pretty good with calc, aren't you?"

Carl turned to face the attractive blond, fighting to keep his eyes from drifting to the floor. His attempt at a nonchalant shrug looked more like a spastic twitch.

"I do okay."

"Well, Mr. Goody lost me again. I was wondering if you could give me some help sometime. I'm pretty sure the stuff he went over today is going to be on the final, and I don't understand any of it."

"Uh, okay. I have class now, but I'll be at the library at three."

"Great," Vanessa said, flashing her biggest, warmest smile. They made plans to meet at the reference desk, and Vanessa walked off after a cheery, "See ya."

St. Martin's Preparatory School was situated on a sprawling pastoral campus a few miles inland from the Pacific Ocean. The school had been established in 1889, and the ivy on the buildings looked as if it had never been pruned. Though they were in the same class there, Carl Rice and Vanessa Wingate might as well have been on different continents. Vanessa was rich, beautiful, and the lead in Carl's most intense sexual fantasies. She ran with a clique that drove the newest and fastest cars, wore the coolest clothes, and was into the latest fads before anyone else in America even knew that they existed. Carl was a scholarship boy who ran with no crowd and bought his clothes off the rack at JCPenney. Being able to spend two hours with Vanessa—even if they were only studying calculus—was the answer to his teenage prayers.

Carl had trouble concentrating in class and was at the library fifteen minutes early. His heart raced every time the front doors opened. After a few minutes of tortured waiting, Carl accepted the fact that he was a fool. Vanessa wasn't going to show up. She had so many friends and so many activities that he couldn't picture her missing out on any of her fun to spend time being tutored by him. He was just starting to gather up his books when he saw her standing near the reference desk, waving.

The school library, a huge stone building, had been built with a donation from a railroad tycoon in the early 1900s. Carl led Vanessa downstairs to a table in the rear of the basement where he worked on his homework nearly every evening. It was dimly lit, but its appeal for Carl was that few other students made their way down to it.

Carl was surprised that Vanessa wanted help with calculus. He'd never pictured her as a serious student. Then again, he didn't really know much about her. He was pleasantly surprised to discover that she was bright enough to understand what he was telling her after he had corrected some basic misconceptions. They were progressing nicely when a large shadow fell across the table. Carl looked up and saw Sandy Rhodes and Mike Manchester looming over them. Mike and Sandy were on the football team. Both boys weighed over two hundred pounds and were in good shape. Carl had heard that Sandy and Vanessa were dating.

"Hey, Van, what's up? I thought we were going out?" Sandy sounded aggrieved that Vanessa was doing schoolwork.

"I tried to tell you I had to study, but I couldn't find you."

"Well I'm here now, so let's go."

Vanessa smiled apologetically. "I can't. I really have to learn this."

Sandy had not acknowledged Carl's presence and wasn't going to accept Vanessa's protestations.

"Come on, Van, it's Friday night. The gang's waiting."

Vanessa's smile disappeared. "I'm studying, Sandy. I am not going out tonight."

"Bullshit," Sandy said. He flipped her book closed and grabbed her arm.

Carl's father had walked out on Evelyn Rice when Carl was five. Carl still had nightmares about his father's rages and his mother's cries of pain. Burned into his memory were images of the vivid purple bruises that darkened his mother's swollen face.

"Let go of Vanessa," Carl said. He sounded frightened, which was to be expected under the circumstances. Carl was wiry, muscular, and in excellent shape, but the two football players were several inches taller and each boy outweighed him by fifty pounds.

Sandy did not release Vanessa's arm. He stared at Carl the way he might regard dog dirt that had attached itself to his shoe.

"Stick your nose back in your book, dork, or I'll break it."

As Sandy turned his attention back to Vanessa, Carl buried his fist in the football player's solar plexus, leaving him breathless. Then he grabbed the tie that all St. Martin's boys were required to wear and jerked his head down. Sandy's chin cracked against the edge of the table, stunning him.

Mike Manchester had been too shocked to react, but the sound of his friend's chin hitting the table snapped him out of his trance. He swung a roundhouse punch, and Carl thrust his thick calculus textbook forward. Manchester's knuckle broke with a crack that sounded like a gunshot. As he recoiled in pain, Carl swung his book like a baseball bat, catching Mike in the back of the head and driving him to his knees. Carl stepped behind Manchester and applied a choke hold, cutting off Mike's air.

"I don't want to fight. Will you call it quits?" Carl asked the struggling boy.

Mike tried to pull Carl's arm away, and Carl tightened his hold. By now Sandy Rhodes had regained his wits and was struggling to his feet. Carl cut off Mike's air and dropped the unconscious boy to the floor before drop-kicking Rhodes in the jaw. Sandy collapsed beside his buddy.

"Holy shit!" Vanessa said as she leaped to her feet. "You have to get out of here. They'll be furious when they come to."

"I don't have a car," Carl admitted, embarrassed to tell Vanessa that his mother picked him up at school.

"I do. Grab your stuff," she said as she gathered up her books. Carl hesitated. Mike Manchester moaned. Vanessa grabbed Carl's arm. "Come on."

"Won't Sandy be pissed that you're helping me?"

"Sandy is a pig. We've only gone out three times and he thinks he owns me. I'm glad you kicked his ass."

Minutes later, Carl was seated in the passenger seat of Vanessa Wingate's Corvette and they were roaring down the coast highway.

"That was awesome," Vanessa said. "Where did you learn to fight like that?"

Carl didn't feel good about the beating he'd administered, and he was ashamed of the pleasure he felt from defeating the two boys with Vanessa looking on, but he could not abide any man inflicting pain on a woman, because of the way his father had treated his mother.

"I've been practicing karate since I was little. I go to a dojo every day after school."

Vanessa turned toward him. The top of the car was down and the wind was whipping her long blond hair and bringing color to her cheeks.

"There's more to you than meets the eye, Carl Rice," she said before turning back to the road.

Carl blushed. "Where are we going?" he asked to cover his embarrassment.

"My house."

They drove in silence for a while. Carl sneaked glances at Vanessa while pretending to watch the ocean. She was so beautiful. He couldn't believe that he was by her side in this amazing car.

"You're on scholarship, right?" Vanessa asked.

Carl colored again and nodded. Evelyn Rice was highly intelligent, but her husband had never permitted her to work or finish school. As soon as Carl's father walked out of their lives, his mother had enrolled in a community college. She earned an AA degree in accounting and was hired as a receptionist at the local branch of a national accounting firm. Eventually, she finished her bachelor's degree and moved up to the position of office manager. One of the firm's partners was an alumnus of St. Martin's and had used his contacts to get Carl a scholarship.

"I envy you," Vanessa said.

"Why would you envy me?" he asked incredulously. Almost every other student at St. Martin's was wealthy, and his poverty made him feel small. He couldn't imagine why anyone like Vanessa would be interested in, much less envious of, someone like him.

"No one handed you everything," she replied. "You've earned what you have with your brains and drive."

"I've had to because I'm poor, Vanessa. Believe me, it's not romantic."

"Neither is living with my father."

"At least you've got one. Mine walked out on us when I was five."

"He didn't murder your mother, did he?"

"What?" Carl wondered if she was joking. "What are you talking about?"

"My mother died in a car crash when I was thirteen. I'm certain it wasn't an accident."

"Did you tell the police?"

"They didn't believe me. Neither did the insurance investigators. I don't blame them. I don't have any proof. I just know the way that bastard operates. He thinks he's above the law. I'll tell you this, he definitely knows people who can make a death appear to be an accident."

Carl didn't know what to say. "Have you told the FBI?"

Vanessa laughed bitterly. "Ten minutes after I walked out of their office someone called my father. The General took me into the library and told me that he would have me committed to a mental hospital if I didn't stop spreading vicious rumors. He said he'd have me sedated and put in a straitjacket and I would stay locked up for the rest of my life."

"Your father's a general?"

Vanessa nodded.

"He couldn't get away with that, could he, locking you away for no reason?"

"You don't have any idea of how powerful my father is. So I gave up and he stopped paying any attention to me. He's not home that much anyway. He spends most of his time in Washington, and he leaves me here to do whatever I want, as long as it doesn't embarrass or annoy him."

Vanessa turned off the main road and punched in a code on a keypad that stood in front of a high electrified gate. The road from the gate twisted through a meadow that was bounded by woods until it crested at a viewpoint that revealed the Pacific Ocean and an immense Spanish-style villa with a red tile roof. Carl had never been this close to a house like the one that stood before him. It was white as snow and looked larger than his entire apartment complex. Terraces brightened by fresh cut flowers fronted the windows on the second and third floors. There was a stable off to the right. Carl had daydreamed about being rich, but he'd never imagined anything like this.

"You live here," he asked, awestruck. "This is yours?"

"Home sweet home," Vanessa answered as she turned onto a circular drive and parked in front of a huge carved wooden door that was shaded by a portico. As she pulled up, the door opened and a man dressed in a white jacket and black slacks came out to greet them. Vanessa tossed him the keys.

"I'm through for the night, Enrique," she said, leading Carl inside. The door closed, cutting off the powerful sound the Corvette's engine made as Enrique drove it to the garage.

"Can I use your phone? My mom is going to worry if I don't call."

There was a phone on an inlaid table in the cavernous entryway. Carl called his mother's office and caught her just before she was about to leave. Vanessa listened as he explained that he was at a friend's house and would get a ride home. Vanessa tapped him on the arm. He told his mother to hold on for a second and broke out into a sweat when Vanessa whispered in his ear.

"Uh, I'm invited to spend the night. Is that okay?"

After a little discussion over curfews and deadlines for returning home, Carl hung up.

"You'll stay?"

"Mom's thrilled that I finally made a friend at St. Martin's."

"I wish my father gave a shit about the people I hang out with."

Carl looked around the entry hall. It was paved with reddish-yellow tiles, and the main attractions were an immense crystal chandelier and a curving marble staircase.

"It's early for dinner," Vanessa said. "Want to go for a swim?"

"I don't have a suit."

Vanessa eyed him wickedly. "Don't worry about that."

Carl blushed and Vanessa laughed. "We keep a selection of swimsuits in the pool house. Leave your school stuff in the entryway and come on."

Vanessa led the way through a large living room lit by sunlight that streamed through high French doors. She pushed open one set, and Carl found himself on a wide tiled patio bordered by a manicured lawn that separated it from a twenty-five-meter pool. There were two dressing rooms on the far side of the pool. Vanessa pointed out the men's changing room and went into the women's. Ten minutes later, Carl came out clad in a black boxer-length swimming suit. Vanessa was stretched out on a lounge in a tiny yellow string bikini. Her lean, tanned body took his breath away. Vanessa's stomach was flat with a hint of muscle, and her legs were long and smooth. He felt himself growing hard and fought with all his might to contain himself. Vanessa gave no sign that she'd noticed his discomfort. Instead, she rose from the chair holding a T-shirt, a sweatshirt for Carl, two big terry-cloth towels and a large beach towel.

"Let's get wet," she said leading him toward the far end of the lawn, where a set of weathered wooden stairs took them down the face of a rugged cliff to a narrow beach three hundred feet below. The tide was coming in and large waves crashed on the shore. Vanessa spread the beach towel on the sand, dropped everything she was

holding on top of it, and ran into the water before
flattening out and swimming into the surf with a
practiced crawl. Carl dove into a wave, then
swam hard to warm up. Vanessa was nowhere in
sight when he came out of the other side of the
wave. He treaded water and turned in place, looking for her, momentarily panicked. Then Vanessa
rose from the sea with the grace of a dolphin, put
her arms around his neck, and pulled him to her.
Her kiss startled Carl, but he overcame his shock
when she kissed him again.

Carl had wanted Vanessa from the first moment he saw her. It was too much to believe that
she wanted him, too, but how else to explain
Vanessa clinging to his body, wrapping her long
legs around his waist and pressing her beautiful
breasts against his chest?

Vanessa broke the kiss and dove under the
waves, leaving Carl dizzy with desire. When she
surfaced, she was almost onshore. Carl swam
after her. When he struggled out of the surf, she
was wearing her T-shirt.

"I'm freezing," she said, tossing him a towel
and the sweatshirt. "Let's go in."

Carl followed, afraid to speak, overwhelmed by
desire at the sight of Vanessa's buttocks moving
rhythmically up the stairs. His erection made it
difficult to think. He tore his eyes away, afraid
that he would fall if he did not concentrate on
climbing the narrow steps.

When they entered the house, Vanessa led Carl
up the winding staircase to the second floor.

"You're here," she said, opening the door to a

guest room. Carl walked in and Vanessa followed him. The room was furnished with a chest of drawers, two end tables, a floor lamp, and a queen-size bed.

"Dinner won't be for an hour." Vanessa shut the door and stripped off her T-shirt. "What should we do until then?"

## 2

Carl woke up before dawn. It took him a moment to remember where he was and another moment to assure himself that yesterday was not a dream. The proof was lying beside him, naked, hair tousled, and achingly beautiful. Carl crept out of bed and slipped on the swimsuit and the sweatshirt Vanessa had lent him. While Vanessa slept in the guest room bed, Carl followed the steps down the side of the sheer cliff to the beach. He needed time to sort out what had happened between him and Vanessa, and to do that he had to clear his head.

In a few hours, the Southern California sun would bake the beach, but at this hour the sun was just rising in the east and the cliff cast a cooling shadow across the sand. Carl stretched for twenty minutes before practicing kata, the dancelike formal exercises of karate. Each kata was a ritual battle fought against imaginary opponents. The moves of the kata had to be performed in a specific order. Carl liked practicing katas more than he liked fighting. For Carl, kata was more than exercise. It was a ritual that imposed a framework of certainty on a life riddled from birth with uncertainty.

Carl glided across the sand just out of reach of the incoming waves. Each kata was more complex than the one that preceded it, and he performed them three times at increasing rates of speed. The kata performed in slow motion and at half speed flowed softly, one movement drifting into the next. Carl was a blur at full speed, but he saw each strike, kick, and block clearly in his mind. As he exercised, the sea, beach, and newborn sun faded away until there was only the blow that he was delivering.

Carl was sweating freely by the time he finished his last kata and started to cool down. He was almost done stretching when he saw a figure descending the stairs to the beach. The sun had risen above the rim of the cliff. Carl raised his arm to shield his eyes from the glare and made out a ruggedly handsome, solidly built man in a T-shirt and shorts. His black hair was sprinkled with silver and worn in a military cut.

"I've been watching for the last twenty minutes," the man said. "I hope you don't mind."

"I didn't know you were there," Carl answered truthfully. The katas had absorbed all his attention.

"You're very good," the man said. "How long have you been studying?"

"I started when I was eight."

"You must be a black belt by now."

Carl nodded, embarrassed. "The belts don't mean much," he said, so that the man wouldn't think he was bragging. "Anyone can earn a black belt by practicing hard enough."

"I'm Morris Wingate, Vanessa's father," the General said, extending his hand.

Carl forced himself to shake it. The peace achieved by his workout was instantly replaced by shame, because he had just had sex with Wingate's daughter in Wingate's house—and fear, because Vanessa had told him that her father was a cold-blooded murderer.

"And you are?" the General asked.

Carl managed to keep his voice steady when he told Wingate his name.

"I assume you're a friend of Vanessa."

"We're classmates. I . . . I've been helping her with calculus."

"Really? An academic and a dedicated student of karate—not my daughter's usual type. I assume you stayed over, last night. After the tutoring session."

"Yes, sir. It was late," Carl answered lamely as his gut churned. He wondered if Wingate had looked in the guest room and seen his naked daughter and Carl's clothes.

"I got in very late myself, around two this morning. I find that exercise wakes me up better than a cup of coffee. Care to join me for a run?"

Carl couldn't think of any way to refuse, so he fell in beside the General. The older man set a steady pace that Carl had no trouble keeping. The beach seemed to stretch forever, and Carl wondered how far Wingate would go. He decided that it didn't matter. In the distance, high up, a solitary tree with a thick, gnarled trunk had dug its roots into the side of the cliff. It tilted precariously toward the sea, but Carl got the feeling that it had been getting the best of gravity for a very long time. He set his sights on the tree and glided along.

Carl and Wingate ran in silence for a while, then Wingate asked, "How is Vanessa's calculus?"

Carl wasn't sure if Wingate was being sarcastic, so he decided to give him a straight answer.

"She picked up on what I was saying pretty fast."

"Vanessa is smart, but she doesn't give school her full attention. I wish her grades reflected her IQ."

The General's confidences made Carl uncomfortable. He wouldn't want his mother discussing his shortcomings with his friends.

"Rice isn't a name I'm familiar with. Do you live around here, Carl?"

"No."

"Where do you live?"

"San Diego." Carl decided to cut short the General's probing into his lineage. "I'm on scholarship."

"You sound defensive."

"I'm not," he said a little too quickly.

"Good. You shouldn't be. I'm pleased that Vanessa has a friend who hasn't had everything in life handed to him. St. Martin's is an excellent school. I wouldn't have permitted Vanessa to attend if it wasn't. But many of the students are there because their parents bought their way in.

They are spoiled and worthless. You should be proud that your admission was based on merit."

The General's speech surprised Carl. He certainly didn't sound like the ogre Vanessa had made him out to be.

Wingate picked up the pace after a mile, but Carl still had no trouble keeping up. At two miles a stone jetty blocked the beach and the General turned back toward the house. With a half mile to go, Wingate started to sprint. Carl could have outrun the older man easily, but he did not want to race. He sensed that this was some sort of test, but he just matched his pace to the General's and pretended that they were not competing. They were two hundred meters from the stairs when Carl saw a man in jeans and a plaid shirt walking along the edge of the cliff. The sun shone in Carl's eyes and he had to look away, but there had been a moment when the man's body blocked the sun and Carl thought he saw an automatic weapon.

When they reached the stairs the General was gasping but Carl's breathing was still steady.

Wingate leaned forward and rested his hands on his knees. "You're in good shape, Carl."

"I work out several hours every day. Running is part of my training."

"Do you compete for St. Martin's?"

"No, sir."

"Why not?"

Carl shrugged. "My studies and karate keep me pretty busy. I don't have time."

"What are you doing next year?"

"College, I hope."

"I assume your grades are high."

"I'm doing okay."

"Where are you applying?"

"Cal, some of the other UC schools. Dartmouth is my first choice. But it all depends on scholarships. If I have to I'll work for a year or two."

Wingate stood up straight. His breathing was normal again. "Shall we go up? Vanessa should be awake by now."

Carl found himself drawn to the General. Would Vanessa turn against him if she thought he liked her father? He hoped that Vanessa was still sleeping and wouldn't see him with Wingate, but he hoped in vain. She was on the terrace dressed in tennis shorts and a light green short-sleeved shirt eating a croissant and sipping coffee.

"Engaged in male bonding?" she asked when the men drew close.

"I asked Carl to join me on my run," Wingate responded, ignoring her sarcasm. "He tells me that he's helping you with your schoolwork."

Vanessa stared at Carl long enough to make him nervous. He fully expected Vanessa to tell her father what they'd done in the guest room all night long.

"I was having trouble with math. Carl's a whiz. I think I understand it now."

"Good. I'm going to shower. I'll see you two later."

"So, what did you think of the General?" Vanessa asked when her father was out of earshot.

"He's in good shape for someone his age," Carl answered noncommittally.

Vanessa laughed. "Don't worry. I won't bite you if you say something nice about him. He makes a great first impression, especially with men. Those steely eyes, the firm set of his jaw, his military posture. He's all man, and you guys eat that up."

"Really, Vanessa, I was practicing karate. We talked about that and we ran together. He asked me where I live and about school."

Vanessa leaned forward and took Carl's jaw in her hand. The touch was electric and ignited his desire.

"You're red as a beet and I bet I know what you're thinking." Carl's blush deepened. "Why don't you go up and shower and I'll join you?"

"With your father in the house?" Carl asked nervously.

"Especially with my father in the house," she answered, staring viciously into the dark interior of her home.

As they got up, a man walked around the corner of the mansion. He was not the same man Carl had seen patrolling the edge of the cliff. This time there was no question that the man was armed.

"Don't worry about them," Vanessa said when she noticed where Carl was looking. "My father always travels with guards. He's very important. Even Enrique is ex-military, from some South American country my father had dealings with. Probably from some death squad my father helped train." Carl couldn't tell if she was kidding. "He's always armed."

Carl frowned. He didn't like the idea of armed men patrolling the grounds. It meant that there was a reason for them to be there. Then Vanessa took his hand and Carl forgot about the guards.

The General left the house shortly after breakfast. While he was gone, Carl and Vanessa alternated between screwing their brains out and lolling on the beach. Wingate returned in the early evening for dinner. He tried to conduct a normal conversation during the meal, but his daughter answered any direct questions tersely and was morosely silent when Carl and her father were speaking. Carl was intensely uncomfortable and was relieved when dinner ended.

The couple went to a movie because the General was having company. The visitors were gone when they returned after midnight. Vanessa spent the night in Carl's room, which made him very nervous. He imagined the General wrenching open the guest room door and murdering him in bed, but there were no nocturnal incursions and Morris Wingate was gone when they woke up Sunday morning.

Carl was exhausted when Vanessa dropped him off at his apartment on Sunday evening. He went right to sleep and slept through his alarm, arriving late for class for the first time since he'd started at St. Martin's. Carl hoped he would not run into Sandy Rhodes or Mike Manchester. He lucked out. They weren't in any of his classes and he only saw them in the hall at a distance. Vanessa told Carl that the boys were telling everyone who asked about their bruises that they'd received their scars while successfully fighting off a gang of bikers in an alley behind a bar.

### 3

The first semester of Carl's senior year was a blur. He wanted to spend every minute he could with Vanessa but explained that he had to keep his grades up if he was going to have a chance at a college scholarship. She understood and never interfered with his studies. When they went to the beach after class, Vanessa had him home by seven. If he stayed at her house on the weekends, she insisted that he bring his books.

At first, Carl dreaded the weekends at the Wingate estate if the General was in residence because there was so much tension between Morris Wingate and his daughter, but he soon began looking forward to Wingate's appearances. The General was charming and intelligent. He had a wide range of knowledge and seemed to have been everywhere. Carl felt guilty because he didn't hate Vanessa's father the way his daughter did. He was careful not to mention his feelings to Vanessa. She must have noticed that Carl and her father got along, but she never said anything to him about it.

Sometimes Carl and the General worked out together. Usually they ran on the beach, but one day Wingate suggested that they spar. He was not in Carl's league, but he wasn't bad. Thinking about it later, Carl realized that he should not have been surprised. Wingate was military, and soldiers fight for a living. For the most part, Carl played defense, content to block Wingate's punches and kicks while occasionally landing a light blow of his own. Carl was sure that the General knew he was holding back, but he couldn't bring himself to go all-out.

Two nights after their sparring session, the phone rang in Carl's apartment. He took the call in his room, hoping that it was Vanessa, but the caller was Morris Wingate. The General had never phoned him before, and he worried that something had happened to Vanessa.

"I'm glad I caught you," Wingate said. "I'm in D.C., but I'll be back in California on Thursday night. Do you have any plans?"

Actually, he didn't. He and Vanessa both had midterms and had agreed to study all week and not see each other.

"Good," Wingate said. "I have a surprise planned for you on Thursday night. I'll send a car at seven. Don't tell Vanessa."

The General hung up before Carl could ask him any questions. He wished that Wingate had not told him to keep their meeting a secret from Vanessa. What if he obeyed and she found out? If you loved someone—and Carl thought he might be in love with Vanessa—you shouldn't have secrets. But Carl didn't know why he wasn't supposed to tell Vanessa. What if the General was planning a surprise for her and wanted him in on it? He'd be ruining everything if he told. Carl decided to wait and see what the General was planning. He could always tell Vanessa what had happened afterward.

A black town car parked in front of Carl's apartment complex precisely at seven. Chauffeur-driven cars were a rarity in Carl's neighborhood, and it drew stares.

"Where are you going?" Evelyn Rice asked her son.

"I don't know, Mom. I told you, the General said it's a surprise."

"Why isn't your girlfriend going with you?"

"I don't know that either." Carl put on his jacket and kissed his mother on the cheek. "I've got to go."

Evelyn wrapped her arms around her body to keep her emotions in as Carl closed the apartment door behind him. Her son had been tight-lipped about this girl he was seeing. All Evelyn knew was that Vanessa was very rich, her mother was dead, and her father lived in Washington, D.C., most of the year and ran an intelligence agency. Evelyn did not approve of leaving a child unsupervised for long periods of time, and she thought it was odd that someone as important as General Wingate would invite her son out for an evening without asking his daughter along; but Carl had been so happy lately that she had kept her forebodings to herself.

Some of the neighborhood kids made remarks when the chauffeur opened the door for Carl, and he felt self-conscious as he slipped into the backseat next to the General. A bodyguard sat in the front seat next to the driver. Both men wore their hair long and were dressed in civilian clothes. Wingate was wearing a black shirt and dark slacks.

"How are your exams going?" the General asked when they were under way.

"Okay, I think. I took two this week and I have three more next week."

"Vanessa thinks she did well on her calculus test. She credits you with her improvement."

Carl colored. "She would have done okay without me."

"She also told me how you protected her from Sandy Rhodes." Carl looked away. "That took courage. I've seen Sandy and his friend. They're much bigger than you."

"I surprised Sandy, and they didn't know how to fight," Carl mumbled.

The General studied Carl for a moment before speaking. "Modesty is a good trait, Carl, but you shouldn't overdo it. Using surprise in a fight is admirable. Men only fight fair on TV. Fighting is not a game. In any event, I am indebted to you for protecting Vanessa."

Carl didn't know what to say, so he said nothing. The General dropped the subject, and they rode without speaking until the car turned off the highway and headed east into farm country.

"I think you'll find tonight interesting."

"Where are we going?"

"To a sporting competition," Wingate answered with an enigmatic smile. "Your fight with Sandy and his friend wasn't your first, was it?"

"No," Carl answered suspiciously, not sure where Wingate was going.

"Did you ever join the Marauders?" Carl's eyes widened. "I know you've participated in some of their gang fights but it's not clear how far the association goes."

"How did . . . ?"

Wingate smiled. "I'm the head of an intelligence agency, Carl. How good an agency would it be if it couldn't even run a background check on my daughter's boyfriend?"

Carl darkened. "I don't think that's right, sir."

"My daughter hates me. She blames me for her mother's death and she goes out of her way to hurt me. On occasion she takes up with boys who could hurt her badly. She dates them simply to cause me pain. I love Vanessa very much. Sometimes I have to protect her from herself. That means finding out what I can about her friends and, on occasion, dealing with boys who could be a problem."

The General read the alarm in Carl's eyes. He smiled warmly. "You're not someone who's bad for her, Carl. I'm greatly relieved that she's finally found someone like you, someone with character."

Carl felt the tension drain from his shoulders.

"I still have to know about the Marauders, though," the General insisted.

"There's not much to know. I have friends from my old school who are in the gang. I'm not. When I earned my black belt I wanted to see how I would do outside a gym, you know, on the street where there weren't any rules. I was in one fight and the cops picked me up. They couldn't prove anything, so they let me go. There weren't any charges, but being arrested shook me up. I told my friends I wasn't going in with them. We're still friends."

"How did you do without any rules?"

Carl looked the General in the eye. "Very well."

Wingate smiled and dropped the conversation. In the east, the hills slowly faded in the growing darkness and the sky filled with stars. The town car turned onto a dirt road and drove through an orchard. Carl saw a light in the distance flickering through the trees. Moments later they were in front of a large barn, parking beside a sleek limousine. Several other expensive cars were parked nearby. When the driver opened the door for the General, Carl heard noise coming from the interior of the barn. The General's bodyguard had gone ahead. He knocked on a door. It opened an inch and a fat man who was smoking a cigar peered out. Wingate's bodyguard gave the fat man a wad of cash and said something that Carl could not hear. The fat man slipped the money into his pocket and broke into a smile.

"General, it's a pleasure."

"It sounds like you've got some interesting contests planned."

"We'll keep you entertained," the fat man assured Wingate as he stepped aside to let Carl, the General, and Wingate's protection into the barn.

A series of spotlights were focused on a cleared sand rectangle in the center of the barn, leaving the majority of the interior in shadow. Thick clouds of cigar and cigarette smoke created a haze, and excited exchanges took place between the people seated on folding chairs that ringed the open space. They were an odd mix of men and women. Some were dressed in formal attire, others in casual clothes. There were men in cowboy boots, plaid flannel shirts, and jeans and a few men who looked as if they'd just left a Vegas casino.

At the far side of the barn several men were exchanging money in front of a portable bar. Wingate led Carl to some chairs in the first row. There were "reserved" signs on the seats. The driver and the bodyguard stood behind the last row of chairs, where they could keep an eye on everyone.

"What's going on, sir?" Carl asked.

"The man who let us in is Vincent Rodino. He organizes unorthodox sporting events. I learned about this one a few days ago and thought it might interest you."

Carl was about to ask another question when the lights dimmed and Rodino walked to the center of the sand rectangle that the seats surrounded. Two men were entering the rectangle from opposite sides. The man who entered from the left was stocky and his thick chest was matted with black hair. His legs were short and heavily muscled, as were his arms. There was a layer of scar tissue above the man's eyebrows, and his nose had been broken more than once. He wore boxing trunks and footgear but no gloves.

Carl recognized the other man from a recent karate tournament. He was tall, slender, and bare-fisted and wore only the black bottoms of his karategi.

"Let's get started, folks," Rodino said in a loud voice. He waited to say more until the people who were standing found their seats. The fighters moved around, loosening their muscles and shadow-boxing.

"We have an exciting card tonight," Rodino said when the crowd quieted down. He raised his arm and pointed at the boxer. "This is Harold Mc-Murray. He's ranked sixth by the California State Boxing Commission in the light heavyweight division. He's got a pro record of thirteen wins, two losses, and six knockouts."

Rodino turned to the other fighter. "Over here we got Mark Torrance, the western states karate champion for the past two years."

The crowd applauded, and Rodino motioned the fighters to the center of the arena.

"You boys know the rules." Rodino paused for effect. "There ain't no rules." Several people in the crowd laughed. "It's winner takes all, no holds barred. You fight until one man is out or quits. No rounds. You can bite, gouge, wrestle. No weapons, though. You got it?"

The fighters nodded. Wingate turned to Carl. "Do you think a karate man can take a professional boxer?"

"It depends on the fighters."

Rodino stepped out of the arena, and the two men circled warily. The boxer was flat-footed, moving straight forward slowly while feinting with his head and shoulders. Torrance danced lightly on the balls of his feet.

The crowd was keyed up, yelling encouragement and waiting for the first blow.

McMurray tried to close, but Torrance used his reach and speed to stay just out of range, teasing the shorter man with jabs that dotted the boxer's face with red welts. Frustrated, McMurray charged. The black belt sidestepped and swept the boxer's feet from under him. McMurray instinctively reached out for support as he went down, leaving his head unprotected. Torrance set himself and delivered a roundhouse kick to McMurray's face. The snapping kick opened a cut on the boxer's cheek. The crowd roared, excited by the blood. McMurray hit the sand and rolled, frantic to get away. Torrance seemed in no hurry. The boxer scrambled to his feet.

"What do you think?" Wingate asked without moving his eyes from the fighters.

"The kick was well executed," Carl answered quietly. He was concentrating on the men with an expert eye.

Torrance landed a few more jabs and got cocky. He started to taunt his opponent, but the boxer fought for a living and he did not anger easily. He was also in good shape and showed no sign that the punishment he'd taken had weakened him.

Torrance jabbed again, and the boxer slipped the punch, shuffled forward, and drove a hard right hand to the black belt's ribs. Torrance flinched, and McMurray followed with a quick left that grazed

Torrance's neck. Torrance clinched, encircling the boxer's powerful shoulders with his long arms. McMurray brought his knee up toward Torrance's groin. As soon as the knee rose Torrance shifted his weight. The judo throw was executed perfectly, and McMurray was flat on his back before he knew what happened. Torrance speared a hand into McMurray's groin, rendering the boxer helpless. Rodino came back into the arena and raised the winner's hand. Torrance danced around the ring, arms raised in triumph, while McMurray writhed on the ground.

Wingate stood up. "Let's get some air before the next fight."

Carl followed the General to the door at the back of the barn. When they passed Wingate's driver, the General told him to place a bet on the next fight.

A crowd had gathered just outside the door, and the General led Carl to a stand of trees. The night air was refreshing after the smoke-filled barn.

"What was your opinion of the fight?" Wingate asked.

"Torrance is good, but that boxer was made for him. He was too slow, too stationary, and he wasn't used to fighting someone who wrestles and kicks."

"How do you think you would do against Torrance?"

There was something about Wingate's tone that made Carl pause before answering. "What do you mean?"

"If you had to fight him, say tonight. How do you think you'd do?"

"You want me to fight him?" Carl asked.

"I think it would be an interesting match."

"Tonight?" Carl asked, searching Wingate's face in an attempt to understand what was behind the General's questions, but Wingate's chiseled features were in shadow.

"Not tonight," he answered with a laugh just as his driver walked up and told them that the next fight was going to start.

"This should be a good bout," Wingate said. He turned his back on his guest and headed for the barn. Carl was in turmoil. What had Wingate been after? Carl frequently felt that Wingate wanted something from him, but he had no idea what it was.

Carl had trouble concentrating during the rest of the bouts. Did the General really want him to fight Torrance, or was Wingate just curious about Carl's opinion? During a break in the action, Carl wandered off by himself. He glanced across to the bar where a man was paying off the winners and Wingate was talking to Rodino in a dark corner.

The General was so powerful, so self-confident. What he wouldn't give to have a father like that—a friend, but more than a friend. The General knew so much about so many things. Carl loved his mother. She worked so hard for him. But he yearned for something more. He missed having a father, a man who could advise him and guide him.

Carl knew that Vanessa believed the worst of her father, but Carl was certain that she was wrong. In the time he'd known him, Morris Wingate had never had a bad word for Vanessa. Carl was certain that he loved her and forgave her for the terrible opinion she had of him. Carl thought that the General was trying very hard to be a good father despite Vanessa's efforts to alienate him. But he knew he couldn't talk to her about his feelings; honesty in this matter would destroy his relationship with Vanessa, and the General's daughter was the most important person in Carl's world. But he wished that there could be a truce between Vanessa and her father. Even more, he wished that Morris Wingate would begin to think of him not only as Vanessa's boyfriend but also as a son.

# 4

Two days after his outing with the General, Carl paid for a month of lessons at Mark Torrance's dojo. Torrance ran the dojo for a national franchise called International Karate, which had headquarters in Chicago. The school was located in a ghetto on the second floor of an old wood frame building. Most of the students were black or Chicano. A few whites traveled to the school because of Torrance's reputation. Carl registered under a false name and pretended to be a beginner with some prior training. He took every opportunity to study Torrance's technique. He concluded that Torrance was a good fighter with weaknesses that were apparent only to someone with Carl's abilities.

Torrance's last class ended at ten every weekday. Occasionally, the sensei would go out for beers with some of his students; but he never went out on Wednesday night, because that was when he did the books. This Wednesday evening, Carl was dressed in black, which helped him blend into the shadows in the alley across from the dojo. Twenty minutes after the last student descended the wooden steps from the second floor landing Carl pulled on a ski mask and raced across the street and up the stairs. His mouth was dry and his heart was pounding when he reached the landing. He knew how insane he was to come here. He was a boy and Torrance was a seasoned fighter. There was still time to stop. He wasn't even certain that Morris Wingate wanted him to fight Torrance. The General hadn't brought up the subject again. But what if this was a test; what if the General wanted to see what Carl was made of? Fear churned in him and he almost turned away, but something stronger—his desire to please General Wingate—forced his hand to grasp the doorknob and push the door inward.

The dojo was a large room with hardwood floors. There were warm-up mats in one corner, and punching bags of various sizes hung from the ceiling along the near wall. Across the dojo, next to the locker room, was a wall of floor-to-ceiling mirrors. The small office where Torrance was working was on the far side of the room across from the front door. The dojo was dark, but there was a light in the office. Carl could see Torrance seated at his desk.

Carl crossed to the other side of the dojo quietly, hugging the wall and staying in the shadows. When he was in position he could see Torrance entering the amounts from a stack of checks into a ledger. Seated at the desk, concentrating on his books, Torrance presented an easy target. Carl remembered what the General had said about surprise being admirable in a fight and fighting fair being something one did only on TV, but he wanted a true test of his abilities.

Carl was no stranger to combat, but his fights had always been with boys like Sandy Rhodes and Mike Manchester, who had no training. Torrance would not quit and he was used to fighting through pain. Carl wondered if he was making a mistake. Was he overmatched? There was only one way to find out.

Carl spotted a rack of dumbbells near the mirrored wall. He decided to draw Torrance into the open space in the dojo. He took a heavy weight from the top of the rack and dropped it. The metal hit the hardwood floor with a loud clanging sound that was amplified by the silence. Torrance leaped to his feet and stared into the darkness.

"Who's there?"

The black belt walked to his office door and looked around the dojo. Carl backed into the shadows. When Torrance walked into the gym, Carl would confront him. But Torrance did not leave his office. He walked to his desk and bent down. When the black belt turned around he was holding a handgun.

It was suddenly crystal-clear to Carl that he was no modern-day samurai on a mission for his master. He was a fool on a fool's errand, a teenage boy who was living out a fantasy. General Wingate was not proposing a test when he asked Carl how he thought he would do in a fight with Torrance; he was making conversation. Unfortunately, Carl's epiphany might have come too late. If Torrance caught him skulking in his dojo dressed like a ninja he would call the police, and Carl would be expelled from St. Martin's. Carl realized that he had one chance to get out of the ridiculous situation he had made for himself.

As Torrance waited for his eyes to adjust to the dark, Carl slipped into the locker room. Torrance flipped on the lights in the dojo a second after the locker room door had swung shut. Carl nudged the door open and watched Torrance walk over to the rack that held the weights. The sensei knelt down and examined the dumbbell that Carl had dropped. Then he looked at the rack. He picked up the weight and placed it where it had been before. Carl heard the sound of metal on metal as Torrance tested the dumbbell's stability to see if it could have fallen unaided. As soon as he concluded that it could not, Torrance moved to the center of the dojo and surveyed the gym, pointing his weapon as he turned. His eyes passed over the locker room door, then swung back to it. The black belt hesitated for a second, then headed for the lockers.

The locker room was long and narrow. Lockers lined the four walls and a row of lockers divided the room. At the end farthest from the door were showers in an open tiled area. The room offered few places to hide. Carl could dodge around the lockers, but how long could he keep that up? There was a section of the shower room that provided concealment from anyone standing near the lockers, but if Torrance looked into the shower area, he would be able to see Carl. If there was any distance between them, Carl would not stand a chance against a gun.

Suddenly the locker room lights went on. Carl had only seconds to act. The door to the locker room swung open and Torrance walked in. He paused by the door. From the end of the row of lockers in the middle of the room he could see all of the locker room except the shower area.

"Come out now and no one will get hurt. I've got a gun and I'll use it."

Torrance sounded unworried. Carl had to fight to keep calm.

"I'll give you a three count. If you're not out I'm going to shoot to kill."

Carl considered surrendering. Maybe he could convince Torrance that he'd come in for extra practice. Then he remembered that he was hiding, dressed in black and wearing a ski mask, and he hadn't gone to the office to ask Torrance for permission to work out. Torrance would turn him over to the police, or else just shoot him. The police would discover that he'd registered at the dojo under a phony name. He'd be expelled from school. It would kill his mother.

Torrance counted to three. He sighed. "Okay, pal. Don't say I didn't warn you."

The karate instructor moved down the row of

lockers toward the showers. It was the only part of the locker room he could not see completely. He was three-quarters of the way down the row when Carl dropped on him from the narrow space between the ceiling and the top of the lockers that ran down the center of the room. Torrance stumbled forward and dropped the gun. The space between the lockers was too narrow for Torrance to turn. Carl hit the karate instructor from behind, bringing him to his knees, and applied a choke hold. Torrance was groping for the gun when he blacked out.

# CHAPTER **TWELVE**

Talking about his battle with Mark Torrance had worn Carl out. He reached for the glass of water on his bed stand and took a sip.

"Did you tell General Wingate what you'd done?" Ami asked.

"Not directly. There was a story in the newspaper, a novelty item about a black belt being beaten up. I cut it out and mailed it to him anonymously."

"What happened after you mailed the clipping?"

Carl's lips twisted into a cynical smile. "The General never mentioned the news story, but he must have received it, because I was drafted a few weeks later."

"And you think Wingate was responsible for your draft notice?"

"I didn't at first. I even went to him for help. I had a scholarship to Dartmouth by then, a full ride. The General was the only person I could think of to ask for help. It took a while to get through to him. I kept calling and calling, but he didn't get back to me for weeks. I'd almost given up when he phoned to say that he'd be in California for the weekend. I went out to the estate. I had all my hopes riding on our meeting."

"What did he say?"

Carl looked as if the memory of the meeting had exhausted him. He shut his eyes when he spoke.

"Wingate was very blunt. He told me that he couldn't help me avoid the draft. He thought that I should go. He reminded me that we were in a fight to the death against Communism. He asked me how I could justify going to fraternity parties and football games while boys my age were giving their lives for their country. He said that I'd make an excellent soldier and I could always go to school when my tour was up."

"How did you feel about his advice?"

"I was very confused, but Wingate . . . the way he put it, he was so positive and he made it sound cowardly to try and get out of my duty to my country."

"Did you fight to stay out of the army?"

"No. In the end I just gave in. The General convinced me that it was my duty and that I would regret shirking it for my whole life. He talked so glowingly about the army and what I could accomplish. He asked me if I hadn't had enough of school, if I wasn't ready to test myself in the real world."

Carl rubbed his eyes. "The thing I regret most was what going in did to my mother. She had sacrificed so much for my future; my going to an

Ivy League school was her dream come true. When I turned down the scholarship she aged overnight." Carl's voice became hoarse, and he could not go on for a moment. "She died while I was on a mission, thousands of miles away. I never knew if she forgave me."

"What did Vanessa say when you told her that you were going into the army?" Ami asked softly.

"She went ballistic. She was convinced that Wingate had engineered my draft notice to break us up. When I decided to go in, she stopped talking to me. She wouldn't take my calls, and she avoided me at school. By the time the school year ended I was cutting class so I wouldn't have to be around her. I just couldn't take it. To tell the truth, it was a relief to go into basic training."

"If Wingate did engineer your notice, do you think he did it to break up your romance with his daughter?"

"It might have been one reason, but mostly I think he wanted me in the Unit. You know those special tests I took in basic, the way I was singled out for Special Forces. I think Wingate manipulated my career every step of the way."

Ami was puzzled. "What is the Unit?"

Rice laughed. "It's the little man that wasn't there."

# CHAPTER **THIRTEEN**

## 1

The pony team had been double-timing since the river, hours before, slowing only where the jungle was too dense to permit the pace. They stopped every hour for five minutes to rest and rehydrate; even with their superior conditioning the men could not go on forever in the heavy humidity of the monsoon season.

A few days earlier, Carl had been at Fort Bragg when a sergeant roused him from a deep sleep. He'd been loaded into a jet and flown to Vandenberg Air Force Base in California, where he had joined up with Neil Carpenter, an electronics expert, and boarded a plane bound for Nha Ha, the Special Forces base in Okinawa. Carl had never been on a real mission, and he was buzzing with energy by the time they landed. At Nha Ha, he learned that he was going to be part of a team

that would be inserted into North Vietnam to re-
cover special electronics equipment from a
downed navy plane. The plane they were searching for had been located by heat-seeking radar in
a low, undulating, sparsely populated section of
the North Vietnamese jungle fifteen miles from
the nearest navigable entry route, a river tributary. Visual reconnaissance had been impossible
because the canopy was triple-thick and fifty to
sixty feet high. Not even the sun penetrated in
many spots.

There were eight men on the team: Carl, Carpenter, five Green Berets they had picked up in
Da Nang, and Captain Molineaux, the team
leader. All the men except Carl had combat experience and were experts in jungle warfare, but
Molineaux stood out. He was a little taller than
Carl but seemed to tower over him. Where Carl
was a bundle of nerves, Molineaux showed
none. He spoke softly when he briefed the team
in a Quonset hut in Da Nang shortly before the
choppers lifted them out, and his calm demeanor
never changed during the mission.

The choppers dropped the team as close to the
river as the helicopter pilots dared. There was a
mad dash through the jungle, then a silent vigil
at the river until a navy gunboat materialized out
of the mist. The boat ferried the team upriver to
the opposite shore, then they were moving again,
double-time. By the time the gunboat disappeared around a bend in the narrow tributary the
team was lost in the thick undergrowth.

They had to move fast. The flybys that had located the downed plane had also recorded heavy troop movement in the area. For all they knew, the Vietnamese were looking for the same plane at the same time. Molineaux said that it was imperative to retrieve or destroy the electronics gear. No one asked why, and Carl never learned what the equipment did, though he wondered about it from time to time.

The team had one advantage over the enemy troops. Before bailing out, the pilot had set off a homing device that broadcast a signal over a top-secret band. Molineaux carried a triangulation device that picked up the signal. They could use it to make a beeline to the plane while the North Vietnamese would have to comb the entire area.

There were no trails leading from the river, and the men were forced to hack their way through the jungle with machetes. No one spoke. All communication was carried on with hand signals. The humidity sapped their strength. Sudden downpours were often thick enough to drench them and hide the nearby forest behind a curtain of water.

The ground rose gradually from the river. After two hours, the undergrowth began to thin. During the hour that followed, the team skirted small bands of Montagnard tribesmen who lived on the hillsides in bamboo huts. In these areas game trails made travel easier, but the men had to be on the lookout for booby traps and ambush sites.

The last rest period had been almost an hour before. Carl knew that it was counterproductive to

think about resting, but he couldn't help it. The
pace was grueling and the rest periods didn't produce much rest. The need to be constantly alert
kept everyone tense. Carl had drawn the job of
babysitting the electronics expert, the only person on the mission who was not expendable.
They were moving forward in a blinding downpour that made Carpenter appear to be jogging
behind a shower curtain, and Carl had to speed
up to keep him in sight. Almost as soon as he did,
Carpenter stopped and dropped to one knee. Carl
stepped in front of his charge, M-16 at the ready,
and one of the other men moved in behind Carpenter.

Senders, the Green Beret in front of Carpenter,
materialized out of the rain and jogged up the
trail coming back to join them. McFee, the point
man, and Captain Molineaux soon followed him.
Molineaux signaled them off the trail and knelt
under cover of a sky-high tree's thick foliage. The
rain still fell but the roof of leaves thinned the
downpour. Settles, Morales, and Shartel, who
was bringing up the rear, joined the others.

"McFee spotted the pilot," Molineaux whispered. Carl thought they could shout at the top of
their lungs without anyone hearing them in this
deluge, but he noticed that Molineaux never
took chances. "We're close, so stay on your toes.
We'll regroup at our last rest point if we get split
up. You'll wait fifteen minutes and no more before going straight back to the river. You all know
the primary and secondary pickup points. If you
miss the boat you're on your own. Understood?"

Everyone nodded. Molineaux stood and they followed. He hadn't said another word about the pilot, and Carl found out why a few minutes later. The rain had not let up and he was concentrating on the trail, the trees, and the brush ahead when Carpenter slowed and looked up. Carl followed his gaze through the dark green foliage until he spotted the pilot swaying back and forth in the upper branches like a marionette. His parachute had snagged on the numerous thick limbs. A sharp-tipped branch had speared through his armpit, puncturing an artery. As he passed under the body, Carl thought about the man hanging far above the ground, bleeding to death. He hoped that the shock of the fall had killed him. He didn't look back after he was past the body. The need to be alert focused all his energy on staying alive, and the pilot was soon forgotten.

They found the plane half an hour later. It had skidded along the ground for a few hundred yards after crashing, creating a small clearing. Parts of the plane were strewn through the trees, but the fuselage was on the ground, tilted at an angle with the nose embedded in the foliage.

"We're going to do this very quietly and very quickly," Molineaux ordered before sending four men into the jungle to establish observation posts. Senders set up his M-79 grenade launcher near the plane. Carpenter climbed inside and Molineaux followed him. Carl and Senders watched the jungle.

Carl could hear Carpenter working inside the plane. He worried that anyone close by would also hear the electronics expert and he wondered how long it would take Carpenter to accomplish his task. Carl caught himself. He could not think about anything but the jungle. He had to concentrate—only he was so tired.

They had not yet encountered the enemy, so the mission was no different from the many exhausting training exercises. Carl hoped things would stay that way: fast in, fast out, and no casualties. Still, a part of him wanted to meet the enemy so he could test himself in combat. He knew that was stupid. Action was glamorous in the movies. In real life, men lost arms, legs, or their lives. The men on this team were combat veterans who had been involved in the personal combat peculiar to the Special Forces. They had killed hand to hand. Yet none of them had told a war story. Maybe their war was too grim and provided the stuff of deep, unsettling dreams instead of the romanticized war stories that a man might talk about stateside over a beer. Even so, a part of Carl wanted to know how he would stack up.

Fifteen minutes after Carpenter and Molineaux had entered the fuselage Settles whistled a prearranged signal and appeared in the clearing. Molineaux stepped down from the plane and conferred with Settles in whispers. Settles disappeared into the jungle, and Molineaux walked back to the plane and told Carpenter to speed it up. Then he began attaching booby traps and thermite grenades with timing devices to the plane. Moments before Carpenter jumped down from the fuselage, Settles reappeared with the other guards. Molineaux told them that there were enemy soldiers in the vicinity. They started double-timing toward the river.

The sun was setting, and Molineaux wanted to cover as much ground as he could before it got dark. Occasionally, Carl heard Vietnamese soldiers calling to each other in the jungle. That worried him. If he could hear the soldiers, they were close; and if they weren't bothering to keep their presence hidden, the force was probably large.

An hour out, they heard a series of dull whumps. The dense forest had muffled the sound of the plane exploding. No one broke pace. The Vietnamese now knew that enemy soldiers were in the area. Once they found the plane, they would find the team's trail.

The seventeen-year-old Vietnamese soldier was hungry and tired of tramping through the soggy jungle, and his bladder was bursting. When Carl rounded the bend, the boy was standing with one foot on the narrow game trail and the other still in the undergrowth. His fly was unbuttoned and he was holding his penis as he prepared to pee. Carl and the soldier stared at each other, eyes wide and openmouthed. It seemed that time had stopped in this ridiculous situation.

Carl knew that it was out of the question to let

the soldier scream, but he couldn't shoot the man without revealing their position, so he thrust the butt of his rifle into the soldier's solar plexus, driving the air out of his lungs, then broke his windpipe. Settles rounded the bend and instantly figured out what had happened. He covered Carl while Morales raced by to tell Molineaux. Moments later, the team was grouped around the dead man. Molineaux ordered Carl and Settles to move the body off the trail.

"Empty your packs of everything except water and ammo," Molineaux said as Carl and Settles concealed the soldier in the underbrush. "Morales, you hump the radio. McFee just told me that there are enemy troops between here and the river.

"This man will be missed soon. Then we're in for it. We have to move through the enemy in the dark. It's five now, and the first pickup is at midnight. You know the routine."

No one said anything. No one even nodded. They knew what Molineaux meant by "the routine." There would be no way they could take a wounded brother with them if he couldn't keep up, and no one was to be taken alive. That was Molineaux's job.

"Let's go," the captain said. The men emptied their packs of food, dry clothes, and first aid kits. Then they concealed the dead man in the undergrowth and took off.

The sniper got Carpenter just before twilight. Carl saw the electronics expert sag and stumble.

If he had not seen the red stain on Carpenter's neck he might have thought that Carpenter had tripped over a root. The red stain saved Carl's life. He dived behind a tree and the bullet meant for him only grazed his side. Carl waited awhile before peeking from behind the tree to try to locate the sniper. As soon as he moved, a bullet chipped the bark inches from his eye. Carl knew that time was on the side of the Vietnamese. If the sniper stayed where he was, Carl would have to move back into the jungle and hope he wasn't seen. Circling around the sniper without giving away his own position would take a long time. He might miss the pickup. But staying put was out of the question because the gunfire would draw the sniper's troops. Carl might even run into them while he was trying to get away.

Several gunshots broke the silence.

"Rice," Molineaux shouted. "Get your ass out here."

Carl was back on the trail in an instant. Molineaux handed him Carpenter's pack, which held the electronics gear Carpenter had taken from the plane. The sniper lay crumpled on the trail a few yards ahead of him.

"Go," Molineaux said. As Carl sprinted ahead he heard voices shouting in Vietnamese behind them. The enemy knew where they were.

Darkness descended and the pursuit stopped. The Vietnamese were content to surround the Americans, putting a wall between them and the river until daybreak. The hours after sunset were filled with fear and confusion, and the team did not reach the river until four in the morning, well past the first pickup time. Molineaux pulled the men into a star perimeter as close to the river as he dared. All the men lay flat on their stomachs with their feet touching. Carl was exhausted, but he was too well trained and too keyed up to sleep.

Ten minutes before the gunboat was due Molineaux moved them out. A fog bank covered the river, and tendrils of mist curled through the jungle. Molineaux saw movement in front of them and called a halt. The Vietnamese were facing away from the river because they thought the team was deeper in the jungle. The sound of a motor brought the troops around. Molineaux raced into a clearing near the riverbank and opened fire just as the gunboat appeared. The boat crew laid down fifty-caliber covering fire. When he dived into the river, Carl saw a face flying away and a slender boy split in two. Strong hands jerked him onboard as bullets smacked into the side of the boat. As Carl flopped over the side of the boat he saw the other men clambering onboard. Then Settles jerked back and fell toward the water. Carl started for him but was pulled away from the rail just as Settles disappeared in the foaming wake. Someone pushed him down and he lay with his face pressed against the deck, smelling death and deafened by the firefight until the jungle muffled the noise and the gunfire faded away.

# 2

During his debriefing in Okinawa, Carl was ordered to discuss his mission with no one, not even his commanding officer. As far as anyone was concerned, the last few days had never happened. After the debriefing, Carl flew back to Fort Bragg, where he remained for a few weeks before being sent to Washington, D.C., on courier duty.

When Carl landed, Morris Wingate's driver was waiting to take him to the Pentagon so he could drop off the documents he was carrying and then take him to meet the General. Carl's orders had not mentioned Wingate, and he wondered how the General knew that he would be on assignment in D.C. Carl had not thought about Morris Wingate much during his time in the army, but he experienced childish feelings of insecurity at the thought of meeting him again.

Wingate's car stopped in front of a three-story redbrick town house that was squeezed between two similar homes on a quiet side street in a wealthy residential area of Alexandria, Virginia. Carl walked up a short flight of stone steps to the front door. Before he could ring the bell Enrique opened the door.

"Nice to see you again," Enrique said before leading Carl down a dimly lit hall to a spacious dining room that was brightly illuminated by a crystal chandelier. A long antique dining table covered with white linen dominated the room. Twelve antique high-backed chairs were arranged around the table, but there were only two table settings.

Carl walked around the room, studying it as he had been trained to study any environment in which he found himself. He stopped when he got to an oak sideboard, above which hung a portrait of a somber, bewigged eighteenth-century male. A door opened behind him, and he turned to find Morris Wingate striding toward him dressed in a charcoal-gray pinstripe suit, white silk shirt, and wine-red tie. Wingate's shoes were polished and his skin was deeply tanned.

"You look great, Carl. I was right, the military agrees with you."

"Thank you, sir."

"Sit down. I'm glad you could come."

Carl hadn't realized that he had a choice. "How did you know I'd be in D.C.?" he asked.

Wingate smiled enigmatically. "Being the head of an intelligence agency has its uses."

A servant entered and ladled lobster bisque from a silver tureen.

"How is Vanessa?" Carl asked as soon as the servant left.

"Fine," Wingate answered. "She's near the top of her class and she's made the tennis team."

Carl sensed that he was not getting the full story. "Will she be home for the summer?"

"I'm not sure. She's been talking about Europe. Some program the university has in Paris. But tell me what you've been up to."

Carl gave the General a sanitized version of his army experience.

"I've been to Airborne and Special Forces training and I'm at Fort Bragg now," he concluded as the servant entered wheeling a dining cart. The servant cleared the soup plates and placed a serving of beef Wellington in front of Carl and his host. Carl had never eaten lobster bisque or beef Wellington before, and the meal was delicious, but a simple home-cooked meal would have been fabulous after months of army chow.

"The last time we talked, you were reluctant to join the army. How do you feel now?" Wingate asked.

The truth was that Carl's training and his experiences made him feel special. He could do things that none of his classmates at St. Martin's could do and he'd had experiences that few St. Martin's boys would ever have. He was confident that he could survive anywhere and could kill if he had to. That was heady stuff for someone still in his teens.

"I'm satisfied with my choice, sir," Carl answered.

"Have you been in combat yet?"

"No, sir," Carl answered without hesitation. He had anticipated the question.

"I heard that you've been in North Vietnam," the General stated quietly.

"You've been misinformed," Carl answered, looking the General in the eye and holding the older man's gaze until Wingate smiled and looked away.

Wingate took an object out of his pocket and laid it on the table. He pushed it over to Carl. It was Carpenter's dog tags. Carl felt himself choke up with emotion but his features did not betray his feelings for his fallen comrade.

"You've done very well, Carl. Far better than even I anticipated."

Carl ran his thumb across the raised lettering and remembered Carpenter falling and the red stain that had spread across his neck.

"I'm afraid I . . . " Carl started, a catch in his voice betraying the lie. Wingate cut him off with a raised hand.

"Your target was a downed navy plane carrying top-secret electronic equipment. The team leader was Paul Molineaux. You had two casualties. Do I have to go on or are you convinced that I know all about your mission?"

Carl didn't answer.

"I've been in the military for a good part of my life and I've served with many men. As young as you are, as new as you are, you are among the finest soldiers that I have ever known."

Carl's chest swelled with pride.

"I have a proposition for you," the General went on. "I don't want you to feel any pressure to accept my offer. However, I do need your promise that you will never repeat what we discuss to anyone, under any circumstances.

"Good," Wingate said as soon as Carl nodded. "You know that I'm the head of the Agency for Intelligence Data Coordination. My agency has as its documented function the collection and coordination of intelligence data from other intelligence agencies. The AIDC charter does not include a provision for active intelligence gathering. On paper, the AIDC has no operatives."

Wingate paused to make sure that Carl was following him.

"What I have told you so far is public knowledge, but there are aspects of the agency that neither the public nor the vast majority of the government, including employees of the agency, knows about. Working within the agency under my direction are a small group of highly trained individuals who perform services for this country of highly unusual and, on occasion, officially illegal nature."

"I'm sorry, sir. What does 'officially illegal' mean?"

"Against the laws of the United States," Wingate answered firmly. "The Unit operates internationally and domestically. No records are kept of our operations and all orders are verbal. The members of the Unit don't know the identity of the other members, and they usually carry out missions as individuals. If a mission requires support personnel we use Special Forces with the Unit member representing himself to be Special Forces."

"I'm confused, sir. Are these men CIA or military intelligence or . . . "

"These men do not exist, Carl."

Carl cocked his head and stared at Wingate. "Where do their orders come from?"

"You don't need to know that, but I can assure you that all orders are legitimate and decisions are made at the *highest* levels of government. I will also tell you that neither the CIA nor any branch of the military knows of the existence of this Unit."

"Then how do you get the support of Special Forces?"

"I speak of the CIA and the military as organizations. These organizations are not aware of the existence of the Unit. However, there are a few—a very few—individuals within these organizations who are in positions of command and know that we exist. These individuals are able to supply our needs."

Wingate waited a beat. Then he looked Carl in the eye. "I want you to join us. Your professional skills are exceptional; you have high intelligence and strength of character. I spotted your potential soon after I met you. I take a certain amount of pride in the fact that you have far exceeded my expectations, a pride that could be no greater if you were my son."

Carl was stunned. He had always been a loner, and the sense of mystery surrounding this invisible team of elite soldiers appealed to him. He was also overcome by Wingate's praise. What worried him was that he only had Wingate's assurance that the actions of the Unit were legitimate, even when its members violated the law.

"What if I decline, sir?"

"The work we perform is too sensitive to entrust to any but volunteers."

"Can I have some time to think this over?"

"Of course." Wingate took a business card out of his pocket. "Call me when you've reached a decision. If you accept, simply tell me that you'll be in town soon and would like to have dinner. I'll arrange for weekend leave."

The General changed the topic of conversation and called for an after-dinner drink. Carl declined but accepted a cup of coffee. He wanted to be clearheaded. Half an hour later he was in the backseat of the General's town car on the way to the airport. Carl did not sleep during the flight back to Fort Bragg.

# CHAPTER **FOURTEEN**

"How long did it take you to decide to join the Unit?" Ami asked.

"About a week. The General had been up-front with me. He told me I would be breaking the law at times. That bothered me."

"But you went ahead anyway?"

"I was young. I was excited about the Unit's elite status. And there was Wingate. You have no idea what that man's approval meant to me. I was thrilled that he'd been watching my progress and had chosen me for this special duty. I couldn't disappoint him."

"What happened after you contacted Wingate?"

"Nothing for about a month. Then I was transferred to the Army Language School at Fort Meyer, Virginia. I lived off post in an apartment. Most of the time, I studied Thai and Vietnamese. I needed the flexibility a student has because my orders came at irregular intervals. In my free time I kept in shape, kept up my martial arts training, and lived the type of life most students lead."

"How did you get your assignments?"

"I would receive a phone call. It would be a wrong number or a solicitation call. I'd drive to a prearranged location, usually very late at night, sometimes after midnight. A lot of times it would be a room at a motel or a parking lot of a crowded mall. We never met at the same place twice."

"This is Wingate you're talking about?"

"Oh, no, not the General." Rice's features darkened. "There was only one time that I received an order from him."

"Then who . . . ?"

"The man who acted as my control was General Peter Rivera."

"Do you know where I can find him? Would he help you?"

Rice looked at Ami. "General Rivera was murdered in 1986. The police think I killed him."

"Did you?"

"No, but there is a lot of evidence connecting me to the crime."

Ami felt uneasy. She didn't completely believe Carl's protestations of innocence.

"What were your first assignments like?"

"They were mostly in Vietnam. I told you about ambushing the mule trains. I did that a few times. I also infiltrated North Vietnamese villages on several occasions. Twice I was teamed with Special Forces pony teams who thought I was with the Phoenix program. On one mission I was led to my target by a North Vietnamese national who worked for the CIA."

"What did you do on these missions?"

"I used a sniper rifle to take out a military officer during one mission. In the other two, I terminated Communist Party officials."

"By shooting them?"

Carl shook his head. "I crawled into their huts at night and slit their throats."

Ami turned pale.

"My war was very personal, Ami. I looked into the eyes of the men I killed."

"Were . . . were you still in the Unit when you went AWOL in 1985?"

"Yes."

"But the Vietnam War must have ended a few years after you joined."

"The Unit still had its uses after we left Vietnam. The communists didn't go away. There was still the cold war."

"How did your missions change?"

"There was more espionage. I investigated suspected spies; I used my intelligence skills to bug embassies." Rice smiled coldly. "I also bugged congressmen and officials of the United States government."

"Americans?"

Rice nodded. "I wasn't told what use was made of the information I collected, but I noticed that some of the senators or representatives I had under surveillance changed their votes on certain bills or initiated legislation that went against their former voting patterns. I also found it interesting that the General remained the head of the AIDC no matter who was president."

"Did you ever . . . were there more assassinations?"

Rice nodded.

"Was this in Vietnam still?"

"No. The focus changed. There was a Russian agent in Madrid, some people who were working for the Chinese."

"How did you . . . ?"

"I stabbed the Russian to death in an alley behind a bar and I . . . I shot the two subjects who were working for the Chinese."

"How many people have you killed, Carl?"

"I don't know."

"Didn't it . . . bother you?"

Carl took a sip of water while he considered her question.

"At first, no. I had never killed anyone before we went after the electronics equipment in that Navy plane. During the mission I was so scared and exhausted that I was running on instinct, like an animal. Then the patrol boat rescued us. I was fed, I was given dry clothes, and I got some sleep. After I woke up I went on deck. I remember sitting with my back against the pilothouse wall, feeling safe for the first time in days. The jungle was quiet and beautiful. I was completely at peace. That's when it occurred to me that I had killed several men.

"In training, I wondered if I would freeze, but I hadn't panicked. I realized that I hadn't thought about the killing at all. I'd just done what I was trained to do. The act of killing had not been a cosmic event. There was nothing philosophical about it. In the heat of battle it was simply a choice between them and me."

"This was in combat, though," Ami said. "You told me that you killed the Russian by . . . you stabbed him to death. And the Chinese spies, that wasn't in the heat of battle. Did you feel differently about those killings?"

"You want to know if I felt remorse?"

"Yes."

"The people I killed were the enemy, and it was my job to kill the enemy, but I never enjoyed it. I believed I was doing the right thing. That helped me deal with what I'd done. But the longer it went on . . . " Carl paused. His eyes dropped to the covers on his hospital bed. "I had bad dreams. I had doubts."

# CHAPTER **FIFTEEN**

WASHINGTON, D.C./ LOST LAKE, CALIFORNIA/
ALEXANDRIA, VIRGINIA—1985

## 1

Carl had met his date in a singles bar the previous
Saturday. She was attractive and shy and sweet.
Even if their relationship got off the ground, Carl
knew that it would end within months, as always. Usually the women called it quits when
they grew tired of his sudden disappearances, his
moodiness, or his inability to display any real
emotions. Whenever the woman wanted something permanent, Carl would pull the plug. Sex
without strings was a good way to forget, if only
for a short time, the vivid memories that were
starting to creep into his head more frequently,
even when he was not asleep.

Carl always chose an upscale Vietnamese restaurant near Dupont Circle for the first date. He had just
finished impressing the young woman by ordering

in Vietnamese when Vanessa Wingate came in on the arm of a man who could have stepped right out of *GQ*. She was more beautiful than his memory of her. The years had given Vanessa's youthful features character and turned her teenage figure into the body of a mature woman.

Carl's date was asking him where he had learned Vietnamese. They all did, so he was able to tell her his programmed answer while he stood up.

"Will you excuse me for a minute?" Carl asked. "I just spotted an old friend I haven't seen in years."

Carl's date followed his gaze. She kept smiling and said, "Sure," but Carl would have known that she wasn't happy if he'd been paying any attention. By the time he was halfway to the maître d's station he had forgotten that he was on a date.

Seconds before he reached her, Vanessa saw Carl pushing through the crowd. They hadn't seen each other since high school, and confusion flickered across her face at first. Then Carl saw amazement and finally what he had been hoping for, a wide smile of welcome.

"My God!" Vanessa said. Her date looked at her, then followed her eyes and saw Carl.

"Vanessa," Carl said, smiling as broadly as his former lover.

"What are you doing here?"

"I live in D.C. Well, in Virginia, really. Are you living here or just visiting?"

"I'm in Georgetown."

"Aren't you going to introduce me?" Vanessa's date asked, annoyed at being left out of the conversation.

"Sorry. Bob Coyle, this is Carl Rice, an old friend."

"Glad to meet you, Carl."

Coyle's crushing handshake told Carl firmly and clearly that Coyle was an alpha male protecting his mate. Carl let Coyle stake out his territory by submitting to the painful pressure. He could see that Vanessa's date wanted him to leave, and he didn't want to spoil her evening.

"Look, I'm with someone," Carl said, "but I'd love to catch up on old times. How can I get in touch with you?"

Coyle scowled when Vanessa told Carl her home phone number.

"Nice meeting you, Bob," Carl said as he returned to his table. As soon as he was seated, Carl explained that Vanessa was an old high school friend. His date accepted the explanation and renewed her question about Carl's knowledge of Vietnamese. Carl kept her entranced with war stories—most of them lies—but he could not stop thinking about Vanessa.

## 2

Vanessa was sitting at a quiet table in the back of a bistro just a few blocks from her apartment in Georgetown. She was dressed in a tan pantsuit and white silk blouse and looked terrific. Carl was wearing gray slacks, an Oxford blue shirt, and a blazer. His hair was shaggy and he looked more like a young lawyer than a member of the armed forces.

When Carl reached the table Vanessa stood up and hugged him. It was the type of brief, businesslike hug that you get from the hostess at a cocktail party who doesn't know you very well. Carl deduced that Vanessa had gotten over the shock of seeing him appear out of nowhere and had remembered the circumstances of their parting.

"Gee, you look great," he said.

"So do you. Still keeping up with your karate?"

He nodded. "And you played tennis in college, right?"

"College was a long time ago, Carl. I started the year you went off to war."

Vanessa spoke the last sentence with a trace of bitterness. Carl looked her in the eye.

"The military has been good to me, Van."

"It must have been if you're still in."

Carl changed the subject quickly. "So tell me, in twenty-five words or less, what have you been doing for the past—what is it—twelve, thirteen years?"

"Something like that." Vanessa thought for a moment. "Well, I guess the biggie was my marriage."

"To that guy at the restaurant?"

Vanessa laughed. "No. Bob's a lawyer for a congressional committee. I'm working for a congressman. I met him about a month ago at a hearing."

"So you're not married now?"

Vanessa looked solemn. "It didn't take. I should have known it wouldn't. His main qualification was that the General despised him. Inertia kept us together for years, but the marriage was over almost as soon as it started."

"On the phone you said that you're back at school?"

"Nights."

"What are you studying?"

"Law. Isn't that what every divorcée studies after the marriage goes south?"

"Working and going to night school must be tough."

"It's a grind but school comes easy to me."

"It always did," Carl said, "except for calculus."

Vanessa looked sad. "Yeah, except for calculus. So, what are you doing in the army?"

"I'm teaching at the language school at Fort Meyer."

"Oh? What languages?"

"Vietnamese and Thai."

"I guess I know where you learned them."

Carl lowered his eyes when he answered, the way he'd practiced it.

"I had some bad experiences in 'Nam, very rough times. Once I got back stateside, a teaching assignment sounded pretty good." He smiled. "Actually, I'm glad I took it. I've enjoyed teaching at the language school and I've made some good contacts at a number of universities. I'll be retiring pretty young and I should be able to teach at any number of places."

"Well, I'm happy for you."

"Are you happy, Van?" Carl asked softly.

"That's a very personal question, Carl. At one time I would have given you an answer, but that time was long ago. I don't think we know each other well enough now."

Carl felt his façade begin to crack. He hadn't expected the old feelings to come back with such intensity.

"I know I hurt you, Van, but that was a long time ago. I would like to get to know you again," he said.

"You're seeing me now, aren't you?" she said.

## 3

Carl and Vanessa started eating dinner near the House office building once or twice a month. Sometimes he would wait for her at the law school when her classes let out and they would go for coffee. The meetings were infrequent and were get-togethers rather than dates. There were times when Carl was tempted to try for something more, but being with Vanessa stirred conflicting feelings in him. When they were together he soared but he also struggled with guilt because he had not told her that he was still working for her father and he was keeping her in the dark about the true nature of his service. He also harbored an irrational belief that he was betraying the General because he had not told him about seeing his daughter. Not that he had many chances to talk to Morris Wingate. Since joining the Unit he had met Wingate on only a few occasions. Wingate had explained how dangerous it was for any member of the Unit to be seen with him. There were spies everywhere.

Carl had been thinking about quitting the Unit for a while. He had been risking his life for more than ten years and he wondered if he was losing his edge. If he quit now he could get a teaching job at a good university. Maybe Vanessa would marry him and they could settle down. They would have kids and she would have an interesting career. It would be a quiet existence, but Carl thought that he could get used to life with two point five children, a dog, and a house in the suburbs with a white picket fence. He fooled himself into believing that he could move from hell to Eden without Vanessa's learning about his secret life.

## 4

A persistent knocking on her front door awakened Vanessa from a deep sleep. She called out, "I'm coming," as she struggled into her robe. When she looked through the peephole she saw Carl Rice standing in the hall. Vanessa was surprised because she had not seen or spoken to Carl for three weeks.

"Please, Vanessa, open up," Carl begged after knocking again. Vanessa didn't want Carl to wake her neighbors so she unlocked the door. Carl staggered in. He was unshaven, his clothes looked as if he'd slept in them, and his eyes were wild.

"What do you want, Carl?" Vanessa asked.

"I have to talk to you."

"It's after midnight. Couldn't this wait until to-morrow?"

"I'm sorry. I know it's late, but I don't know what to do."

Vanessa took a hard look at her visitor. Carl looked like a man who might do something desperate.

"Do about what?" Vanessa asked.

"Can I sit down?" Carl asked. "I'm exhausted. I haven't slept in days."

Vanessa stepped aside and Carl slumped onto the couch and laid his head back.

"I can't do it anymore," he said. "I've got to get out."

"Get out of what?"

"I lied to you," he said. "I couldn't tell you the truth, so I lied, but I don't want to do that anymore. I want you to know what I am, Van. I'm a killer. I kill for your father, and I want to stop."

Vanessa couldn't breathe.

"You're the only one who can possibly understand," Carl said.

"What is it you want me to understand?"

"I've done terrible things."

"And you want what, forgiveness?"

"I'm beyond that."

Vanessa felt a twinge of fear. Aside from a general explanation of the work of the AIDC her father had never told her what he did. She'd had her suspicions—why did he need armed guards wherever he went?—but she never allowed herself to think beyond that.

"I've been so happy since we reconnected," Carl told her. "I thought I could start over with you. But almost everything I've told you was a lie. Then they gave me another assignment. It was very bad. I want to stop now. I don't want to do this anymore."

"What did you do?"

"I went to Texas. There was a Chinese woman. Her parents immigrated to Massachusetts when she was nine. She worked on a top-secret project. I don't know what she did exactly." Vanessa realized that Carl was talking about the woman in the past tense and started to feel sick. "They said she was a spy, a very dangerous spy, who was passing secrets to the Chinese. The Chinese had co-opted her. She was a threat to our country."

"And you . . . ?"

Carl forced himself to look at Vanessa. He had vowed to tell her everything and he would not back down.

"I shot her in the eye. She was sleeping. I broke into their house and killed them."

"There was someone else?"

Carl nodded. His voice cracked. "Her husband. He was a captain in the army."

"But he was a spy, too?"

Carl shook his head slowly from side to side. "They aren't certain but they couldn't take a chance that he was working with her. That's what I was told."

Carl started to cry. "He was an American, Vanessa. He might have been completely innocent. He was a captain, just like me."

"A captain? You told me you were a sergeant."

"That's my cover. So is my job at the language school. My whole life is a lie."

Carl's head dropped into his hands and he sobbed. Vanessa was appalled by what he'd told her and she could not bring herself to comfort him.

"My father gave you your orders?"

"I've worked for him for more than ten years."

Vanessa looked confused. "The AIDC is involved in the coordination of intelligence data. It doesn't have agents who do what you do."

"It does, Van, but only a handful of people know about my Unit."

Carl explained what he had been doing since he had been recruited by the General. Vanessa grew angrier as he spoke.

"The bastard," she said when he was done. Her eyes shone. "Do you realize what would happen if we exposed him?"

"Don't think that way. Your father is a very dangerous man. I have no idea how far he would go if he thought that you were a danger to him."

"Don't you want to help me? Don't you want to stop being his puppet?"

"I want to stop but I don't want you to die. Your father will kill us if he feels threatened. What you're thinking of doing isn't practical, anyway. There is no proof that the Unit exists. General Wingate would deny it and so would everyone else connected to the operation. And if by some chance you were able to get evidence that the Unit exists, you would endanger anyone who knew about it. Killing is considered a method of problem solving to these people—to me. I'm one of them, Van. It's how we think. If you have a problem and killing will solve the problem, you kill."

Vanessa was quiet for a few moments. Then she looked at Carl.

"What are you going to do?"

"I want to leave the army. I want some peace."

"Will my father let you go?"

"I don't know. But I've got to ask."

Vanessa thought for a moment. "That could be very dangerous, Carl. My father hates weakness. Think of how much you know and how much you could hurt him. Once he knows you want out, you'll become a problem he has to solve."

Carl stared at Vanessa with empty eyes. "I don't care anymore. I have to stop. If he lets me go, I'll be through with it. If he kills me, I'll be at peace too." He laughed. "I guess I'm in a win-win situation."

**5**

Carl phoned Vanessa the evening after he had made his confession, and her answering machine took the call. He phoned several other times but Vanessa didn't pick up. The next day, Carl called Vanessa at work and was told that she was not in. She didn't show up at her law school class either. Carl wondered if Vanessa's apartment was bugged. Had the General reviewed a tape of his conversation with Vanessa? Was she dead be-

cause of him? Carl drove to the apartment. It was
dark. He jimmied the lock and entered. She
wasn't there, and her mailbox was stuffed with
mail.

The next night Carl received a call from a
polling service. He had never been given an assignment so soon after returning from one, but
the call signaled a meet. Five hours after he de-
coded the message he parked in front of room
105 of a motel on the outskirts of Baltimore. Carl
expected to find General Peter Rivera waiting for
him, but the room was unoccupied. A vicious
snowstorm was pummeling the east coast, and
any number of weather-related possibilities could
explain his late arrival.

Carl threw his pea jacket and watch cap on the
bed and went into the bathroom. He started
brewing coffee in the pot provided by the motel.
As the coffee perked he wondered what he
would do if Rivera had another assignment for
him that required him to kill. Before he could
sort out his thoughts, the door opened. Carl drew
his gun and pressed against the bathroom wall.
He could see the front door in the mirror that
hung over the sink. A brutal wind blew
snowflakes into the motel room. A man who was
too tall to be Rivera followed them in. His face
was hidden behind the upturned collar of his
overcoat.

"Your tax dollars pay for those bullets, Carl,"
Morris Wingate said. "Don't waste them."

Carl holstered his weapon and stepped into the
bedroom carrying two mugs of steaming coffee.

"Cold enough for you?" Carl asked nonchalantly as he handed Wingate one of the mugs.

"Cold enough," the General said as he stomped the snow from his shoes.

"I've been trying to get through to you," Carl said.

"I've been away," Wingate answered, and Carl knew that this was the only explanation he was going to get. The General sat down in the room's only easy chair and warmed his hands on the coffee mug. Carl turned the desk chair around and set his mug on the blotter. He forced himself to look Wingate in the eye as he cut to the chase.

"I've been thinking about leaving the service."

"Does this have anything to do with Vanessa?"

Carl was trained to hide his emotions, but his training failed him.

"You are an extremely important person, Carl. We keep track of you."

Carl felt sick.

The General shook his head sadly. When he spoke he did not sound angry, only hurt and disappointed.

"I wish you'd confided in me before now. You know that you and Vanessa mean a lot to me."

Carl waited, unsure of just how much Wingate knew.

"Have you told her what you do for a living?" the General asked.

Carl's mind raced to find the right answer. If Wingate had overheard his confession, a lie could sign a death warrant for him and Vanessa. The same result might follow if Wingate didn't know what Carl had told his daughter and Carl told Wingate the truth.

"I haven't told her about the Unit and I don't plan to," he lied. "We both know that she wouldn't approve."

Wingate nodded. "Why have you decided to abandon your career?" he asked.

Carl looked down at his hands. "I'm losing my edge. I'm burned out."

"You should take some time to think about this. You're a shooting star, Carl. You're going to keep rising if you stay in the service. There are people who are watching you with big things in mind. Will you promise me that you won't act precipitately?"

Carl wanted out now, tonight, but he didn't have the strength to say so.

"I'm not jumping into anything," Carl said.

"Good, because I have important work for you." Carl was surprised. General Rivera had always briefed him. "When you're through with this mission, take some R and R and figure out what you want to do with your life. I'll back your decision one hundred percent, no matter what you decide."

Wingate opened a briefcase he had been carrying. Inside were cash, false identification, a weapon, and other items that he needed on an assignment. The General handed Carl a slim file. Inside was a photograph of a handsome man with windblown hair standing in front of an office building. He looked familiar, but Carl could not place him.

"Who is this?"

"You don't need to know that."

Carl was puzzled. General Rivera had always told him the names of the people who were the subject of an operation.

"That's unusual, sir."

"Yes, it is," Wingate replied as he moved the photograph aside and opened a map.

"Lost Lake is an upscale community of summer homes in northern California." Wingate pointed at a lot that had been circled in red. "Your subject lives here. You'll be able to get to the property by boat." The General handed Carl a slip of paper. "This is the security code. The subject should be alone tonight."

"What do you want me to do?"

"You're dealing with a spy for a foreign intelligence organization. He has in his possession the military records of every member of the Unit, including yours."

"How . . . ?"

"I'm not at liberty to tell you, but you can imagine what would happen if an unfriendly foreign power knew your identity. I want those papers back. The existence of the Unit is at stake. When you have the papers I want this man eliminated, and I want the method of execution to be graphic and brutal."

Carl was surprised. A kill was usually carried out as quickly and quietly as possible.

"If I may ask, sir, why do you want the subject terminated in this manner?"

"I'm not going to explain my orders, Carl. Assume that there are good reasons for everything I tell you." The General stood up. "You'll fly out immediately. There's a car waiting at the airport. Bring me the papers. Remember, the existence of the Unit depends on you."

## 6

The normal procedure for undertaking a mission involved an extensive briefing and time to prepare, but Carl had flown west with no more information than he'd been given at the motel. He landed at an airstrip in California after dark. A little before two in the morning he anchored his boat just off a shallow beach that was screened from the subject's house by trees. Carl worked his way through the woods until he could see the back of a modern log cabin. The house was dark. He crossed the lawn quickly, invisible in his dark clothes, camouflage paint, and navy blue watch cap.

Carl jimmied the lock, punched in the security code, and was inside in seconds. He had memorized the layout of the house and knew where to find the stairs to the master bedroom. The man in the king-size bed lay curled on his side slumbering peacefully. His eyes sprang open when Carl slapped a piece of tape across his mouth. Carl stunned him with a blow and bound his hands and ankles. When he was done, Carl showed the man a large hunting knife with a serrated blade. A scalpel was lighter and easier to wield, but he used the big knife to inspire terror.

"I want the army records you stole. Give them to me and I'll let you live," he lied. "Hold out and you'll suffer until you break, and everyone breaks eventually."

The man's chest heaved from fear. He was sweating and his muscles were twitching involuntarily.

"I'm going to remove the tape. You will tell me where to look. We'll go together. If you've lied I'll remove your left eye."

Carl took the tape away and the man said, "You're making a mistake . . ."

Before he could finish, Carl slapped back the tape, ripped away his pajama top and sliced a piece of flesh from the man's chest. The subject arched back as if struck by an electric charge. His eyes squeezed shut and he threw his body from side to side, trying to ease his pain. Carl usually felt nothing in these situations, but he felt sick this time. He swore that this would be his last mission.

"We'll try this one more time. I'll ask you for the location of the papers and you'll give it to me. That's all I'm interested in. Remember the pain you just suffered, because that was the least amount of pain you will endure. Every time you fail to obey instructions I will escalate your discomfort. I have all the time in the world. Don't increase your suffering needlessly. When I remove the tape, tell me where to find the army records."

"They're downstairs in my office," the man gasped when Carl peeled back the tape. Carl hoped the man was telling the truth. He wanted this mission over with. Carl taped the man's mouth again.

He thought they were far enough from the neighbors so a scream would not be heard, but he wasn't taking chances. He helped the subject to his feet, sliced away the tape that bound his ankles, and supported him as they walked downstairs. The chest wound was bleeding freely and the pain made the man stumble. When they reached the office Carl turned on the lights. Then he secured the subject to a ladder-back chair and removed the tape from his mouth.

"Where are the army records?" he demanded.

The man gave him the combination to a wall safe. Carl knew that he was not lying because the combination was included in the file he'd seen at the motel. He opened the safe and took a sheaf of papers from it. It only took a moment to find his records in the stack.

Carl took out the knife. Wingate wanted this bloody, and he would obey the General's orders this one last time. He made several quick cuts, working fast so the subject would not suffer too long. He tried to keep his eyes off of the struggling man's face while he worked. When he felt that the body looked horrible enough he mercifully cut the subject's throat. His hand trembled when he made the kill and he felt tears welling in his eyes. Then he heard a sound behind him and whirled around, holding the bloody knife in a combat position.

"Carl?"

Vanessa Wingate was standing in the doorway dressed in a long white T-shirt, her hair tousled from sleep. They stared at each other for a moment before Vanessa saw the man in the chair. When she backed away, her eyes never left his. Carl knew that he should grab her, but the horror he saw on her face paralyzed him. Vanessa bolted down the hall and into the night. On any other mission, Carl would have pursued a fleeing witness and silenced her, but the only thing Carl could make his body do was race to his boat. He was running across the lawn when Vanessa screamed.

# 7

The General's driver took Carl from the airport to Wingate's town house in Alexandria, Virginia. Carl was barely holding it together when he was shown into the study. General Wingate was sitting near the fireplace, reading. He stood up when Carl walked in.

"Did you get the records?" he asked anxiously.

"Who did I kill?" Carl answered.

The General studied Carl for a moment.

"Did something happen?"

"Who did I kill?" Carl repeated, more emphatically.

Wingate sighed. "A congressman. You'll read about it in the paper tomorrow."

"What was his name?" Carl asked certain that he knew already.

"Eric Glass."

Carl stared at the General. "You used me."

"What are you talking about?"

"Vanessa was there, you bastard. She was staying at the house."

"It's not what you think."

"Then explain the situation to me, General, because I'm confused. For the first time ever you give me an assignment instead of Peter Rivera. And this assignment just happens to involve your daughter and the man she works for. Also for the first time I'm told to murder a man in the most violent way possible. Did you use me to get revenge against Glass for sleeping with your daughter?"

"You're right about Glass and Vanessa being lovers, but that's not why Glass had to die. There was one set of records of the men in the Unit. It was in the safe in my den in California. Glass was a sleeper agent. He seduced Vanessa and tricked her into stealing the records. Vanessa stole the records because she hates me. You know that. She wants to destroy me and she thought that Glass would help her do it. But she didn't know that he was a spy. She thought he'd hold hearings and expose the Unit."

"Why didn't you tell me Vanessa would be at Glass's house?"

"I didn't know. I would never have sent you if I thought that she would be there. That's why I didn't tell you the name of the man you were sent to eliminate. I knew you'd never met Glass, but you knew he was Vanessa's employer."

"Why did you send me at all?"

"Because you're the best I've got, and this is the most important assignment I've ever given out."

Carl wandered over to a leather armchair and sat down in front of the fire. He felt the heat on his face as he stared at the flames.

"She saw me. She knows what I did."

"That's a problem, but I'm going to deal with it. I've received a call from Lost Lake. Vanessa is in shock. She's in the local hospital. I'm going there as soon as we finish. I wanted to be here for you when you got back because the sheriff told me that Vanessa had identified you."

"What will I do? I'll be arrested if I go back to Fort Meyer."

"You're right about that. The police are looking for you. I'm sure that the FBI will be involved soon. But I have a solution. I'm going to send you someplace where no one will look for you."

Carl looked up. "Where is that?"

"We've received intelligence that American MIAs are being held in a secret jungle prison camp in North Vietnam. I'm sending all the members of the Unit to rescue them."

The chance to meet the other members of the Unit distracted Carl. "What will happen when I get back?"

"Carl, I love you like a son. I want to protect you. I have a few ideas of how I can do that but I don't know if they'll work. If they don't, you'll go away. When you come back you'll be a wealthy man with a new life and a new face. Now, let me have the records."

# CHAPTER **SIXTEEN**

"Did you rescue the MIAs?" Ami asked.

Carl laughed. "The mission was a setup, and I was so naive that I didn't see it coming."

"What happened?"

"There were ten of us. I'd seen their pictures when I looked through the records I took from Congressman Glass's safe, so I knew that everyone was there. Paul Molineaux, who led my first combat mission, was the only man I recognized. He was the team leader this time, too. He showed us pictures of the camp and briefed us. We had to take a boat in-country but Molineaux said that there were copters waiting to take us out. He had pictures of the MIAs. It looked real. We all believed him."

"But it wasn't true? There were no MIAs?"

Carl shrugged. "There might have been, but I doubt it. I think the General phonied up some pictures to fire us up. There wasn't a man in the Unit who wouldn't have died willingly to bring an MIA home. But we never got the chance to find out if there were MIAs.

"Molineaux stayed on board the boat that took us in-country, which was strange. He gave me command. He said that there were a lot of soldiers in the area because of the prison camp and he had to make sure that the boat, which was our alternative escape route, was protected. We accepted his word blindly. We were so stupid."

"What happened?"

"The Vietnamese knew we were coming. They ambushed us. The place we were headed was at the end of a valley. We were caught at the base of these hills. An eighty-deuce—uh, eighty-two-millimeter round—exploded about fifteen feet from me. There was shooting all around. I tried to get out of the clearing where they trapped us and into the forest to apply first aid."

"You were wounded?"

"In the stomach, but not bad. It burned. You know, like if you were jabbed with a hot poker, and my leg was numb and I was nauseated, but after a while the pain became steady, a sharp, burning sensation I could handle. Besides, when it happened I was just moving and I was scared because there was so much shooting.

"I crawled along a washout and into the jungle. I could hear the men fighting and dying. Then I heard one of the Vietnamese soldiers order some of his men to hunt me down and the others to check the bodies to make sure they were dead. I managed to slip past my pursuers and head for the boat. When I got to the river the boat was gone. If it had been there, I would have escaped, but I wasted so much time getting to the river that the soldiers caught up to me. By that time I was too weak from my wound to put up a fight."

"What happened after they got you?"

"They cleaned the wound and removed a lot of the shrapnel. They took most of my clothes. I had to walk barefoot and they would go in circles to make the trip longer."

"How long was the march?"

"I have no idea. I just know it took a long time to get to the prison."

"What did they do to you?"

"It wasn't Club Med." He laughed harshly. "The Vietnamese had a penchant for torturing my feet. Once they tied my arms behind me with wet leather strips so my shoulders were pulled clear back around. At one point I was put in a steel box in the sun and left."

"What did they want from you?"

"That was the funny thing. They didn't question me. They just tortured me. It was like they didn't need the information because they knew everything I knew."

"How did you get out?"

"We were in a village. They didn't have cells. I was in a hut with guards out front. At night, my hands were placed in front and shackled to a post. They shackled my feet, too. I managed to dig under the post to the hard packed earth. I'd replace what I'd dug up and smooth it out when I saw daylight. Eventually I got under the pole and worked the chains out from under it. When the guard made his rounds I used the chain like a garrote and broke his windpipe. He had a knife in his boot. I used it to kill the guard who was outside the hut. Then I found what looked like a roller skate key that fit the locks on my chains. I got out of the camp and started running. I had a general idea where I was and I know how to live off the land."

"How did you get back to the states?"

"I headed for Thailand. When I crossed the border I stole some money, bought a fake ID, and sailed back as a deckhand. It was almost a year before I landed in San Francisco. I figured I was owed, so I went looking for Peter Rivera. Only Rivera was dead, murdered the same way I had killed Eric Glass. And there was evidence that pointed to me as his murderer. That's when I figured out what must have happened. Wingate shut down the Unit and stole the money from the secret fund. He framed me for Rivera's murder and the theft. Everyone bought it because Vanessa had seen me kill the congressman.

"A few months after Rivera was murdered the General retired from the army and moved to his estate. He lived quietly for five years. Then he made a very large investment in Computex, Simeon Brown's software company. I think he used money from the secret fund. With his contacts in the military, Wingate was able to get contracts for Computex. He was living off his dead wife's money until Computex took off. Once the company got hot, Simeon Brown died. A lucky break for the General, no?"

"Did you ever try to get even?"

Carl shook his head. "I was tired, Ami. I was

sick of it. Living in the jungle all those months changed me. I didn't want revenge. I wanted peace. I went underground and I was happy living off society's radar screen. Hell," he said with a smile, "I haven't paid taxes for years, and solicitors never call me. What more can you ask?"

# CHAPTER SEVENTEEN

Ami had not seen Vanessa standing with the other reporters when she rushed across the hospital lobby with her head down and her shoulders hunched, obviously uncomfortable with the size of the crowd, the television lights, and the shouted questions. Even if Ami had studied the mob of reporters, she would not have recognized her client, who wore a black wig, makeup, and dark glasses and looked more like a society reporter than a haphazardly dressed representative of a sleazy tabloid.

While the other members of the press waited for the return of the reporters who had been chosen for the pool that was to be allowed to record Morelli's arraignment, Vanessa slipped away from the press corps and stationed herself around the corner from Leroy Ganett's office. Shortly after the arraignment ended, Ganett returned with Brendan Kirkpatrick at his side. Fifteen minutes later, the two men walked out of the doctor's office, and Vanessa heard Ganett tell the prosecutor that he was going to the cafeteria to get something to eat. She waited until the elevator doors closed and took the next car to the basement.

Vanessa pretended to look over the hot dishes while Ganett put a sandwich, an apple, and a soft drink on his tray. As soon as the doctor paid the cashier, Vanessa followed him. He was unwrapping the cellophane from his sandwich when she spoke.

"Dr. Ganett, I'm Sheryl Neidig," Vanessa said as she slipped onto a chair opposite the doctor. "I flew in from LA to look into the Little League case."

"I'm sorry. I can't talk about that."

"And I don't expect you to, right now. I know that you have to honor the doctor-patient privilege."

Dr. Ganett looked confused. "What do you want with me, then?"

"I'm an executive with Phoenix Productions. We're an independent production company based in Hollywood and we're exploring the possibility of making a television movie-of-the-week about Daniel Morelli's case."

"I still can't discuss my patient with you."

"Actually, you can if Mr. Morelli agrees to waive the physician-privilege. And, I assure you, it will be in his financial interest to do so. Yours too, in fact. If he sells us the rights to his story, our movie would have a character based on you."

"On me? Well, I don't know . . ."

"We wouldn't use your name, unless you wanted us to, but Mr. Morelli was wounded and he is in a hospital. Naturally, there would be a doctor in the movie, and we would need a technical consultant to help us make the film as realistic as possible." Vanessa flashed her sexiest smile. "Would you be interested?"

"Uh, well, I don't know. What would I have to do?"

"Oh, it would be a snap for you. You'd supervise the technical aspects to make sure our actors behave like real doctors; you'd explain medical procedures, stuff like that. We might even arrange a cameo role, if you're interested. You know, give you a small part in the film." Vanessa smiled. "Who knows, this could be the start of a whole new career."

Ganett looked interested and nervous. "I'd have to clear this with the hospital administrator."

"Then you are interested?"

"I might be."

"You'd be paid, of course."

"Oh?"

"We'd have to negotiate the fee, but—and don't tell anyone I told you this—ten to twenty-five thousand wouldn't be out of the question."

"That sounds, uh, fair. When can I tell you if I can do it?"

Ganett sounded eager now. Vanessa smiled. "Why don't I call you tomorrow?"

"Okay."

"Great. What's your office number?"

Dr. Ganett told her, and Vanessa made a show of writing it down in a spiral notebook she took

out of her purse. When she'd put away the no..
book Vanessa stood up.

"I'll call LA and tell them you're interested. My
boss will be excited. And we'll touch base soon."

# CHAPTER **EIGHTEEN**

Ami had trouble containing her excitement on the drive back to her office. George French had warned her about the dangers of investing too heavily in the type of story that Carl was telling, but she was certain that he wasn't lying.

As soon as Ami was seated behind her desk, she dialed her expert's number.

"George, it's Ami. I just got back from the hospital."

"How did it go?"

"Morelli opened up to me, only his name isn't really Daniel Morelli."

"Who does he say he is now?"

"This is highly confidential, George. You'll understand why you can't breathe a word of this to anyone once you hear what he told me."

"You don't have to worry about me, Ami."

"Okay. Morelli says that his real name is Carl Rice and that he went AWOL from the army in 1985. He told me some other things, George. If he's telling the truth, this is huge."

"What does that mean?"

Ami told French about Carl's claim that he worked in a secret unit run by Morris Wingate. She recounted his missions and ended with Rice's claim that Morris Wingate had ordered him to murder Congressman Glass.

"What do you think, George?" Ami asked when she was done.

"Either our boy has a very active imagination or you're sitting on top of the biggest scandal in the history of American politics."

"Which do you think it is?"

"Honestly? I go with door number one. The whole story is too fantastic. One of the leading candidates for president of the United States is out to get him. That's right out of the introductory chapter to *Paranoid Behavior for Dummies*. And I've seen that prison escape in several movies."

"We should be able to check on some of his story now that we know Carl's real name."

"If it is his real name."

"Can you ask your friend to find Carl Rice's military record?"

"Yes, but this is the last time."

"No, I agree. If Carl lied about this, then I'll wash my hands of him."

"I'll call you when I know something."

Ami hung up and thought about calling Vanessa Kohler, but she decided against it. She wanted to meet with Vanessa face to face and she wanted to be prepared for their meeting. Ami booted up her computer. Moments later, she had found a story about a black belt in San Diego named Mark Torrance who had been beaten up during a burglary.

Next, she searched the Web for articles about the murder of Congressman Eric Glass. The results were encouraging. The congressman had been murdered at Lost Lake, California, in 1985; and a witness, whose identity had been kept secret by the police, had named Carl Rice as a suspect. There were more stories about the case, but they added no new information.

Ami brought up articles about the murder of General Peter Rivera. One of them contained disturbing information. General Rivera had been tortured and killed in his home in Bethesda, Maryland, in a manner similar to the way that Congressman Glass had been killed, and Carl Rice was named as a suspect. An enterprising reporter for the *Baltimore Sun* had connected the cases of Rivera and Glass and had looked into the background of Carl Rice. According to a follow-up written by the reporter, Rice had been discharged from the army for psychological reasons.

Ami's intercom buzzed, and her receptionist announced that Brendan Kirkpatrick was calling. Ami toyed with not taking the call from her least favorite lawyer, but she was still representing Carl Rice until another attorney took the case off her hands.

"Hello, Mr. Kirkpatrick."

"Hello, Mrs. Vergano. Recovered from your first arraignment yet?"

Ami's blood pressure started to go up until she realized that the question was not a taunt but had been asked in a friendly tone. Still, she wasn't ready yet to forgive and forget.

"What can I do for you?" Ami asked.

"It's what I can do for you. I met with my investigator. He's talked to some more witnesses, and I have a better picture of the case now. I have a proposition for Mr. Morelli."

"And that would be?"

"I'm willing to drop the charge of attempted murder in exchange for a plea to the assault on the officer. I'll recommend a sentence of three years. With good time, Morelli will be out in about a year."

"Why the change of heart?"

"I'm convinced that Morelli was trying to protect the coach when he fought with Barney Lutz."

"So why not dismiss, if he was acting in self-defense?"

"Your client used too much force and he attacked a cop."

"Morelli was attacked from behind. He didn't know he was fighting with an officer."

"He could see he was fighting a cop after he threw the cop over his shoulder. The other officer says that he shot Morelli because Morelli was about to spear his partner in the throat."

"He was acting in the heat of passion."

"Maybe, but he didn't stop when he saw the uniform, so that's the best I can do."

"I'll relay the offer to my client," Ami said.

"There's another condition."

"What's that?"

"To get the deal, your client has to tell us his real name."

"Why does he have to do that?"

"So we can be sure that he's not wanted for other crimes. We've reached a dead end trying to identify him. That's a little spooky nowadays. Someone like Morelli should have fingerprints on file."

"He's a drifter. He doesn't hold regular jobs, and he gets paid in cash."

"Tom Haven, the cop that shot Morelli, was in the military and knows something about self-defense. He told me that no one handles himself the way your client did without serious training. Haven thinks that there's a good chance Morelli is ex-military, which makes it even odder that his prints aren't on file." He paused. "You may not want to believe it, but your boy is probably a trained killer. I need to know if he's hurt other people the way he hurt my cop and Mr. Lutz."

"I'll talk to Dan and get back to you."

"Good. One more thing."

"Yes?"

"I want to apologize for coming on so strong that first day. I didn't know you, and I honestly thought that you were trying to chase Morelli's ambulance. I shouldn't have jumped to conclusions."

Ami was surprised by the apology but was still angry with Kirkpatrick.

"That's right, you shouldn't have," she answered.

"I said I'm sorry. I checked around. You've got a good rep."

"I'll get back to you," was Ami's terse reply.

Ami hung up and stared out her window. "Well, well," she thought, "miracles do happen." Maybe she'd been wrong about Kirkpatrick and he wasn't a total prick. She remembered what Betty Sato had said about the prosecutor's wife. Ami knew what it was like to lose a spouse you really loved. It changed you.

Ami picked up a picture of Ryan and held it in front of her. He was so beautiful and so good. She had lost Chad, but she was so lucky to have Ryan to love. Kirkpatrick didn't have a child to soften the blow of losing his wife. Kirkpatrick's work had become his life, and his work was dealing with the horror that the worst people in society imposed on innocent men, women, and children. You would have to become hard and mistrusting if that was all you thought about every day. Ami closed her eyes and thanked God for Ryan. After Chad died, Ryan had kept her sane and given her hope. Without him she could have easily slipped into despair. Despite everything that had happened to her, she knew that she was fortunate to be the mother of someone as special as her son.

Ami turned back to her desk and opened Carl Rice's file. Inside was the number of Ray Armitage's hotel in Boulder, Colorado. She wasn't experienced enough to know if the plea offer Kirkpatrick had made was good or bad. That would be a job for a seasoned criminal defense attorney. Fortunately, Armitage was in his room. Ami didn't tell him about any of the new developments in the case except for Kirkpatrick's plea offer. The defense attorney said that the offer sounded okay but he couldn't advise Rice about it until he'd studied the facts thoroughly. Then he told Ami that there had been a new development in the case of the Olympic skier that would keep him in Colorado for three more days. He promised to call her as soon as he knew when he was returning to Portland and assured her that he was very interested in Rice's case.

Ami hung up. She was disappointed that she would have to stay on as Rice's attorney. The case was too big for her, and the story in the *Baltimore Sun* bothered her. If Rice had been discharged from the military because of mental problems, maybe Dr. French was right and Carl's wild tale of a secret unit run by a presidential candidate was pure fantasy. She had been hoping that she would be able to hand off the job of figuring out the truth about Carl Rice to Ray Armitage. Now she had to soldier on.

# CHAPTER **NINETEEN**

When Ami arrived at work the next morning she found a message from George French asking her to come to his office as soon as possible. Ami was nervous during the crosstown trip and she didn't feel any better when she saw how grim Dr. French looked when he greeted her in his waiting room.

"My friend faxed me a copy of Rice's military record," the doctor said as he escorted Ami to his office. "You're not going to like it."

As soon as Ami was seated French handed her a government document titled "Report of Transfer or Discharge." While Ami read it the psychiatrist gave her a quick synopsis of the report.

"Carl Rice was drafted into the service from the San Diego area and was in Special Forces. After a year of learning Vietnamese at the Army Language School at Fort Meyer, Rice was sent to Vietnam, where he saw combat. After this mission, Rice was hospitalized for combat-related stress. After his discharge from the hospital, Rice returned to the states and was assigned to be a language instructor at Fort Meyer. After his tour in Vietnam his records show no further service overseas."

French pointed at a section of the form that indicated the soldier's rank.

"Remember Rice told us that he was a captain?"

Ami nodded.

"This says that he was a sergeant."

"I don't know anything about military ranks. Is that a big difference?"

French laughed. "Night and day, Ami. A sergeant is a noncommissioned officer. A captain is a commissioned officer. Captain is a much higher rank."

French handed Ami another document and pointed to a section marked "Conduct."

"Here's the really bad part. Rice was kicked out of the army because he wore the insignia of a captain and an improper uniform when he wasn't authorized to do so."

French handed Ami a psychiatric report from Walter Reed General Hospital signed by Captain Howard Stienbock.

"Read this," the doctor said.

Ami started to feel queasy as she read Dr. Stienbock's report.

*I certify that Carl Ellis Rice, a 31-year-old Caucasian male with approximately 14 years of active-duty service, was seen by me on 7 March and 15 March 1985 at Walter Reed General Hospital NPOP Clinic at the request of his company commander.*

1. *Pertinent history:* On several occasions Rice was alleged to have worn a captain's bars and com-

bat ribbons to the class he was instructing in Vietnamese. Rice stated that these episodes occurred following rejection by a woman whose identity Rice chose to keep secret, other than to say that she was the daughter of a general in the United States Army. Rice stated that he had worn the bars because he was secretly a captain, although he is listed in official military records as a sergeant. When asked to explain this discrepancy Rice refused on the grounds that I was not cleared to receive this information, but he did state that he was frequently sent on top-secret missions. My attempts to get Rice to clarify his remarks were met with smiles or vocal refusals made on grounds of "national security."

2. *Mental status:* Rice presents as a hyperalert 31-year-old with no evidence of organic brain dysfunction. His mood was depressed and his speech slow and difficult to hear. There is no evidence that the episodes in which he allegedly wore the captain's bars occurred during dissociative states. Rice was hospitalized during a tour of duty in Vietnam for combat-related stress and depression.

3. *Findings and conclusions:*

A. Diagnosis—Paranoid personality disorder coupled with possible paranoid delusions as a result of combat-related stress, exacerbated by recent personal problems. I have concluded that Rice may feel that he was a failure in combat and may have created a delusional construct in which he is a cap-

tain who has been sent on secret missions
to compensate for his feelings of inadequa-
cy. Without more information I cannot
form a definitive diagnosis, and Rice
refused to be forthcoming with me.

B. Subject is able to distinguish right from
wrong and is able to adhere to the right. He
is mentally capable of participating in his
own defense.

C. Subject is cleared for action deemed appropriate by command.

"What does this mean?" Ami asked.

"This is strictly a guess, but let's assume that Rice
wanted to reestablish a relationship with Vanessa
Wingate when they met again in D.C. Only she's
not interested in him the way she was when they
were teenagers. Rice knew she hated her father
and suspected he had done all sorts of terrible
things, including murdering her mother, so to win
her back to his side he made up this story about
her father ordering him to commit all sorts of
crimes. Maybe—if he's in a paranoid state—he
even believes it."

"I checked the St. Martin's Prep yearbook,"
Ami said. "Rice did graduate in the class of 1970
with Vanessa Wingate."

"That doesn't mean that he was her lover in
high school," French said. "But, true or not, it
looks as though he believes that she was his
lover. If he was obsessed with Vanessa, he may
have seen her with Congressman Glass and decided that they were lovers. He may have imag-

ined that Glass was a rival who was standing between him and the object of his desire. That might explain why he was depressed. He may also have convinced himself that Vanessa would be his again if he removed this obstacle. That would be one explanation for why he murdered the congressman."

# CHAPTER **TWENTY**

Vanessa wasn't in when Ami called her hotel, so she left another message. Her client called her back just before noon and they arranged to have lunch at Brasserie Montmartre, a restaurant that was a few blocks from Vanessa's hotel and within walking distance of Ami's office. Ami reserved a booth so that they would have privacy. Vanessa was waiting for her when she arrived.

"We have a lot to discuss," Ami said as soon as they ordered. "First, I spoke to Ray Armitage. There's been a new development in his case in Colorado so he won't be back in Portland for two more days. Second, the district attorney has made a plea offer."

"What is it?"

Vanessa looked tense as Ami explained what Brendan had told her.

"So Dan will have to go to prison if he takes the offer?" Vanessa said.

"I'm afraid so."

"What if he turns it down? Will he still be locked up?"

"Yes, unless Armitage persuades the judge to set bail that's low enough for Dan to meet. Otherwise he'll be in jail, unless he's acquitted."

"How soon will we know about bail?"

"Armitage told me that he'll set a bail hearing right away, but he'll need some time to digest the facts, talk to Dan, line up witnesses, etcetera. It might be a week or so."

Vanessa was pensive while the waitress placed their orders on the table. When the waitress left, Ami looked directly at her.

"Are you Morris Wingate's daughter?"

Vanessa hesitated.

"Did you go to high school with Carl?"

Vanessa could not hide her surprise. "He told you his real name?"

Ami nodded. "And I know that both of you graduated in 1970. I've checked the St. Martin's yearbook."

"What else have you been up to?"

"I've consulted a psychiatrist. He's interviewed Carl. We're concerned about his mental health."

"I see."

"Vanessa, Carl has told me a number of things that are very unsettling. If I'm going to help him I have to know if they're true."

"What did he tell you?"

"I can't reveal what he told me, because our conversations are protected by the attorney-client privilege; and I don't want to tell you, because I want to see if you both tell the same story. It will help me judge Carl's mental state."

"What do you want to know?"

"What was your relationship in high school?"

Vanessa looked sad. "It was very intense our senior year," she answered softly. "It ended when he was drafted."

"Why?"

Vanessa looked down at the tabletop. "Carl had a full scholarship to Dartmouth. It was his dream to go there. If he'd tried, he could have gotten a deferment so he could go to college and avoid the draft. My father talked him into going into the army. I felt that he had chosen my father over me."

Vanessa raised her eyes and looked into Ami's. "I hated Carl for that," she said.

"When was the next time you saw him?"

"In 1985 in Washington, D.C. It was a coincidence. I was on a date and so was he. We were at the same restaurant. He recognized me and came over. A week later, we had dinner together."

"So you started dating Carl again?"

"I wouldn't call it dating. We met for dinner every once in a while. Sometimes he'd wait for me after class and we'd go for coffee. It was strictly platonic."

"How long did this go on?"

"A few months."

"Why did you stop?"

"Carl disappeared for a few weeks." Vanessa ate a forkful of her salad. It was obvious that she was stalling while she debated with herself what she would say next.

"Did you worry when Carl stopped coming around?" Ami prompted.

"Not at first. As I said, we weren't dating. He was just an old friend. We'd had a teenage love affair, but that was a long time ago in a different life. I'd been married, divorced; a lot had happened since high school. I missed seeing him, because he was a nice guy; but I also thought that he wanted more out of the relationship than I did. I assumed that he had sensed the way I felt and wanted to be the one to break it off rather than face rejection."

"So you didn't have any romantic feelings for Carl when you met again in D.C.?"

"If he'd asked me to go to bed with him I would have turned him down." Vanessa sighed. "Honestly, at that time, I liked being with Carl, but, well, he was a sergeant in the army. If he retired he was going to be a language teacher who might become a professor someday. I was spending my days in Congress with dynamic men and women who were doing big things on a national or worldwide stage and my evenings with brilliant law students who were going to run the world. Carl was fun but I didn't see a future with him."

"Did you see Carl again?"

Vanessa got very quiet.

"Did he show up at your apartment in the early morning?" Ami asked.

"Yes."

Ami smiled. "This is like pulling teeth."

Vanessa did not return the smile.

"He told me about the Unit," Ami said.

"Thank God," Vanessa said. Then she started to talk.

"Carl told me that he was in a secret army group composed of a small number of highly trained men that was run by my father. It was concealed within the Agency for Intelligence Data Coordination, and the men carried out assassinations, among other illegal activities. He said he'd just returned from a mission in which he had followed orders and murdered two people. He wanted to get out of that life. He was desperate."

"Did you try to help him?"

"Yes. I knew that my father conducted business in our house on the California coast. There's a safe in his den. One day I was in the den when he opened it. He wasn't careful, and I memorized the combination. Father was in Washington, so I flew home on a red-eye and searched his den. I found the records of ten men in the safe."

"Were these the records for the Unit?"

"Nothing in the records connected the men to the Unit Carl had told me about, but I guessed that these were the members because Carl was in the group and they had a very high level of training."

"What did you do with the records?"

"You know very well what I did with them."

"I need you to tell me."

"I took them to Eric Glass." Vanessa's voice broke. "He was a very decent man." She took a sip of water. "Eric was on the House committee with oversight of the intelligence community. I told him what Carl had told me about the Unit. Eric was going to have one of his staffers run a check on the men whose files were in my father's safe."

"This meeting was at Lost Lake on the night the congressman was murdered?"

"Carl did that," she said in a voice that was barely above a whisper. A tear trickled down her cheek. "He tortured Eric for the records, then he cut his throat."

"You saw him?"

Vanessa nodded slowly.

"There was so much blood. And the look on Eric's face . . . "

"What happened to you after the police came?" Ami asked.

"That night is a blur. I've blocked out most of it. All I can remember are flashes, little snapshots. But I remember very clearly what my father did to me." Vanessa's sorrow was rapidly replaced by bitterness. "He put me in a mental hospital, and I spent a year in hell. He made certain that no one would ever believe a word I said about the Unit." Vanessa pointed to her forehead. "I have a big red stamp right here. It says 'Ex-Mental Patient, Nutcase.' When I came out of that place I was addicted to the drugs they gave me, unemployable." Vanessa gritted her teeth. Ami could see the rage building. "You have no idea what I've been through."

"Vanessa, I know you don't want to believe it, but there is another possible explanation for the Unit that doesn't involve your father. The psychiatrist who interviewed Carl thinks that he may be suffering from a rare form of mental illness called a paranoid state. According to my expert, it's a possible explanation for his story. Carl may be so disturbed that he actually believes he was in a secret Unit run by your father. That's why his story sounds so plausible."

"You see what I'm up against?" Vanessa said. "No one believes me! But I know that my father did run the Unit. He is evil. And now I've got a chance to set things right. I've got a witness who can tell the world what my father is really like. But I've got to get him out of jail before they kill him. Any minute now my father will learn that Carl Rice is alive and send his men after him."

"Carl is perfectly safe, Vanessa. He's locked in the secure ward of the hospital. There's a policeman guarding him. No one can get to him."

For a moment, Ami thought that her client was going to argue with her, but suddenly Vanessa calmed down.

"I guess you're right," Vanessa said. "Carl is probably safe in a guarded, locked ward."

"He is. Try to keep calm. Ray Armitage is the best. He'll be on the case very soon. Then we'll get some results. Okay?"

Vanessa nodded. "I'm sorry I got so upset. You're doing a great job."

Ami smiled, but she was certain that Vanessa had not meant a word she said since her rapid mood change.

After lunch Ami walked back to her office and went over everything she knew about Rice's case. She had no new insights until she reread Captain Howard Stienbock's psychiatric report. The doctor had concluded that Carl had a mental problem in 1985. Dr. Stienbock's testimony would establish that her client had a long-standing psychiatric problem if Ray Armitage decided to go with an insanity defense.

Ami dialed Walter Reed Hospital on the chance that Stienbock was still working there. The hospital operator had no listing for a Dr. Stienbock, so she transferred Ami to the personnel department. After being kept on hold for fifteen minutes, Ami was informed that Dr. Stienbock was deceased.

"When did this happen?" Ami asked.

"December of 1985."

That was only months after he'd written the report on Rice.

"How did he die?" Ami asked.

"That's not in his file."

"Was he married? I could call his wife."

"He was single."

"Do you have the name of a next of kin?"

"I'm sorry, but I can't give out that information."

Ami thanked the woman and hung up. Then she turned to her computer and did an Internet search for Dr. Howard Stienbock and Walter Reed Hospital. There were only a few hits, but one was a newspaper story in the *Washington Post* about a hit-and-run accident that had claimed the life of a psychiatrist employed by Walter Reed Hospital. According to the story and Stienbock's obituary, the doctor had been in the Special Forces during Vietnam and had seen combat of an unspecified nature during the war.

Ami turned away from the computer and stared at her wall. Stienbock's death proved nothing. It just meant that he was unavailable as a witness. But the connection to the Special Forces did give her pause. So did the fact that the driver of the car that killed the doctor had never been apprehended.

Still, Ami had no more proof now that Carl Rice was part of a secret army unit than she had before she'd tried to find Dr. Stienbock. Vanessa based her belief in the existence of the Unit on the statements of Carl Rice, who might be delusional. Vanessa's only supporting evidence was a collection of army records she could not produce, which may have been in the General's safe for a purely innocent purpose. But what if Carl wasn't lying? How could you prove that the Unit existed when all trace of it had been erased?

A thought occurred to Ami. According to Vanessa and Carl, after Carl confessed his activities in the Unit, they had seen each other only one time, for a few seconds, in Congressman Glass's house. Carl said that Vanessa spoke his name, then ran away. So how did Carl know about the army records Vanessa had stolen from her father's safe? If the records existed, and Vanessa hadn't told him about them, there was only one other person who could have—General Morris Wingate.

Ami tried to think of another possibility. Maybe Carl saw the records while he was torturing Glass in Glass's office. But why would he take Glass to the office? Why not torture Glass in bed where he found him?

Ami wondered whether there was any mention of the army records in the official reports of the murder. If they were still in Glass's office when the police arrived, it would prove that Carl's story was a lie; but it would be some evidence in Carl's favor if the army records were not inventoried in the police reports.

Ami made a snap decision. Mary O'Dell's son, Bobby, was Ryan's best friend. She would ask if Ryan could stay with Mary for a night or two. If she could get a flight to San Francisco this evening, she could be at the Lost Lake police department first thing in the morning.

# CHAPTER **TWENTY-ONE**

Vanessa knew that Dr. Ganett would be in his office at six in the evening because she'd called earlier, posing as Sheryl Neidig, to tell him that she had exciting news that she wanted to tell him in person. Ganett had been eager for her to come over and had agreed to wait at the hospital. Vanessa put on her wig and dressed in black slacks and a blue silk blouse that showed off her figure. She was also wearing sunglasses and hoped that Ganett would assume that they were a Hollywood affectation.

When Vanessa conceived her plan, she did not realize how nervous she would be when the time came to execute it. When she knocked on Ganett's office door, she felt slightly nauseated, and her hand was shaking. The doctor told her to come in and motioned her to a chair.

"I just received fabulous news from LA," Vanessa said, fighting to keep a tremor out of her voice. "Fox is crazy about doing a made-for-TV movie about Daniel Morelli and the whole problem of Little League parents, and they are very hot about you consulting for us. They're also considering—very seriously, I might add—the possibility of a role for you, and I don't mean a cameo."

Ganett brightened. "That is exciting."

"Here's the thing, though. When you do these movies based on real events you have to move fast so the events are still fresh in the viewer's mind when the movie airs."

Ganett nodded knowingly.

"Bob Spizer—he's my boss—Bob wants me to start location scouting right away." Vanessa fished a digital camera out of her large purse. "I've already taken pictures of the hospital, but I need a few of the secure ward to send to LA. It's for the screenwriter." Vanessa leaned forward and lowered her voice. "Nick Battaglia is on board. We were so lucky to get him. Usually he's impossible to tie down, but he's between projects."

Ganett nodded again, even though he'd never heard of Nick Battaglia—which was not surprising, since Vanessa had made up the name.

"Nick visualizes the scenes before he writes them. He's like that, a real artist. Tough to work with sometimes, but his finished product is always first-rate. Anyway, I know it's late, but I was wondering if you could take me up to the ward where they're holding Morelli."

"I couldn't take you into his room," Ganett said.

"Of course not." Vanessa paused as if she'd just gotten an idea. "Are there any empty rooms on the ward that look like his?"

"Yes. I could let you see one of them."

"Terrif. I'll have a contract for you in a day or so. You may want to have a lawyer look it over. I can't tell you how much they're going to offer for the consulting fee, but I put in a good word for you."

On the way up to the ward Vanessa asked question after question to keep Ganett occupied and to give herself time to review the plan that had come to her after Ami told her how easy it had been to get in to see Carl.

When the elevator stopped, Vanessa let Ganett lead the way. She felt light-headed and she hoped that the doctor would not notice that she was perspiring.

"Hey, James," Ganett said to the slender black man who was manning the desk.

"Evening, Dr. Ganett."

"This is Sheryl Neidig. She's with a production company in Hollywood. They're going to make a movie about the Little League thing."

"No kidding?"

"Dr. Ganett is going to be our technical consultant," Vanessa said, flashing James her brightest smile.

"Let us in, will you?" Ganett asked. "Sheryl has to take a few photos of the ward for the screenwriter."

Vanessa wondered if the guard would want to search her purse. She was certain that she could get to her gun before he could react.

"Sure thing," James said. He grinned at Vanessa. "If you need an extra, I'm available."

"I'll keep that in mind," she answered as James

talked into his radio. A moment later, another orderly—this one tall and blond with a weight lifter's physique—opened the door from the inside.

"What's the routine for getting out?" Vanessa asked with a laugh. "I'd hate to be stuck in here."

"Mack's got the keys to the kingdom—right, Mack?" Dr. Ganett said.

"Don't worry," Mack answered with a grin, "we'll probably let you out."

Vanessa laughed and asked Ganett another question. Ganett answered it, then gave a running commentary about the type of patient who was treated on the ward as Mack led them down the hall toward Carl Rice's room.

"How do you open these doors?" Vanessa asked when they had almost reached the policeman who was guarding Carl's door. It was all she could do to keep her voice even.

The orderly pulled out a ring of keys. "Like the doc said, I've got the keys to the kingdom."

"Do those keys open all the rooms?"

"There's a master key," Mack answered as he showed it to her.

They arrived at Carl's room and Ganett introduced "Sheryl" to the officer and told him why she was in the ward. The officer seemed impressed.

"Can I look in the room?" Vanessa asked the policeman.

"Sure."

Vanessa looked through a small window that was inserted a third of the way up the door. Carl was lying in bed staring back at her but he gave no sign that he recognized her. She stepped back from the door.

"Could I see inside one of the empty rooms?" Vanessa asked. Mack looked at Ganett. He nodded. The orderly opened the thick metal door of the room next door. It was identical to Carl's except for the bed, which had only a bare mattress. As they walked inside, Vanessa asked Ganett and the orderly a few questions. Then she paused as if she'd just been struck by an interesting idea.

"Officer," she called to the policeman, "could you step in here for a moment so I can get a shot for the screenwriter? He'll want to be able to describe Morelli's guard for the costume department."

"Sure," the policeman answered. He was ripe for anything that broke up the monotony of guarding a locked hospital room.

Vanessa's breathing was so rapid that she was certain the policeman would hear it as he walked by her. As soon as the three men were in the room Vanessa closed her eyes for a moment to regain her composure, but she was still shaking like a leaf when she took her gun out of her purse.

The men stared uncomprehendingly. Then the officer started for his weapon.

"I'll kill you if you touch that gun," Vanessa said, surprising herself by how calm she sounded. "If you cooperate, no one will be hurt."

Time stopped as the three men decided what to do. Vanessa prayed that they wouldn't attack her, because she wasn't sure that she could pull the trigger.

The officer froze, but Mack looked as if he was tensed to spring.

"Don't do it, Mack," Vanessa said, shifting the gun so it pointed at his stomach. "I don't want to leave you dead or crippled."

Mack hesitated, and Vanessa knew she'd won.

"Get down on your stomachs with your hands and feet spread wide."

The men did as they were told, their eyes never leaving her weapon.

"Sheryl, what's going on?" Ganett asked as he lowered himself to the floor.

Vanessa ignored him. "Mack, push your keys and radio over here, and no sudden moves."

Mack did as she was told.

"Officer, please slide your gun to me."

The officer complied.

"Cell phones next."

Vanessa could see Ganett calculating the odds and she shifted her weapon toward him.

"Leroy, I'd hate to see you die for your cell phone. I promise it will be right outside the door. I won't even use any of your minutes."

The doctor slid the cell phone to her.

"Okay, here's the drill. I'm locking you in, but I'll check on you before I leave. If you've changed position, I'll kill you. If you don't cause trouble you'll be okay."

As soon as she locked the door, her legs almost gave way from relief. After a brief look through the window to make sure that the men hadn't moved, she unlocked Carl's door. He stared at his visitor.

"Get up, Carl, we're leaving."

"Who . . . ?"

"I'm Vanessa. Now, move it. We don't have time to talk. I just locked your guard, an orderly, and your doctor in the room next door. We've got to get you out of here."

Carl struggled out of bed. He'd been walking for the past few days, but his legs were still stiff from inactivity.

"Stay next to the wall when we get close to the front door," Vanessa said. "The orderly on the other side is about your size. You'll switch clothes with him once I lure him into the ward." She pulled a second weapon from her purse and handed it to Carl butt first. "Take this."

Carl checked the weapon, chambered a round, then held it at his side with the muzzle pointing down. When they were at the entrance to the ward he pressed himself against the wall so that he would not be visible to someone looking through the window in the door. Vanessa was amazed at how alive she felt now that Carl was with her. She used the master key to open the door. James looked surprised when she walked out alone.

"Where's the doctor?" he asked.

Rice stepped out. James's jaw dropped when he saw the prisoner training a gun on him. He started to get up and Rice cracked him across the temple with the gun barrel. The orderly's legs wobbled from the blow and he almost fell.

Vanessa blanched when she saw the blood, but she kept a grip on her emotions. Rice grabbed the dazed orderly by his collar, shoved him through the door, and swept his feet out from under him. James fell to the floor.

"Strip, and do it fast," Rice ordered. He grabbed the orderly's pants and shirt as they came off. While Vanessa kept her gun on James, Rice put on the outfit. Then they took the orderly down the hall and locked him in the room with the other prisoners, who were still on the floor.

"Why are you doing this?" Carl asked when they were headed down in the elevator. "Don't you know how much trouble you're in?"

"I know that you'll be dead if you stay here. If I could break you out this easily, think how easily my father's men will be able to break in when they learn you're alive."

"I wish you'd left me on my own. I told Ami Vergano that I didn't want you involved."

Vanessa smiled. "When did I ever do anything anyone ordered me to do?"

Carl smiled back. "Point taken. So, Captain, what's the plan?"

"My car is gassed up and we're going to get out of town. After that, I have no idea."

# CHAPTER **TWENTY-TWO**

Ami caught a night flight to San Francisco and rented a car at the airport a little after midnight. It took two hours to drive to Lost Lake, and she spent what was left of the predawn hours in a motel on the outskirts of town. When her travel alarm went off at eight o'clock that morning, she felt as if her head were filled with cotton. She felt a bit better after her shower and better still when she stepped outside into the crisp mountain air.

Behind the motel was an arm of Lost Lake, and Ami could see a slice of blue through the pine trees. She wandered down to a dock that had been weathered gray. A few boats bobbed at anchor, and some early risers were fishing near the far shore. Ami stared across to the green hills that rose up behind the crystal-clear water. A hawk glided above her and puffy white cumulus clouds floated above the hawk. The idyllic scene made the violence that had brought her here seem all the more incongruous.

Downtown was three parallel streets of one- and two-story buildings named Main, Elm, and

Shasta. As she drove along Main, Ami spotted
numerous curio shops and art galleries and three
cafés that advertised caffe latte, sure signs that
the town survived on tourist dollars. A one-story
dull-brown concrete building at the far end of
Main housed the Lost Lake sheriff's department.
Ami parked and waited to cross until a shiny
tanker and a pickup with a cord of wood stacked
in the back drove by.

The reception area consisted of several chairs
upholstered in scratched, faded faux leather. A
low metal fence ran between the reception area
and an open space filled with metal desks. Uniformed sheriff's deputies were sitting at some of
the desks. The receptionist—a large, cheerful
woman dressed in a Hawaiian print muumuu—
occupied the desk next to the rail. When Ami
came in, the receptionist was transferring a call
about a bear that was scavenging in a resident's
garbage pails. She hung up and flashed Ami a
welcoming smile.

"What can I do for you, honey?"

"I have an appointment with the sheriff."

A few minutes later, a tall, broad-shouldered
man with close-cropped salt-and-pepper hair and
hazel eyes walked out of a corridor that led to the
rear of the station. He wore the tan uniform of
the Lost Lake sheriff's department and seemed to
be in his late forties.

"Mrs. Vergano?" he asked as he held open the
gate that blocked access to the rest of the building.

"Yes," she answered extending her hand.

"Aaron Harney," the sheriff said as they shook

hands. "Why don't you come on back to my office?"

Ami followed Harney to the rear of the station house and into a wood-paneled office. The walls were covered with framed plaques, certificates, and pictures of Harney with the governor and other celebrities; dominating the view was a mounted moose head. A glass bookcase filled with law books stood against a wall. On top of the bookcase and on other level surfaces were bowling and softball trophies that the department had won. On Harney's large scarred desk were pictures of his wife and five children.

Harney offered Ami a seat and settled into a chair behind his desk.

"Last night, on the phone, you said that you wanted to talk to me about Congressman Glass's murder, but you weren't very clear about why," Harney said.

"I'm involved with a case that may be related," Ami said. "I'd like to learn more about the Glass case, maybe see the old files, if that's possible."

"It might be if you can tell me why a twenty-year-old case interests you."

"That's a little tricky, Sheriff. You know that the law forbids me to reveal the confidences of a client."

Harney nodded. "And you know that there's no statute of limitations on prosecuting a murder suspect."

"Last night, I left my son with a neighbor and flew down here. I've got to get home today, so I don't have time to go to court for the files. If you don't want me to see them you'll win."

Harney liked his visitor's honesty. Most lawyers would have threatened him with the fury of the law.

"Did you know that I was the first officer on the scene the night the congressman was murdered?" the sheriff asked.

Ami's surprise showed on her face.

"I've been the sheriff here since Earl Basehart retired, and I was a deputy for a bunch of years before that. Counting my experiences as an MP in the military, that makes about twenty-five years of crime fighting. During those twenty plus years I've seen a thing or two, but that was the worst. The way Congressman Glass looked when I found him is something I can't forget. It shook me up when it happened, and it still disturbs me. So you can see why I was real interested when you called."

"The case is *State v. Daniel Morelli*," Ami said. "You may have heard about it on the news. My client is accused of stabbing a parent during an argument at a Little League game."

"I have heard of that case. It's a hell of a thing. But what does it have to do with the murder of Congressman Glass?"

Ami sighed. "I really wish I could tell you but I can't. I'm bound by law to keep my client's confidences."

Harney studied Ami and she held his gaze. He stood up.

"Let's take a drive. When we come back you can read the file."

"Thank you, Sheriff."

"You can thank me by calling me when you feel you can talk about my case."

They took the sheriff's cruiser on the fifteen-minute drive from the station to the Lost Lake Resort. As soon as they were under way, Ami asked Harney what he remembered about the night Eric Glass was murdered.

"I remember the scream." He shivered involuntarily. "I was clear across the lake, but sound carries out here at night. That scream cut through me. I felt like someone had run ice up my spine."

"Was it the congressman who screamed?"

"No." Harney looked grim. "I imagine he did a lot of screaming, from the look of his wounds, but the scream I heard was from a woman. Vanessa Wingate, the General's daughter."

"What did you do after you heard the scream?"

"I drove around the lake as fast as I could and radioed for backup. When I got to the house I went around back and Miss Wingate wandered out of the woods in a daze. She scared the hell out of me. I thought she was a ghost, to be honest. She had on this long white T-shirt, and her eyes were vacant."

"Did she say anything?"

"Yeah, she kept on repeating over and over, 'Carl killed him, Carl Rice.'"

"So there was never any doubt that Rice was the murderer?"

Harney hesitated.

"Do you have some doubts, Sheriff?"

"Not many, but we never found any physical

evidence to confirm Miss Wingate's story. It did look like someone had pulled a boat up on the shore, but when that happened and who did it we couldn't say. People take boats out on the lake all the time. I thought I heard an outboard motor when I got out of my car, but it wasn't necessarily the killer. It could have been anyone taking advantage of the moonlight."

"Did you question the people who live around the lake?"

"Of course. No one admitted being out there, but local kids sneak onto the property all the time and they wouldn't have come forward."

"Who were your other suspects?"

"That's obvious. Vanessa Wingate was staying at the house and she was acting very strange."

"But you didn't arrest her."

"We didn't have probable cause. There was no blood on her, and we never found the knife, which suggested that the killer had taken it with him. If she and the congressman were lovers she might have had a motive, but she denied it. When we searched the house it looked like she was staying in the guest room. Glass slept in a king-size bed and only one side looked like it had been slept on. We wanted to ask more questions, but General Wingate spirited Miss Wingate away before we could interrogate her."

"What do you mean?"

"What I said. I found Miss Wingate's name and a California address in her purse. It took a while to track down the General, but we notified him as soon as we could. He told us he was coming to the hospital, and he was there a few hours later."

Harney shook his head, still awed by the memory of the General's arrival.

"That was some entrance. He came in by helicopter with two bodyguards and a psychiatrist who worked at a place called Serenity Manor. The General just took over. He was like that. One of the most forceful and charismatic men I've ever met. I don't doubt he'll be our next president. Being in his presence is like standing next to bottled lightning."

They drove around a curve, and Ami saw large black metal letters that spelled out "Lost Lake Resort" attached to a low stone wall. Harney turned onto a paved two-lane road that wended its way through an evergreen forest for a quarter-mile. Blocking access to the grounds was a gate that could be raised or lowered by an access card or by a security guard in a small brick gatehouse. The gate and the guard didn't look as if they afforded any real security—anyone could sneak through the woods on either side, and the guard was old, fat, and slow-moving—but they gave the illusion of protection and an air of exclusivity to the wealthy owners of the expensive homes that dotted the lake.

"Hey, Ray," Sheriff Harney said.

"Sheriff," the guard replied with a nod.

"Going to take a ride around, if that's okay with you."

The guard nodded again, raised the gate, and waved them through. After another eighth of a mile Ami saw signs for the lodge. The road forked and Harney turned left, away from the lodge, toward a range of low green hills. Every so often a driveway appeared. Most of the houses were screened from view by trees, but occasionally Ami could see one of the summer homes. For the most part, they were overbuilt—massive ranches, imitation Spanish villas, or huge stone fortresses. Ami felt as if she were in the midst of an architectural battlefield.

"What happened to Vanessa after her father arrived at the hospital?" she asked, her eyes turned toward the landscape but her mind on the sheriff's story.

"All hell broke loose. She started screaming when the General walked into her room. They had to sedate her. Then the psychiatrist who was with the General had a conference with the doctors at the hospital. Next thing we knew, our star witness was lifting off in that helicopter and that's the last we saw of her."

"Didn't you try to stop them from taking her away?"

"Not really. We're just small-town cops. The General, he was something else. Earl did say something about her being our only witness, and the General promised he'd make his daughter available whenever we needed her. What could Earl say? Wingate was her father, and Lost Lake Hospital couldn't provide the type of psychiatric care Wingate's doctor said she needed." Harney shrugged. "That was that, except for the FBI man."

"Who?"

"Name was Victor Hobson, a real tough guy. The FBI was involved because Glass was a congressman and Hobson had been assigned to the case. He showed up a few hours after the General left, and he was furious when he heard what the General had done."

"Was any progress ever made with the case?"

"Not really. The General brought Rice's army records with him. Rice had been discharged for psychiatric reasons. Wingate said he was a very disturbed young man. Seems he and Miss Wingate went to high school together, and he had a crush on her. Then they'd met again in D.C. where Miss Wingate was going to law school and working for the congressman. Wingate thought that Rice was obsessed with his daughter and probably killed Glass because he imagined the congressman and his daughter were lovers."

"Was Rice ever arrested?"

"No. We put out an APB, and the FBI had him on the ten-most-wanted list for a while, but I never heard anything else about him except for a second murder of some General on the east coast where Rice was a suspect. After that, nothing."

A driveway appeared and Harney turned into it. At the end of the driveway was a two-story log cabin set back behind a manicured lawn and some flower beds.

"I thought you might like to see the place. The Reynolds family owns it now. He's a banker in San Francisco. They come out a lot in the summer, but they're in Europe now. I can't let you in."

"I understand."

"The place was hard to sell after Glass died. You can imagine the problem. When the Reynoldses got it, they redecorated, knocked down a few walls. I've been inside, and it doesn't look the same. But the grounds are pretty much the way they were that night."

Ami got out. It was hot and the midday air was still. She stared at the house and turned slowly in a circle, trying to imagine the way it would look in the dead of night. The sheriff waited patiently, then followed Ami when she walked around to the back. The house had blocked the breeze from the lake, and it felt cool and welcome.

"That dock was there then," Harney said, pointing out a short wooden pier. "Glass had a speedboat he tooled around in. And that's the path to the tennis court where I first saw Miss Wingate."

Ami looked at the dock for a moment before turning her attention to the path that led to the tennis court. She imagined Vanessa Wingate wandering out of the darkness in her white nightdress.

"The path goes past the tennis courts to a narrow rocky beach you can swim off or picnic on. We think Rice put it there."

"It's all so peaceful, so beautiful," Ami said. "It's hard to imagine a murder happening here."

"It's our first and only one, thank God."

Ami wandered back across the lawn. The curtains were closed, but there was a slit between the curtains and the sill. She looked into the kitchen.

"That's new," Harney said. "The Reynoldses put in the island and the convection oven. Those marble countertops weren't there either."

Ami wondered how much remodeling you would have to do before the ghosts left you alone. She turned away from the house.

"Thanks for the tour."

"Did you learn anything helpful?" the sheriff asked.

"No. Maybe there'll be something in the files."

# CHAPTER **TWENTY-THREE**

The file for the Glass murder was waiting for Ami when she and Sheriff Harney returned from the lake. She went through everything, including the pictures from the crime scene. Ami had never seen a murdered man, and the way Glass had been killed was so horrible that she felt light-headed after looking at the photographs.

The only new information Ami gleaned from the file was that no army records were inventoried during the search of Glass's house. Either Vanessa was lying and she had never brought the files to Glass or Rice had taken them with him when he fled. One thing in Vanessa's and Rice's favor was the fact that they had both told the same story about the records, and Ami was certain that they'd had no opportunity to talk since Carl had been arrested. Of course, the fact that Vanessa had found records of military personnel, including Carl, in her father's safe didn't necessarily mean that the secret unit existed.

Ami had just finished her review when her cell

phone rang. It was Mary O'Dell, the friend who was watching Ryan.

"Thank God I got you," Mary said. "You've got to come home."

"What happened?" Ami asked, terrified that Ryan had been hurt.

"The police were here. They're looking for you."

"Me? What for?"

"That man who was staying with you escaped. It's all over the news."

Ami raced to the San Francisco airport and caught the first flight to Portland. Detective Walsh had left a number with Mary, and Ami had phoned him while she waited for her flight to leave. Walsh confirmed that her client had escaped from the security ward but was unwilling to give Ami any more information over the phone.

Walsh had sent a policeman to the airport and he was waiting at the gate when Ami landed in Portland. TV crews and a larger than normal contingent of police cars had ramped up the usual chaos that was endemic to any hospital. Ami's escort led her through the media mob in the lobby and into an elevator. Their car stopped and Ami walked into a crowd of forensic experts, uniformed officers, and men in suits. She spotted Brendan Kirkpatrick talking to a police officer near the door to the security ward. He stopped in mid-sentence when he saw Ami.

"Mrs. Vergano. Nice to see you," he said coldly.

"What happened?"

"Your lodger escaped with the help of a woman. You're lucky you were in California, or I'd have you in custody."

Ami's eyes widened with fear and her breath caught in her chest.

"I don't know anything about this. I didn't help him escape."

"Who didn't you help escape, Mrs. Vergano? What's your client's real name, and who is the woman?"

Ami felt awful. "I can't answer your questions, Brendan. My client told the answers to me in confidence. They're privileged."

"We'll see about that. I'm going to haul you in front of a judge first thing in the morning."

"You have to believe me," Ami pleaded. "I'd help if I could."

Kirkpatrick's shoulders sagged and he let out a deep breath. "There I go yelling at you again. I'm sorry. I'm just exhausted and frustrated."

"Believe me, I'd cooperate if I thought I could. I'll tell you everything I know if the judge orders me to talk to you."

It suddenly dawned on Ami that Carl had been locked in the ward and guarded by a policeman and at least two orderlies.

"Was anyone hurt?" she asked.

"Your client pistol-whipped one of the orderlies. He had to have some stitches. Everyone else is okay."

"How did he escape?"

"The woman posed as an aide to a television

producer and conned Dr. Ganett into taking her into the ward. I guess he didn't learn anything from his experience with you."

Ami flushed.

"The orderlies were so excited about being on TV that they didn't search her. She had two guns in her purse. Rice and the woman locked everyone in an empty room and disappeared. As of now, we have no idea where they are or what they're driving."

Kirkpatrick was starting to say something else when Detective Walsh walked out of the elevator. He looked upset.

"Excuse us, Mrs. Vergano," Walsh said as he pulled the prosecutor out of earshot. As Walsh spoke, Ami could see Kirkpatrick getting more and more agitated. She heard him swear. Then the two men strode back to her.

"No more games, Ami," Kirkpatrick said, his temper barely under control. "We need the name of the woman, and anything else you can tell us, now."

"What happened?"

"Dr. George French is dead, murdered," Walsh said.

Ami blanched and her legs gave out. Kirkpatrick grabbed her arm to keep her from falling.

"Get her some water," the DA told Walsh as he helped Ami to the chair at the orderly's station. By the time Walsh returned with a cup of water tears were coursing down Ami's cheeks.

"He was such a good man," she sobbed. Kirk-

patrick looked at sea but Walsh knelt next to Ami
and helped her sip from the cup.

"You've got to help us, Ami," the detective said.
"Do you know who the woman is? Do you have
any idea where they're going?"

"What makes you think my client killed Dr.
French?" Ami asked. The question sounded more
like a plea for help.

"We don't, but this is a hell of a coincidence."

A horrible thought suddenly occurred to Ami.
"How . . . how was George . . . ?"

Walsh seemed reluctant to answer her. "It looks
like he was kidnapped from his home and taken
to his office," he said.

"Was he shot?" Ami asked, hoping that Walsh
would say that this was the way that the psychiatrist's life had been taken.

"No." Walsh hesitated again.

"Please, it's important."

"He was tortured, then his throat was cut."

Ami squeezed her eyes shut. She felt sick. She
wanted to take Ryan and run somewhere, far away,
but there was something she had to do first.

"Will you take me to the murder scene?"

"I don't think . . . " Walsh started.

"Please," she said, remembering the crime
scene photos in the Glass file. "I can't explain
why, but I've got to go to the crime scene."

On the ride over, Ami learned that one of the
cleaning crew in French's office building had discovered the doctor's body. A police car had been

sent to French's house, where the body of his wife had been found. Walsh thought that the Frenches had been asleep when the killer broke in. His bedroom and den had been ransacked, but Walsh didn't think that the killer found what he was looking for because he had brought the psychiatrist downtown and the safe and the filing cabinets in French's office were open and files were strewn about.

When they arrived at French's office building, Ami was escorted to French's suite. As they walked from the reception area to the doctor's office, Kirkpatrick became aware of the nauseating stench exuded by the newly dead that permeated every murder scene. He glanced at Ami. Her complexion was pasty and she was unsteady on her feet.

"Are you certain that you want to do this?" he asked.

Ami nodded because she was holding her breath to block the smell. She hoped she wouldn't be sick.

When they arrived at the door to the office Ami squeezed her eyes shut, then opened them slowly to control her view of the body. The office could have passed for a slaughterhouse. Blood had sprayed across the coffee table and the rug. Her stomach churned. Bile rose in her throat.

Ami focused on two bare feet that were taped to the base of a chair in the center of the room. The feet were bloodstained. Someone had beaten them. Ami remembered what Carl Rice had said about the penchant his Vietnamese captors had for torturing his feet. Her eyes moved upward. French was wearing blood-spattered pajama bottoms. Ami gulped some air and vowed to get this over with. She raised her head and looked at what was left of George French. He had been taped to a chair. He was bare-chested and there were cuts all over his torso. His throat had been cut. She was looking at a mirror image of the crime scene in the home of Congressman Eric Glass.

Ami stumbled out of the room. Kirkpatrick half-carried the attorney to the reception area. He settled her on the couch and handed her a bottle of water he'd had the foresight to bring with him. Walsh and Kirkpatrick waited anxiously for Ami to calm down.

"Can you tell us the name of the woman and Morelli's real name?"

Ami looked as if she was on the verge of a nervous breakdown. "I don't know what to do. I'd have to break their confidences," she said, her voice a tremor away from a sob.

"Can you at least tell us if something you saw in French's office makes you think Morelli did this?" Walsh pressed. "That would be your idea, not something your client said."

"He did it," Ami said. "I can't tell you how I know, but I know."

"Brendan, get this in front of a judge first thing. In the meantime I'm putting some men outside Mrs. Vergano's house tonight."

"Why?" Ami asked in disbelief.

"Morelli didn't run," Walsh answered. "He

stayed in Portland knowing that every policeman in the city was looking for him. I think he's trying to destroy the record of what he told you and French. If you hadn't been out of town, I think you'd be dead too."

Ami was already frightened. Now she was terrified.

"Surely, he won't come after me now. He'll think I've spoken to you."

"He can't be certain that you've told us what you know. He may take the chance that you've honored the attorney-client privilege and kept your mouth shut. If he plans to kill you to keep you quiet, he'll have to move tonight. I've already sent a car to Mary O'Dell's house to make sure your son is protected."

"Oh, God," Ami moaned. She slumped forward. "What do you want me to do?"

"Go home and try to rest," Kirkpatrick said. "You'll collapse if you don't."

"No, I want to see Ryan."

"That's not a good idea," Walsh said. "If Morelli is coming after you, you don't want to be anywhere near your son."

# CHAPTER **TWENTY-FOUR**

Emily Hobson, Victor Hobson's wife of fifteen years, had supper waiting when he arrived home a little after eight. Two years before he met Emily, Victor had been engaged to a teller he'd met while investigating a bank robbery. His fiancée had broken off the engagement because she couldn't put up with his erratic hours and his refusal to discuss the details of his work. Emily was a fingerprint examiner in the FBI lab. She'd retired after their second child was born. Victor worried that she would be bored silly if she stayed at home, but she had surprised him by being perfectly content to raise their children and put up with him. Victor knew that he'd been lucky to find someone who understood his job from the inside.

After dinner, Victor checked on his children. His son was working furiously at a video game, and his daughter was talking on the phone with her best friend. They both grunted at him—a clear indication that they wished to be alone—so Victor walked downstairs and turned on CNN.

The Supreme Court had heard another case involving *Miranda* rights; a suicide bomber had killed seven people in a café in Jerusalem; and there had been a surprise development in the Little League case.

As the newscaster discussed the breaking story in Oregon, the station ran a clip of the brawl that had led to the arrest of a Little League coach on multiple assault counts. Victor stood up when the handheld camera focused on the face of the man the announcer identified as Daniel Morelli. The announcer explained that an unknown woman had helped Morelli escape from the security ward at the county hospital where the defendant had been imprisoned. A police artist's sketch of the woman and a mug shot of Morelli flashed on the screen.

Hobson had flown to Lost Lake shortly after the murder of Congressman Eric Glass. Vanessa Wingate had already been removed from the hospital by her father. The only positive result of his trip had been an opportunity to look through Carl Rice's army records, which had been supplied to the sheriff by Vanessa's father. Hobson still had a copy of the file, which contained the only photograph he had been able to locate of Rice. The face in the mug shot was older and careworn, but there was no question in Hobson's mind that Daniel Morelli was Carl Rice.

The newscasters started talking about a plane crash in Brazil, and Hobson turned off the set. The day after Morris Wingate had declared his intention to challenge President Charles Jennings for his party's nomination, Hobson had received a call from Ted Schoonover, an ex-CIA man who was the president's chief troubleshooter. Schoonover had invited him to breakfast at a Greek restaurant in a strip mall in a Maryland suburb. Hobson was willing to bet that no one with any clout in D.C. had ever set eyes on the place. Schoonover was a short, chubby man with thinning hair and a double chin, certainly not the type of person you would notice in a crowd. After their meeting, Hobson had run a check on him. Except for some basic employment information, Schoonover's file was eerily blank. Hobson had been able to determine little more than the fact that Schoonover had served with Charles Jennings when Jennings was the director of the CIA. When Hobson tried to get more information about the ex-spook he was told that he was not cleared to look at the relevant files.

Over breakfast, Schoonover had asked Hobson if he'd heard Wingate's announcement. Then he asked the FBI man to brief him on the events at Lost Lake and their aftermath. When Hobson was finished, Schoonover asked if there was any new information on the whereabouts of Carl Rice. Hobson had told Schoonover that he'd had no new information about Rice since the mid-1980s. Schoonover told Hobson that the president wanted to know immediately whenever there were any developments in the case.

Hobson had not contacted Schoonover after his phone conversation with Vanessa Wingate, because he had nothing concrete to report. Now he took Schoonover's business card out of his wallet and dialed the cell phone number that the president's aide had written on the back.

"Talk to me," Schoonover said after three rings.

"This is Victor Hobson. There's been a new development in that matter we discussed."

"You up for a late-night snack?"

"The same place?"

"See you in a half hour."

A sign on the door said that The Acropolis closed at eleven P.M., but Ted Schoonover was sitting inside eating baklava and sipping thick Greek coffee when Hobson parked outside at eleven-thirty. Before Hobson could knock, a balding man wearing a white apron let him in, then relocked the door.

"You want some coffee? The baklava is the best," Schoonover said.

"I'm fine."

"Then fill me in."

"Vanessa Wingate called me a few days ago and said that she knew how to find Carl Rice, but she wouldn't tell me anything else. I had her call traced to a motel, but the clerk said that she'd checked out. I questioned her boyfriend. He says that he has no idea where she went. I didn't call you, because I didn't have anything solid and Vanessa is—well, to put it charitably—odd. She was raving about her father trying to kill her. The boyfriend told me that she'd called 911 and told the cops that he was being attacked in their apartment when that wasn't true."

"Where is this going?"

"Have you heard about the brawl at that Little League game in Oregon?"

"I read something about it."

"I think Carl Rice is the man the police arrested at the game. I'm pretty sure that he was in Portland, Oregon, as of last night."

"What do you mean, 'was'?"

"A woman broke him out of the security ward of the county hospital."

Schoonover stopped eating and gave Hobson his full attention.

"On TV tonight, they showed a mug shot of the man who escaped. The newscaster called him Daniel Morelli. I can't be certain, because the photo in Rice's file was taken when he was in his twenties and the man in the mug shot is years older, but it definitely looks like Rice, and the artist's sketch of the woman looked a lot like Vanessa Wingate."

"What are you planning to do?"

"I thought I'd send an agent out to Portland to keep tabs on the manhunt."

Schoonover thought while he dabbed at his lips with a napkin.

"No," he said after a moment's reflection. "You take care of this personally."

"I'm an assistant director. I can't go running off to Oregon for God knows how long. Rice has hidden successfully for twenty years. I have no idea how long it will take for the police to find him."

"Don't worry about your other work. I'll take care of that with the director. You'll offer FBI assistance on this. Once Rice is arrested, you'll call me and I'll take over. Your job is to make certain that no one gets to this guy before I do. No one, is that understood?"

# CHAPTER **TWENTY-FIVE**

Ami nodded off twice during the ride home, but fear erased her fatigue when the patrol car parked in front of her house. Ami and Ryan lived in a yellow-and-white farmhouse surrounded by dense woods. It had a quaint front porch with a swing that she and Chad had rocked in on warm summer nights after Ryan went to sleep. In daylight, it was a picture-postcard house. Tonight, when Ami looked at the woods she painted and the home she knew so well, she saw dark places where a murderer could hide.

One of the officers stood watch while Ami waited in the car. The other officer used Ami's keys to unlock her front door. When he was satisfied that no one was hiding in the house, the two policemen escorted her inside. While Ami went upstairs to get ready for bed, one officer took up a post in the living room and the second went outside to patrol the grounds. Ami felt better after a shower, though she was certain that she could not possibly fall asleep. For a while her thoughts kept her in turmoil, but she was so exhausted physically and emotionally that she soon drifted off.

Ami's eyes snapped open. She stared bleary-eyed at the clock on her end table. It was one-forty-six in the morning, and the room was pitch-black. The thud of a heavy object falling had jerked her out of her deep sleep, but she wasn't certain that she hadn't dreamed the sound.

Ami sat up and listened. She heard nothing but the ticking of the grandfather clock in her downstairs hallway. The clock was an antique that Chad had loved. The metallic tock of the moving hands could be heard clearly in the middle of the night and had always bothered Ami, but she could not bring herself to get rid of the clock after Chad died. Now it was the only sound she could hear. She had almost convinced herself that the sound that had awakened her was a figment of her imagination when a floorboard creaked.

Someone was walking up the stairs and trying to be quiet about it. Ami got out of bed. Her heart beat furiously until she remembered that there was a policeman in the house. She was chiding herself for being a fool when her doorknob started to turn.

Ami rushed to the door and braced against it. The knob stopped turning.

"Who's out there?"

The wooden door shattered and flew into the room. Splinters stabbed Ami, and the sharp edge of the door struck her forehead, knocking her onto the bed. A shadow loomed over her. Dressed all in black, the man seemed part of the darkness. He raised a brutal knife whose serrated blade shone in the moonlight. Ami rolled off the bed to the floor and had scrambled to her knees when she was jerked up by her hair. The pain was excruciating. She screamed and the grip on her hair relaxed. Ami rolled to her back, her hands up in self-defense. Her attacker collapsed on top of her. Ami screamed again as she shoved at the weight that crushed her to the floor. The killer did not strike at her and his body barely moved. Over his shoulder, Ami saw another man whose face was concealed by a ski mask identical to the one the first assailant had worn. Ami scuttled from under the first man's body until her back was pressed against the wall.

"It's me," a familiar voice said.

The man peeled back his ski mask. Carl Rice stood above her, a large, blood-covered knife in his right hand. Rice saw where she was looking and laid it on the floor.

"It's okay. I'm not going to hurt you. I heard about Dr. French on the radio and I knew they'd come for you."

Ami had never been so close to death and she was having trouble breathing.

"I'm going to help you stand up," Rice said. "Let's get you away from the body."

Carl reached down and helped Ami to her feet. She moved sideways so she would not have to touch the corpse but she could not take her eyes off of the dead man.

"Who is he?" Ami asked, terrified that she knew the answer.

"It's one of Wingate's men."

"Oh, no," Ami moaned, overwhelmed by the idea that someone as powerful as the General was after her.

"This is the worst possible time for me to come back from the dead," Rice said. "Wingate knows that eventually the police will figure out that I'm wanted for the murder of a general and a congressman. He's got to be terrified that I'll barter information about the Unit for a lighter sentence. If President Jennings raises serious questions about the Unit, Wingate's presidential hopes go down the tube. That's why Dr. French was killed. Wingate had to find out what I told you and the doctor, and who else knows. Ami, did you tell the police about our conversations?"

Rice's reference to the police made Ami remember her guards.

"What happened to the two officers who . . . ?"

Carl shook his head. "I was too late."

"Those poor men, they were only here to help me."

Ami started to sob. Rice gripped her upper arms. "You've got to pull yourself together. We don't have time for this."

"*We* don't have time?" Ami yelled as anger replaced her despair. "You're the cause of all this. Those men would be alive if it weren't for you."

"And you would be dead," Rice answered calmly, "and you may be dead soon if we stand here debating who's responsible for what. When

Wingate's men don't report in, he'll send more. Now tell me what you told the police about the Unit."

"The police don't know anything. I told them what you said was privileged." Suddenly a picture of George French's ravaged body flashed in Ami's mind and she shuddered. "Wingate's men must know what you told us. George was tortured just the way you tortured Eric Glass."

"Do the police think I killed French?"

Ami nodded. "I saw the crime scene photographs at Lost Lake. I thought . . . "

"Of course you did. What else were you supposed to think?" Rice placed his hands on Ami's shoulders. "There's only one way you can save yourself. You have to tell that DA, Kirkpatrick, about the Unit. Wingate won't have a reason to kill you if other people know my story. Get dressed. I'll take you to police headquarters and drop you off." Rice pointed at the corpse. "He's your proof."

Ami grabbed some clothes and a pair of sneakers and went into the bathroom while Rice searched the dead man. When she came out he was holding a pistol that he'd taken from the killer.

Carl led Ami downstairs in the dark and out the back door. They circled through the woods that bordered her property and came out on a logging road about a quarter-mile from the farmhouse. Ami saw the outline of a car in the dark. Carl aimed a penlight at the front window and turned it on and off. The engine started, and Carl raced to the car with Ami in tow. Ami jumped into the back, Rice got into the front passenger seat, and Vanessa started driving.

"We're going to drop Ami at police headquarters," Rice said.

Vanessa was about to respond when Ami pointed down the road. "What's that?"

A car was barreling toward them with its lights off. Carl opened his window and fired across the hood. An answering shot blew out Vanessa's left front headlight. Carl fired again and the other car's windshield shattered. Almost instantly the car careened off the road. When they sped past, Ami saw the driver slumped over the steering wheel.

"Move!" Carl ordered Vanessa. She floored the accelerator and Ami flew back in her seat.

Two men had leaped out of the wrecked car and were firing at them. Carl pushed Ami to the floor as a bullet ricocheted off the trunk leaving a trail of sparks. Ami rolled back and forth on the floor as Vanessa sped out of range.

"You can sit up now," Rice said when he was sure that they were safe.

"Where are we going after we drop off Ami?" Vanessa asked.

"I don't know," he answered. "We need a place to hole up until the hunt dies down. Then we can try to figure out how to get out of the country."

"I have an idea," Ami said. "When I was at my old firm I bought a cabin with two other couples. It's on the coast. I'm pretty sure no one is using it this week. You can stay there."

"Thanks for the offer but I'll pass," Rice said.

"Why? It's pretty isolated. No one will look for you there."

"If the police find out you helped us they'll arrest you. I'm not going to risk that."

"You just saved my life, Carl. I'd be dead and Ryan would be an orphan if it weren't for you." Ami took a key off of her key chain. "I'm willing to take a chance for someone who took a big one for me. Use the cabin."

# CHAPTER **TWENTY-SIX**

Ami was drinking a cup of coffee when Walsh and Kirkpatrick burst into the interrogation room where she had been waiting for the past half hour. She was wearing jeans and a sweatshirt and looked like hell.

"Is Ryan safe?" she asked before they could say anything.

"He's fine," Walsh assured her. "I sent an extra car over there to be sure. Tell us what happened at your house."

"The policemen who were guarding me are dead. I would be dead too if Carl hadn't saved me."

"Who is Carl?" Walsh asked.

"My client's real name is Carl Rice, not Daniel Morelli. The woman who helped him escape is Vanessa Wingate. She's the daughter of General Morris Wingate."

"The Wingate who's running for president of the United States?" Walsh asked.

Ami nodded.

"Holy shit."

Brendan Kirkpatrick imagined the consequences to his career of issuing an APB for the daughter of a man who was the front-runner for his party's presidential nomination.

"Okay, Ami," he said. "Let's start at the beginning. What does the daughter of a presidential candidate have to do with an itinerant carpenter who got into a fight at a Little League game?"

For the next half hour Ami told the prosecutor and the detective the stories Carl and Vanessa had told her. They both listened intently, and Walsh took notes. When Ami was almost finished an officer came into the interrogation room and started to speak to Walsh. The detective stopped him and they left the room. Moments later Walsh reentered the room. He looked concerned.

"The men I sent to your house just reported in. They found the officers. They're dead. But there aren't any other bodies at your house."

Ami was stunned. "That's impossible."

"Did you see the men who murdered the officers?" Walsh asked.

"Weren't you listening? One of them attacked me with a knife!"

"Calm down," Kirkpatrick said.

"Do you think I'm lying? Do you think I made this up?"

"No one is accusing you of lying," Kirkpatrick said. "It's just that . . . Well, the whole story sounds . . ."

"Unbelievable?" Ami finished for him. "Don't you think I know that?"

There was an uncomfortable silence in the room. Ami used the moment to think.

"Vanessa was parked on a logging road behind my house when Carl saved me. After we got out of the house, Carl and Vanessa drove me here. While we were still on the logging road, men in another car attacked us. Carl shot the driver and they crashed. The car must not have been too badly damaged and they must have driven to my house and taken the bodies away."

Before Kirkpatrick could respond, the door to the interrogation room opened and a large man with granite features walked in followed by two other men in crisp blue pinstripe suits.

"Who are you?" Kirkpatrick snapped.

"I'm Victor Hobson, the executive assistant director for law enforcement services at the FBI. These are agents McCollum and Haggard. I understand that you had Carl Rice in your custody and you let him escape. I'm here to help you get him back."

Walsh and Kirkpatrick exchanged glances.

"How did you know our prisoner's name was Carl Rice?" the DA asked.

"I've been hunting Rice since 1985. He's wanted for the murders of United States Congressman Eric Glass and General Peter Rivera. The woman who helped him escape is probably Vanessa Kohler, General Morris Wingate's daughter."

"Mr. Hobson," Kirkpatrick said, "I've got a question to ask you, but I'd like to hear what you

can tell us about Rice and Vanessa Wingate first.
Will you fill us in on what you know?"

"In 1985, Congressman Eric Glass was tortured
and murdered in his summer home on Lost Lake,
California. A deputy sheriff found Vanessa
Wingate wandering around the grounds in a
daze. She identified Carl Rice as the killer, but
there was nothing beyond her statement connecting Rice to the crime. I was sent to investigate because the victim was a member of
Congress. By the time I got to Lost Lake, General
Wingate had taken his daughter out of the local
hospital and had committed her to a private
mental hospital. She was there for a year and the
medical staff prevented me from talking to her
during her stay.

"I learned that Rice had dated Ms. Wingate when
they were in high school and had bumped into her
again in Washington, D.C., a month or so before
the congressman was killed. I also learned that
Rice had recently been discharged from the military for psychiatric reasons. The prevailing theory
is that if Rice murdered Glass, he did it out of jealousy.

"Several months after Eric Glass was murdered,
General Peter Rivera was tortured and murdered
in Maryland. The MO was identical to the
method used in the Glass killing. Physical evidence at the scene of the Rivera murder linked
Rice to the crime.

"I interviewed Ms. Wingate after her release
from the hospital. She was estranged from her fa-

ther and calling herself Vanessa Kohler. Kohler
was her mother's maiden name. Ms. Kohler confirmed that she saw Rice kill the congressman.
She denied that she and Glass were lovers but refused to tell me why she was at Glass's house."
He paused for a minute, then shrugged. "And
that's the sum total of my knowledge about the
case. You said you had a question for me."

"Mr. Hobson, did you ever hear that Carl Rice
was a member of a secret army unit run by General Wingate?" Kirkpatrick asked.

"That's what Vanessa claimed in an unpub-
lished book she's written, but Rice's army records
don't support her accusations. From what I've
learned Vanessa hates her father. She believes
that he murdered her mother. She also believes
that he killed John F. Kennedy."

Kirkpatrick and Walsh stared at each other in
disbelief.

"You've got to be kidding," the prosecutor said.

"Then she's nuts?" the detective added.

"Vanessa is a very troubled woman with a lot of
odd ideas. She works for one of those supermarket tabloids that run stories on alien abductions
and Elvis sightings."

"We've just learned that Carl Rice claims that
the Unit is real and that he worked in it for the
General," Walsh said.

"Yes, well, I'm inclined to think that we're dealing with two mentally disturbed individuals who
are feeding off each other's fantasy. It's even possible that Vanessa murdered the congressman and
framed Rice for it."

"Then why would he help Vanessa?" Ami asked.

"And you are?" Hobson asked.

"Ami Vergano. Carl was renting an apartment over my garage. He was helping out at my son's Little League game when he hurt Barney Lutz and that officer."

"Ms. Vergano is Rice's lawyer," Kirkpatrick added.

"I see," Hobson said. "Well, Ms. Vergano, if Rice is crazy, and he's in love with Vanessa Wingate, he might do anything."

"Mr. Hobson," Ami said, "a man broke into my house tonight. He murdered two policemen and tried to kill me. Carl saved me. Doesn't that make you think that Carl and Vanessa might be telling the truth about the General and the Unit?"

"Morris Wingate's company has its own security force. If the General thought that Rice was a danger to his daughter, he might have sent them after him."

"But they killed the policemen."

"Did you see them do that?" Walsh asked.

Ami paused. When she answered she was less sure of herself. "I saw Carl kill the man who broke into my room. He told me that the men had murdered my guards."

"There you have it," Hobson said. "Isn't it possible that Rice killed the policemen and Wingate's men arrived at your house shortly afterward? Rice could have ambushed them and told you that he saved you."

"Look," Walsh interrupted, "this speculation is

getting us nowhere. It doesn't matter whether or not this Unit exists. Rice broke out of jail and Vanessa Wingate helped him. They're fugitives and they're armed and dangerous. We need to arrest them. We can sort out these big issues once they're locked up."

# CHAPTER **TWENTY-SEVEN**

Vanessa drove west from Portland on back roads until she hit US 101, the narrow highway that runs from Washington to California along Oregon's scenic coastline. If it had been daylight Carl and Vanessa would have seen stunning rock formations jutting out of the Pacific, massive sand dunes, and stands of evergreen, but they drove in the dead of night and all they saw was the eerie glow of whitecaps floating like ghosts in the darkness when the highway drew close to the ocean.

Ami had told them where the unpaved dirt road to the cabin joined the highway. Her directions were good and they found the turnoff easily. The car bounced along for a quarter of a mile. Then the headlights illuminated a two-story house with gray siding that had been weathered by the constant battering of the sea air. The cabin backed on the beach and was surrounded by woods.

Carl and Vanessa realized that they were starving. Vanessa had planned ahead. She had a duffel bag filled with provisions in the trunk, along with another bag filled with clothes. The first thing they did when they were inside was check the refrigerator so that they wouldn't have to waste their food. They found cold beer and soda, some frozen food in the freezer compartment, and canned goods in the pantry. Carl fixed dinner using some of the food from the duffel bag and some of the food that was already in the house.

When they were finished eating, Carl cleaned up while Vanessa walked through the rest of the cabin. Besides the kitchen, there was a small living room and a half bath on the first floor. A back door opened onto a sandy yard that overlooked the beach. Upstairs were three small bedrooms. Vanessa was standing in one of them when she heard Carl come up behind her. He placed his hands on her shoulders. She felt the warmth through her shirt and turned into his arms.

"I don't think I've thanked you yet," he said.

Vanessa smiled. "We've been a little busy."

Carl slid his arms down to Vanessa's waist and kissed her. His kiss was tentative but her answering kiss was not. Carl took a deep breath.

"You need to get some rest," he said.

Vanessa ran her hand along his chest. "Care to join me?"

"Not tonight. I have to stand guard."

"No one is going to find us here. You need sleep, too."

"I dozed in the car. And we don't know what type of surveillance equipment Wingate has. For all we know, he's been using a satellite to track

us." Carl kissed her forehead. "So get to sleep.
One of us has to be fresh in the morning."

Vanessa opened the window and let in the cold
sea air, suddenly exhausted. She kicked off her
shoes and slid between the sheets. It seemed to
her that she had slept only a few minutes when
an insistent tapping on her shoulder brought her
out of a dark dream. There was a hand across her
mouth and she panicked until she realized that it
was Carl's.

"They're here," he whispered.

Vanessa stepped into her shoes, took her Magnum out of her purse, and followed Carl to the
back door. On the way down the stairs, Carl told
her that they couldn't take the car because they
would have to drive through Wingate's men,
who would blow it to pieces.

"We'll get into the woods behind the house and
keep moving," Carl said. "I didn't see a landing
party on the beach. They'll come at us from the
front and circle around."

"I'll slow you down, Carl. I'll make noise.
They'll hear me."

"You didn't forget about me and I'm not leaving you."

She gripped his shoulder and stared into his
eyes. "Be smart. My father will kill you, but he
won't kill me. I'm his daughter. Get away, then
come for me if you can."

Carl started to argue but she sealed his lips with
a finger. "We don't have time. Go."

Carl realized that Vanessa had sized up the situation correctly. He could move through the woods like a ghost, but Vanessa had no training and she'd give them both away.

"I'll come for you," Carl said. Then he kissed her hard and ran out the back door. Vanessa looked over her shoulder and saw him disappear into the woods heading north as she headed south, hoping to bring as many men as possible after her.

The backyard was small, and she was into the woods in no time. Over the years, a footpath had been worn through the underbrush, but she was afraid to follow it because that's where her pursuers would go. Vanessa left the trail and tried to push through the thick foliage without making noise. A little light, cast down from a quarter-moon, filtered through the upper branches. Vanessa had gone only a few steps in the dark when a branch snapped across her cheek, drawing blood. She gritted her teeth against the sharp pain and stumbled over a root, tumbling to the ground. She was about to stand when a man materialized out of the darkness a few feet from her. He carried an automatic weapon that was only slightly larger than Vanessa's Magnum.

Vanessa gripped her gun tightly as the man disappeared into the foliage. She didn't know what to do. She had made a lot of noise during the short time she'd been in the woods. She would make more if she left her hiding place. After some thought, she decided to stay where she was and hope Wingate's men would go away if they

didn't find her. She had just made her decision
when her gun was plucked from her hand.
Vanessa swung around.

"It's me, Vanessa. Don't be afraid."

Vanessa rose unsteadily. Her legs were shaking
and her breath was tight in her chest.

"Sam?" she asked.

"Everything will be okay now."

Vanessa took a step back and bumped into another man who was right behind her.

"Don't worry," Sam Cutler said. "You're safe.
I'm going to take you to the General."

Vanessa's mouth gaped open and her eyes
widened. "You work for my father?"

"Your dad was worried about you, especially
when he made his decision to run for president.
He was afraid you'd do something crazy and he
wanted to protect you."

Vanessa's eyes blazed with hate, and her rage
built like a hurricane. She had cared about this
man; she had taken him into her bed and her
heart. She remembered how frightened she'd
been when she thought that her father might
hurt him. Now she felt like a fool.

Vanessa drew her arm back to hit Sam and the
man behind her caught her wrist in an iron grip.

"You bastard," Vanessa screamed as she struggled to break free.

"Please try to understand, Van. I know you're
angry but . . . "

Vanessa lashed out with her foot and caught
Cutler on the shin. The blow should have hurt
like hell but he didn't move.

"We don't have time for this, Vanessa. You're in great danger."

Vanessa tried to kick Cutler again, but he stepped out of range and she writhed with frustration.

"Please calm down. I know Rice has convinced you that he was a member of some secret group that your father ran, but it's not true. Carl Rice is a seriously disturbed man."

"Tell this ape to get his hands off me."

"I can't while you're like this. Now, please, tell me where Rice has gone."

"So you can kill him?"

"So we can capture him and return him to custody. Do you realize how much trouble you're in? You broke a killer out of jail."

"The General made him a killer."

"You've got that all wrong. I was in charge of Carl's first mission in Vietnam. We lost two men and Carl was in the middle of some terrible combat. He couldn't take it. He cracked up and had to be hospitalized. I don't think he ever recovered."

"No. Carl told me about that mission. He was very brave . . . "

"That's true, but a lot of brave men have breakdowns after combat situations. It's nothing to be ashamed of. For Carl, though . . . Well, I'm no shrink, but I guess he made up this fantasy world with this secret unit so he could handle it. He was at the language school until the army discovered how sick he really is and discharged him."

"No. Those army records are false. My father

made them up," Vanessa said, but some doubt had softened her conviction.

"Look, we really don't have time to discuss this now. Carl Rice is out there and he's armed. He killed two policemen and two of my men at Ami's house. I've got to get you to safety before he hurts you or any more of my men. So where is he?"

Vanessa was confused, but she was determined to protect Carl.

"I have no idea where Carl is. We split up. I told him to go. I knew I'd slow him down."

Cutler studied her for a moment and Vanessa held her breath.

"Okay, I believe you," Cutler said. "Carl's got to be out of practice. My boys will find him soon enough."

Sam looked at the man who was holding Vanessa. "Bring her to the car, and I'll join the hunt."

"How did you find us?" Vanessa asked to stall for time, knowing that every minute might help Carl get away.

"You made it easy. Remember when you called me from your hotel to tell me that you were okay?"

Vanessa nodded.

"After you hung up I hit Star 69 and read out your number. A pleasant young woman told me that I had reached the Portland Hilton. Once I knew where you were, one of my men followed you to your car and put a tracking device on it."

"So that's how you knew we were on that logging road behind Ami's house," Vanessa said.

Instead of answering, Sam Cutler nodded to the man who was holding Vanessa and she felt a needle prick her skin. She wanted to ask Sam what he'd done, but the words wouldn't come. Seconds later, she was unconscious in her captor's arms

Vanessa was semiconscious and disoriented when the car stopped. She thought she heard a small plane engine but couldn't be certain that she wasn't imagining the sound. The back door of the car opened. Cool air swept in and swept away a little more of the drug's effects. Before she could gather her wits, strong hands grabbed her and she was lifted out of the car. She stood unsteadily and looked around. The sun was just rising behind a hangar at a small airport. Several yards across the tarmac stood a black helicopter with a Computex logo.

"She's coming out of it," said the man who was propping her up.

"That's okay," Sam Cutler answered. "She's still too groggy to cause trouble. I'll give her a booster shot before we take off."

Vanessa was led across the tarmac. As she was lifted into the copter, Cutler pulled a cell phone out of his pocket and punched in a number.

"Mission accomplished," he told the person on the other end of the line. "See you tomorrow."

Cutler jumped into the copter and took the seat beside Vanessa.

"Where are we going?" she mumbled as Cutler strapped her in.

"Home," Sam answered. Then Vanessa felt a needle prick her skin and once again she slid into a velvet darkness that lifted hours later when the chopper set down on the helipad at her father's estate. Moments later, she was helped out of the plane and led across the lawn to the rear of the mansion. She knew she was home, but it felt as if she were dreaming.

"We've got a room waiting for you," Cutler said as he helped her up the back staircase to the second floor and down the hall to a room that had been used by the maids when her mother was alive. The General's staff was all male and former military.

"Your father is campaigning in Cleveland," Sam said as he took off her clothes and put her into a pair of pajamas. She vaguely recognized them as nightclothes she'd worn when she still lived at home. "He'll be here tomorrow and you two can get reacquainted. He's really worried about you."

Sam lifted the covers and helped Vanessa under them. It felt so good to lie down on soft sheets. Sam whispered, "Get a good rest, Van." Then there was another needle prick and the door closed. Vanessa heard a lock click into place. The last thought she had before she drifted off was that her father had kept her pajamas all these years.

# CHAPTER **TWENTY-EIGHT**

It was almost six-thirty when the strategy session ended at police headquarters. Adrenaline had kept Ami alert for hours, but Brendan Kirkpatrick saw her eyelids droop and her head nod more than once.

"You must be wasted," he said.

"It's starting to catch up with me," she conceded with a weary smile.

"I've arranged a room for you at the Heathman," Brendan said, naming a fine hotel that was only a few blocks from the Justice Center.

Ami looked alarmed. "I can't afford to stay there."

"Don't worry. The county ·is paying the tab until we're sure that it's safe for you and your son to go home. I also asked a policewoman to pick up some of your clothes from your house. They're in your hotel room along with your toothbrush, a comb and brush, and some other stuff from your bathroom. She also packed some of your son's clothes. If you need anything else, I'll send you home with a police escort."

"Thank you, Brendan."

"Hey, you're an important witness."

"It was very thoughtful."

"I'm glad you approve. Just don't drink too much booze from the minibar."

"I don't think I have the strength to open it, right now."

"Then I'd better walk you over to the hotel."

"You don't have to do that."

"I know, but I'm starving and we can both use some breakfast."

Ami had not realized how hungry she was until Brendan mentioned eating. Suddenly the prospect of a decent meal and clean sheets sounded like heaven.

Outside the Justice Center commuters were drifting into downtown Portland, but the streets were still quite empty. There were no lines at the parking garages, and only a few pedestrians, many clutching steaming lattes, walked toward their office buildings. Ami paused and blinked in the sunshine. She found the cool breeze blowing inland from the Willamette River refreshing after being cooped up in the interrogation room all night.

"It feels good to move," Brendan said.

"It would feel better to sleep."

"I know what you mean, but I don't think I'll be indulging in that luxury much until we catch Rice."

Brendan was being so nice that Ami felt guilty about not telling him that Carl and Vanessa were staying at the cabin. She had debated telling him where to find the fugitives more than once since walking into the Justice Center, but—despite what Hobson said—she believed that Carl and Vanessa had risked their lives to save her and she wasn't prepared to give them up.

"Do you agree with Hobson's take on what happened at my house—that Wingate sent men to rescue Vanessa and Carl killed them and the officers?"

"It makes sense."

"Why do you think Carl let me live? Why kill Dr. French and the policemen and not me?"

"Who knows how the mind of someone with his mental wiring works? Maybe French said something that made Rice think he was working with Wingate. Maybe Rice distrusts psychiatrists but sees you as one of the good guys."

"I guess that's as good an explanation as any, but I still think it's possible that he did save me. If he's telling the truth, General Wingate has a powerful motive to kill Carl and anyone else, like George and me, who Carl told about the Unit."

"If the Unit exists. We only have Rice's word for that."

Ami was too tired to argue and she was relieved when she saw the Heathman across the street. The hotel restaurant had just opened and there were only a few other diners. The hostess seated Brendan and Ami by the window and a waiter brought them water. Ami ordered a light meal and Brendan ordered pancakes.

"I want to see Ryan," Ami said as soon as the waiter left.

"He can stay with you until it's safe to go home. I bet he'll get a kick out of living in a hotel for a few days."

"He will. He's very curious." Ami smiled. "Sometimes he drives me crazy with all his questions."

"I understand he was pretty upset after the game."

"He's better now, but it's been tough on him. He really likes Carl and he still has nightmares about what happened. He doesn't need more violence in his life. It took him a long time to get over the death of his father."

"That must have been tough for both of you."

"Chad was a great father. A great husband, too."

Ami choked up for a moment. She was tired and it was tough to control her emotions.

"I know. Betty Sato told me," Kirkpatrick said so that she wouldn't have to talk about something that obviously still hurt.

"Ryan was my lifeline, Brendan. He kept me going. If he hadn't been there I don't know what I would have done."

"You would have done okay. You're tough. You don't take shit from anyone, certainly not from me."

He smiled. Ami thought of Brendan's own situation, carrying on bravely despite losing someone he loved.

"How did you do it, all by yourself?"

"I put one foot in front of the other and kept walking. I'm still walking. I'm afraid to stop. I guess I don't have to tell you."

The waiter appeared with their order. They both looked grateful for the interruption.

"I'll check you in after breakfast," Brendan said as soon as they were alone. "Then I'll arrange to have Ryan picked up from school and brought here."

"This is awfully nice of you."

"I'm trying to make up for the way I treated you when we first met. I feel guilty about that."

"Yeah, you were a bit of a shit," Ami answered with a grin. "But I forgive you."

"Good. I don't want you mad at me, at least, not when we're out of court."

# CHAPTER **TWENTY-NINE**

Carl had doubled back after laying a false trail that he hoped would lead his trackers south. From his position behind a tree several yards away, he'd heard everything that Sam Cutler said to Vanessa and he'd seen Cutler give the order to inject her.

Carl was certain that he had met Cutler twice before, only Wingate's man had called himself Paul Molineaux during Carl's first combat mission and the mission to rescue the MIAs. Carl debated killing Cutler and the man who was holding Vanessa, but he rejected the idea. Cutler was right. Carl was out of practice. In his twenties, he could have taken both men out with a handgun from this distance, but Vanessa might die if he couldn't get his shots off quickly enough or—which was equally possible—if he missed. Carl decided that his best course of action was to wait until Vanessa's guard took her to the car, but he had to reject that plan when two more men materialized at Cutler's side.

"We lost him," one said.

"Okay," Sam answered. "We'll never get him in the dark after he's had this much time to get away. Let's bring the General's daughter home."

Carl watched them go. He'd heard what Cutler had said about the tracking device. When he was certain that Cutler and his men had gone, he disabled it. As he drove, he started working on a plan for rescuing Vanessa.

Carl abandoned Vanessa's car in a supermarket parking lot, stole a nondescript Chevrolet, and headed south using back roads. It took him a full day to drive down the coast. On the way, he listened to the radio for the political news. Wingate was giving a speech in Cleveland. If the General went straight home, he and Carl would arrive at the mansion at about the same time.

After nightfall, Carl broke into a sporting goods store in a small town near San Diego and stole a pair of stiff-soled trail shoes, binoculars, a wetsuit, a fishing bow and arrows, several lengths of sturdy rope, and the strongest fishing line he could find. He put his booty into one of Vanessa's duffel bags and drove toward a beach a few miles south of the General's estate, where he'd hung out when he was a student at St. Martin's Prep.

There were no cars in the narrow lot when Carl parked around midnight and changed into his wetsuit. The beach was deserted, too. Carl strapped the duffel bag across his back and started swimming up the coast. Fighting through the rolling water was exhausting, but thoughts of Vanessa kept him plowing ahead. Carl knew that getting into the mansion and rescuing her would be much harder than the swim. No matter how many times Carl fine-tuned his plan, it sounded suicidal.

"Getting old is a bitch," Rice thought as he dragged his aching body and the duffel bag out of the surf and onto the beach behind the stone jetty at the end of Morris Wingate's property. He flopped down on the sand to catch his breath. For most of his life, Carl had been in the type of shape that let him endure almost any physical hardship with a minimum of wear and tear; but now he was almost fifty and his body did not hold up the way it used to, no matter how much he worked out. Then there was the fact that he had still not fully recovered from being shot. The only thing that kept him going was Vanessa. He had betrayed her once, when he went into the army without resisting, and he wasn't going to let her down again.

When his breathing was back to normal, Carl peeked over the jetty and surveyed the three-hundred-foot cliff that marked the boundary of the Wingate estate. When he saw the old tree still jutting out from the side of the cliff, he breathed a sigh of relief. His plan depended on that tree, and he hoped that he was half as tough as it was.

Carl's main problem was the condition of the cliff. Centuries of a relentless assault by nature had made the surface he was about to climb very unstable. The face of the cliff was constantly sloughing. Vegetation grew in cracks in the shale, loosening it. Wind laden with moisture and salt from the sea beat at the rock mercilessly. The net result was a facade that was always crumbling and falling away. Each toe and handhold would be treacherous enough in the daytime. At night, every inch of the climb was going to be a surprise.

Carl struggled out of his wetsuit and put on his jeans, shirt, and trail shoes before scanning the top of the cliff with the stolen binoculars. When he was satisfied that there were no guards patrolling, he slung the duffel bag across his back. He was about to sprint across the beach when he heard the sound of rotary blades whipping through the night. Rice pressed himself against the jetty and scanned the sky until he fixed on a dot of light moving toward the Wingate estate from the north. Moments later the landing lights on Wingate's helipad came on and a Computex helicopter dropped out of the sky. The General had come home.

Carl knew that the arrival of the helicopter was bound to distract the guards, so he ran across the sand to the base of the cliff, then stood in the shadows listening for any sign that he had been detected. When he was convinced that he was safe, he began his ascent directly under the tree.

Despite arms and legs that ached from the swim, pain from his wounds, and wind that buffeted him mercilessly, Carl scaled the first hundred feet with only minor problems. Then two successive handholds crumbled and a foothold gave way, sending him sliding several feet down the face of the cliff.

Carl stopped his fall on a narrow ledge and broke out his gear. After attaching a long length of fishing line to an arrow, he fitted the arrow to the fishing bow. From the beach the old tree was three hundred feet straight up, but now the tree was a little less than two hundred feet above him—still a long shot, but he had no choice but to go for it.

Carl aimed so that the arrow would clear the back of the tree. His first shot was short and he had to reel the arrow back. Wind blew his second shot away from the face of the cliff. Carl waited patiently for the wind to die down before taking his third shot. His muscles strained as he pulled back on the bowstring. He sighted and released. This time the arrow arced through the air, sailing over the north side of the tree and across the back. The weight of the arrow pulled the fishing line down the south side of the tree past Carl, and it fell almost to the beach.

Carl scrambled back down the cliff while letting out more line. When he reached the arrow, he took a long length of rope out of the duffel bag and attached it to the fishing line above the arrow using a fisherman's knot. Then he let go of the arrow, moved to the north side of the tree, and pulled the fishing line back over the tree until the attached rope hung from both sides of the trunk.

After detaching the arrow and the fishing line from the rope, Carl tied a bowline loop at one end of the rope and passed the other end of the rope through the eye of the bowline, creating a noose around the trunk of the tree. Carl pulled on the rope until it tightened around the tree, providing a fixed anchor.

Now, using separate pieces of rope, Carl made a sling that looped around his chest and a seat harness that he secured around his waist, under his buttocks, and through his crotch so that it fitted like a diaper. Then he removed from the duffel bag two more pieces of rope that were roughly twice the length of his body. He tied the first piece around the rope that dangled from the tree using a prusik knot and attached a second prusik beneath the first. The prusik was a clever device that could slide up or down the rope when there was no tension on it, but would tighten and not slide when tension was applied. Carl ran the top prusik under his chest sling and attached it to his seat harness. When Carl sat on the seat harness, the tension on the prusik kept the harness secured to the rope. Carl could dangle in space without fear. If Carl put his foot in the loop formed by the lower prusik he could stand up straight and the tension on the lower prusik would keep him from sliding when he was standing. Additionally, when he stood, the upper prusik loosened and he could slide it up the rope as far as he could reach. Carl had created a simple system that allowed him to slide up the rope by alternately standing and sitting. This allowed him to climb up the tree with a minimum of effort because he could rest by sitting or standing.

When Carl reached the tree, he paused below the edge of the cliff, sagged back in his seat harness, and rested. As soon as he regained some of his strength, he peered over the edge. No guards were in sight. Carl hauled himself over the lip of the cliff. He left the rope secured to the tree so that he and Vanessa could rappel down it if they were able to escape, but he covered it with dirt and leaves so a guard would not see it.

Carl had taken two silenced nine-millimeter Glock automatics, ammunition, and a combat knife from the men he'd killed at Ami's house. The knife was already in a sheath he'd strapped on before the climb. He took the pistols from the duffel bag before concealing the duffel in the underbrush a few yards from the tree.

Carl thought about the task that was facing him. He had to get past the guards and Wingate's surveillance equipment, break into the mansion, and find Vanessa without getting killed or captured. Then he had to escape with her, which meant that Vanessa would have to rappel to the beach and swim down the coast in choppy seas. The whole thing seemed impossible to pull off.

The next time Vanessa drifted into consciousness a man was standing by the door, watching her, and someone else was sitting beside her bed. It was dark in the room. She closed her eyes. Thinking was such a strain.

A warm hand covered Vanessa's. She forced her eyes open again. The lights went on and she blinked.

"Thank God you're safe."

It took Vanessa a moment to realize that it was her father who had spoken and a moment more for her to remember that she hated him. Anger-triggered adrenaline cleared away most of her drug-induced stupor and she tried to sit up.

The General touched her shoulder. "No, rest, you need your strength."

"Get your hands off me."

"Vanessa, I love you. I did what I had to do to protect you."

"From who, daddy? You're the only person I'm afraid of."

"You don't know what you're saying. Everything I've done has been to help you."

"Like locking me up in that asylum and keeping me drugged for a year so I couldn't tell anyone that you ordered Carl to murder Eric Glass?"

She pointed at Sam Cutler, who was watching from the door. "Like having your little spy kidnap me? Tell me daddy, while he was living with me, did Sam give you a blow-by-blow version of how we fucked?"

Vanessa's words were slurred and lacked force. Even so, the General flinched.

"Carl Rice is an insane killer," Wingate said. "I have no idea how many people he's murdered. I had to get you away from him."

"You have to murder him because he's the only man alive who can tell the truth about the dirty little secret that can keep you from becoming president."

Wingate sighed. "He's delusional, Vanessa. That's what makes him so convincing. He really believes everything he's told you. But none of it is true. There was no secret army. I did not arrange for Carl to be drafted, and I never ordered Carl to kill Eric Glass. That was all in Carl's head, and you believed him because you hate me. But I've always loved you, even when you've hurt me. Do you have any idea how badly I feel knowing that my daughter believes I'm so evil that I could murder my wife, a woman I loved dearly?"

The General ducked his head, and his voice caught. "I've never told you, but there have been nights where I've cried myself to sleep because of you, knowing that you . . . have such a low opinion of me that . . . "

Wingate shook his head. To Vanessa it appeared that he had been overcome by emotion, and that shocked her. She had never seen her father lose control—not even at her mother's funeral. It was one of the things that had convinced her that Morris Wingate did not love his wife. Was the General's display of emotion genuine or manufactured? Everything she believed about her father convinced her that he was faking.

"Are you hungry?" Wingate asked. "I'll have dinner sent up." He smiled in an attempt to lighten the conversation. "I have a new chef. He's French. I stole him away from a four-star restaurant in Los Angeles."

"It looks like kidnapping is becoming your new hobby."

"Yes, well you've got a few interesting hobbies of your own," he answered wearily. "You've put me in a terrible situation, Vanessa. You're a wanted criminal. You helped Carl Rice, a multiple murderer, escape from jail. I'm your father and I love you and want to protect you, but I'm also running for my party's presidential nomination, not to mention the trouble I could get into for harboring a fugitive. What should I do?"

"Your political ambitions are no concern of mine," Vanessa said.

"I know you don't believe me, but Rice is a very dangerous man. I had to get you away from him."

"So, are you going to turn me in?"

"No one knows you're here, and I'm going to keep it that way. I have plenty of connections worldwide from my government days and Computex. It would be an easy matter for me to get you a new identity, even a new face. You could start over in another country. You'd be safe and I'd make sure you had plenty of money."

"So that's it. You want me tucked away in some backwater where I can't rock the boat."

"I do not want you in jail because your delusions led you to help a murderer."

"What do you have planned for Carl?"

"Carl is a problem for the police. They may never catch him. He's very resourceful. He's managed to elude capture for years. Maybe his luck will hold out. Did he tell you where he was going, what his plans are?"

"We didn't know where we were going. We were going to hole up at the cabin where Sam found us and figure out our next move in the morning, after we'd gotten some rest."

"So you have no idea where he might be?"

"No."

Wingate glanced at Cutler. He straightened up and took a hypodermic out of his pocket.

"What's that?" Vanessa asked.

Wingate moved quickly and pinned Vanessa to the bed.

"Something that will help you rest," he said. "It won't hurt."

"I don't want any more drugs," Vanessa screamed as she struggled to get free.

Wingate and Cutler ignored her pleas. Sam stood over Vanessa. She bucked and threw herself from side to side.

"Hold her still, General," Cutler said as he bent forward to administer the injection. "I don't want to miss the vein."

It was a little over two miles from the jetty to the mansion through the woods on the south side of the General's property. Charlotte Kohler liked to stroll along paths she'd had a landscape architect lay down through her private forest, but Carl avoided them because they would be a natural place for motion detectors. After a while, Carl saw the lights of the house through breaks in the foliage. He crept forward cautiously until there were only a few trees between him and the lawn at the back of the mansion. The grounds directly behind the house offered few places to hide, and two guards crossed on the back lawn while Carl had it under surveillance.

Carl watched carefully as the guards walked their route. One of the men crossed the pool deck near the cabana where Carl had changed into a bathing suit on his first visit to the estate. As soon as the guard disappeared, Carl made a decision.

It took the guards twelve minutes to complete their circuit. Carl worked his way through the woods as close to the cabana as he could. Everything depended on getting behind it undetected. He sprinted from the woods to the pool and dove low behind the cabana.

Carl checked his watch. Three minutes to go. He visualized the attack, going over possible scenarios. With a minute to go, Carl withdrew the combat knife from its sheath. He had made several silent kills, and he knew that he had to act without hesitation. He had already seen in such circumstances a certain phenomenon that convinced him that human beings had some kind of electrical field around them to warn them when there were other humans in close proximity. Though he didn't know if there had been any scientific studies to support his notion, no matter how stealthy an approach, an intended victim would sense when an attacker entered this field. A moment's hesitation was all it took to turn a sure kill into a fight to the death.

The guards passed on the lawn, and Carl's target arrived at the pool just as the other guard disappeared around the side of the house. Carl moved as soon as the guard's back was to him. The guard was turning as Carl attacked, but he had no chance. The knife struck home and he died without making a sound. Carl dragged the guard's body into the cabana and changed into his clothes. Now, in addition to the Glocks and his knife, Carl had the guard's automatic rifle and two extra clips of ammunition.

To make up time Carl walked a little faster than the pace his victim had kept, but he was still late. He spotted the other guard when they were on the north side of the mansion near the door to the cellar. This was fortunate because they were away from any windows. Carl knelt and pretended to tie his laces. He kept his head down to conceal his face.

"What's up, Rick?" the guard asked as he came in range.

Carl shot him with the silenced Glock and dragged him against the side of the house. He tried the cellar door. It was locked. He rifled the guard's pockets and found a key chain. The third key he tried opened the door.

In high school, Carl and Vanessa had made love in the basement's cool darkness on a discarded Persian rug while Vanessa's father was meeting with movers and shakers above them. The basement was still cool and dark, but those erotic moments were forgotten as Carl moved between the stacked furniture and abandoned art and up the steps to the first floor. He remembered that the basement door led to a short hall near the kitchen. He opened the door wide enough to see into the corridor.

A guard walked past the entrance to the hall, and Carl ducked behind the basement door. As soon as the guard was past, Carl moved down the hall toward him. When he reached the end of the hall,

Carl stooped down and peered around the corner. The guard had stopped with his back to Carl. It looked as if he was taking a break. Carl stunned the man with a blow to the back of the skull, then choked him unconscious. He dragged him back into the basement, cuffed him with plastic cuffs he found in the guard's back pocket, sat him against a stack of mildewed cardboard cartons, and slapped the guard back to consciousness.

The man's eyes flicked open. They tried to focus on Carl's face but the taste of metal in his mouth brought the guard's eyes down to the gun barrel that was wedged between his lips.

"You have one chance to live," Carl said in a calm, authoritative tone. "When I take this gun barrel out of your mouth you'll tell me where the General is holding his prisoner or I will shoot you and find someone else who will tell me. Understood?"

The man nodded. Carl withdrew the barrel past the man's lips.

"Second floor, maid's room."

Carl hit the man fast and much harder than he had the first time. The guard slumped sideways as Carl headed for the stairs. He knew the location of the maid's room. He and Vanessa had screwed there one summer evening. Now that he thought about it, almost every memory he had of Wingate's mansion was connected to sex.

Carl used the back stairs to get to the second floor. He moved down the hall without making a sound. As he drew close to the maid's room, he heard voices. Then Vanessa screamed, "I don't want any more drugs."

When Carl wrenched open the door the General was pinning Vanessa to the bed and Sam Cutler was poised over her with a hypodermic needle.

"Put down the hypo or die," Carl said.

Cutler froze. Wingate turned his head toward the door. His mouth opened, but he stifled whatever he had intended to say.

"Put it down, now," Carl commanded. Cutler laid the needle on the end table next to the bed.

"Get away from her and stand against the wall. Quick!"

Both men obeyed.

"I knew you'd come," Vanessa said.

Carl moved to the side of the bed. For a brief second, his eyes left Wingate and Cutler and moved over Vanessa. In that instant, Sam Cutler slipped a Shirken out of his sleeve. The Japanese throwing star had six knife-sharp points. Cutler hurled it across the bed like a discus into Carl's right shoulder. The shoulder went numb and he dropped the Glock. Cutler leaped across the bed. Vanessa raised her leg, catching Cutler across the knees. As he stumbled over her, Vanessa grabbed the hypodermic and rammed the needle into Cutler's thigh.

"You bitch!" he screamed. Then his eyes started to lose focus. Vanessa knew exactly what was happening to Cutler's body. It had been happening to hers with regularity ever since Cutler had injected her in the woods.

Wingate took a step toward Rice, then changed direction and charged out of the room when Carl grabbed the Glock with his left hand and started to aim. The shot went through the open door and into the wall, sending plaster chips spraying across the hallway. The General was shouting at the top of his lungs. Rice peered into the hall. It was empty but it wouldn't stay that way long.

"Get up, Vanessa."

Vanessa struggled to her feet. She wanted to move faster but her legs felt like noodles. Carl helped her stand. He knew it was going to be impossible to fight his way out of the house and escape down the cliff with Vanessa in this condition, but he didn't dwell on the future. He would complete his mission one step at a time and whatever happened, happened. And the first step was getting out of the room.

Carl held the Glock in his left hand and gripped Vanessa's elbow with his right.

"Concentrate, Van. We have to get out of here fast."

"Okay," she answered in a sleepy voice.

Carl took a step into the corridor, and a bullet almost took his head off. He ducked back inside the maid's room as wood splinters from the door frame flew through the air. Carl slammed the door shut and jammed the chair under the knob. Then he dumped Sam Cutler on the floor and pushed the bed onto its side.

"Get behind the bed and hug the floor. There are going to be a lot of bullets coming through the door and walls."

Carl joined Vanessa behind the bed and set out all his weapons and ammunition on the floor beside him. He had enough firepower to hold out for a while, but then what?

"What's going to happen?" Vanessa asked. She still sounded a little spacey.

"I don't know. We're trapped in here. There's only one way out—the door—and your father has that covered. Even if we got out the door, we'd have to fight our way down the corridor to get to the stairs. Then we'd have to fight our way down the stairs and through the house."

Carl shrugged. Vanessa forced herself to focus. She was getting sharper every second and during one of those seconds she'd had a glimmer of an idea, but she'd been too groggy to hold on to it. She had figured out one thing, though. She had wondered why, if her father loved her enough to save her old pajamas, he had put her in a deserted wing of the mansion in the maid's room instead of her old room. Now she knew the answer to her question. The General had expected Carl to come for her. All she'd been to him was bait, and this room had always been a trap.

"Carl, be reasonable," the General called out. "There's no way out of there. Throw out your weapons. That way, Vanessa won't get hurt and neither will you."

"That does sound reasonable, Morris," Carl answered sarcastically. "I'm sure we can trust you. Maybe we can grab a bite to eat and reminisce about old times, too, like the mission to rescue the MIAs that your flunky led. You sure looked out for me and the rest of your boys then."

"I don't know what you're talking about, Carl.

The only time Sam led a mission with you as a member of the team was your first mission, and you cracked up after it. You're a sick man, Carl. I'll tell that to the authorities. Maybe we can have you hospitalized instead of sent to prison."

"That's it," Vanessa said, as she suddenly remembered her idea.

"What?" Carl asked her, but Vanessa didn't answer. Instead, she started searching Sam Cutler. Just before they'd taken off from the airport in the Computex helicopter, Cutler had made a call on a cell phone, which he'd put in his pocket.

"Yes!" she said when she found it.

# CHAPTER **THIRTY**

Victor Hobson had crawled under the covers of his hotel bed a little after midnight at the end of a fruitless day spent shuttling between the Portland police bureau and the FBI office. Then he had tossed and turned all night. At five in the morning, he dragged himself out of bed feeling more exhausted than he'd been when he went to sleep. On the east coast it was eight o'clock. If he were home, he would be at least an hour behind his usual schedule.

Hobson went into the bathroom. The mirror in his hotel room was not kind to him. Shaving, brushing his teeth, and taking a cold shower raised his spirits a little, but his failure to make any progress in the manhunt was still depressing.

Carl Rice had been as insubstantial as a ghost for the past twenty years, and there were times when Hobson had wondered if Carl was just a figment of his imagination. Now, just when it appeared that Rice was in his grasp, he had disappeared again. Victor could not understand how a man could vanish so completely.

It had been too late on the east coast to call Emily before he went to bed, so Hobson decided to call her now, knowing that she'd be up with the kids. He was reaching for the hotel phone when his cell phone rang. Hobson tried to remember where he'd put it and finally found it on the desk after several unnerving rings that sounded to his tired brain like metal dishes clattering on a tile floor.

"Hobson," he barked as he turned on the desk light.

"Victor, this is Vanessa Kohler."

Vanessa's voice acted on Hobson like a strong cup of coffee.

"Where are you?" he asked, trying to hide his excitement.

"I'm with Carl Rice in my father's mansion. You know where that is, right?"

"Yes."

"My father's men kidnapped me and he's been using drugs to keep me a prisoner. Carl broke into the mansion to rescue me but we're trapped. We've barricaded ourselves in a maid's room on the second floor. My father's men are trying to kill us. We're armed, and we'll fight if we have to, but we'd rather turn ourselves in."

"I can arrange that."

"Then you'd better move fast. I don't know how long my father will wait before he tells his men to storm the room. Now, here's what I want you to do. First, you have to tell the local police where we are and that we want to surrender to them. They'll have to come to the room. We're

afraid to step into the hall if we're not protected.
My father's men have already fired several shots
at us."

"I'll call the police immediately," Hobson assured her.

"As soon as the police are on the way I want
you to call my father. I'll stay on the line so you
can hear him if he tries to break into the room.
Tell him that you're talking to me and that the
police are coming. Tell him to stop shooting.
He'll kill us if the police aren't here soon."

"Give me the number of the estate."

As soon as Vanessa rattled off the phone number, Hobson dialed Detective Walsh on the hotel
phone. Walsh answered almost immediately. He
sounded half-asleep.

"Howard, this is Victor Hobson. I've got Vanessa
Wingate on my cell phone. She's barricaded in a
second-floor room in General Wingate's mansion
in California. Carl Rice is with her and they're
armed, but she assures me that they'll surrender
to the police if the police go to the room and escort them out. Call the police in San Diego and
get them to Wingate's estate immediately. Explain the situation. Vanessa says that her father's
security guards are shooting at her. I'm going to
call General Wingate and try to cool things
down."

Once Hobson told Walsh where Wingate's estate was located, he disconnected and dialed the
Wingate mansion.

"Answer that, General," Hobson heard Vanessa
yell as soon as the phone started to ring. "I'm

talking to an assistant director of the FBI on Sam's cell phone. We've offered to surrender to the police. He can hear everything that's going on. He wants to talk to you now."

"Did you hear that?" Vanessa asked Hobson.

"I can hear you," Hobson assured her.

"My father knows you're on the line. If he shoots us it will be murder."

There was a click on the hotel phone line. "Who is this?" General Wingate asked.

"Victor Hobson, General. I'm an assistant director of the FBI. We spoke many years ago when I was investigating the murder of Congressman Eric Glass."

"Yes, I remember. You were an agent then."

"You've got a good memory. Your daughter called me. She's on the line now on a cell phone and can hear what I'm saying. I understand we have a situation at your mansion."

"My daughter is a sick woman, Director Hobson. Carl Rice—the man who murdered Eric Glass—was in jail in Portland, Oregon. Vanessa helped him escape. He's insane but very clever. Rice has convinced Vanessa that I'm some master criminal who is trying to kill them.

"My men rescued Vanessa from Rice but he got away. She was brought here so that I could get her the help she needs. I was going to call the authorities after I contacted a lawyer to represent her, but Rice broke into my home. He's killed several of my guards and he tried to kill me. I managed to escape and my security force has them pinned down. He's holding one of my men hostage, if he hasn't killed him already."

"Yes, well, I want you to tell your men to hold their fire," Hobson said. "We've contacted the San Diego police and they're on the way. Vanessa says she and Rice are willing to surrender to them, so there's no need for you to take any action aside from making certain that they stay put."

"Did you hear that?" Hobson heard Vanessa yell at her father. "You better not try anything now. Director Hobson will hear everything you do. Carl and I will lay down our weapons when the police come. We won't hurt anyone, so there won't be any 'killed resisting arrest,' or 'killed in self-defense.' If you shoot us you'll be charged with murder."

The second line in Hobson's hotel room started blinking.

"I'm going to put you on hold for a moment, General" he said. "I'm getting another call. It's probably an update on the police situation."

"I'll hold," Wingate said. "And don't worry. My men won't shoot. I don't want Vanessa hurt."

Hobson spoke to Detective Walsh long enough to be briefed. Then he reconnected with Wingate.

"The local police are minutes away, General. Please have your gate man let them in."

"Of course. Now, Director Hobson, will you ask my daughter, as a show of good faith, to send my man out?"

"Vanessa?"

"Yes."

"Your father says that you have a hostage."

"He's not a hostage. He's the bastard who kidnapped me. You've met him. He's Sam Cutler."

"Your boyfriend?"

"Ex-boyfriend. My father paid him to keep an eye on me. He's the one who's been giving me drugs, and he tried to murder Carl."

"Will you send him out as a show of good faith?"

"I should kill the bastard, but I'll give him back to his master if Carl says it's okay."

Hobson held on the phone. He could hear Vanessa and Rice conferring, but he couldn't make out what they were saying.

"Okay. Tell the General to keep his men back and we'll drag him out. He's still unconscious."

"Vanessa has agreed to send out your man, but you have to keep back from the door."

"I'll tell my men to back away and hold their fire."

"Good."

"And I have a favor to ask you."

"What is it?"

"Please tell the police to treat my daughter gently. She's a sick woman. I'm certain she has no real grasp of reality. She belongs in a hospital, not a jail."

Vanessa could hear Victor Hobson's half of the conversation, and she could imagine what her father was saying. He would be lying, of course, telling Hobson that she and Carl were crazy, but crazy was better than dead.

As soon as Hobson told her that the General had pulled his men down the hall, Carl gave Vanessa his gun.

"He looks like he's still out," Carl said, "but don't hesitate to kill him if he's faking."

Vanessa kept the gun trained on Cutler. Carl grimaced from the pain in his shoulder as he pushed the bed out of the way and pulled the chair from beneath the doorknob. Then he grabbed Cutler under the arms and dragged him to the door. Vanessa followed him, keeping the gun trained on Cutler. He still looked unconscious, but Vanessa wasn't taking chances.

Carl wrestled Cutler to the door and Vanessa opened it. The area in front of the door was empty. Carl laid Cutler on the floor and shoved him into the hall. Vanessa slammed the door shut and Carl wedged the chair under the knob again before pushing the bed back into place.

"We did what you asked," Vanessa told Hobson. "Sam's in the hall, safe and sound. Now it's your job to keep us alive."

"The police are almost there," Hobson said.

Vanessa sat down with her back to the far wall and pulled her knees to her chest.

"How are you holding up?" Carl asked.

"I'm fine, just tired. It's probably the drugs."

"They'll wear off soon."

Vanessa closed her eyes.

"I'm sorry I got you into this," Carl said.

"You didn't get me into anything. I'm the one who broke you out of jail."

"And now it looks like we'll both go to prison. I never meant for it to be this way."

"Why did you come for me, Carl? You could have been well away from here, on your way to freedom."

"I betrayed you once, Van, and I wasn't going to do that again. I let the General seduce me. That decision has haunted me my whole life."

"You think we would have stayed together if you went to college? I was pretty screwed up back then." She laughed. "I still am."

"I have no idea what would have happened. I just know that I let you down."

"So you were trying to set things right by storming the General's castle?"

"I was keeping my word. You saved me and I told you I'd come for you. That's what I did. Sorry it didn't work out like it does in the movies."

"Oh, I don't know. In the movies, the cavalry always comes to the rescue."

Vanessa pointed to the outer wall. Rice heard the faint sound of sirens.

"We'll be out of here soon and we'll be alive," Vanessa said.

"But we'll both be in jail."

Vanessa reached over and held Carl's forearm. "Don't give up. We'll beat him. I know it. I just haven't figured out how, yet. But we'll beat my father."

Vanessa swore this with conviction, but Carl knew he was doomed to spend the rest of his life behind bars. Vanessa's father could probably keep her out of jail, though she would spend years—if not a lifetime—in a mental hospital.

Carl put his good arm around her shoulder and pressed his lips to her forehead. "Sure we will, Van. Sure we will."

# CHAPTER **THIRTY-ONE**

Ami's wake-up call shocked her out of a deep sleep shortly after six in the morning, but Ryan slept through the jangling noise. Ami hung up the phone, flopped back in bed, and watched her son sleep. Last night, he had been so excited about staying in a hotel, eating in the fancy dining room, and watching a Disney movie in their room. Now, he looked so peaceful that she had to smile. Death and destruction were all around, but they barely touched her boy.

Ami wished that she could let Ryan sleep, but she had to get him to school. Then she would go to her office. The Morelli case had consumed most of her time since the General's daughter had barged into her life, but Ami had other clients with pressing problems and she could not afford to laze around her hotel room all day. She had explained this to Brendan Kirkpatrick after they had finished breakfast yesterday morning. The prosecutor had arranged for the policeman who was guarding her to drive her to her office after she woke up around noon. The officer had stayed in the reception area until it was time to pick up Ryan at school.

"Hey, Tiger," Ami said as she gently shook Ryan's shoulder. "It's time to get up."

Ryan grunted and rolled away from her. She leaned over and planted several disgustingly wet kisses on his cheek.

"Yuck, Mom, don't," he begged.

"Then get your butt out of bed. It's a school day."

"Do I have to? Can't I stay here with you?"

"Nope. I'm not even staying here. I'm going to work, and you're going to school. Now, if you move fast enough, we can have breakfast in the dining room."

Suddenly Ryan was wide awake. "Can I have pancakes?"

"If you don't dillydally. Now scoot."

As Ryan grabbed the clothes that Ami had laid out for him and ran for the bathroom, there was a knock at the door. Ami knew that the guard would not let anyone hurt her if he could help it, but she remembered what had happened to the policemen who had guarded her at her house.

Ami slipped on the terry-cloth robe that the hotel provided and peered through the peephole. Brendan Kirkpatrick was standing on the other side of the door looking as if he'd just stepped out of a men's fashion magazine. She, on the other hand, looked like a woman with no makeup who had just gotten out of bed and had not even brushed her teeth. For a moment she debated pretending that she wasn't in, but that wasn't practical. The guard knew she hadn't left the room. It wasn't a particularly adult way of handling the situation, either, so she opened the door and let the prosecutor in.

"To what do I owe this honor?" Ami said, clutching the edges of the robe together at her neck.

Brendan didn't seem to notice how awful she looked. He flashed a wide grin. "You're safe. They got them."

"Where?" Ami asked, afraid that the arrest had been made at her cabin.

"California. I don't know the whole story, but Howard Walsh tells me that Wingate's security force rescued the General's daughter and brought her to his estate near San Diego. Rice broke into the mansion to get her back. He killed and injured several of Wingate's men, but the General trapped them in the house and they surrendered to the police."

Ami felt a weight lift from her shoulders. Kirkpatrick thought it was because Rice was behind bars where he could not hurt her or her son, but Ami was thankful that the police had not figured out that she had abetted the fugitives' escape.

"Anyway," Brendan went on, "you're safe. And you can go back to your house tonight."

"That's great."

"You must be relieved."

"I am. Ever since Vanessa walked into my office, this case has been a nightmare. I should never have been involved in the first place. I never intended to represent Rice, anyway. I was just in it until someone competent could take over."

Brendan smiled. "For a neophyte Perry Mason, you certainly gave me a hard time."

"Good. I'll consider this outing to be a success if you've learned a little humility. Maybe the next time you won't be so quick to pick on a defenseless woman."

Brendan held up his hands. "Hey, I give. I learned my lesson. And you're anything but defenseless. Anyway, I just wanted to give you the good news personally."

"Thanks."

"Well," Kirkpatrick said awkwardly, "I have to get to the office. I actually have other cases. Maybe I'll see you around."

"Maybe you will."

"I might have to call you as a witness, you know."

"I'll be ready."

"Well, see you."

Ami stared after Brendan Kirkpatrick as the door closed. Was she imagining it, or was the stone-cold DA showing the type of nervousness around her that was reminiscent of an adolescent boy with a crush? Did he like her? She sure had not liked him. Not at first, anyway. But he was growing on her. She wondered what she would say if he asked her out. Oh, well, no use speculating. He hadn't, and she would cross that bridge if she ever came to it. Right now all she wanted to do was take Ryan to school. She'd had enough excitement to last a lifetime, and she was looking forward to living a normal, boring existence again.

# CHAPTER **THIRTY-TWO**

Patrick Gorman, the owner of *Exposed,* lumbered into the visiting room at the San Diego jail and dropped into a chair across from a dejected Vanessa Kohler. Vanessa's initial euphoria at escaping from her father's mansion had given way to despair as it slowly dawned on her during the numerous police interrogations that everyone believed General Morris Wingate's version of events and no one gave any credence to her fantastic tale of secret armies and government conspiracies.

Gorman forced a smile, but he was sad to see one of his reporters in such a sorry state.

"When I hired you, did I forget to tell you that your job is to report the news, not be the news?" he asked.

"I probably wasn't paying attention."

"That, I can believe. So, how are you doing?"

"Okay. I'm isolated from the rest of the prisoners so I don't have to worry about being gang-raped. My biggest problem is boredom and the shitty food. Of course, with what you pay me, all

I can afford is shitty food, so I guess boredom is my main problem."

"Hey, I pay top dollar for a scandal sheet. See if they'd pay you any more at *The Enquirer*."

"How's the paper doing? I can't get it in here."

"It's gone downhill since you left. No one writes a giant rat story like you."

Vanessa smiled for a moment. Then she sobered. "Have you heard anything about Carl? They won't tell me a thing."

"I know he's in federal custody. They're not letting anyone near him. He hasn't even been arraigned yet."

Vanessa leaned forward and lowered her voice. "Did my lawyer bring you my manuscript?"

"I read it yesterday."

"Are you going to publish it?"

Gorman shook his head slowly. "I can't, Vanessa."

"This will be bigger than Watergate, Pat. You'll be the next Woodward and Bernstein all by yourself. They'll be talking about *Exposed* in the same breath with *The New York Times*."

"*Exposed* can't afford to go legit. We'd lose our readers," Gorman joked in an attempt to lighten things up, but Vanessa wasn't biting.

"Do you really want someone like Morris Wingate running this country?"

"My politics have nothing to do with my decision. You've been in the newspaper business long enough to know that you can't print the stuff you're writing about without heavy-duty corroboration."

"You've got resources, Pat. Use them to corroborate my charges."

"I don't have the contacts to verify something like this. You're talking about decades-old black ops that are buried so deep that no one else has ever heard of them."

"Carl Rice knows all about them."

"We can't base our story on the word of an escaped convict who's murdered a congressman, a general, and . . . " Gorman shook his head. "I forgot the body count at your father's house."

"You've got to show everyone what my father is really like."

"I can't do that without rock-solid proof. We'd be sued into oblivion."

"You're afraid, aren't you? Did he get to you?"

Gorman looked tired. "Neither your father nor anyone connected to him has talked to me, Van. We just can't print unsubstantiated stories accusing presidential candidates of murder."

"Then why are you here?"

Gorman looked uncomfortable. "Like I said when I came in, you've gone from writing the news to being the news. You and Carl Rice are the biggest story in the country, and *Exposed* would like an exclusive."

"I can't believe you, Pat. I never thought you'd take advantage of our friendship."

"Your defense is going to be expensive. We'll foot the bill for the best lawyer."

"What's the headline going to be? 'Love-Starved Spinster Seduced by Serial Killer,' or will you go with 'Maniac Lovers on the Run'?"

"You'll get to tell the story anyway you want. You can even talk about your father. Our lawyers tell me that we can't be sued if you're the one making the accusations."

Vanessa looked sad. "I am so disappointed in you, Pat. I thought you were my friend."

"I am your friend. I want to help."

"You want a story. I've become another giant baby-eating rat."

"That's not true," Gorman protested feebly, but he looked ashamed.

"Please go."

"Will you think it over?"

Vanessa seemed on the verge of tears. Gorman could not look her in the eye.

"Just go, Pat."

"Van . . ."

"Please."

Vanessa closed her eyes. She felt more tired and defeated than she had since her arrest. She never believed for a moment that Patrick Gorman would betray her. Now she knew that he was like everyone else. For a brief moment, she gave way completely to despair. But that moment ended when she recalled something that Gorman had said. The guard entered to take her back to her cell, but she didn't even know that he was in the room. Without realizing it, her boss had given her an idea that might save her and Carl.

# CHAPTER **THIRTY-THREE**

The Justice Center is a sixteen-story concrete-and-glass building in downtown Portland, separated from the Multnomah County courthouse by a park. In addition to the central precinct of the Portland police bureau, the Justice Center is home to a branch of the Multnomah County district attorney's office, several courtrooms, the state crime lab, state parole and probation, and the Multnomah County jail. Ami Vergano had already been on the thirteenth floor of the Justice Center when she was interrogated in the detective division of the Portland police bureau, but she had never been inside a jail and she found her first visit to this part of the building unnerving.

The jail occupies the fourth through tenth floors of the Justice Center, but the reception area is on the second floor. To reach it, Ami walked through the center's vaulted lobby, past the curving stairs that led to the courtrooms on the third floor, and through a pair of glass doors.

"I'm Ami Vergano, Vanessa Kohler's attorney,"

she told the sheriff's deputy who was manning the reception desk. "I'd like to visit her. She may be here under the name Vanessa Wingate."

While the deputy checked her ID, Ami looked around the room. A jittery teenage girl with tattoos and a nose ring was casting anxious glances toward the door where released prisoners left the jail. She smelled as if she hadn't bathed in days, and there were dark circles under her eyes. The only other person waiting in the reception area was a heavyset attorney in mismatched sports jacket and slacks, who was reading over police reports in preparation for a visit to a client.

The guard returned Ami's ID and searched her attaché case. When the search turned up neither weapons nor contraband, he motioned Ami toward a metal detector that stood between her and the jail elevator. Ami passed through without setting off an alarm and the guard walked her to the elevator and keyed her up to the floor where Vanessa was being held.

After a short ride, Ami found herself in a narrow hall with concrete walls. The moment the elevator doors closed, she started to feel claustrophobic. The guard in the reception area had told Ami to summon the guard on this floor by using the intercom that was affixed to the wall next to a thick metal door at one end of the corridor. Ami punched the button anxiously several times before the box crackled and a disembodied voice asked her about her business.

Moments later, a jail guard peered at Ami

through a plate of glass in the upper half of the door, then spoke into a walkie-talkie. Electronic locks snapped, and the guard ushered Ami into another narrow corridor that ran in front of the three contact visiting rooms in which prisoners met face to face with their attorneys. Ami could see into the rooms through large windows outfitted with thick, shatterproof glass.

Vanessa was already waiting for her in the room farthest from the elevators. She was dressed in a shapeless orange jumpsuit and sitting in one of two molded plastic chairs that stood on either side of a round, Formica-topped table that was bolted to the floor. The guard opened another metal door and stepped aside. Ami walked into the room, and the guard pointed to a black button that stuck out of an intercom affixed to the pastel-yellow concrete wall.

"Press that when you're through, and I'll come and get you," he told her before closing the door.

Vanessa's hair was uncombed, and she looked even thinner than Ami remembered. Endless days in jail in San Diego, while Oregon and California fought over which state had the right to prosecute her first, had turned her complexion ashy-gray and beaten down her spirit.

"Are you okay?" Ami asked.

"No. I'm really down," Vanessa answered honestly. She seemed exhausted.

"I'm so sorry, Vanessa."

"Don't be. None of this is your fault. I have only myself to blame." Suddenly a flash of Vanessa's determination and self-confidence showed on her face. "But I don't regret what I did. Carl would be dead if I hadn't rescued him." Then her shoulders slumped and she looked lost. "I just hope he survives in prison, but I don't think he has much of a chance. He's too much of a threat to the General."

Ami did not argue with Vanessa. She was finally convinced that the secret army was a fantasy and her client a seriously deluded woman, but what good would it do to challenge Vanessa's delusions now? Instead, she opened her attaché case and took out several legal documents.

"I have a substitution of counsel for you to sign," Ami said, sliding the papers and a pen across the table.

"You're not going to represent me?"

"I can't. Remember, we talked about this the first time we met. First off, I have no experience as a criminal defense attorney. Second, it's unethical for a lawyer to represent two people in the same case. It's a clear conflict of interest. One of the ways a lawyer helps a client is by negotiating a deal for her with the district attorney. If there are two defendants, it's normal for the lawyer for one of the defendants to tell the DA that her client will testify against the other defendant in exchange for a lighter sentence. I can't do that for you or Carl if I represent both of you.

"And there's another problem. I helped you hide out. Do you know how much trouble I'd be in if that came out? I aided and abetted your escape. If I become a codefendant, it's obvious that I'd have to drop off the case.

"Not to mention that I'm a witness to Carl's attack on Barney Lutz and the police officer at Ryan's game."

Ami smiled ruefully. "I've got so many conflicts of interest that I feel like a human law school exam question. But don't worry. Ray Armitage is still willing to represent Carl and I've lined up Janet Massengill to represent you. She's excellent. She thinks there's a good chance that she can get you released at a bail hearing."

"No, no," Vanessa said as she shook her head back and forth. "I wouldn't be safe out of jail. I'm in solitary here. Unless he bribes a guard, my father won't be able to get to me."

Ami held her tongue. It was sad to see such a strong woman reduced to this state of terror.

"That's something you can talk over with your new lawyer. You don't have to ask for bail if you don't want it. As soon as you sign this substitution, Janet will take over. She's tied up today, but she can visit you tomorrow."

Vanessa reached across the table and placed her hand on top of Ami's.

"Don't desert me, Ami."

"Haven't you been listening? I have no choice."

"You have to stay on as my attorney. It's my only chance."

"To do what?"

"Expose my father and save Carl."

"How can you possibly do that, Vanessa?" Ami asked, finally exasperated by her client's refusal to face reality.

"I can demand a hearing in open court with the

press and the public present. I can call witnesses.
I can subpoena my father, and you can cross-
examine him under oath with the whole world
watching."

"It won't work. He'll just deny everything, and
the prosecutor will trot out your mental history.
Your lawyer won't have any evidence to contradict anything the General says."

"Carl will contradict him."

"No one is going to believe Carl without corroboration. Think of how he'd look after Brendan Kirkpatrick got through with him on cross.
There is overwhelming evidence that he has
killed a congressman, a general, several of your
father's guards, and my friend George French."

Vanessa looked Ami in the eye. "Carl swears
that he wasn't even in the United States when
General Rivera was murdered, and he didn't kill
George French. I was with him from the time I
helped him escape until I was kidnapped."

Ami shook her head. "That's going to be a hard
sell, Vanessa. I saw the photographs of the crime
scene at Lost Lake. George was killed the same
way that Carl killed Congressman Glass. If you're
the only alibi he has . . . " Ami held out her
hands, palms up. "You see the problem?"

"I do have a way to defeat my father that
doesn't depend on Carl, but you have to stay
with me. I don't trust anyone else to pull this
off."

"Pull what off?"

"There may be a way to prove that the Unit existed and that my father was involved, but it's a

long shot." Vanessa looked down at the tabletop. "If this doesn't work . . . "

She looked so defeated that Ami could not help feeling sorry for her.

"I can't, Vanessa. I just explained why I have to step down from your case and Carl's case. Tell Janet Massengill your plan. She can do anything I can do, and better."

Vanessa looked up. Her features looked set in stone, and her eyes blazed with insane determination.

"You are my only hope, Ami, and you are not going to desert Carl or me."

"Vanessa . . . "

"I'll tell the police that you helped us escape."

Ami's jaw dropped, and she flushed with anger. "I'd be ruined," she said. "I'd be arrested and disbarred."

"I didn't want it to come to this, but I have no choice. I must stop my father. I can't let him become the president of the United States. He has to pay for what he's done to me and Carl."

"Please, don't do this, Vanessa. I've only tried to help you. I've never done anything to hurt you. Why would you want to hurt me and my son?"

"I don't want to hurt you or Ryan, but I will if I have to. Remember one thing, Ami. I am my father's child, and I can be just as ruthless as he is if I have to."

"What do you want me to do?" Ami asked, hoping that she would find a flaw in Vanessa's plan that would persuade Vanessa to drop it and let her go.

"Write down this number. It's for Victor Hobson's cell phone. Arrange a meeting. If I'm right, there is proof that the Unit existed and he can help me prove it."

# CHAPTER **THIRTY-FOUR**

The guard ushered Ami, Brendan Kirkpatrick, and Victor Hobson into the visiting room and closed the door behind them. Vanessa was already seated at a table with three extra chairs.

"You know Mr. Hobson," Ami said. "This is Brendan Kirkpatrick. He's prosecuting you. I want to make sure you understand that."

"I have no illusions about Mr. Kirkpatrick's interest in me."

"Good," the prosecutor said as he placed a tape recorder on the table. "I'm going to insist on recording everything that goes on here."

"I expected that," Vanessa answered.

While the prosecutor played with the tape recorder, Victor Hobson sat across from the prisoner.

"It's been a long time," he said.

"Almost twenty years."

"Sorry we have to meet again under these circumstances."

"You and me both," Vanessa answered with a wry smile. "But you're going to help me change my circumstances."

Brendan spoke into the tape recorder, stating the date, explaining where the recording was taking place, and giving the name of everyone present.

"Look, Vanessa, I've got to say this before we go any further," Victor Hobson said as soon as Kirkpatrick's introductory remarks were finished. "I'm with the FBI, which means that I'm a law enforcement officer. So is Brendan. Our job is to put you in prison."

"No, Victor, your job is to get the bad guys. That's not Carl or me. My father is the bad guy here and I'm going to help you get him."

Brendan Kirkpatrick shook his head. "I don't like this. I'm here only because of Mrs. Vergano, who should not be representing you."

"I've waived any conflict in writing."

"She showed me the paper," Brendan said. "I still think you're making a huge mistake. You realize that I will definitely use any incriminating statements you make to convict you, and I'll call Mr. Hobson and your attorney as witnesses to everything you say, if that becomes necessary?"

"Yes."

"If I call Mrs. Vergano as a witness she will definitely not be able to represent you anymore."

"I know that, but I'm hoping it won't be necessary." Vanessa leaned forward and focused on Kirkpatrick. "My bail hearing is next week . . . "

"And I'm opposing your motion. I want to be up front with you, Miss Kohler. I regard you and Mr. Rice as dangerous criminals. Not only am I going to oppose bail, but there are very few concessions that I can make if you're thinking about plea negotiations."

"Would you still feel that way if I could prove that my father ran a secret army unit during and after Vietnam that committed any number of illegal acts in the United States, including murdering Congressman Eric Glass on my father's orders?"

Kirkpatrick sighed. "I've read your statements to the California authorities, and Mr. Hobson has told me about your book. I find your charges against General Wingate incredible and totally unsubstantiated. And even if they were true, how would that change the fact that you broke Rice out of jail at gunpoint? I think we should end this meeting before you say something that makes your situation even worse than it is."

"My father is an unprincipled killer. Do you want a man like that running this country?"

"Of course not—if he is an unprincipled killer," Kirkpatrick answered, "but you can't prove your accusations, and I would not consider anything you or Carl Rice said without independent corroboration."

Vanessa looked at Victor Hobson. "Well, there might be corroboration, and you might be able to get it, Victor. If you find it, we can use my bail hearing to get my father. We can call him as a witness and put him under oath."

"What are we talking about here?" Hobson asked.

"I think we should cut this short now," Kirkpatrick said.

"Let's hear what Vanessa has to say."

Kirkpatrick looked surprised, and Vanessa almost sobbed with relief when she realized that the FBI man was going to listen to her.

"Patrick Gorman, my boss at *Exposed* visited me when I was in jail in San Diego. We were joking around about the jail food, and I told him that I couldn't afford much better with what he paid me."

"What does jail food have to do with proving that your father was in charge of a team of assassins?" Kirkpatrick asked.

"Let me tell you."

# CHAPTER **THIRTY-FIVE**

The Multnomah County courthouse occupies an entire block across from Lownsdale Park in downtown Portland. Built in 1914, the gray concrete and riveted-steel building contrasts sharply with the modern architecture of the Justice Center on the other side of the park and promises uncompromising justice to those who break the law.

A small jail on the seventh floor of the courthouse houses prisoners who are making court appearances. The elevator that transports them from the jail stopped in an alcove in the back of the courthouse on the Fifth Avenue side. Judge Ruben Velasco's courtroom, where Vanessa's bail hearing was going to be held, was in the front of the courthouse on the Fourth Avenue side.

Ami was wearing a tasteful strand of pearls and was dressed in a black pantsuit and a white silk blouse, one of her few decent outfits and the outfit she always wore to important court appearances. Vanessa was wearing a severe gray suit that Ami had purchased for her. If it were not for the handcuffs, she would have been mistaken for part of the defense team. Ami walked a few steps behind the guards who escorted Vanessa out of the jail elevator when it opened on the fifth floor. As soon as they stepped into the corridor a mob raced toward them.

"Keep moving forward and don't answer any questions," Ami instructed as the reporters and television cameras converged on them. The sheriff's deputies plowed through the shouting crowd. Ami shielded her eyes from the glare of the television lights as she followed behind the guards.

"Were you and Carl Rice lovers?"

"Why do you hate your father?"

"Are you going to vote for President Jennings in the primary?"

The questions thundered toward her like a stampeding herd, but Vanessa did not flinch from the onslaught. Where Ami shunned the attention of the media, Vanessa welcomed it as a chance to get her message about her father to the public. She squared her shoulders and stared back at the journalists.

"My father is a murderer," Vanessa shouted, ignoring Ami's advice. "He should be in jail, not the White House."

Ami was concerned that Vanessa's statements to the press might be used against her, but that didn't concern Vanessa. She knew that she'd spend years behind bars if Victor Hobson didn't come through for her. She wasn't afraid. She had survived the asylum by believing in herself, and she would survive prison. She had nothing to lose, anyway. If Hobson failed, she was no worse off than she'd been the minute she surrendered to the police. But Hobson might find her proof. If he did, her father would be destroyed. If that happened, she was willing to face the consequences of breaking Carl out of jail.

A line of spectators was filing through a metal detector that had been set up outside Judge Velasco's courtroom. A guard held up the line to let Ami, Vanessa, and the guards into the courtroom. Brendan Kirkpatrick and Howard Walsh turned in their seats at the prosecution table and watched the women walk down the aisle. Ami did not notice them. She was too busy scanning the crowded benches. Several reporters occupied a section reserved for the press at the front of the courtroom. Leroy Ganett, who was under subpoena by Ami and the DA, was seated in the rear of the courtroom. The doctor turned red and looked away when he spotted the women who had scammed him. Victor Hobson, the one man Ami and Vanessa hoped would be present, was missing.

One other man was not present in the courtroom. General Morris Wingate was waiting in the DA's office guarded by a contingent from the Secret Service and his own security force. Kirkpatrick had brought the General into the building before court convened to avoid the mobs of protestors, supporters, and reporters who had converged on the courthouse when the General's appearance as a witness was made public.

Just as they reached the low fence that separated

the spectators from the area where the attorneys and the judge conducted business, Vanessa noticed a slender, bookish, nattily dressed man in his mid-fifties.

"See that guy in the seat by the window in the third row from the back?" Vanessa whispered to Ami. "That's Bryce McDermott, my father's chief political adviser. He's probably going to report everything that happens in here."

There was an undercurrent of whispers—some hostile, some sympathetic—when the guards unlocked Vanessa's handcuffs. The women took their seats as soon as Vanessa's hands were free. Ami tried to ignore the hum of conversation that drifted through the gallery by concentrating on the outlines of direct and cross-examination that she had made for each witness. She had managed to block out most of the noise when the rap of the bailiff's gavel announced Judge Velasco's entrance. Ami rose to her feet and signaled Vanessa to do the same as the judge took the bench.

"Good morning," Velasco said to everyone in the courtroom. "You may be seated."

The judge waited to address the spectators until his bailiff had read the name and number of the case into the record.

"Before we begin this bail hearing, I want to make it clear to the members of the public who have been granted the privilege of watching this court proceeding that I will not tolerate improper behavior in my court under any circumstances. Anyone who causes a disturbance will be taken from the court immediately and will face criminal sanctions, including contempt of this court.

"One reason why I have made this announcement is the possibility that General Morris Wingate, a candidate for his party's presidential nomination, may be called as a witness. If that happens, there will be a heavy police and Secret Service presence in addition to the guards who would normally maintain order in this court. If anyone is contemplating any type of political protest during his testimony, I warn you that you will go to jail. I hope that is clear."

The judge paused to let his message sink in.

"Now to business. Are the parties ready?"

"The state is ready, Your Honor," Brendan Kirkpatrick said, standing to address the court.

Ami stood. "Ami Vergano for Miss Kohler. We're prepared to proceed."

"Very well. Mr. Kirkpatrick, what is your position on bail for Miss Kohler?"

"The state wishes bail to remain as it is. The defendant used a gun to help Carl Rice escape from the secure wing of the county hospital. She terrorized four people during the escape. Since his escape, Mr. Rice has murdered and assaulted a number of people. Miss Kohler may have aided and abetted some of these crimes. After she is prosecuted in Oregon, the defendant will be sent to California where she is facing charges of murder and assault growing out of the invasion of General Wingate's home. Her actions prove that she is a danger to others and a flight risk.

"One more thing. Miss Kohler has a pathological hatred of her father, General Morris Wingate. If she were free, she would be a danger to a presidential candidate."

Kirkpatrick sat down, and Ami stood. Inside, she cringed at the argument she was about to make, but she had a duty to present her client's position even if she did not believe it. More important, Vanessa still held the power to destroy Ami's life and Ryan's by telling the authorities that Ami had helped her hide.

"First off, Your Honor, Miss Kohler has no criminal record. She is employed with a newspaper in Washington, D.C. I'm going to offer into evidence an affidavit from her employer stating that he will continue to employ Miss Kohler. She has also had the same residence in Washington for many years. Except for this incident, Miss Kohler has been a model citizen.

"More important, Miss Kohler did not help Mr. Rice for criminal reasons. Miss Kohler believes that her actions in rescuing Carl Rice from the hospital were justified by a theory of defense of another, as were Mr. Rice's actions in California when he rescued Miss Kohler, who had been kidnapped and assaulted by her father and his agents.

"Carl Rice and General Morris Wingate have known each other since Miss Kohler and Mr. Rice attended high school together in California. Mr. Rice received a draft notice during his senior year in high school and went into the army instead of seeking a college deferment, even though he had earned a scholarship to Dartmouth. He eventually became a member of the Special Forces during Vietnam, and that is when his path and the General's path crossed again.

"During Vietnam, General Wingate was the head of the Agency for Intelligence Data Coordination, which has a charter that does not permit it to have active intelligence agents. Despite this clear prohibition, General Wingate ran a small and highly select army unit out of this agency. The Unit was financed by money obtained from illegal activities, such as drug smuggling."

There was a stirring in the audience, and Judge Velasco gaveled for silence. When the courtroom was quiet he turned his attention to Ami.

"I hope you have evidence to support these sensational claims, Mrs. Vergano."

"I have subpoenaed witnesses who will testify about the Unit and the General's connection to it."

Velasco looked incredulous but told Ami to continue.

"Soon after Mr. Rice returned to the states after completing his first combat mission, General Wingate arranged a meeting during which he recruited Mr. Rice into the secret unit. From the early nineteen-seventies until 1985 Mr. Rice was a member of the Unit. Under orders, he completed several missions including assassinations in Europe and on American soil.

"In 1985, Vanessa Kohler was living in Washington, D.C., where she became reacquainted with Mr. Rice. One evening, he confessed to killing two people in Texas under orders. These individuals were supposed to be spying for the Chinese. He was very upset and told Miss Kohler that he wanted to get out of the Unit.

"Miss Kohler found evidence in a safe in the General's house that proved the existence of the Unit. She presented it to Congressman Eric Glass at his summer home in Lost Lake, California, in hopes that the congressman would expose the activities of the Unit and her father's involvement in this illegal activity. When he discovered that the files were missing, General Wingate sent Mr. Rice to kill the congressman and retrieve the papers. After Mr. Rice murdered Congressman Glass and recovered the documents, General Wingate arranged for the murder of Mr. Rice. He survived, without the General's knowledge. Mr. Rice went underground for years, but his picture was on national television as a result of his arrest in the Little League assault case. When Miss Kohler recognized him, she knew that it was only a matter of time before her father learned that Carl Rice was alive.

"Miss Kohler helped Mr. Rice escape from the hospital because she was certain that General Wingate would have him killed to keep his secret."

The noise in the courtroom increased in volume. The judge rapped his gavel again.

"Please approach the bench," he said.

The judge leaned down and lowered his voice as soon as Ami and Brendan Kirkpatrick were standing at the side of the dais.

"I'm warning you, Mrs. Vergano. I will not permit my courtroom to be turned into a platform for political character assassination. Your charges are going to be carried by every television station and newspaper in this country and could affect the outcome of the primary election. I will report you to the bar association and place you in contempt if these charges prove to be unfounded or unconnected with the purpose of this hearing."

"I understand, Your Honor," Ami answered meekly. She felt sick to her stomach and light-headed with fear.

"And you, Mr. Kirkpatrick—I haven't heard a single objection."

"I don't see how I can object, Judge. Mrs. Vergano claims to have witnesses who will testify to what she has alleged. Personally, I don't think they have any credibility, but you're the only person in this court who can decide the credibility of a witness."

"And I will, Mrs. Vergano, I will. And if I decide that you or your client has misused the judicial process there will be consequences."

Even in ill-fitting orange jail clothes with his legs and hands shackled Carl Rice commanded respect. He walked with dignity and—like a caged panther—he radiated a sense of danger that made you want to keep your distance.

"May Mr. Rice have his shackles removed during his testimony?" Ami asked the judge.

"Sergeant Perkins?" the judge said, addressing the ranking jail guard.

"We would prefer that the irons stay on, Your

Honor. Mr. Rice is considered a high-risk prisoner. We've been informed that he's trained in
martial arts and is ex-Special Forces. The sheriff
knew this might come up, and he thinks the
handcuffs and leg irons should stay on."

"I'm going to follow the sheriff's recommenda-
tion, Mrs. Vergano. I might rule differently if this
were a trial, but I know he's a prisoner and that
will not prejudice my decision on bail."

Carl shrugged to show that it made no difference to him. Judge Velasco ordered his bailiff to
administer the oath, and the guards helped Rice
into the witness box.

"Mrs. Vergano," Judge Velasco said, "before
you examine Mr. Rice I want to inquire of him."

Ami nodded. She had expected this.

The judge turned toward the witness. "Mr.
Rice, Mrs. Vergano was your attorney . . . "

"She still is, Your Honor," Rice answered
calmly.

"That troubles me. Normally, one lawyer does
not represent two defendants who are charged in
the same case."

"Mrs. Vergano explained all the problems that
could arise from her representation of Miss
Kohler and me. I have waived any conflicts because Miss Kohler and I believe that it is in our
best interests to have Mrs. Vergano representing
both of us."

"This decision of yours makes me very nervous,
but I will accede to your choice. However, I must
discuss another matter with you. Are you aware
that you are testifying under oath and that every-

thing you say will be recorded by the court reporter
and can be used against you in every court proceeding that occurs in your cases here, in California, and
in federal court?"

"Yes, sir, I have discussed this thoroughly with
Mrs. Vergano."

"You could be convicting yourself of murder,
assault, escape, what have you, out of your own
mouth."

"I appreciate your concern, Your Honor, but
I'm willing to risk my life to let the American
people know the truth about Morris Wingate."

Judge Velasco was visibly agitated. For a moment it looked as if he might say more. Instead,
he turned toward Ami.

"Go ahead, Mrs. Vergano."

"Thank you, Your Honor. Mr. Rice, did you serve
in the United States Army?"

"Yes."

"Was that during the Vietnam War?"

"And after."

"When did your service end?"

"Officially, I don't think it ever did, but I left on
my own accord in 1985."

"What were the circumstances that caused you
to leave the service?"

"General Morris Wingate sent me and the other
members of an illegal unit that he was running out
of the AIDC to North Vietnam. We were supposed
to be rescuing American MIAs, but the whole thing
was a setup. The North Vietnamese knew we were
coming. There was an ambush. Everyone in the
Unit was killed except me. I was captured, but I

escaped. After a year, I made it back to the states and went underground. I figured no one would look for me, because the General would assume that I was dead."

"You testified that you were set up. By whom?"

"By General Wingate. He wanted to eliminate everyone who was in the Unit, and he nearly succeeded."

Ami asked Rice to tell the judge how he was recruited into the Unit and to recount some of his missions. The noise from the gallery ceased as Rice hypnotized the spectators with testimony about ambushing mule trains in the Shan Hills, cutting the throats of village chiefs in Southeast Asia in the middle of the night, and assassinating spies in Europe and America. Ami heard the scratch of pencils on steno pads behind her in the press section, which was packed with reporters from every major newspaper in the country and several members of the foreign press.

"Mr. Rice, you testified that you were recruited into General Wingate's Unit after your first combat mission."

"Yes, Ma'am."

"Were you wounded during that first mission?"

"I was grazed by a bullet. It wasn't anything serious."

"Were you hospitalized as a result of your wound?"

"Well, I was sent to a hospital to have the wound checked, but they kept me less than a day."

"Were you hospitalized for combat-related stress?"

"No, Ma'am."

"Did you receive a more serious wound during the mission to rescue the MIAs?"

"Yes. A shell exploded near me and I was hit by shrapnel."

"Let's move to another subject. From what high school did you graduate?"

"St. Martin's Prep in California."

"Was Miss Kohler a student at the school?"

"We were in the same class."

"Who is Vanessa Kohler's father?"

"General Morris Wingate."

"Did you meet General Wingate while you were dating his daughter?"

"Yes, on many occasions."

"Did Miss Kohler break up with you while you were in high school?"

"Yes."

"Why?"

"I was drafted. She wanted me to resist the draft. I'd been accepted to college and could have gotten a deferment. She was upset when I didn't try to get one and chose to serve."

"Did Miss Kohler believe that her father was responsible for your draft notice?"

"Yes. She thought he had engineered my draft to interfere with our relationship."

"After high school, when was the next time you saw Miss Kohler?"

"In 1985."

"Where did you meet?"

"In Washington, D.C. I was teaching at the army language school at Fort Meyer, and she was attending law school and working for Congressman Eric Glass of California."

"At some point after you met Miss Kohler in Washington, did you tell her about your involvement with her father and your missions?"

"Yes."

"Did you find out sometime later what she did as a result of your confession?"

"Yes. She stole the files of the ten members of the Unit from her father's safe and gave them to Congressman Glass, who had a summer home on Lost Lake, California."

"Were you given any instructions by Morris Wingate concerning the congressman and the files?"

"General Wingate told me that Congressman Glass was a traitor who was going to sell the files to a foreign government. He instructed me to go to Lost Lake, retrieve the files, and torture the congressman to death."

There was a loud reaction in various parts of the spectator section, and Judge Velasco gaveled for silence. Ami continued her questions as soon as silence returned to the courtroom.

"Was murder by torture unusual even in your line of work?"

Rice's composure cracked for the first time. He licked his lips and looked ill.

"Was torturing someone to death unusual?" Ami repeated.

"Yes," Rice answered, his voice barely audible.

"Did you follow the General's orders?"

"Yes."

"Did anyone see you kill Eric Glass?"

Rice looked over at Vanessa. "Miss Kohler was in the house. I didn't know that she would be there until I saw her. The General hadn't told me that his daughter had given the files to the congressman."

"What did you do after you saw Miss Kohler?"

"I panicked. I ran. When I got myself together, I took the files to the General and asked him to explain why Vanessa was at Lost Lake. He told me that Glass had seduced her into stealing the files. He said that she'd told the police that I killed the congressman. Then he told me that he would hide me in North Vietnam by sending me on a mission to save a group of American MIAs who were being held captive. He promised me that he would have a plan in place when I returned to ensure that I would not be arrested. He was going to arrange plastic surgery and a new identity."

"But that never happened?"

"No," Rice answered bitterly. "The mission was a trap. I could prove that the Unit existed and so could the rest of the men. He needed us dead to protect himself. All those brave soldiers who would have given their lives for their country . . ."

Rice stopped. He was trying to maintain his composure, but he was on the verge of tears. He asked for a glass of water. Judge Velasco no longer looked skeptical. There were whispers in the gallery. Ami chanced a glance behind her. The spectators looked subdued and serious.

"How did you survive?" Ami asked, her voice so low that the court reporter had to strain to hear her.

"I escaped."

"Would you please tell the judge how that happened?"

Carl gathered himself and told Judge Velasco how he was captured and tortured, and how he escaped, survived in the jungle, and made his way back to America. While he was speaking, Carl's eyes never left the rail of the witness box. When he finished, he was totally spent.

"Why did Miss Kohler break you out of the hospital?" Ami asked when Rice was ready to continue.

"She believed that the General would try to kill me as soon as he learned that I was alive."

"So she rescued you to save your life?"

"Yes."

"Were her fears for your safety justified?"

"I believe they were."

"After you left the hospital, did you murder Dr. George French, a psychiatrist I was using in your case, and his wife?"

"No."

"Who killed them?"

"General Wingate had his men murder Dr. George French."

"How do you know that?"

"Because his men tried to murder you also, Mrs. Vergano."

"And you rescued me?"

"Yes."

"Why do you think General Wingate murdered Dr. French and tried to kill me?"

"You were the two people who had access to me at the hospital. He was afraid I'd told you about the Unit and his involvement in it so you could use the information as a bargaining chip in plea negotiation."

"Why did you break into the General's mansion in California?"

"His men had kidnapped Vanessa. I saw them. I was afraid for her life."

"So Miss Kohler did not go to her father's house voluntarily?"

"No, Ma'am."

"No further questions, Your Honor."

Brendan Kirkpatrick rose slowly and approached the witness. On the way to the stand, the prosecutor handed Ami copies of several documents.

"Your Honor, I've just given counsel copies of State's Exhibits 1, 2, and 3, which I have previously marked. Mrs. Vergano is willing to stipulate, for purposes of this hearing only, that they are Mr. Rice's army records from his official file. I move their introduction into evidence."

"You're willing to stipulate, Mrs. Vergano?" Judge Velasco asked.

"Yes, for this hearing only, Your Honor."

"Very well. The documents will be admitted."

"I just have a few questions for you, Mr. Rice," Kirkpatrick said as he handed the witness copies of the exhibits. "You've testified that you were in this so-called secret unit from the early nineteen-seventies until 1985, when you went AWOL?"

"Yes."

"And you had numerous missions overseas?"

"Yes."

"Look at your records. After your first combat mission, do they show any more overseas service?"

"No, but these records are false. My missions were never on paper when I was in the Unit."

"So you have testified. Still, your official records do not support your testimony, do they?"

"No."

"What was your rank in 1985?"

"I was a captain."

"But the records list you as a sergeant, don't they?"

"Yes."

"Look at Exhibit 3. That's the psychiatric evaluation written by Dr. Howard Stienbock."

"I was never interviewed by this man. This is false."

"But it does say that you were discharged from the service for pretending to be a captain and the doctor does conclude that you may have been experiencing delusions as a result of the stress you suffered in your only combat mission."

"It was not my only combat mission. These documents were prepared by General Wingate to cover up my membership in the Unit."

"I see. They were written as part of the conspiracy against you?"

"They were prepared as part of a cover-up."

"And you no longer have the records you took from Lost Lake?"

"I gave them to the General."

"And the men in the Unit are all conveniently dead? Their bodies are in North Vietnam?"

"It wasn't convenient for them, Mr. Kirkpatrick. They were brave men and they died a hard death."

"So you say, but you can't prove your story, can you?"

Rice paused for a moment before shaking his head.

"We need you to speak up for the record, Mr. Rice. Do you have any proof to support your accusations against General Morris Wingate?"

"Other than my word, no," Rice said, his voice barely above a whisper.

"Then the judge pretty much has to take your word for the existence of this secret unit, your exploits in it, and the falsity of the official army records, doesn't he?"

Rice stared at the papers he held in his hand and did not answer. Kirkpatrick let the matter drop and introduced a new subject.

"When you and the defendant were in high school, did she ever tell you how she felt about her father?"

"Yes."

"Would it be fair to say that the defendant hates her father?"

"Yes."

"Did she ever tell you that she believed that General Wingate murdered her mother?"

"Yes."

"And was part of the conspiracy to kill President John F. Kennedy?"

There was a gasp in the courtroom and some laughter. Judge Velasco gaveled for order.

"She never told me that she thought her father was involved in the Kennedy assassination."

"But she does hate her father?"

"Yes."

"And she would do anything—say anything—to hurt her father, wouldn't she?"

"Objection," Ami said. "That question calls for speculation."

Before the judge could rule, Kirkpatrick said, "I'll withdraw the question, and I have no further questions for the witness."

The guards helped Carl out of the witness box. When he passed by the defense table, he looked at Vanessa and she smiled. He smiled back as he was led out of the courtroom, but the smile lacked conviction.

"Call your next witness," the judge instructed.

"Miss Kohler calls Dr. Leroy Ganett," Ami said.

Dr. Ganett walked to the stand without looking at Ami or Vanessa. He was upset when he took the oath.

"Dr. Ganett," Ami asked after establishing the doctor's credentials and his position at the county hospital, "you were Carl Rice's treating physician, were you not?"

"Yes," he answered tersely. It was obvious that

he wished he were anywhere other than in the witness box being questioned by Ami on behalf of Vanessa Kohler.

"And you knew him as Daniel Morelli?"

"Yes."

"Let's refer to him by his true name—Carl Rice—from now on, okay?"

"If you wish."

"Why were you treating Mr. Rice?"

"He was brought to the hospital with gunshot wounds. I operated on him, and after he was placed in the security ward I continued to treat him."

"Doctor, I'm handing you defense Exhibit 1. Please identify it for the court."

"It's my medical report on Morelli's—uh, Rice's—condition."

"Did you write it after examining him?"

"Yes."

Ami pointed at a line in the report. "Would you read this sentence to the court, please?"

Dr. Ganett saw where she was pointing and cleared his throat.

"Uh, this sentence says that an X ray of Mr. Rice's abdomen showed metal fragments compatible with shrapnel."

"And shrapnel is a metal fragment from a bomb or grenade that is exploded during war, is it not?"

"Well, not necessarily wartime, but from a bomb, yes."

"Most shrapnel wounds are received during war, aren't they?"

Dr. Ganett thought for a moment then nodded.

"I would say that you would see a larger number of shrapnel wounds during a war."

"No further questions."

"Dr. Ganett," Brendan Kirkpatrick said, rising from behind the prosecution table, "you used the term 'compatible with shrapnel' in your report, didn't you?"

"Yes."

"Why didn't you just say that the metal fragment was shrapnel? Why use the word 'compatible'?"

"We have no way of knowing that the fragment is shrapnel. It is a metal fragment, it is consistent with shrapnel, but it could be something else."

"It could be a metal fragment that penetrated Mr. Rice's body during an explosion in this country?"

"Yes."

"An auto accident could result in the creation of a metal fragment like the one you found in his body?"

"I suppose so."

"Or a water heater could have exploded? That could result in the creation of a fragment like this one, couldn't it?"

"I suppose."

"So there's no way of knowing where Mr. Rice received this wound, or under what circumstances, just from looking at an X ray, is there?"

"I guess not."

"Assuming for the sake of argument that Mr. Rice did receive this wound in combat, is there any way that you can tell if it was inflicted in 1985 as opposed to the early nineteen-seventies?"

"No, I don't think you can do that."

"Thank you, Doctor."

Relief flooded Dr. Ganett's features when Ami said that she had no further questions and he hurried out of the courtroom.

"Any more witnesses, Mrs. Vergano?" Judge Velasco asked.

Ami stood again. "Miss Kohler calls Detective Howard Walsh."

After Walsh took the oath, Ami established that he was the detective in charge of the Little League case.

"Detective Walsh, when Mr. Rice was arrested in connection with the incident at the Little League game, did you take his fingerprints?"

"Yes."

"Is that routine when a person is arrested?"

"Yes."

"What did you do with the fingerprints?"

"We ran them through AFIS, the Automated Fingerprint Identification System, to see if he had a criminal record."

"Was AFIS able to match Mr. Rice's prints?"

"No."

"Mr. Kirkpatrick has entered records from Mr. Rice's army file into evidence. Weren't the fingerprints in the file?"

Walsh hesitated.

"Well, Detective?" Ami prodded.

"There appears to be some kind of clerical error, because his prints aren't on record with the army."

"Thank you, Detective."

"No questions," Kirkpatrick said.

"My final witness is Miss Kohler, Your Honor."

This was the moment that Vanessa had been waiting for. It was her chance to tell the world that her father was pure evil. Yet the moment her name was called, doubts assailed her. Was everyone else right? Was the Unit a figment of Carl's imagination? Did her father really love her?

"Miss Kohler," Judge Velasco said. "Please come up here and be sworn."

Vanessa steeled herself and willed herself to her feet. She was right. Her father was evil. She threw her shoulders back and walked to the witness box, convinced that justice would be done today.

Before Judge Velasco would allow Ami to examine her client, he reviewed the problems that Ami's dual representation of her and Carl Rice created and gave her the same warning about incriminating herself that he had given Rice. When Vanessa told him that she wanted to testify, the judge told Ami to continue.

"Miss Kohler," Ami asked after a few preliminary questions, "in 1985 in Washington, D.C., did Carl Rice tell you about his involvement in a secret military unit that your father was running out of the AIDC?"

"Yes."

"After this conversation, did you try to find proof that the Unit existed?"

"Yes."

"What did you do?"

"My father had a safe in his office in our house

in California. He didn't know that I knew the combination. Inside were the army records of ten men, including Carl's records."

"What did you do with the records?"

"I was working for Congressman Eric Glass, who was on the House committee that oversees the intelligence community. I knew that he was at his summer home at Lost Lake in Northern California. I took the records to him. I wanted him to look into what these men had been doing during and after Vietnam."

"What happened to the records?"

"I gave them to Eric, and he agreed to have someone on his staff look into them. It was late. Eric let me use one of the guest rooms. A noise woke me up in the middle of the night. I went downstairs."

Vanessa paused. Even after all these years and numerous retellings, the horror of what she had seen was still fresh.

"Do you want some water or a brief recess?" Ami asked.

"No. I'm okay." Vanessa coughed, then took a deep breath. "Eric was tied to a chair. He . . . There was blood all over. Carl was standing over him with a knife. He'd killed the congressman, and he took the records."

"Let's move on to the events at the county hospital. Why did you rescue Mr. Rice from the security ward?"

"Objection," Kirkpatrick said. "This was not a rescue. Miss Kohler aided and abetted an escape from custody."

"That's to be decided by Your Honor," Ami responded. "Our position is that Miss Kohler's bail should be lowered because Mr. Rice was in danger and she rescued him. We believe that Miss Kohler is not guilty of any crime if Mr. Rice's life was in danger if he stayed in the hospital."

"Objection overruled, Mr. Kirkpatrick. Mrs. Vergano is entitled to her theory. Whether I accept her theory is another matter entirely."

"You may answer my question," Ami said.

"My father thought that he'd gotten rid of the evidence that could prove that the Unit existed. With Carl alive, he faced the possibility that his criminal activities would be exposed. And even if there wasn't enough proof for a criminal conviction, what Carl knows could derail his presidential bid. I knew my father would go to any lengths to get rid of Carl, so I broke him out of jail."

"Why not just tell the authorities about the danger to Mr. Rice?"

Vanessa laughed. She pointed around the courtroom. "You can see how much credence the police give to what I have to say. My father had me committed to a mental hospital after Lost Lake in order to destroy my credibility. I knew no one would take me seriously, so I saved Carl before the General's men could kill him. As it was, we just escaped in time. My father's killers murdered Dr. French and his wife shortly after we escaped and they tried to kill you."

"How do you know that Mr. Rice didn't kill Dr. French and his wife?"

"I was with him from the time he left the hospital until I was kidnapped by my father's men."

"Did you know any of the men who kidnapped you?"

"Sam Cutler."

"Who is Sam Cutler?"

"I can't be certain that's his real name. Carl knew him as Paul Molineaux. He works for my father, but I didn't know that when I met him."

"What was your relationship with Mr. Cutler before he kidnapped you?"

"He was my lover," Vanessa answered bitterly. "When my father decided to run for the presidency, he instructed Sam to get close to me to make sure I wouldn't cause his election campaign any trouble." She paused. "I only learned this recently."

"Was Mr. Cutler alone when he kidnapped you?"

"No. He had several members of my father's security force with him. They tried to kill Carl, but he escaped."

"Where were you taken by Mr. Cutler?"

"To my father's home in California."

"Is this the house in which you grew up?"

"Yes, but I don't go there anymore."

"Did Mr. Cutler use force to bring you to the mansion?"

"He used physical force and he drugged me."

"So you did not go to the mansion of your own free will?"

"No."

"Was Mr. Rice trying to kidnap you when he broke into the mansion?"

"No. He was rescuing me. My father was keeping me there against my will."

"So Mr. Rice was trying to rescue you from kidnappers when he broke into the mansion, and you would have left with him voluntarily?"

"Yes."

"If the judge lowers your bail or releases you on your own word, what will you do?"

"I'd follow the court's instructions. If he lets me return to Washington until the trial, I'll go back to work. Patrick Gorman, my employer, is keeping my position open. I have an apartment. I've been living there for close to fifteen years."

Ami handed a document to Judge Velasco.

"This is a signed affidavit from Patrick Gorman attesting to the fact that Miss Kohler has been a valued employee for many years and that he will continue to employ her if she is released from custody. I've given a copy of the affidavit to Mr. Kirkpatrick, and he has agreed that it can be a substitute for Mr. Gorman's testimony at this hearing."

"Is that so, Mr. Kirkpatrick?" the judge asked.

"Yes, Your Honor."

"Very well, any further questions of your witness?"

"No," Ami said.

"You may examine, Mr. Kirkpatrick."

When Brendan walked over to the witness box he looked subdued, as if he were sad to have to ask his questions.

"Were you and Carl Rice lovers in high school, Miss Kohler?"

"Yes."

"And you broke up in high school?"

"Yes."

"Then you renewed your acquaintance in D.C. in 1985?"

"Yes."

"Did you become lovers in Washington?"

"No."

"Who made the decision to keep the relationship platonic in D.C.?"

"Me."

"Why was that?"

"We hadn't parted on the best of terms in high school, and we'd both changed over the years." Vanessa shrugged. "I just didn't feel like getting involved in that way with Carl again."

"And Mr. Rice knew how you felt?"

"Yes."

"He also knew that you hated your father, didn't he?"

Vanessa laughed. "Everyone knew that."

"Did Charlotte Kohler, your mother, die in a car accident when you were in middle school?"

"It was no accident."

"You believe that your father murdered your mother, don't you?"

"I know he did."

"But you have no proof that she was murdered, do you?"

"No," Vanessa answered as she glared defiantly at the prosecutor.

"And the authorities concluded that your mother's death was an accident, didn't they?"

"My father has people on his payroll who can make any death look like an accident."

"Nonetheless, the official verdict was that your mother's death was an accident?"

"Yes."

"You testified that Sam Cutler was living with you in Washington?"

"Yes."

"Did you tell him that you thought that your father may have been involved in the Kennedy assassination?"

"My father's military career took off soon after Kennedy was murdered," she answered belligerently.

"And you think that's because he was involved in some sort of cabal that was responsible for the assassination?"

"I don't have any proof about that. It's . . . The coincidence is . . . " Her voice trailed off as she realized how insane she sounded. "Yes."

"You testified that you and Mr. Rice had once been lovers, but you decided to keep the relationship platonic when you met again in 1985."

"I just said that."

"What if he wanted more, Miss Kohler? He knew you hated your father and that you'd believe any outlandish story he made up as long as the villain in it was General Morris Wingate. What if he concocted a story about a secret army headed by your father to bind you to him?"

"No, the Unit existed," Vanessa insisted stubbornly.

"If Mr. Rice hadn't told you about the Unit, would you have known about it?"

"What about the records in the safe?"

"Please answer my question, Miss Kohler," Brendan asked patiently. "If Mr. Rice had not told you about the Unit, would you have known of its existence?"

"No."

"Did any of the records you took from your father's safe mention the Unit?"

"No, but Carl's army records were with the others."

"Couldn't your father's possession of these records have had an innocent explanation that had nothing to do with a super-secret team of assassins?"

Vanessa shook her head from side to side. She was growing very agitated.

"My father is a killer. He ordered Carl to kill Eric Glass for those records."

"You cannot produce these records for the court, can you?"

"My father has them, if he hasn't destroyed them."

Brendan looked at the judge. "Would you please instruct Miss Kohler to answer my question?"

"Yes, Miss Kohler. You're not allowed to argue with counsel. If there is a point you wish to make, your attorney can ask you about it during redirect. Do you understand?"

"Yes," Vanessa answered grudgingly.

"Do you want the court reporter to read back the question?"

"That's not necessary." Vanessa turned to the prosecutor. "No, Mr. Kirkpatrick, I can't produce the records."

"Miss Kohler, did it ever occur to you that Mr. Rice may have murdered the congressman out of jealousy because he thought that Eric Glass was your lover?"

"I don't believe that. You don't know my father. You have no idea what he's capable of doing."

"Have you ever seen your father kill someone?" Kirkpatrick asked.

Vanessa hesitated.

"Have you?"

"No."

"Have you ever seen him order someone to commit a crime?"

"No," Vanessa answered softly.

"Has your father ever hurt you?"

"He had me kidnapped."

"Or did he rescue you from a man who is a confessed mass murderer?"

Vanessa glared at the prosecutor. "My father had me locked away in a mental hospital." Her eyes blazed with hate and her body was rigid. "He kept me in a drugged stupor for a year just to shut me up."

"Or to help you. Didn't the doctors at the hospital make the diagnosis that kept you there?"

"They did what he ordered them to do."

"Did the doctors tell you that?"

"No."

"Did you ever hear your father give such an order?"

"He's too smart for that. He was always telling me how much he loved me and how it hurt him to have to hospitalize me. He made certain that there were witnesses. He may be evil but he's also very clever."

"Or very caring, Miss Kohler, or very caring. I have no further questions, Your Honor."

"He made me look like a fool," Vanessa told Ami, who was seated across the table from her in the jury room following the noon recess.

"Brendan is an excellent attorney. He knows that you have only Carl's word that the Unit exists."

"What about the murder of Dr. French and his wife?"

"Brendan doesn't believe you or Carl. He thinks that Carl killed the Frenches and that you're covering for Carl."

"Carl saved your life. What does he think about that?"

"He thinks that your father's security people came to my house looking for you and Carl killed them and my police guards. That explanation fits Brendan's theory of the case."

Vanessa shook her head. "We don't have a chance, do we?"

"I'm sorry, but I told you that this would happen. You've been in a mental hospital and your father is a national hero. You're very open about your hatred for him. That gives you a strong motive to lie or distort the truth."

"Still no word from Hobson?" Vanessa asked.

"No."

"I knew I'd never beat him. He always wins."

Vanessa closed her eyes and tilted her head back. Her pain was so visible that it hurt Ami, but Ami knew of no way to stop the pain. They had lost, and Vanessa and Carl Rice were going to go to prison for a long time.

# CHAPTER **THIRTY-SIX**

After Ami Vergano rested her case, Brendan Kirkpatrick began the prosecution's case by questioning Dr. Ganett and the other men who'd been taken prisoner at the hospital. Shortly before noon, Judge Velasco recessed court until two.

The prosecutor was feeling a little down when he walked into the Multnomah County district attorney's office on the sixth floor of the courthouse. He usually felt elated after a great cross-examination, but his demolition of Vanessa Kohler had been too easy. Her irrational belief in General Wingate's mythical secret army was a product of hate and a deep-seated mental illness. Beating up on someone who was irrational and sick was not something he relished.

"Mr. Kirkpatrick," the receptionist called out. "I have an important message from Mr. Stamm about your bail hearing. He wanted me to make sure you got it as soon as you came back from court."

Jack Stamm, the Multnomah County district attorney, was Kirkpatrick's boss. Brendan took

Stamm's note from the receptionist. His brow
furrowed with confusion as he read it. He was
tempted to go to Stamm's office and ask for an
explanation of the instructions, but the note
was very clear. It ordered him to do as he was
told without question.

Brendan walked down a narrow hallway that
began at the reception desk and ended in a large
open area that housed the workspaces of the
deputy district attorneys and their staff. General
Wingate was waiting in the conference room.
Two Secret Service men were guarding the door.
They searched Brendan and his briefcase before
letting him in.

General Wingate's pale blue eyes fixed on the
prosecutor the moment the door opened.
Seated beside him was Bryce McDermott, the
General's political adviser. Mr. McDermott had
returned to the conference room as soon as
Vanessa was through testifying, to brief the
General on what Carl Rice and his daughter had
said. At the end of the table was a compact,
muscular man wearing a leather jacket that was
open enough to give the deputy DA a clear view
of a large handgun. The man's eyes were on
Kirkpatrick as soon as he entered the room.

The General still wore his gray-streaked hair in
a military cut. He had on a white silk shirt, a
solid maroon tie, and the slacks from a charcoal-
gray suit. The suit jacket was folded neatly over
the back of a chair.

Wingate looked upset. "Bryce tells me you
were pretty rough on Vanessa."

"It's my job to win this bail hearing, but I can assure you that I didn't enjoy myself."

The General sighed. "I know you're just doing your job, but I hurt whenever Vanessa hurts. Do you have children, Mr. Kirkpatrick?"

"No," Brendan answered. His expression didn't change but he felt an ache in his heart. He and his wife had started talking about a family shortly before she died.

"They're amazing, but they play havoc with your emotions. Every little thing they do brings you either ecstasy or pain. Sadly for me, Vanessa's actions over the years have brought me little pleasure. Still, I can't stand to see her suffer."

"Then I'm sorry to tell you that I need you to testify."

"Surely that's not necessary after the job you did examining Carl and Vanessa. What possible questions could the judge have about their sanity? He's got to realize that Vanessa is too irrational to release on bail."

"General Wingate, if there's one thing I've learned in my years in practice it's that you never assume a judge or jury is going to act in any particular way. I've seen the most bizarre decisions made in this courthouse, and the only thing I know for sure is that you always cover your ass.

"Besides, I need you to tell the judge why you had your daughter brought to your home and what happened when Rice broke in. And I think it's essential that you deny Rice's allegations about this secret army he claims you ran when you were with the AIDC."

The General turned to McDermott. "What do you think, Bryce?"

"I agree with Brendan. The press is all over the courtroom. They took down every word Rice and your daughter said. We need to defuse this thing. If you don't answer their accusations, the media is going to speculate about why you're keeping mum. Let's put this bullshit to rest, right now."

Wingate sighed again. "You're right. I'm just not happy about sitting across from my daughter and saying things that will reinforce her belief that I'm trying to destroy her life."

"I understand completely, and I'll try and make this experience as painless as possible," Brendan said.

"I don't suppose Mrs. Vergano shares your sentiments?"

"No, sir, I don't believe she does."

Brendan Kirkpatrick and General Wingate pushed through the courtroom doors surrounded by the General's bodyguards and followed by Bryce McDermott. Suddenly, the back benches were flooded by the glare from the television lights and there was an explosion of sound from the corridor. Then the doors swung shut and the General walked to the witness box, back straight, eyes forward, as if he were on parade. When he drew even with his daughter, he paused to send a sad smile her way. Vanessa met the smile with a look of pure hatred. Wingate's smile faded and he shook his head sadly.

As soon as the bailiff swore him in, the General took his seat in the witness box.

"Have you ever been married?" Kirkpatrick asked as soon as he had walked Wingate through his educational, military, and business history.

"Yes, to Charlotte Kohler, a wonderful woman."

"What happened to her?"

Wingate dropped his eyes. "She died in a car accident."

"When did this happen?"

"In the mid-sixties, when Vanessa was still in middle school. Her mother's death hit her very hard."

"You're referring to the defendant, Vanessa Kohler?"

"Yes."

"Is the defendant the only child of your marriage?"

"Yes."

"How would you characterize your relationship with your daughter?"

"We were close until her mother died. Then she got it into her head somehow that I was responsible for the automobile accident that killed Charlotte. She was in her teens, a very vulnerable age. Our relationship became strained."

The General looked up at the DA. "I take a lot of responsibility for that. Vanessa and I lived in California but I worked in Washington, D.C."

"You were in charge of the Agency for Intelligence Data Coordination?"

"Yes. I should have been home more, but I

couldn't be, especially after Vietnam started. The workload was punishing."

"Was there a specific event that further affected the relationship between you and Miss Kohler?"

Wingate nodded. "In 1985, Vanessa saw Carl Rice murder Eric Glass. It was a terrible murder—very gruesome. She had a breakdown and had to be hospitalized. I checked her into an exclusive private sanatorium where she would get the best care possible. She fought her hospitalization. She insisted that locking her away was part of some plot against her."

Wingate paused and took a sip of water before continuing.

"Putting Vanessa in a mental hospital was very painful for me, Mr. Kirkpatrick, but sending her to Serenity Manor was absolutely essential for her mental health." The General looked down. "After I had her committed, she refused to speak to me."

"How long have you known Carl Rice?"

"I believe we first met at my home in California in 1969. It was the beginning of Vanessa's senior year in high school. Carl was a classmate."

"What was your initial impression of Mr. Rice?"

"I liked him. He was bright, articulate, and a serious student and athlete."

"What was Mr. Rice's sport?"

"Karate. He'd been studying since he was young and he was very good, a black belt."

"You know that Mr. Rice has accused you of being the head of a secret army unit that recruited him during the Vietnam War."

"Yes."

"Are you aware that he alleges that this army unit committed illegal acts, including murder, at your command?"

"Yes."

"Are you also aware that Mr. Rice has testified that you ordered him to torture Congressman Eric Glass to death in order to retrieve documents which your daughter took from your safe in California? These documents were supposed to prove the existence of this secret army."

"I've heard about the testimony."

"Did you order Carl Rice to kill the congressman?"

"No, absolutely not."

"Did this secret army unit ever exist?"

"No. The Agency for Intelligence Data Coordination is an intelligence-gathering organization that works with data supplied by other intelligence agencies, like the CIA and the Defense Intelligence Agency. The agency's charter does not permit it to have agents of its own."

"What about these records that your daughter claims she took from your safe that prove the existence of this secret army—the records Mr. Rice said he took from Congressman Glass after torturing him? What do you have to say about them?"

"Mr. Kirkpatrick, those documents are a figment of my daughter's and Mr. Rice's imaginations. They were never in my safe, because they never existed."

"Do you know why Mr. Rice made up this story about the secret army?"

General Wingate hesitated. "I have a theory," he said at last.

Judge Velasco looked at Ami because he expected an objection. When she didn't make one, he chalked it up to her inexperience.

"Please tell it to the court."

"I'm not particularly proud of what I'm about to say. At the time I believed that I was doing what was best for all concerned."

Wingate paused to collect himself. Ami thought that he looked like a man who was being forced to perform a necessary, but regrettable, duty. From the silence in the courtroom, it was obvious that he had captivated the spectators and the judge.

"As I've said, Mr. Rice was an extremely bright young man who made an excellent first impression. Unlike most of the children at St. Martin's Prep, Carl was on scholarship, and I admired his grit. I came from a poor family and was also a scholarship boy. I knew how hard it was for someone who is poor to be around other children who have everything. It was only later that I discovered that he was deeply confused, especially about his relationship with me.

"Mr. Rice's father deserted his family when Carl was very young, and his mother raised him. There was no significant father figure in his home while he was growing up. It soon became apparent to me that he envied Vanessa her wealth and wished that he could be part of our family. He began relating to me as if he were my son. I didn't realize that this was happening at the time, or I would have distanced myself from Carl."

"Did a particular incident make you realize that there was a problem?"

"Yes. In those days I knew a man who organized fights between combatants from different martial arts disciplines: boxers would go up against wrestlers, judo players would fight Thai kickboxers. I took Carl to one of these matches because he was a serious student of karate.

"One of the fighters was a black belt named Torrance who ran a dojo and was a local karate champion. After he won, Carl and I discussed the fight and I asked him how he thought he would do if he went up against Torrance. It was a casual conversation, and I didn't think anything of it until several weeks later when I received an envelope in the mail. There was no name on it and no return address. There was no letter inside either, only a newspaper clipping about Torrance. Someone had broken into his karate studio and beaten him almost to death. I was certain that Carl was the assailant and had sent me the clipping to impress me. It didn't. I felt terrible that I might have inadvertently caused Carl to attack Torrance, and I was deeply concerned that someone this unbalanced was close to my daughter. But there was no way I could talk Vanessa into breaking up with Carl. By her senior year in high school our relationship was very strained. If I'd even suggested that she stop seeing Carl, she would have intensified the relationship just to spite me."

"What did you do?" Brendan asked.

"I thought about calling the police, but I had no

proof that Carl was involved. Besides, he had a scholarship to an Ivy League school by this time and I knew that an arrest would ruin his chances of going to college. And, as I've said, I felt terribly guilty about what had happened. Then fate intervened. Carl received a draft notice, and he came to me for advice."

"Did you have anything to do with his being drafted?"

"I did not. This is another one of Vanessa's delusions."

"Go on."

"Carl wanted to know if I thought that he should serve or get a student deferment. I should have helped him go to college, but I wanted to get Carl as far from Vanessa as possible, so I persuaded him to go into the army. I shouldn't have taken advantage of the fact that he saw me as a father figure, but I did it to protect my daughter. I also thought that spending time in the military might help Carl mature.

"When Carl saw Vanessa again in 1985, he knew that she hated me. I think he made up this story about a secret army so she would take him back. He may still have been in love with her."

"Did you ever meet with Mr. Rice between his senior year in high school and this year when he invaded your home?"

"No, we had nothing to do with each other."

"You did not have him come to your town house in Virginia soon after his first combat mission so that you could recruit him into this secret army?"

"No. He was never at my town house in Virginia, and, as I've testified, there was no secret army."

"And you did not meet him in a motel in Maryland and order him to torture Congressman Eric Glass to death?"

"Certainly not."

"Okay, let's move forward to more recent events. Please tell the judge how the defendant came to be at your home after she helped Mr. Rice break out of the county hospital."

"You have to remember that Carl had murdered Congressman Glass in 1985, and was also the main suspect in the murder of an army general named Peter Rivera around the same time. Then there were the two men he nearly killed at that Little League game. Needless to say, I was horrified that Vanessa was on the run with someone that dangerous. So I instructed some of my people at Computex . . ."

"This is your company?"

"Yes. We have a highly trained security force of former Green Berets, Delta Force, and Rangers, who I used to rescue my employees in Afghanistan. I sent them after Vanessa because I knew how dangerous Carl could be. They were lucky enough to find her before Carl hurt her. My men were under orders to bring Vanessa to me. I was planning to call the authorities after I arranged for legal representation and psychiatric care."

Wingate paused. He looked pensive. "Maybe I should have had my men take Vanessa directly to the police, but I have been able to do so little for her since her mother died and I . . . Well, I may have used poor judgment, but I would probably do the same thing if I had a second chance. Honestly, I just wanted my daughter safe and with me."

"What happened after you learned that Vanessa had been rescued?" Kirkpatrick asked.

"I was in Cleveland making a campaign speech. I flew directly home."

"Tell the court what Carl Rice did when he learned that your daughter was in your home."

"Soon after I arrived, Carl invaded my house."

"Was anyone hurt during this invasion?"

"Yes. Several of my guards were either killed or injured."

"Once inside, what did Mr. Rice do?"

"He broke into the room where Vanessa was staying. I was talking to her when Carl attacked. One of my men distracted Carl, and I escaped and summoned the guards. We kept him pinned down until the police arrived. My daughter had called an FBI man named Victor Hobson, and he negotiated their surrender. I'm very grateful to him because Vanessa was not harmed."

"I have no further questions for General Wingate," the DA said.

The judge nodded to Ami. "Mrs. Vergano," he said, "your witness."

Ami slid a list of ten names out of her file. "Thank you, Your Honor," she said, rising to her feet. "General Wingate," Ami said, "who is Arthur Dombrowski?"

"I have no idea."

"Who is Fredrick Skaarstad?"

"I don't believe I've ever heard of him."

Ami read seven more names. The General denied knowing all of them.

"But you do know Carl Rice?" she asked after glancing up from the last name on the list.

"Yes."

"Would it surprise you to know that I've just read you a list of the ten men whose records your daughter took from the safe in your home in California and gave to Congressman Glass?"

"Mrs. Vergano, those records never existed except in my daughter's imagination. I assume she gave you those names, but I have no idea where she got them."

Ami stared intently at the General, who braced himself for more cross-examination. After a moment, however, she shook her head.

"No further questions, Your Honor."

The General looked surprised. He cast a quick glance at Kirkpatrick, who shrugged.

"Do you have any more witnesses, Mr. Kirkpatrick?" Judge Velasco asked.

"I may have one more. Can we recess so I can speak with him?"

"How long will you need?"

"Twenty minutes, half an hour."

"Very well. We'll adjourn for half an hour."

As Wingate and Kirkpatrick walked up the aisle toward the courtroom doors, two Secret Service men and the General's bodyguard formed a protective circle around him. More members of the General's security force waited outside the courtroom. Kirkpatrick pushed through the doors, and the television lights flashed on as the reporters began firing questions at the candidate.

"The General will hold a press conference in an hour at his hotel," Bryce McDermott said loudly enough to be heard over the din. "He won't take any questions until then."

"Let's get you upstairs and away from this mob," Brendan said.

They double-timed it up the marble staircase to the district attorney's office, and Kirkpatrick led the General back to the conference room.

"Before you leave, there's someone who wants to meet with you," Brendan told Wingate.

"We don't have much time," McDermott said. "The General has to be in Pittsburgh tomorrow, and we still have the press conference."

"I'm afraid this is important," Brendan insisted as he opened the conference room door.

"Good afternoon, General," said Ted Schoonover, President Jennings's chief troubleshooter. He was seated at the conference table with Victor Hobson. "You know the assistant director, don't you?"

McDermott pointed at Schoonover. "What's he doing here?" he asked Brendan angrily.

"Mr. Kirkpatrick has no idea why I'm here, Bryce," Schoonover said. "And the reason for our meeting is something I can discuss only with General Wingate. So, everyone but General Wingate and Director Hobson will have to step outside."

"No fucking way," McDermott answered.

"General, we don't have time for a chat with Jennings's hatchet man."

"You don't have a choice, Mr. McDermott," Hobson said. "This meeting is part of a criminal investigation and I'm exercising my authority as a federal agent to clear this room. You, the General's bodyguard, and the Secret Service will have to wait outside."

McDermott started to protest, but Wingate held up his hand.

"Wait outside, Bryce."

"But . . . "

"I'll be fine."

As soon as the door closed behind Kirkpatrick, McDermott, and the General's bodyguards, Wingate took a seat across from Schoonover and the assistant FBI director.

"We have a problem, General. Or, rather, you do," Schoonover said.

"What problem?" Wingate asked.

"I'm afraid that some of your testimony under oath wasn't true and I thought that you'd like to clear it up before the press finds out."

"I'm not following you," General Wingate said.

"You testified that you had no contact with Carl Rice between the time he was in high school and the time he invaded your mansion."

"That's correct."

"During her cross-examination, Mrs. Vergano read you a list of names of men who were supposedly in the secret unit you ran out of the AIDC. You said you'd never heard of them."

"That's right."

Schoonover took a sheaf of papers out of an attaché case and pushed them across the table.

"Then how do you explain these?" he asked.

The General shuffled through the papers for a moment. They were covered with numbers and letters and appeared to be some kind of code.

"What are they?" he asked.

"Do you want to explain, Victor?" Schoonover said.

"Sure. Your daughter took the personnel records of the men in your secret unit from your safe."

Wingate smiled. "There were never any records, Mr. Hobson. They are . . . "

"Yes, yes," Hobson interrupted, "figments of the imaginations of two very disturbed people, as you testified, and I'm sure the originals don't exist anymore. You'd have been a fool to keep them after Carl Rice killed Eric Glass to get them, and you are definitely not a fool. But neither is your daughter. Vanessa wrote down the names of the men before she gave the documents to the congressman, and that enabled me to track down the documents Ted just gave you."

"These don't look like personnel records," the General said.

"They're not. I did serve a search warrant at the army records center in St. Louis, Missouri, for the personnel records, and they found records for all the men on Vanessa's list. They were similar to Carl's official records. The men were all listed as having few if any combat missions, and most of those were early in their careers. They were also shown as having stateside duty for most of their time in the service. None of them had a rank over sergeant.

"But the personnel records weren't the main thing I was looking for. Carl always claimed that he was a captain. A captain's pay is significantly higher than a sergeant's. Vanessa told me to look for the pay records, too. Strangely, none of the pay records for these men existed in St. Louis. The clerk I spoke with told me that a fire of mysterious origin destroyed a lot of their records in 1973."

Hobson paused and stared at the General, but Wingate did not react. Hobson smiled.

"A lot more microfilm was destroyed in the mid-nineties when the information was upgraded to digital media," he continued. "I thought that I'd reached the end of the line when the clerk remembered that the Defense Finance and Accounting Service in Indianapolis kept copies of the original pay records on microfilm."

Hobson shook his head. "I had a hell of a time finding them. The microfilm was in old moldy boxes filled with thousand-foot rolls. My men and I thought we'd go blind, but we finally got the pay records for all ten men."

"I can't make heads or tails of these numbers and letters," Wingate said.

"But you do recognize the names at the top. They're the same names that Mrs. Vergano read to you, the names you testified under oath rang no bells."

Hobson placed a document on the table. "This

is Carl Rice's pay record for his time in the army from 1970 until 1985. You should have a copy in that stack."

Wingate found his copy and stared at it.

"I couldn't make any sense of this either," Hobson said, "but I got a subject-matter expert at the DFAS to interpret the code. What's important is the pay rate for each man. Carl was paid as a captain right after he claimed to have started working for you. And he received hazardous-duty pay, which he would not have received for teaching at the language school. But most important, someone had to authorize the promotion of these men so they could receive the pay increase. On the page for each of these men is a code that authorizes their promotion to captain so they could be paid as captains. The papers promoting these men were with their pay records."

Hobson pushed them across the table.

"They were all signed by you, General," Schoonover said.

Wingate looked at the documents but did not touch them.

"Victor, would you step outside?" Schoonover asked.

Hobson got up without a word. As he circled the table, his eyes never left Wingate. The General was pale. He seemed disoriented, like a man awakening from a deep, troubled sleep.

"So, what does Jennings want?" Wingate asked as soon as he and Schoonover were alone.

"He'd love to see you on California's death row

awaiting execution for the murder of Eric Glass. Actually, we both would."

"That's not going to happen." Wingate picked up the papers he'd stacked in a pile. "This jumble of numbers and letters won't get you anywhere. And neither will testimony from my daughter, the ex-mental patient; or Carl Rice, the mass murderer."

"Carl passed three polygraphs since we took him into federal custody. Vanessa passed her tests, too."

"Polygraph evidence isn't admissible in court."

Schoonover smiled. "You're right, but newspaper reporters are. The bail hearing is only in recess. What do you think the papers will print when these documents are admitted into evidence? You've testified under oath that you've never heard of these men and that you had no contact with Carl after he graduated from high school. Your signature on the pay records proves that you're lying."

"These documents are forgeries. Jennings probably had someone from the CIA doctor them."

"Right, the CIA. That reminds me. Do you remember getting a visit from a CIA agent shortly after Eric Glass was murdered?"

"No."

Schoonover nodded. "Charles told me you'd deny any knowledge of the meeting, and Gregory Sax, the agent, is dead—the victim of an armed robbery that occurred shortly after Peter Rivera was murdered."

"Where is this going?"

"Sax was the Unit's liaison with the White House in 1985. When Vanessa told the police that Carl Rice murdered Eric Glass, Sax knew that a member of the Unit had killed the congressman, and he had a crisis of conscience. He'd been leery of some of the Unit's missions, but there had always been some sort of national security justification that let him rationalize the assassinations, the drug dealing, and all the other sordid activities in which your men engaged. But Glass's murder was the last straw. He's the one who went to President Reagan and told him that the Unit had to be shut down. He's the man who carried President Reagan's order to shut down the Unit back to you in 1985. And you really shut it down, didn't you? You sent those fine soldiers to their deaths. Then you made it look like Carl Rice had murdered Peter Rivera for the codes to the secret fund, but you killed Rivera and took the money, didn't you?"

"It's convenient for you that this Sax person and the president he allegedly told about Vanessa's secret army are dead. Where is this fairy tale going?"

"When Sax was murdered, President Reagan put a bright young CIA agent in charge of a secret investigation of the Unit. The agent was Charles Jennings."

"Ah, and I suppose that Charles is going to get on TV and tell the world about his secret investigation that just happens to prove that the man who is running against him is a murderer and a thief."

"You know better than that. But the president

knows you're dirty, Morris. He doesn't have to be convinced that you betrayed your men in Vietnam, that you stole the millions in the secret fund and used that money to buy into Computex, and that you were behind the murders of Sax, Glass, and Rivera. Unfortunately, with Rice missing and Sax dead, he could never prove anything. Then Carl Rice returned from the dead. And now we have the pay records of men that you swore under oath you didn't know, with your signature authorizing their promotions to a rank their official files say they never attained."

"This is all very interesting but I've got a statement to make to the press and a plane waiting to take me to Pittsburgh."

"Use the press conference to announce that you're dropping out of the race."

"Not a chance."

"Then we'll go public with the pay records, the Justice Department will look into where you got the money you used to finance Computex, and we'll investigate the plane crash that killed Simeon Brown. With all the negative publicity, you'll be lucky to get any votes in the primary, and the president will have four more years to make your life hell."

"This is what happens in banana republics, Ted," Wingate replied calmly. "The person in power arrests his opposition. If Charles tries that with me, I'll win the primary in a landslide."

"You'll be able to count the votes in jail, if the other prisoners vote to watch the news that night," Schoonover answered.

Wingate stood up. "I'm calling your bluff, Ted. If you persist with these outrageous demands, I'll hold a press conference, all right, and I'll use it to expose the blackmail threats you've just made. I'll have Brendan Kirkpatrick and the Secret Service agents in my guard detail tell the world how the president's hatchet man insisted on this private meeting. Then I'll get the best experts money can buy to prove that these documents are false."

Schoonover smiled. "When I was in 'Nam, we had a name for guys like you who sent other people to die doing their dirty work. We called them REMFs. It's an acronym that stands for rear-echelon motherfuckers. We despised them, just like I despise you. That's why I'm going to take great pride in bringing you down."

Sam Cutler was working on the details of security for an appearance in Madison, Wisconsin, when the General stormed into his hotel suite. Wingate had been calm and self-assured when he spoke to the reporters at his press conference, but he was seething now.

"Sam," Wingate barked. Cutler cut short his phone conversation and followed the General into the bedroom.

"Has this room been swept?" Wingate asked.

"We can talk," Cutler assured him.

As he changed into casual clothes for the trip to Pittsburgh, Wingate told Cutler about his meeting with Ted Schoonover.

"The documents can hurt us," the General said,

"but our real problem is Carl Rice. Vanessa knows only what he told her. Carl is the key."

"What do you want me to do?" Cutler asked.

Wingate stared at his aide. "Don't be obtuse."

"Rice is going to disappear, General. Jennings will stash him in a safe house."

"Then find him. Use our contacts at Justice, the CIA. Pay what you have to, but find him. And remember, Sam, I'm not the only person who's in danger. You have a lot to lose as long as Carl Rice is alive."

# CHAPTER **THIRTY-SEVEN**

Ryan was supposed to go home with Bobby O'Dell's mother, so he was surprised when Ami picked him up at school and told him that they were going to the Multnomah County courthouse. The last time Ryan had been to the courthouse was on "Bring Your Child to Work" day. Before court convened, a nice lady judge had let him sit in her chair and hold her gavel. Then he'd had to sit in the spectator section for an hour and listen to his mom and another lawyer talk. Ryan liked sitting in the judge's chair, but the other stuff was pretty boring. Ryan asked Ami why they were going downtown. Ami said it was a surprise. She didn't tell him that this meeting had been one of Carl Rice's conditions for helping Ted Schoonover and President Jennings bring down Morris Wingate.

The courthouse was still busy when Ami and Ryan arrived, but the only people in the corridor outside Judge Velasco's courtroom were a hard-looking man and woman in plainclothes, who Ami guessed were FBI agents. Inside the locked courtroom, two other agents watched the door to the judge's chambers.

Ami knocked on the hall door to Judge Velasco's chambers. It opened into the anteroom where the judge's secretary worked. The secretary was gone, her place taken by two FBI agents who watched alertly as Ami and Ryan entered.

"Go on in, Mrs. Vergano," said the agent who had unlocked the door. Ami thanked him and ushered Ryan into the judge's office where Carl Rice waited, free of his shackles and dressed in tan slacks and a plaid cotton shirt.

Ryan hesitated when he saw Carl, suddenly shy and tentative.

Carl flashed a big smile. "Hey, Champ, how's the team doing?"

"Okay," Ryan answered quietly.

Ami placed a hand on Ryan's shoulder. "They won one and lost two, but Ryan had a single and a double in the last game."

"Not bad," Carl said. "How's the curveball coming?"

"I haven't really been practicing," he mumbled.

"That's not good. You won't master the curve if you don't practice. Have your mom catch for you."

Ryan shrugged. Carl knelt down so that he was closer to Ryan's height, and Ami stepped back.

"You're upset by what happened at the ball game, right?"

Ryan shrugged again but wouldn't look Carl in the eye.

"That's okay. It shook me up, too. It's no fun

being shot, and I feel very bad about hurting Barney Lutz and that policeman. That was wrong."

Ryan shifted uneasily.

"But I didn't ask your mom to bring you here to talk about that. There's something I want to tell you."

Ryan looked at Carl expectantly. "Are you coming home?"

"I wish I could." Ryan's face fell, and Carl put his hand on Ryan's shoulder. "If I tell you a secret, will you promise to keep it to yourself? It's important that no one but you and your mom know."

Ryan hesitated. He looked confused.

"My real job isn't being a carpenter, Ryan. I'm a spy. You know what that is, right?"

"Like James Bond."

Carl nodded. "I work undercover for our government, and I was on assignment when I was living at your house. I can't tell you what the assignment was, because it's top-secret, but it was very important. When I got shot, it loused up everything, but my bosses squared it with the police and I'm not in trouble anymore."

"If everything is okay, why can't you move back?"

"I wish I could. I really like your mom, and you're terrific, but spies don't get to settle down like regular people."

Carl leaned forward until his lips were close to Ryan's ear. "This is something even your mom doesn't know," he whispered. "I work directly for the president, and he just gave me new orders. I can't tell you what they are, but it's my most important assignment ever."

"Really?"

Carl nodded. "I'll tell you something else that isn't a secret. If I had a son I'd want him to be just like you, but spies don't get married. We have to be on the move all the time, and we don't want to put the people we love in danger."

"Don't you get lonely?" Ryan asked.

"Yeah," Carl said. He felt a tightening in his chest and had to struggle to hide his sadness from Ryan. "But, from now on, when I start to feel down, I'll remember the fun I had at your house and I'll cheer right up. I'll be able to keep track of you guys, too. My intelligence agency will let me know how you're doing in school and Little League. That's why I want you to practice that curve. It would be great if I heard that you'd won a few games with the pitch I taught you. What do you think?"

"I'll work on the curveball."

"Will you help him, Ami?" Carl asked.

"Definitely," she said, her voice choked with emotion.

"School, too. I want you to do your best. Okay?"

"Okay," Ryan answered solemnly as a tear trickled down his cheek.

Carl stood up. It took all his training to stay calm. "Let's shake on it, then."

Ryan held out his hand, and Carl's engulfed it. Then Carl drew Ryan to him and gave him a hug.

"Wherever I am, you'll be in my heart, Ryan." His eyes met Ami's. "You and your mom."

"Will we ever see you?" Ryan asked, tears coursing down his cheeks now.

"I'd sure like to see you again, someday. Meanwhile, you take care of your mom, okay? She needs you, and you need her. And work on that curve."

Carl tousled Ryan's hair.

"I've got to go now. The president sent a special plane for me, and I can't keep him waiting."

Ryan wiped a forearm across his eyes.

"Keep safe," Carl said. Then he touched Ami on the shoulder and walked through the door to the courtroom. The door closed behind him, and Ryan didn't see the agents secure his handcuffs before leading him away.

"He'll be okay, Ryan. You don't have to worry," Ami assured her son, her eyes still on the door to the courtroom. Then she looked at Ryan.

"Are you going to be okay?" she asked.

Ryan nodded, embarrassed to be crying but unable to stop.

Ami knelt beside him. She had tears in her eyes, too. "It's okay to be sad. He's a good friend. And maybe he'll get some time away from his job someday and you'll see him again. The important thing is to know that he cares about you very much. You understand that, don't you?"

Ryan nodded.

"And you also understand about keeping what Carl told you a secret."

"I won't tell," Ryan answered solemnly.

"And I'll help you with the curve and your schoolwork so Carl will be proud of you, okay?"

Ryan nodded.

"You know it's a little late for me to shop for dinner. How about going to the Spaghetti Factory? You'll need those carbs for tomorrow's game. Coach is letting you pitch, isn't he?"

"Yeah."

"Gonna try the curve?"

"I don't know if I have it right, yet," Ryan answered. Ami heard the worry in his voice. She smiled and gave him a hug.

"You'll never know if you don't try, right?"

"I guess."

"Then let's go eat and you can practice with me before you go to bed."

One agent had stayed behind to lock up. He let them out of the judge's chambers and turned off the lights at the same moment an unmarked car with tinted windows drove out of the parking garage with Carl Rice in the backseat. The car headed for the airport where an FBI jet was waiting to take Carl to an undisclosed destination.

# CHAPTER **THIRTY-EIGHT**

It took Sam Cutler a week, and the small fortune he had paid to Robert Bloom—an FBI agent with a cocaine habit—to discover where Victor Hobson had stashed his star witness. After viewing aerial surveillance photographs of the Nebraska farm, Cutler told Wingate that he did not like the setup one bit. Wingate had answered that the FBI used this remote spot for a safe house because it was difficult to attack. The farm was miles from the interstate, so anyone driving to it would stand out like the Rockies in the flat landscape. A locked gate separated the dirt road that led to the farmhouse from a paved state road. On either side of the gate were miles of barbed wire. The dirt road ran like an arrow through fields of corn that could provide cover for the attack force, but the fields ended a distance from the farmhouse where Carl was living with an FBI security detail, and there was open land between the house and the cornfields that provided no cover.

Wingate and Cutler had discussed their options and decided that they had none. They didn't know how long Rice would be kept at the farm. If Hobson moved him, they'd have to start all over again. So Sam Cutler had assembled the team of six men he'd used to grab Vanessa and had driven to Omaha, eschewing air transport because of video surveillance and paper trails that could eventually lead back to the General.

There was no moon on the evening of the assault. Cutler parked half a mile from the entrance to the farm. One of his men cut a hole in the barbed wire and the team moved into the shelter of the cornfield, where the tall stalks blocked the cold wind that had cut through the men as soon as they left the shelter of their car. Using a Global Positioning System, Cutler maneuvered through the rows of corn, stopping just before the open ground. He scanned the farmhouse through night-vision binoculars. A guard was smoking a cigarette on the porch. Another guard was patrolling the perimeter. Cutler was disgusted by the sloppiness of the security detail. Two of his men were deadly accurate with a sniper rifle and would be able to pick off the guards without making a sound before the attack force ever left the cover of the cornfield.

How many guards would that leave inside? The overflight that had given the team the aerial surveillance photos had registered heat signatures for six human beings: Carl and five guards. But the overflight had been more than twenty-four hours earlier, and more agents could have arrived.

Just as Cutler was about to command the snipers to kill the guards, the agent on the porch snuffed out his cigarette and walked inside, and the man who was patrolling the perimeter walked out of sight behind the farmhouse. Suddenly, no one was watching the ground between Cutler's position and the farmhouse. He made a split decision.

"Double-time to the house," he commanded. If they could cover the ground fast enough, they could use the element of surprise to take out everyone inside.

The men were halfway across the open space when Cutler's two snipers went down and the assault team was bathed in light. Cutler was temporarily blinded and threw a forearm across his eyes.

"Order your men to throw down their weapons, Mr. Cutler," a voice, amplified by a bullhorn, boomed out. "You're surrounded and you have no chance of escape."

Soldiers were beginning to emerge from the cornfields just as it dawned on Cutler that his wounded men had been shot from the farmhouse.

"We've had you under surveillance since you paid Robert Bloom for the location of this safe house. He's under arrest, by the way. You've been set up, Sam, and there's only one way out for you and your men—cooperation. So throw down your weapons. We'll take care of your wounded, and you and I can have a talk."

Cutler knew that he and his men would die if he opted for a shoot-out, so he told them to lay down their arms. Several medics attended to the wounded snipers. His men were cuffed and led toward the barn, while three soldiers walked Cutler to the farmhouse.

Ted Schoonover was sitting in the parlor in an overstuffed easy chair. A fire was roaring in the grate. Tiffany lamps sat on oak end tables, and an embroidered antimacassar covered the back of a sofa decorated with a floral pattern. On the wall was an oil painting of cows grazing in a field. Cutler would not have blinked if Ma and Pa Kettle had appeared out of a side room. Instead, Carl Rice and Victor Hobson joined the president's aide.

"Sit down, Sam," Schoonover said, indicating a hard wooden ladder-back chair. Cutler settled in and his guards stood by, on the alert even though he'd been disarmed and his hands were cuffed behind him.

"Can I have these cuffs off?" Cutler asked.

Schoonover smiled. "Not a chance, Sam. You're way too dangerous even with them on. Now, let me explain the program. I'm going to make you an offer. Then, whether you accept or not, you're going to join your men in one of those secret locations where we interrogate terrorists. Don't ask for a phone call or a lawyer. Your civil rights don't exist anymore—but all is not lost."

"I'm listening."

"I'll make this simple, Sam. We want Morris Wingate. I'm sure he explained about the pay records. Coupled with his lies at his daughter's bail hearing and Carl's testimony, that gives us a shot at convicting him of something—perjury at a minimum. But I'll be honest, that might be all

PHILLIP **MARGOLIN**

we can nail him on—unless we can produce a witness who will corroborate Carl's testimony."

"Me," Cutler said.

Schoonover nodded. "One or more of the men we just captured might also be helpful. We'll know soon. They're tough, but we'll break them eventually if they decide not to cooperate. But you're the prize, the inside man, Wingate's chief lieutenant."

Cutler didn't say a thing, but everyone could see that he was thinking hard.

"As of now, you've disappeared, Sam, and the General is not going to help you. He can't. So, you're on your own."

"This is sort of like the mission to rescue the MIAs," Carl said. "The General wrote off the men in the Unit, and he'll do the same to you. The moment you were captured you became expendable."

"Thanks for your concern, Carl," Cutler said.

"Don't become confused," Carl said. "I'd as soon see you dead after what you did to the Unit, but I want to see Wingate destroyed, and you're the key."

"So, what do you say?" Schoonover asked.

"I'll want more than life in a cage, if I'm going to cooperate," Cutler said.

"We have to know what you can do for us before we can talk about concessions."

"I can do plenty, believe me," Cutler said.

# CHAPTER **THIRTY-NINE**

Two weeks later, Ami Vergano closed the door of a small, windowless room in the federal building in San Diego and set her briefcase and a package wrapped in brown paper on the floor before taking a seat across the table from Carl Rice and Vanessa Kohler. Carl's hair was short, his beard had been shaved off, and he was dressed in casual clothes. Vanessa was wearing jeans and a white T-shirt.

"Mission accomplished," Ami said as she took copies of several documents out of her briefcase and gave them to the couple.

"This first set of papers dismisses all state and federal charges against you, and grants you immunity from prosecution, in exchange for your testimony against Morris Wingate in any state or federal proceeding."

Vanessa looked at her incredulously. "Are you saying that you got us full immunity?" Vanessa asked. "They have me dead to rights on the jailbreak, and Carl admitted under oath that he killed Eric Glass."

"Remember during the trial when Brendan went to the DA's office to bring General Wingate to court to testify?"

"Yeah," Vanessa said.

"Victor Hobson took me aside and explained what was going on. Brendan was in on everything. His job was to get your father to testify that he hadn't seen Carl between high school and the rescue attempt at your father's mansion. But they still needed me to get your father to deny he'd ever heard of the men in the Unit. I told Victor that I wanted immunity before I'd help. I reminded him that you'd both been victims and had taken a terrible chance in testifying in order to bring down your father; furthermore, without the two of you, there'd be no case. He agreed to come through with immunity in exchange for Carl's complete cooperation in the government's case against Wingate."

"I was happy to oblige," Carl said.

"Did they have second thoughts after Sam Cutler agreed to testify against my father?" Vanessa asked.

"Some," Ami answered, "but it was too late. Carl and I had already followed through on our part of the bargain.

"Here's something else I want you to read," Ami said as she handed the couple more documents.

"This second group of documents is the paperwork that will get you into the federal witness protection program," she explained.

As Vanessa examined the paperwork, she

showed none of the joy or excitement that Ami had expected to see.

"Is there something wrong?" Ami asked.

"Do you remember the last scene in *The Graduate*?" Vanessa asked.

"I think so. I saw it on TV a year ago. Dustin Hoffman has just spirited the girl away from her wedding, right?"

"Katharine Ross played the girl," Vanessa said, "and she and Dustin are sitting on the bus and they're together, but they have this scared look on their faces when they realize that they have no idea what they're going to do next. I feel like that. My entire adult life has been dedicated to getting revenge on my father. Now I've won, but the life I've built for myself during the past twenty years is what I've had to sacrifice to get him. I have no idea what I'm going to do from this day forward."

"Was it worth it?" Ami asked.

"I guess I'll find out, only I'll never be able to tell you or anyone else I've ever known the answer to your question. I'll have to cut all my ties to the people and places I used to know."

"Once your father is in prison you'll be safe."

"We'll never be safe, Ami," Carl said. "The General has a network that stretches back to the nineteen-sixties. He'll have people on our trail until he's dead, and maybe even after that."

"Are you sorry you agreed to testify against him?"

"I had no choice," Carl said. "Besides, my life won't be so different. I've been on the run so long I don't remember any other life. It's Van I worry about."

Vanessa reached out and took Carl's hand. "I'm tough, Carl. I made it through the asylum. I conquered drugs. I'll live through this."

Carl squeezed her hand. "We'll get through it together."

Vanessa smiled at Ami. "At least your life will go back to normal now that you've gotten us out of your hair."

Ami laughed. "I'd be lying if I said that I wasn't glad this case is over. I don't like being a celebrity. Can you believe that two people stopped me in the airport this morning and asked for my autograph?" She shook her head. "Drawing up a simple will is going to seem like heaven after being attacked by assassins and groupies."

"I bet people are asking you to handle more than a simple will after the publicity you've been getting," Vanessa said.

Ami blushed. "I have been asked to handle some bigger cases."

"Are you going to take them?"

"I don't know. I can use the money, but I'm worried about Ryan. I don't want him to turn into a latchkey kid."

"Why don't you hire an associate? With the money you can charge now, you can afford one."

"I'm thinking about it."

There was a sudden silence as the trio ran out of things to say. Ami had promised herself that she would keep this meeting businesslike, but she felt herself tearing up.

"I'm going to miss you guys," she said. "You're both special."

"I'm going to miss Ryan," Carl said.

Ami brightened. "He tried the curveball in his last game."

"How did it go?"

She laughed. "He struck out a batter the first time he threw it. But the next guy hit a homer off him. But he's not discouraged. We practice every day."

An embarrassed quiet settled on the room. Then Ami remembered her package.

"I brought you something. The marshals said they'd make sure you got it when you've settled into your new home."

Ami took off the brown paper. Under it was the landscape that Carl had admired at the Portland Spring Art Fair on the day they'd met.

"This is great, Ami. This is perfect."

Ami reached across the table and placed her hands on top of Carl's and Vanessa's. She was crying unashamedly now.

"You take care of yourselves."

"We will," Vanessa said.

"You've been an important part of our lives, Ami," Carl said. "We'll never forget you."

Brendan Kirkpatrick stood up when the door to the interview room closed. Ami's eyes were red and her face was flushed. He could see that she'd been crying, and he handed her his handkerchief.

"Are you okay?" Brendan asked.

"I'll be fine. I'm just worried about Carl and Vanessa."

"Those two are survivors, Ami. Remember,

Carl escaped from a North Vietnamese prison camp, survived the jungle, and fought his way back to the states. And Vanessa had the courage to challenge her father, who just happened to be a billionaire candidate for the White House. These are two tough guys. They're going to survive this, too."

Brendan pushed the down button and the elevator doors opened. Ami stepped into the car.

"I know you're right," she said. "This whole thing has just overwhelmed me. I'm not used to seeing my face on the front page of the paper. I don't like being the center of attention."

"I know you don't, but you've been magnificent."

Ami blushed. "Thank you, Brendan, but I don't feel magnificent. I feel . . . I don't know . . . exhausted, I guess."

"I don't doubt you're exhausted, but you're also one of the gutsiest women I've ever met."

Brendan laughed.

"What's so funny?" Ami asked.

"I was just remembering that stunt you pulled in the hospital when you kept me from asking Carl if you were his lawyer. You have no idea how pissed off I was at you."

"Oh, I have some idea. What you don't know is how scared I was. As soon as you left, I collapsed. I was so frightened that you were going to arrest me that I was shaking."

The elevator doors opened on the main floor and Ami was shocked to see that it was dark outside.

"Do I still scare you?" Brendan asked with a grin.

"Nah, you're all bark and no bite."

"I'm also famished. I was down here in San Diego about a year ago working with the feds on a drug case and one of the U.S. attorneys took me to a terrific seafood place in the gaslight district. Want to join me? I'm buying."

"I don't have much of an appetite."

Brendan shook his head and laughed ruefully "You *must* be tired."

"What do you mean?" Ami asked warily.

"Because you usually pick up on stuff pretty fast. I'm asking you out on a date, Vergano. I'm not nearly as interested in the seafood—which is really good—as I am in spending time with you."

"Oh!" Ami paused. "Okay, I'll have dinner with you, especially if you're buying."

"You're not a gold digger, are you?"

Ami slipped her arm through Brendan's. She had an impish grin on her face.

"You'll have to figure that out, won't you?"

# ACKNOWLEDGMENTS

The following people were of invaluable help to me in writing *Lost Lake*; the book would not have been possible without them: Ami Margolin, Andy Rome, Earl Levin, Dr. Howard Weinstein, Dr. Jim Boehnlein, Bryan Hubbard, Nicole Dalrymple, Don Nash, Richard Meeker, Steve Perry, Bridget Grosso, and Robin Haggard.

Thanks to Dan Conaway, Jill Schwartzman, Marie Elena Martinez, and everyone else at HarperCollins. A special thanks to Tim Vert, who makes my website a terrific place to browse.

I remain indebted to Jean Naggar, Jennifer Weltz, and the rest of the gang at the Jean V. Naggar Literary Agency who have made my writing career possible. They are a pleasure to work with.

I could not have written this book without the support of my family, my fabulous wife, Doreen, my terrific children, Daniel and Ami, and Daniel's equally terrific wife, Chris.

Finally, thank you to all the readers and book-sellers who have supported me all these years. I love writing, and you make it possible for me actually to earn a living at it.

Coming in **July 2006**
PROOF **POSITIVE**
By Phillip **Margolin**

Doug Weaver had experienced his fair share of bad days during his legal career, but the day Oregon executed Raymond Hayes was one of the worst. Doug tried to convince himself that watching someone die from a lethal injection wasn't like seeing someone stabbed to death or crushed by a train, but that only helped him deal with what he would see. It didn't ease his guilt. Deep down, Doug believed that Raymond Hayes was going to die because he had screwed up.

The fact that Doug liked his client made it even more difficult. Bonding wasn't unusual during a death case where the attorney and his client are thrown together for months or years at a time. Sometimes during a visit at the penitentiary when they were talking about NASCAR races or football games Doug would almost forget why Ray had needed representation. There were even moments when he thought, "There but for the grace of God go I." The slightly overweight attorney with the receding hairline did bear a faint resemblance to his chubby, balding client. Both men were also in their early thirties, and they'd grown up in small towns. But that was where the similarities ended. Doug was a lot smarter than the majority of his high school classmates, while Ray barely graduated. After high school, Doug had gone to college and Ray had stayed home, working the farm for his ailing, widowed mother before selling out and moving with her to the cottage in Portland where she had been brutally murdered.

The last time Doug had made the fifty-mile drive from Portland to the Oregon State Penitentiary it had been to tell Raymond that the justices of the United States Supreme Court had voted against taking up his case.

"Does that mean I'm going to die?" Ray had asked in that lazy drawl that sometimes made you wonder if he was even slower than his below-average intelligence test scores suggested.

The question had caught Doug off guard. It took a shifting of mental gears to accept the notion that a denial of a Writ of Certiorari in Ray's case was the legal equivalent of shooting his client between the eyes.

"Well," Doug had stammered as he tried to think of a tactful way of answering the question.

Ray had just smiled. He'd been seeing Father McCord a lot, and Jesus was now a big part of his life.

"Its okay, Doug," his client had assured him. "I'm not afraid to meet my Lord and Savior."

Doug wasn't so sure that there was a place in

Heaven for a son who had beaten his seventy-
two-year-old mother to death with a hammer so
he could steal her diamond wedding ring and
forty-three dollars, but he kept the thought to
himself. If Ray was convinced that he was
straight with the Lord, Doug wasn't going to play
devil's advocate.

"My life ain't been so great," Ray had said. "I
hope I'm a better person in Heaven."

"You will be," Doug had assured him.

Ray had studied his attorney with a sad, com-
passionate eye. "You still think I killed Mom,
don't you?"

Doug had never told Ray that he didn't believe
his protestations of innocence, but he guessed
that somewhere along the way he'd slipped up
and revealed his true feelings.

"I really don't know, one way or the other,
Ray," Doug had hedged.

Ray had just smiled. "It's okay. I know you
think I lied to you. I appreciate how hard you
worked for me, even though you thought I done
it. But I didn't kill Mom. It's the way I always said
it. So I know I'll go to Heaven and stand by the
side of Jesus."

Doug had handled other capital cases but only
Ray had been sentenced to death. In fact, very
few Oregon inmates had been executed since the
death penalty had been reinstated in 1984. Doug
hated the fact that he would be one of the few attorneys in the state who could say that he'd wit-
nessed the execution of a client.

During the week leading up to the execution

Doug didn't sleep well and felt tired and cranky. Anxiety caused his mind to wander at the office and made it difficult to get any work done. He had been drinking more than usual too, which was always a bad sign.

Doug had never questioned Ray's guilt but his inability to stave off death ate at him. He was constantly second guessing decisions he'd made, especially the decision to convince Ray to plead guilty. It wasn't as if his strategy was unreasonable. He'd consulted several lawyers who handled death cases and most had agreed with his plan. The older, experienced attorneys had convinced him that winning a death case meant keeping your client alive. The evidence against Ray was incredibly strong, and Doug had gambled that Ray's acceptance of guilt and his spotless record would sway the jury in favor of life in the sentencing phase of the trial. He had been horribly, horribly wrong.

Doug worked on the day of the execution but he didn't accomplish much. Before leaving for the prison, he ate a light dinner, put on his best suit, a clean white shirt, and his nicest tie, and even shined his shoes. He wanted a drink badly, but he limited himself to one glass of scotch. Doug was going to be sober at the execution. He figured he owed Ray that.

The day had been out of sync with Doug's mood and the seriousness of the event he was about to witness. Dark clouds should have blocked the sun. There should have been lightning strikes, heavy rain, and a sky filled with ravens. Instead, spring was in the air, gaily colored flowers were in bloom, and nary a cloud hung over the interstate. Doug found the weather profoundly depressing, and he was grateful when the sunset cast shadows over the landscape.

At 9:30 P.M., Doug parked in a lot several miles from the prison. The location of the lot had been shrouded in secrecy to keep all but a select group of reporters from finding the witnesses who were to be shuttled to the penitentiary. Ray and his mother were the last of a small family so, thankfully, there were no relatives waiting. Doug noticed a group of government officials standing off to one side. Among them was Amaya Lathrop, the assistant attorney general who had convinced the appellate courts to affirm the sentence of death, and Martin Poe, a career prosecutor in the Multnomah County District Attorney's office, who had obtained the death sentence at trial. Jake Teeny, the deputy DA who'd second-chaired the case, had moved back east two years ago. Lathrop had always seen the case as a debate about issues of constitutional law far removed from the gore through which Doug and the prosecutors had waded in the courtroom, so Doug wasn't surprised that the AG nodded his way while Poe studiously avoided looking at him.

Marge Cross drove up moments after Doug parked. She was a short, chunky brunette with the courtroom demeanor of a pit bull, who had been unmarried and fresh from a clerkship at the Oregon Supreme Court when she second-chaired

Raymond's case. Marge had been dead set against the guilty plea, but she'd never criticized Doug after the verdict of death and had second-chaired two other cases with him after *Hayes*. The attorneys had talked about driving to the prison together, but Marge's two-year-old daughter had come down with the flu and she'd had to stay with her until her husband finished teaching a class at Portland Community College.

"I see Poe has come to gloat," she said bitterly.

"I don't think he's gloating, Marge. He's not that low."

Marge shrugged. "You're entitled to your opinion. But he and Teeny were snickering all through the trial, and I heard they celebrated with some of the other Neanderthals from the office after the sentencing hearing."

Doug didn't bother to argue. Marge was very political. She saw every case as a battle against the forces of fascism. Motherhood had not softened her. Doug didn't really like conflict, which was odd for a trial lawyer. He got along with the DAs as a rule and thought of the prosecutors as men and women doing a tough job to the best of their ability.

"Hooper's here," Marge said in a tone even more scathing than the one she'd used when referring to Poe. Doug spotted Steve Hooper, the lead detective on Ray's case, talking to a State Trooper near the van that would take them to the prison. The detective was a linebacker in street clothes with wide, bunched shoulders, a thick neck, and the hint of a gut. His head was covered with a thatch of jet-black hair, and a shaggy mustache drooped over his upper lip. The only thing small about the detective were his close-set eyes and his pug nose, which looked out of place on such a broad face.

Hooper was an aggressive cop who believed that he was never wrong. Marge called him "The Fuehrer," and Doug found it hard to disagree. Hooper had certainly used Gestapo tactics when he arrested Ray, and Doug was certain that he had lied about certain incriminating statements that Ray was supposed to have made before the detective switched on his tape recorder in the interrogation room. Ray swore he never made the statements, but there was no way to prove that Hooper had falsified his report.

"Did you talk to Ray?" Marge asked.

"By phone just before I left the office."

"How's he doing?"

"He sounded calm. Spoke about going to a better place, standing by the side of the Lord. I'm glad he found religion. It's helping him accept . . . what's going to happen."

Doug licked his lips. He found it hard to talk about the execution.

"Listen up, people," shouted Thad Spencer, the community relations representative of the Department of Corrections. "We'll be heading out in a minute. Just a reminder. There will be medical people standing by in the viewing room in case any of you needs help, and there's no talking permitted after you enter the viewing room. Any questions?"

Spencer fielded a few from the reporters but the attorneys were quiet and somber. After the last question, Spencer herded the witnesses onto a van. They took back streets all the way to the penitentiary. Along the route, they passed police cars at several locations. They were there to deal with the protestors who were chanting outside the prison. Doug noticed that the police officers stopped talking and stared into the van as they drove by.

The van passed cyclone fencing and razor wire on the way into the penitentiary.

"I saw some old newsreels of East Berlin in the 1960s," Marge said. "There's an uncanny resemblance. Makes you wonder if we're still in America."

Doug didn't respond. He wasn't feeling well and he was thankful that there would be medics in the viewing room. He didn't think he'd throw up or pass out, but he couldn't be sure.

Inside the prison, Doug went through a metal detector and had his hand stamped. Then everyone waited in a comfortable office where coffee and fruit had been provided. Doug didn't touch either. Amaya Lathrop, the assistant AG, walked over and offered that it must be really tough for him to have to see the execution. She was so genuinely sympathetic that Marge loosened up. Soon she and Doug were talking to Martin Poe, who turned out to be as nervous as everyone else. It soon became clear that no one but Steve Hooper was feeling particularly good about what was going to happen. The detective sat by himself looking relaxed and happy as he took bites from a plate loaded with fruit that he was balancing on his lap. Adding to the general unease was the chanting of the demonstrators on State Street that was loud enough to be heard inside the office.

At 11:30, Thad Spencer led the witnesses to the death chamber at the rear of the prison. Each time they were moved to a new location, Doug's tension level skyrocketed and he regretted his decision to come to the prison sober. As they walked down the silent corridors he felt light-headed and worried again about fainting. Talking would have helped but everyone was so uptight that Doug was afraid a single word would sound like the crash of a thousand accidentally dropped dinner plates. He couldn't think of anything to say, anyway.

By the time the witnesses were led into the death chamber it was a little after midnight. The viewing area was claustrophobically small, about eight by twelve. The witnesses stood on a raised platform. In front of them was a window veiled by a curtain. The silence was broken only by the sound the reporters made when their pencils scratched across their note pads.

At 12:20, the curtain lifted. Ray was strapped to a gurney. Intravenous tubes had been inserted in his veins. They were attached to glass tubes that protruded from the wall. The tubes would supply the lethal chemicals that would end Raymond Hayes's life. Behind the wall—unseen—was the executioner.

From his spot on the platform Doug could look down on his client. Ray seemed a little nervous but calmer than Doug had expected. The superintendent of the penitentiary was standing next to the gurney. He laid a comforting hand on Ray's shoulder. Ray turned his head, scanned the room, and fixed on Doug. A microphone in the death chamber must have been activated because Doug could hear Ray clearly when he spoke.

"Superintendent Keene told me you ain't allowed to talk, so I understand if you don't answer," his client said. "Thanks for coming, Doug. You being here comforts me. You too, Marge."

Doug heard Marge's sharp intake of breath.

"Well, these are my last words, so I want to make them good."

He fixed on Martin Poe.

"I am innocent, Mr. Poe, but don't worry. I know you think I killed my mom and that you were only doing your job. I forgive you and God will forgive you, so find peace in your heart."

Ray choked up for a second and had to stop. As hard as he was fighting, he could not stop a tear from trickling down his cheek.

"Mom knows I didn't do her no harm, and she'll be able to tell me so right soon. God bless all of you."

Ray nodded to the superintendent. He nodded back and left the room. Ray closed his eyes and breathed deeply a few times, then all activity stopped. His right eye was completely closed, but, bizarrely, his left lid was slightly open allowing the institutional light to gleam on his dark pupil. Doug could see that no one was in there anymore. He sighed and fought back tears. Poor Ray, he thought. He'd been put down like a dog.

No one said anything during the walk back to the van. Doug guessed that no one could think of anything to say that wouldn't sound forced, trite or false. As soon as they were in the lot, Marge took Doug's hand and gave it a squeeze.

"You did all you could, Doug. No one could have done more. If you ever start thinking that you failed Ray, remember that he didn't think so. And also remember that no matter what he said just now he did kill his mother in a horrible way. I think it's wonderful that he found God, but he was a guilty man no matter what type of man he was when he died."

Doug nodded, afraid to speak. Marge touched his shoulder. "See you in town," she said. Then she walked to her car.

Doug paused for a minute. The air was warm and the night sky was clear and covered with stars. It would be nice to think that Ray was one of them, but he didn't have much hope. The sound of several engines starting up snapped him out of his reverie. He got in his car and was shocked to discover that it was only a little after one-thirty. He thought for sure that he'd missed an entire night. Doug took a few deep breaths, jammed a Rolling Stones CD in the stereo, cranked up the volume until it was so loud he could not think, and headed home. As he drove out of the lot he noticed Steve Hooper standing beside his car, speaking into a cell phone.

When the phone rang, the clock on the fireplace mantle read 1:36. Bernard Cashman had been expecting the call and he picked up on the first ring.

"He's dead," Steve Hooper said.

"Thank you for telling me."

"We couldn't have done it without you, Bernie."

Cashman's chest swelled with pride. "It was a team effort, Steve. I just played a small part."

"Hey, you don't have to be modest with me. You're the best lab guy I've ever worked with. It was the print on the hammer that nailed Hayes, no pun intended."

"Are you calling from the prison?"

"I'm at my car. We just got out."

"You must be exhausted. Go home and get a good night's rest."

"I'll sleep like a baby knowing that scumbag is six feet under. Nice work, and I'm not just saying that."

"I appreciate it. Thanks again for the call."

Cashman hung up the phone and enjoyed the moment. Then he stood. He was in his late thirties, a tall man with a lean face and a dignified bearing who kept himself trim and fit with workouts in the gym and long runs. His ash blond hair was expertly cut, and his manicured beard and mustache gave him the look of an eighteenth-century count. When he moved, it was with the grace of a duelist. His melodic baritone would find a home in the finest choir and was hypnotic in a courtroom.

Cashman went into the kitchen and uncorked a bottle of La Grande Dame 1979 that he'd kept chilled in a bucket of ice. The champagne was outrageously expensive but only the best was suitable for an occasion like this. Bernard Cashman's testimony had put three men on death row, but Raymond Hayes was the first to be executed.

Earlier, the forensic expert had prepared blinis on which he now spread crème fraîche and fine Beluga caviar. There was a ban on the Caspian Sea delicacy because the Russian Mafia was overfishing the sturgeon that produced it, but Cashman had connections that were willing to bend the law when gourmet cuisine was involved.

Cashman filled a slender glass with the sparkling, golden champagne and sipped. He sighed then bit into a blin. A delicate globule of roe burst on his tongue and the explosion of flavor was exquisite. The criminalist closed his eyes and smiled with satisfaction. What a perfect moment!

Open on the kitchen table was a scrapbook in which Cashman kept a record of his courtroom triumphs. The section devoted to Raymond Hayes was filled with articles detailing the guilty plea and sentencing. Tomorrow, he would cut out the article about Hayes's execution and paste it in.

Cashman finished his glass of champagne and ate the rest of the caviar. He wished there were others here to celebrate with him but he knew many people would find his celebration inappropriate, peculiar, or both. They were entitled to their opinions but he did not believe that it was wrong to rejoice when justice was done.

# PREMIUM PLUS

## WHAT IS A PREMIUM PLUS EDITION?

The "Premium" offers you a more readable type and larger page format. The "Plus" is our gift to you.

Log onto www.harpercollins.com/premiumplus, enter code LL0506, complete the entry form, and mail it to us with the original receipt from your purchase and you will receive the FREE PICK OF THE MONTH from HarperCollins Publishers (approximate retail value: $7.50).

This offer is valid for U.S. consumers only from 5/30/06 – 7/30/06. Please allow twelve weeks for delivery. (Shipping and handling are FREE too.) See complete details at www.harpercollins.com/premiumplus.

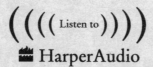